Praise for *Rigged for Murder*

Winner of a 2009 Independent Publisher Award for Best Regional Fiction, and the 2009 RebeccasReads Award for Best Mystery/Thriller

"A winning combination of psychological thriller, police procedural, and action adventure. It's a five-star launch for [LeClair's] aptly named sea-going series and hopefully a precursor in an armada of others to follow…Tightly written and intricately constructed LeClair's *Rigged for Murder* is first-class storytelling in a setting so authentic you can hear the ocean's roar and taste the salt from the sea."

—Mysterious Reviews

"An engaging New England whodunit…Readers will believe they are sailing on the schooner and waiting out the storm at Granite Island as Jenifer LeClair vividly captures the Maine background…With a strong support cast including the capable crew, the battling passengers, and the eccentric islanders to add depth, fans will enjoy *Rigged for Murder*."

—Midwest Book Review

"Brie [Beaumont] is smart and competent, and she uses her brain and not her gun…Jenifer LeClair offers another appealing main character in *Rigged for Murder*, first in her Windjammer Series."

—St. Paul Pioneer Press

"A strong plot, non-stop action, and first-class character development combine to make this an exciting, page-turning adventure novel. Adding to the tension, intrigue and mystery is the meticulous care in researching the details and terminology of sailing, lobstering, and the Maine coastal islands and communities… I have added Jenifer LeClair to my list of 'must read' authors and I am eagerly looking forward to the sequel to *Rigged for Murder*.

—Reader Views

"A debut mystery that is so well written you will hunger for more…Take a female cop on leave from the Minneapolis police force, a good looking sea captain, a crew of seasoned sailors, mix in a lyrically drawn sense of place, an approaching storm, a murder, well-developed characters, and superbly good writing, that's Jenifer LeClair. Read this supremely engaging mystery and enjoy the ride."

—Once Upon a Crime Mystery Bookstore

"Rigged for Murder is an exciting mystery with a little romance thrown in. The setting for this novel is unique and gives the reader insight into life aboard a sailing ship."

—Armchair Reviews

"The story develops logically, with interesting twists… The setting and the weather are well-handled and provide strong context without obtrusiveness. The characters have depth and movement… LeClair gets the sea and the sailing just right."

—Books 'n' Bytes

"The author did a good job of hiding who the killer was… To me that is the sign of a good writer…I recommend [*Rigged for Murder*] to anyone who likes mysteries and has an interest in sailing…This book is a great combination of the two."

—RebeccasReads

"Rigged for Murder is a fast-paced story which rings true both aboard and ashore on island communities. The characters are real, the situations are downright scary, tension is palpable. I'm looking forward to more sailing and better weather aboard the *Maine Wind* in the next book of the series."

—John Foss, master/owner,
Schooner *American Eagle*, Rockland, Maine

DANGER SECTOR

The Windjammer Mystery Series

JENIFER LECLAIR

Conquill Press

This book is a work of fiction. Names, characters, places and incidents either are products of the author's imagination or are used fictitiously. Any resemblance to actual events, or to actual persons living or dead, is entirely coincidental. For information about special discounts for bulk purchases contact conquillpress@comcast.net.

DANGER SECTOR

Copyright 2011 by Jenifer LeClair

Cover Design: Jeff Holmes

Library of Congress Control Number: 2011921462

LeClair, Jenifer.
Danger Sector: a novel / by Jenifer LeClair – 1st edition

ISBN: 978-0-9800017-0-9

Conquill Press/July 2011

Printed in the United States of America

10 9 8 7 6 5 4 3 2 1

For Craig

Who travels this road with me, ever cheerful, warm, and loving

For your reference, the author has included a glossary of sailing terms in the back of the book.

ACKNOWLEDGEMENTS

Thanks first to my family for their support and love. Many thanks to Pat Frovarp and Gary Shulze at Once Upon a Crime Mystery Bookstore in Minneapolis for their support, help, and friendship. We Minnesota mystery authors are lucky to have such fine advocates for our genre. Thanks to mystery author Christopher Valen for his collaboration on the manuscript. In this solitary profession, it is so nice to have a like-minded friend and colleague to work with. Thanks to Lt. Gary Wright of the Maine State Police for his help with information about police procedures in Maine. Thanks to my friend Jeanette Brown for reading the manuscript and offering suggestions. Thank you to Jennifer Adkins, editor and typesetter extraordinaire, and to Jeff Holmes for a wonderful cover. I'd also like to thank Karen Villanueva, my publicist from *Rigged for Murder*, for all her hard work with a then-first-time author. Also, heartfelt thanks to all the bookstore owners and managers in Minnesota, the Midwest, and in Maine, who welcomed me, scheduled events, and helped make *Rigged for Murder* a success. I'm looking forward to seeing you all again this summer as I promote *Danger Sector*. Finally, many thanks to Captain John Foss, master and owner of schooner *American Eagle*, for providing wonderful adventures aboard the *American Eagle* that continue to fuel my imagination.

"Exaltation is the going
Of an inland soul to sea –
Past the houses, past the headlands,
Into deep Eternity…"
                    —Emily Dickinson

DANGER
SECTOR

Prologue

Ocean and forest filled the artist's cottage that occupied a secluded point on the eastern shore of Sentinel Island. Waves slapped the rocky beach, and beyond the porch a red squirrel chattered and scolded from its perch in a tall spruce tree. Sunlight poured through two roof windows, caressing the honey-hued log walls and burnishing the metal castings and copper sculptures that decorated the artist's great room.

The killer paused a moment and smiled at the tranquility before dragging Amanda's body toward the other end of the room. The socks on her limp feet made a dusty sound against the wide pine floorboards. In the corner a large casting of a ship's prow lay overturned, waiting.

The killer maneuvered the artist's body into the hollow base of the casting. Sweat dampened his chest as he strained under her dead weight. "You should like this, Mandy," he belittled; "you're about to become one with your work. Not to worry, though. I'll be back tonight, and we'll go for a nice ride in your boat."

The killer retrieved a few slats of scrap wood from Amanda's fireplace kindling box. He placed them across the opening, wedging them under the lip of the casting to keep the body in place. Taking a rag from his pocket, he wiped down the inside and lip of the casting. He walked to the backdoor, stepped outside, and retrieved a piece of heavy plastic sheeting and a roll of gray tape he'd hidden behind a bush near the door. He returned to the scene, draped the plastic over the base of the casting, and cut it to the shape of the opening. As he worked the tape around the base, the thick plastic distorted Amanda's wide-eyed stare, giving it a Dali-esque twist of horror. Unnerved, the killer's hands began to sweat, and the plastic slipped beneath them. The voice inside his head yammered away, simultaneously berating and cajoling him. *It's taking too long. You have to get out of here. Don't panic, you're almost done. Someone could show up. Calm down. There, see, it's finished.*

The killer stood up and tipped the casting upright. It was easily done with all the weight in the base. Using the rag again, he rubbed down the outside of the cool metal surface and walked over to where Amanda had been sitting, having coffee. He picked the newspaper off the floor, folded it, and tossed it onto the table. He turned slowly in a circle, surveying the room, then moved to the back door and silently slipped out.

Chapter 1

Brie Beaumont shifted on the gray wool blanket. She stretched her arms above her head, laying them on the warm wood of the schooner's deck so the July sun could get at the underside of them. Her long blonde hair lay like an exotic fan on the spruce planking. *A ripe peach of a day—one to make you forget that life is chiefly about supply and demand. It demands and you supply.* Eyes closed behind her sunglasses, she turned the thought in her mind and smiled as it slipped away and drifted lazily down her stream of consciousness.

She turned her head and studied John DuLac. He'd dozed off, lulled by the sun and the motion of the ship at anchor. He was tanned from life at sea, and his dark hair needed a trim. Over the past two months she had come to recognize his presence in her life as a stabilizing force so strong it was almost tangible. The memories that haunted her retreated more and more as the uncomplicated routine of life aboard a sailing ship worked its healing magic.

John shifted as she watched him and, rolling onto his left side, opened his eyes. "Hey, you," he said. "I haven't felt this relaxed since I don't know when."

Brie felt a sudden urge to reach out and touch his face, but restrained herself. The beginnings of romance that had blossomed that night in May, on this very deck, had been put on indefinite hold when she had accepted his offer to become second mate aboard the *Maine Wind*. She had been the one to set the boundaries around what their working relationship would be. But the kiss they had shared that night called to her, the memory of it intruding more and more often when he spoke to her, moved past her on deck, sat next to her in the galley at dinner. And now this break in the cruising schedule so they could sail out to Sentinel Island.

Brie hadn't thought much about being along on this junket. After all, she was part of the crew, and she simply assumed John needed his three crew members aboard to sail the *Maine Wind* out to the island. But to her surprise, they'd dropped anchor midday, and John had come up from the galley with a picnic basket and a blanket. When she'd asked about Scott and George, she was told they were eating below deck. Clearly, John hadn't forgotten that kiss either, and the picnic announced his intention that they'd be sharing these next few days as something other than captain and second mate.

Brie knew that normally the summer schedule allowed for no such breaks. The cruising season for the Maine windjammers was short, and the captains made the most of the few months they had. But John had left time in this summer's schedule to help his friend, Ben, do some repairs to an old lighthouse he had inherited on Sentinel Island.

"Does Ben know when we're arriving?" she asked, staring up at the Atlantic sky. The motion of the ship, combined with her unearthly view, gave her a distinct and not unpleasant sense of floating in space and time.

"I didn't give him a definite ETA. He knows better than anyone that we're at the mercy of the prevailing winds. A part of me is eager to get there and see this lighthouse of his..."

"But?"

John propped himself up on his arm and looked at her. "But this is nice too, Detective Beaumont."

Brie pushed her sunglasses up on her head and stared into his unusually brown eyes. "That would be Second Mate Beaumont to you," she said with a smile.

A large cloud passed over the ship, momentarily blocking out the sun and bringing with it a gust of wind that made Brie shiver. John leaned across and drew the blanket over her shoulder. He lingered for a moment above her, the electricity between them so strong that Brie felt a crushing sensation in her chest. She'd already decided there was no way she was not kissing him. A wisp of hair blew across her face; John tucked it behind her ear, and at that unfortunate moment the radio crackled to life.

"Maine Wind, Maine Wind, Maine Wind."

John froze, and the pained look on his face from the moment being broken was so humorously pathetic that Brie reached up and brushed his cheek, chuckling softly.

He rolled over and sprang to his feet, walked past the wheel, and grabbed the radio receiver. "This is the *Maine Wind* —over."

"Maine Wind, this is the *Honey Bee.* How far out are you?"

"About four hours, Ben. Over."

"There's some weather moving in."

John turned and looked over his shoulder to the south. A dark line of clouds had formed on the horizon. "We'll beat it, Ben. We should be anchoring around six o'clock. Over."

"I'll keep a weather eye out. Don't worry about dinner— I've got it covered."

"Roger that, Ben. Over and out." John turned back to Brie. "We've got to get the sails up and get underway, or that weather will catch us." He helped her pile everything into the picnic basket and rolled up the blanket.

"Thanks for the picnic, John. It was lovely. I'll bring these below." She picked up the basket and blanket and headed down to the galley.

John walked behind her to the galley companionway and called down to the rest of the crew, "Prepare to raise sail."

First Mate Scott Hogan and George Dupopolis, the ship's cook, piled up the companionway ladder, followed by Brie. She and George got busy on the forepeak halyard, hauling up sail. Gaff-rigged sailing ships have a second spar at the top of the sail that sits at approximately a 45-degree angle to the mast. The end of this gaff can be lowered to depower the sail without lowering the entire sail. While learning the ropes, Brie had discovered that Captain DuLac often used this procedure when anchoring for brief periods in a sheltered bay, as they had today for lunch. Now she and George were resetting the foresail. Working aboard the *Maine Wind* the past two months, Brie had drawn on every bit of her police conditioning, and her body had taken on a toughness it hadn't seen since her academy days.

Astern of George and Brie, the captain and Scott were resetting the ship's mainsail. Muscles strained as they hauled up the heavy gaff and canvas to rhythmic shouts of. "Heave—heave."

They were anchored in a wide bay, the shape of a giant scallop shell, off one of the many uninhabited islands that dot the Gulf of Maine. Along the shore, a thick stand of spruce flanked a crescent of sandy beach. Brie loved these unspoiled islands. Undeveloped coastline was a rarity, but Maine had managed to preserve the wildness of many of its islands.

Captain DuLac took the wheel, and the rest of the crew went forward to crank up the anchor. The captain steered the *Maine Wind* to starboard for breaking out the anchor. Getting underway in a windjammer without power to raise sails or anchor required serious teamwork. It comforted Brie to know that, in a world where so much was done with a push of a button, there were still jobs that required hands-on strength and skill.

They cleared the bay and set a southwest heading. John held the schooner on a port tack in the freshening twenty-knot breeze blowing straight out of the south. George went aft to coil the halyards, and Scott and Brie made their way out onto the netting beneath the bowsprit to unlash the jib. As the *Maine Wind* moved off the island, the clean smell of salt air engulfed Brie. She always liked leaving an anchorage and that first blast of sea air hitting her senses. To her it was the smell of freedom.

The downside of never marrying or owning a house or a pet had been loneliness. The upside had been freedom, and now that freedom was all Brie felt she truly possessed.

In April she had left her job as homicide detective with the Minneapolis Police Department. A little over a year before that she had been shot, and her partner Phil had been killed in the line of duty. After a year of physical and psychological struggles, Brie had taken a leave from the force and come to Maine, where her paternal grandmother still lived. Left behind was the analytical world of the homicide detective, where she had lived day to day and year to year, her job serving up one grotesque puzzle after another, many of them with key pieces missing. Often, she had fallen asleep haunted by the images of grisly crime scenes. And though she'd been told years ago that this reaction would go away, it never fully had. And then she had been shot. On that spring night when the world was just beginning to wake up and smell of hope, she'd been taken down by the same bullet that had killed Phil. All the years of hard work, all that she had accomplished, crumbled around her.

Over a year's time her body had slowly healed but her psyche hadn't. Finally, she'd run away—taken the leave she had been offered and gotten on a plane east the same day. But even here in Maine, a place she had always loved, Brie had felt adrift, outside of herself. During the last two months aboard the *Maine Wind*, though, she had reclaimed parts of herself—parts she was sure had died, along with Phil, on that tragic night in north Minneapolis. She almost felt as if her existence were now divided into two separate lives, her before-the-shooting-life and her after-the-shooting-life, as if everything moved from that zero point either backward or forward in time.

Out on the bowsprit, they had finished untying the lace lines. She and Scott moved back to the deck and raised the jib and staysail. Through an odd series of events in May, Brie had become second mate on the *Maine Wind*, which suited her fine. Not only was she an experienced sailor, but for now, anyway, she had no desire to return home. She wanted to live for awhile with no sense of where the next day would bring her—with little more to occupy her mind than wondering if a squall would blow up or if porpoises might race off their bow that day.

Aboard ship life was simple. She kept in her possession only what fit in her sea bag at the foot of her berth. She followed the captain's orders. She ate whatever George cooked and, at night, she fell into bed with the kind of mindless exhaustion that resulted from a working life at sea. There was a lot to be said for that kind of simplicity—where life was reduced to its lowest common denominator. There was a lot to be said for escaping the mind-numbing complexity of modern life. For Brie it had been like taking up the old dust-laden rugs of routine and getting down to the bare boards of her life. And she had finally begun to heal.

But, while the flashbacks of that fateful night had become less frequent since encountering John DuLac and coming aboard the *Maine Wind*, they hadn't gone away. Maybe they never would. Occasionally, one would open a jagged tear in her being with such abruptness it took her breath away. Then she'd be plummeted back into that old familiar darkness and anxiety —symptoms of Post Traumatic Stress Disorder, or PTSD, as the psychologist had referred to it.

Brie turned and watched John at the wheel. Their eyes met for a few seconds, and the beginning of a smile warmed his handsome face. She glanced around the deck, making sure everything was shipshape, before heading for her favorite spot. Now that they were a ways off the island, they had picked up speed. The wind had increased to twenty-three knots, and they were slicing along at twelve to thirteen knots—a speed that felt like flying under sail. Beating upwind, they were heeled enough to be taking seas through the starboard scuppers. The salt water surged in, rolled aft along the wood-planked deck and drained out the scuppers at the back of the ship.

Brie stepped over the gunwale, and with the agility of a tightrope walker made her way toward the end of the bowsprit. The sea spread out before her, a heartbreaking shade of blue. The big wooden spar extended a good fifteen feet beyond the bow of the ship. Known as widow-makers in the old days, it was not uncommon for mariners to fall from this part of the rigging, while furling sail, and be lost in heavy seas. At the end of the bowsprit, Brie turned and leaned against the pulpit. Below her the sea streamed by, creating the effect that it, and not the ship, was in motion. She watched the water foaming away from the ship's bow and took in the beauty of the *Maine Wind* from this vantage point. She had fallen in love with the fine old vessel. And the man sailing her? Well, that was a story yet to unfold.

Brie turned back around and lowered herself onto the tiny platform at the end of the bowsprit. Straddling the small piece of wood, she dangled her legs over the water flying by below her. The sea was a wondrous thing. On its best days it placed a calm around the heart like a giant, undulating tranquilizer. On its worst days it put the fear of God into you. All illusions of control tended to dissolve in its vast presence. For Brie, who felt she had lost control of her life fifteen months ago, surrender to the sea and the life one lived upon it had come as a surprising relief. The contradictory nature of the sea intrigued her. It was a place of constant change but no change; a place of great emptiness or fullness, depending on one's point of view; the great laboratory of life, with no permanent structure to house it. There was a lot of thinking room out here.

"Stand by to come about!"

The captain's voice roused Brie from her thoughts. She hopped up, threaded her way back along the bowsprit, and climbed over the gunwale. They had been on a southwest heading since lunch, and it was time to change course. The main and foresails would take care of themselves, but she and Scott would need to reset the jib. They took their places in the bow, Scott to port and Brie to starboard, to await the captain's order.

"Ready about," he called.

"Ready," came their reply.

"Helm's alee." Stepping to the side of the ship's wheel, the captain spun it hard, pulling the wooden spokes hand over hand. It took several rotations of the big wheel before the *Maine Wind* began to head upwind. When the ship was dead into the wind, Brie released the starboard jib sheet and moved across to the port bow to help haul in the sail and make it off. Scott's short russet-colored hair glowed in the sun as he worked the line around the belaying pin in a figure eight. At the captain's order they moved aft to sweat the foresheet—a process used to trim sail, allowing the *Maine Wind* to perform at peak efficiency. Scott hopped on the top of the cabin and grabbed the sturdy line that controlled the foresail. Tugging on it, he rocked back and forth to create slack in the line, which Brie tightened around the pin.

Brie had formed quite a friendship with Scott Hogan since her arrival on board in May. Scott was mature for twenty-five, so it was easy for Brie to forget that he was eleven years her junior. He came from a wealthy medical family in Providence, Rhode Island, and displayed a kind of deportment rare in young men of his age. At eighteen he'd jumped the family ship, which had him bound for Harvard. Like Brie, he had come to Maine, where he had met John DuLac and shipped out on the *Maine Wind*. She was sure this was part of the reason there was such a vibe between her and Scott. During their past two months of crewing together, they had become fast friends. She had learned that over the past seven years Scott had spent his time in the off-season working at John's boat repair yard and attending the University of Maine, where he had acquired degrees in music and math. Now, when he came back to land in October, he tutored kids in math and gave violin and guitar lessons.

"So, Brie, looks like we're going to spend a few days up to our elbows in paint and plaster dust." Scott's lively green eyes twinkled in the sunlight as he sat down on the cabin top next to her and leaned against the foremast.

"I'm looking forward to meeting Ben. John's talked about him so much I feel like I already know him."

"I felt that same way before I met him. But he took me a bit by surprise. He was sterner than I'd expected."

"Really? That *is* a surprise. From the way John talks about him, I've been expecting someone more Kris Kringlish."

"Don't get me wrong. It's clear he loves John like a son. He's just reserved about it. He was a career Navy man, you know. Maybe that's why he comes across the way he does."

"Well, I'm glad you told me. Forewarned is forearmed."

"I think we're each gonna *need* four arms the next few days to get everything done that John's talking about."

"He hasn't really filled me in."

"Well, there's talk of tearing out a couple walls in the keeper's house to do some plumbing and wiring work. And I guess the roof has some issues too."

"Doesn't sound like we'll be getting in a lot of hammock time."

"I wouldn't bank on it if I were you. I don't mind, though. John's done an awful lot for me over the years."

"Hey, Brie," John called forward. "You want to come back and take the helm for a bit?"

"Sure!" Brie hopped down off the cabin and headed aft. On regular cruises she didn't get this chance often. If John had to leave the wheel, Scott usually took over. She guessed John wanted to spend a little time with her, but she also knew that *he* knew how much she loved sailing the *Maine Wind*.

"I need to go below and pull a chart," he said as she approached.

Brie stepped behind the wheel and took note of their heading on the compass. "Take your time, John. I've been hoping to take a turn at the wheel."

"All you have to do is ask, Brie. I'm always happy to let you sail."

She watched as John went down the companionway in front of the wheel and, at the foot of the ladder, ducked into his cabin on the port side of the ship. She pictured the cabin in her mind's eye. The space was small but functional. The double berth was tucked partially under the deck overhead. To the left of the door sat a chart table, and beneath it, a rack with small, square pigeonholes held rolled-up charts. More long cylindrical charts were stored on a shallow rack suspended from the ceiling of the cabin. A small bookcase next to the chart table held a collection of sea literature. A wood chair in front of the chart table was bolted to the floor. John would have pulled a chart and sat down at the table to spread it out.

She settled in behind the wheel, holding the schooner on its southeasterly heading. Taking the helm of the *Maine Wind* thrilled her. In all her years of sailing, she'd never experienced anything like it. Up until the time her father had died, her family had owned a large cruising sailboat they'd kept on Lake Superior. *Edna Mae* was a trim craft, and they'd tasted many adventures aboard her. But the *Maine Wind*, at 90 feet and carrying 4500 square feet of sail, was a true sailing ship. Her rich history lived in her; every polished spar and plank of decking had a tale to tell. The ship was like a living thing with a heart and pulse — each creak of timber and groan of rigging an inhalation and exhalation. To sail such a ship was to become one with it, to feel its power with each movement and vibration of the wheel, to harness and command an awesome force of nature. For Brie, sailing the *Maine Wind* embodied joy.

She surveyed the horizon line to the south, where a widening band of charcoal smudged the sky. Reaching into the cuddy across from the wheel, she pressed the "WX" button on the radio to hear the NOAA coastal weather forecast. The forecast was for thunderstorms and increasing wind in the midcoast region by later that night. She hoped the bad weather would blow through overnight. John had told her Sentinel Island had some pretty spots. She was hoping to explore the island tomorrow, demolition schedule allowing, and break in her new hiking boots.

Within ten minutes John climbed back up the ladder, chart in hand, to join her on deck. "I ran a plot, and it looks like we're on schedule to arrive at the island around six o'clock."

"I just tuned in the weather. They're saying the front won't arrive until tonight."

"Great. I hope it holds off at least till we anchor and get up to the lighthouse."

John sat down on the starboard side locker and leaned back against the rail, watching Brie steer the ship. She had a typical helmsman's stance, with feet apart for balance on the sloping deck. Her clear blue eyes flashed with pleasure as she held the wheel, and her long hair blew out behind her like pale ribbons of silk. She wore a plain white tee shirt and loose-fitting cargo khakis. The crew preferred these because they allowed for freedom of movement when working on deck or up in the rigging, and also because they dried more quickly than denim, when wet. A leather sheath on Brie's belt held a rigging knife that all sailors wore when on deck. A long, braided lanyard attached the knife itself to her belt so it couldn't be dropped and lost. The wind played with her clothing, so occasionally John caught the outline of her small breasts or her trim waist and hips.

He liked watching her sail the ship. It seemed odd, but there was an intimacy about it. The *Maine Wind* was his life and his home six months out of every year. And here she was, temporarily in control of it. Seeing her there at the wheel—master of ship and elements—stirred something in him.

She was a good sailor, too—every bit as confident and steady at the helm as Scott. That didn't surprise him a bit. He knew what Brie was made of. He'd seen what lay beneath the slim body and shy demeanor. While he'd held back from physical contact with her the past two months, his feelings for her had only deepened as he watched her work with the crew and passengers aboard ship. His real respect for her, though, stemmed from the incident at Granite Island back in May, when they were marooned during the gale. There he had watched the homicide detective at work—seen her strength, both mental and physical. He had also watched her grapple with her inner demons. She was courageous. He'd fallen in love with that, and with her.

Brie glanced over at him, feeling uncomfortable, knowing his eyes were on her. John stood up and moved to the side of the wheel. He unrolled the chart and slipped it under two bungee cords that held it in place on the cabin top.

"So, has Ben made any friends on the island?" Brie asked.

"He's only been out there since April, and he's bit reclusive. According to him, there's not much at that end of the island except for the lighthouse. There is one other cabin out there that's owned by an artist. He's mentioned her a few times, so I guess they've gotten acquainted."

"Hmmm, do you think there's any romance involved?" The minute she'd asked the question, she wished she could call it back. It seemed like prying. She knew Ben had lost his wife to cancer a few years ago, and all of a sudden the comment struck her as inappropriate. She wrote it off to John's proximity, and also to the fact that romance had been on her mind since lunch.

John smiled. "I think they're just friends. At least so far. You never know what might develop, though."

As he said this, he stepped over and stood behind her at the wheel. Actually, a little too close for Brie's comfort. She felt her stomach muscles tighten, and the blood seemed to stop flowing to her head. She noticed Scott had fallen asleep on the cabin top near the foremast, and George was nowhere to be seen. *Oh dear,* she thought. John stepped forward so their bodies were touching and reached around, placing his hands over hers on the wheel. After a brief inner struggle, she decided to go with it.

Leaning into him, she drew in a deep breath that, unintended, slipped out as a sigh.

"It's good for me too," John said into her ear.

Brie felt color wash across her face. Why did he do this to her—reduce her to something like a driveling adolescent? The last time she could remember feeling this dopey about a guy was in college, and that was a long time ago. It was an absolute puzzle to her, and she couldn't help wondering if it had something to do with being shot. *Oh, snap out of it, Brie, and quit pretending you don't like this. And by the way, quit overanalyzing. This isn't a crime scene—it's simple biology. Just let yourself go.*

She let time and thought slip away till nothing but the sensory experience remained—the feel of the wind, the feel of the ship, the feel of John. She didn't know how long they stayed like that, leaning into each other, steering the ship, but when John stepped away, she actually experienced a moment of disorientation. Then she noticed George emerging from the galley companionway. John had reacted to seeing him and moved away from her. Possibly he didn't want George to intrude on the moment, or maybe he didn't want to make *her* feel uncomfortable. Mainly, though, Brie knew that John chose to maintain a certain decorum aboard ship when they were under sail.

George walked aft.

"Hey, George, it's beautiful up here. You should come topside and enjoy," Brie said. She knew George was pretty much married to his galley, though, where he spent endless hours concocting the best meals in the windjammer fleet.

"I was wondering if I need to start some dinner prep, Captain?"

"No need, George. We had a call over the radio from Ben. He said he's got dinner covered."

"Oh," he said, momentarily flustered. He nodded his head seriously, as if he'd just been told the lettuce was bad. "Well, then, I guess I'll just hang out on deck and catch the sailing." He ran a hand through his curly black hair, pulled a ball cap from his back pocket, and put it on.

Brie watched him walk forward, climb onto the cabin top and lay back in the sun. She supposed he already had the dinner plan thoroughly in hand. George came from several generations of Greek restaurateurs in New York City. She knew that letting someone else prepare the food felt as unnatural to him as breathing underwater.

"So, tell me, John," she said, turning to him, "was Ben surprised when he inherited this lighthouse from his friend Harold?"

"Surprised would be an understatement. It wasn't so much the inheriting part. Harold McCann had no family still alive, and Ben was pretty much his only close friend. But Harold's death really shocked him. Harold was only sixty-five, and in peak condition. According to Ben, he ran three miles a day on the island trails and ate a vegetarian diet."

"So how did he die?" It was a morbid question, but one that came as second nature to Brie.

"He fell down the lighthouse stairs. Died from the head trauma. It bothered Ben, Harold being a runner and all, and obviously sure-footed. Ben even talked to the coroner, but there was nothing in the autopsy to raise any questions. I guess it had been raining the night he fell. He'd gone up to the top of the light to watch the storm. His shoes would have been wet. The coroner said that most likely led to the fall."

"So, who found him?"

"It was the artist—Amanda's her name, I think. She came over the following morning because she'd noticed the lights on in the keeper's house all night. Apparently she can see his lights from her place at night."

"How long had Harold lived at the lighthouse?"

"Not very long. About a year, I think. He died last year in the spring."

"Hmmm," was all Brie had to say. But her detective mind was busily turning over the details of John's story and wondering if a little more digging might not be called for.

Chapter 2

They had sailed on in silence for twenty minutes, Brie happy as a clam at the wheel, and John content to leave her there as he followed their progress on the chart. They were approaching Fog Island that lay about forty degrees to starboard.

"Can we maintain course?" Brie asked.

John checked the chart and the GPS for depth readings. "Not a problem," he said.

It had been a near perfect day of sailing. They had departed early from Camden, where the *Maine Wind* made berth. Their heading had taken them east across Penobscot Bay past waters thick with lobster buoys. They'd seen lobsterboats with men in blaze-orange gear hauling up their living in large rectangular traps from the ocean floor. Occasionally, they had spotted another windjammer ghosting effortlessly along in the distance, and known her by the cut of her sails and design of her hull. Off North Haven Island they'd sailed past Pulpit Harbor, where an osprey soared above its blue hunting grounds. On previous cruises Brie had seen osprey nesting atop Pulpit Rock—the miniature Gibraltar that guarded the entrance to the harbor. Beyond North Haven they had set a heading southeast through the waters of Merchant Row and had dropped anchor in a secluded island cove for lunch.

They were now on a heading east southeast, leaving Fog Island off their starboard quarter. They skirted ledges where sea lions basked in the sun and passed a group of low-lying islands thick with creeping juniper, bayberry, and sea roses—plants hardy enough to survive the continual salt spray.

Over the past couple of months Brie had acquired a number of books on seabird habitats, tidal zones, and native vegetation. She had begun learning names and actively looking for various species of plants, birds, and sea creatures. She took particular interest in the tidal and sub-tidal zones with their array of barnacles, crabs, sea urchins, and anemones. The crabs were her favorites. One day in June while out hiking, she'd come upon a stretch of sand, pocked with small holes, near a salt marsh. As she watched, a fiddler crab no more than an inch and a half in size scurried down one of the holes. She squatted low to the ground and waited. One after another the tiny creatures appeared, scuttling in and out of a forest of holes, where they nested. After that, whenever possible, she'd made a study of the mid and low tidal zones, searching for new varieties of the armored crustaceans.

They maintained their heading for another half hour. The wind had shifted to the southwest, and the captain told Brie to come 20 degrees to starboard. A short time later he pointed toward a landmass on the horizon. "There's Sentinel Island."

Brie looked at her watch—four-thirty. She felt a puff of disappointment. *What was that saying? It's all in the journey. Whoever wrote that must have lived aboard a sailing ship.*

John read her lack of excitement. "Hey," he said with a wink. "Shore can be fun too." He held her blue eyes for a moment, hoping to convey his intentions.

"It sounds more like forced labor, if you ask me."

"I'll have to speak to Scott about those loose lips. You know what they say."

Brie smiled and studied the horizon. John was right. This was a chance for them to be together without the ship's schedule to interfere. So why did she feel so conflicted about it? She suspected it had a lot to do with her as-yet-unformulated decision about returning to her job in Minnesota. October wasn't that far off, and a part of her held back from the idea of involvement with John because she didn't want to hurt him. She didn't want to hurt herself either—there'd been enough stress in the past year. But the fact of the matter was that even though she'd kept John at bay physically, he'd crept into her heart and made a little nest there. Those fledgling feelings born back in May had gained strength, and threatened to spread their wings and fly, taking her resolve with them.

She took it as a sign that maybe she needed to do a little more letting go—just let things take their course. She reminded herself that trying to keep tight control over everything in her life had not led to happiness. In fact, it seemed clear to her now that that tendency had impeded her psychological healing after the shooting. So, in the spirit of resolve, she let her current concerns slip away in favor of enjoying the rest of the afternoon.

Sentinel Island grew steadily larger on the horizon. "Where's the lighthouse located?" Brie asked.

"At the southern end. We'll sail down the west side of the island. Ben says there's a sheltered cove deep enough to anchor in along that shore. He moors his boat, *Honey Bee*, there, so it should be easy enough to spot with the binoculars as we approach. From there it's about a quarter mile hike up to the lighthouse."

"Is there a year-round community on Sentinel Island or just summer cottages?"

"There's a small lobstering village—Barnacle Bay—that sits at the north end of the island. Ben said there's a gravel road from the lighthouse to the village. I'm sure there are other cottages on the island as well—both permanent residents and seasonal folks. Like most of the islands, I'd guess the interior is largely uninhabited."

"Maybe there'll be some trails around the island to explore," Brie said hopefully.

"Usually, if there are kids on an island, you'll find some rough trails. Kids like their secret haunts. Teens too."

"How else would they get in trouble?" Brie chuckled.

"Maybe *we'll* look for a secret spot. See what kind of trouble we can get into."

"Don't tempt fate, John. You should know by now, trouble's my middle name."

"This'll be the good kind of trouble," he said. Looking past her, he watched a gull wheel and take a fish a hundred yards astern.

She studied his strong profile for a moment, conjuring up this secret spot, and noticed her heart pumping out way more beats per minute than steering a ship required. She pushed the thought away and glanced at the compass to check their heading.

"Well, I think I'll hand over the helm. Let you take it from here."

"You sure? You're doing fine."

She stepped aside, giving him the wheel, not able to tell him she needed some distance. Over the past couple of months she'd longed for this kind of attention, but their flirting throughout the afternoon had left her feeling a bit conflicted, and she wanted a little space right now to think things over. She went forward, stretched out on the cabin top, and pretended to take a nap.

Within forty minutes they were steering a course along the western shore of Sentinel Island. Brie had gotten a few glimpses of Barnacle Bay as they approached.

"Brie!" John called forward.

"Aye, Captain."

"Rouse Scott and tell him to come aft. Then head out the bowsprit with the glasses and keep a lookout for that cove."

"Aye, Captain."

Brie walked to the galley companionway to get Scott. An hour earlier George had persuaded him to come below and help make a batch of cookies to bring ashore.

Scott climbed up the ladder, and Brie went aft to grab the binoculars and headed for the bowsprit. They had stayed a ways off the island so they'd have a clear view along the shore and know when the cove was coming up. She kept the glasses trained on the shoreline, knowing they'd be on the cove before long.

The terrain rose as they traveled south, the sandy shoreline giving way to granite slabs. John steered the *Maine Wind* around a bend, and Brie saw the top of the lighthouse come into view. She took another look through the binoculars. Toward the end of the island, steep rocky bluffs rose above the sea. She scanned the shoreline and found the cove. Ben's small lobsterboat, *Honey Bee*, was anchored there, its bright yellow hull ablaze in the afternoon sun.

She headed back in from the bowsprit and called aft. "We're coming up on it—about a quarter of a mile. Looks like we can steer straight in if we fall off a bit to the southeast."

John handed the wheel off to Scott and came forward. He took a long look through the glasses, getting the lay of the land.

"That cove is wicked small," he said.

Brie was entertained by this curious Maine-ism, which was frequently used to express the superlative. The weather could be "wicked" hot or a man might be "wicked" hungry. Or a storm could be "wicked" bad, during which one might read a "wicked" good book.

John studied the cove a moment longer before handing the glasses back to Brie. He walked aft and took the wheel. "Prepare to anchor," he called out.

Scott headed forward to join Brie on the forepeak halyard.

John steered the *Maine Wind* to port on a bead with the entrance to the cove. When they were still a good ways from the cove he called out, "Scandalize the forepeak."

Scott and Brie eased the halyard, lowering the end of the gaff and the top of the sail. The ship slowed, and they went aft to repeat the procedure on the mainsail.

John's skill at bringing the *Maine Wind* into an anchorage—well, there was nothing for it but all-out admiration. The forces at play and the cost of a miscalculation boggled Brie's mind. It was not unlike the challenge of sailing a boat up to a dock, but on a much grander scale.

They drifted forward, entering the mouth of the cove. The steep granite shoreline rose to a height of about thirty feet. The rock face glowed pink in the afternoon sun. John steered the ship to port, watching the depth readings on the GPS screen. When they'd drifted nearly to a stop, he gave the order.

"Drop the hook!"

The quarter-ton anchor hit the water. The heavy chain rumbled across the deck through the starboard hull, and the *Maine Wind* nosed up into the wind, coming to rest in the small deep cove about ten yards downwind of *Honey Bee*. They dropped the second anchor off the port side in case the weather got bad. Brie wasn't sure if they'd return to the ship that night or not. She guessed the second anchor was a just-in-case measure.

The four of them got busy lowering and folding the sails and lashing them off to the main and foresail booms. As they worked Brie caught sight of a tall, gray-haired man working his way down a steep path that hugged the side of the rocky bank.

"That must be Ben," Brie said.

John turned from the work and hailed him. "Ahoy, Ben!"

The man looked up from the path. "Ahoy, the *Maine Wind* and scurvy mates," he called out.

"Arrrr," Scott shouted back. He pulled out a belaying pin and struck an Incredible Hulk stance. Ben's laugh floated out to them.

Not too stern so far, Brie thought.

They lowered the small dory that hung from the portside davits. One by one they climbed down the rope-and-slat boarding ladder into the dory. Each of them had packed a small backpack. They stowed these in the bow of the dory. John took the center seat and manned the oars. He pulled for shore, and they soon beached the dory on a small, pebbly spit. They climbed out and tied off to a large rock at the base of the cliff. It was high tide, so they wouldn't have to worry about the dory floating away.

John and Ben exchanged a handshake, followed by the one-armed guy hug.

"Well, you know these two, Ben," John said.

Scott and George each shook hands with Ben and said their howdy's.

"And this is Brie Beaumont, my second mate."

Brie extended her hand and Ben took it.

"Pleased to meet you, Brie," he said. His expression—one of interest coupled with assessment—made Brie wonder how much of her story John had disclosed.

"I've been looking forward to meeting you, Ben. And your lighthouse."

"Well, I hope neither of us will disappoint."

Ben had a commanding presence even in his paint-splotched jeans. He was a square-shouldered six-foot-two with serious blue eyes and a healthy mustache. His silver-gray hair was slightly disheveled from the wind, and it somehow softened a man that Brie sensed still ran on military time.

They started up the rocky trail that rose steeply for about an eighth of a mile. Ben took the lead and John brought up the rear. As they headed south, the root-woven track hugged the edge of the bluff, giving views of the *Maine Wind* anchored below them. The breeze came cool off the ocean, but the sun warmed them. Brie added this to her list of near-perfect Maine days where the temperature hovered around 70 degrees.

The trail rose at a steady incline and she watched for a glimpse of the lighthouse, but so far, it had been shielded from view by the thick growth of spruce. Wildflowers, ones she'd seen on the mainland a month ago, bloomed in the forest and along the trail. Snowy-flowered bunchberry covered the forest floor, here and there punctuated by jack-in-the-pulpit with its blossoms of striped purple and green, and columbine with its delicate bell-like flowers. Brie had seen these species in the forests of Minnesota, and their presence here made her feel welcome.

"It's nice to see the wildflowers still in bloom," she commented to Ben's back as they hiked up the trail. Brie was second in line, with Scott, George and John behind her.

Ben looked around and smiled. "On the outer islands summer comes late, and occasionally, not at all. There's at least one year in Maine's recorded history that missed summer altogether."

"Really?"

"Yup. In eighteen sixteen, there was a hard frost in July and the first snow fell in August. That winter Penobscot Bay froze solid all the way to Isle au Haut, and pack ice filled the waters of Muscongus Bay as far out as Monhegan Island."

"Hey Ben," John piped up, "you're gonna have Brie thinking Maine is part of the Arctic Circle."

"Don't worry, John, I come from the frozen north myself. In winter, Minnesota is pretty much an icebox from top to bottom. In Embarrass, way up on the Canadian border, the temperature has dropped to sixty-four below zero—the coldest temperature ever recorded in the continental United States. I've always wondered if that's how the place got its name."

"That rivals any claims we've got on cold," Scott said from behind her.

"But we make up for it in dampness," Ben said. "Goes right to your bones in the winter."

"Ditto that for New York City," George inserted.

Brie smiled to herself, noting that their first conversation was about—what else?—the weather.

The trail climbed steadily upward, and suddenly the top of the lighthouse rose straight out of the pine. "Oh, look, there it is," Brie said, pointing up. Like a star rising from the forest, the Fresnel lens glittered in the late afternoon sun.

The trail bent sharply to the east, into the forest, and a little farther on came back out onto the southern edge of the island. From atop the granite bluff, a heart-quickening panorama opened before them. The ocean spread out, a deep china blue, here and there punctuated by islands poking their green and brown heads above the surface. The salt breeze came strong off the water, and for a few moments, Brie and the others gave themselves over to the calming sounds of wildness. Wind stirred the forest. Waves pounded the base of the cliff, their hollow reports echoing up the rocks. Gulls cried as they wheeled in sweeping arcs, searching for dinner.

The trail rose gently as they continued east along the edge of the bluff. The forest had retreated, leaving a sparse groundcover of low-lying plants, moss, and lichens. On the last leg of the trail they encountered a short, steep outcropping of granite. They shinnied up the rock using a series of natural footholds, and when they came over the top, there stood the lighthouse, magnificent in its isolation.

Perched near the brink of the tall cliff, the whitewashed stone tower rose thirty or forty feet above the surrounding bedrock. Two small windows like searching eyes sat one above the other on the tower's seaward side. Atop the tower, the sturdy iron gallery with its black catwalk and railings ringed the lantern room. And finally, like a sundae with its crowning cherry, a metal, faceted roof capped the lantern room and was itself topped off with a black iron ball and a lightning rod.

Ten yards north of the lighthouse sat the small house that had been the keeper's quarters. There was a kind of postcard charm about it. The simple two-story dwelling had freshly painted white siding and a tidy black roof. Gingerbread trim of a deep cranberry color gussied up the eaves, and matching shutters brought summery warmth to the winter-white of the structure. Approximately one hundred yards beyond the house, the dense spruce forest ranged from the eastern to the western edge of the promontory, walling off the lighthouse from what lay beyond and assuring both privacy and isolation to lighthouse dwellers.

"Would you like to go up to the top of the light?" Ben asked the group.

"Can we?" asked Brie. She knew lighthouses maintained by the Coast Guard were not open to the public.

"We certainly can. When a taller lighthouse was built on nearby Drake Island back in nineteen thirty-four, this lighthouse was decommissioned and, along with a number of others on the coast, sold at auction. Harold's father—Harold McCann is the man I inherited the property from—bought the lighthouse and keeper's quarters back in the nineteen sixties."

They paused outside the tower, and Ben produced a ring with three keys on it and unlocked the door. Everyone crowded inside the base of the tower and looked up. It was like being at the bottom of a cool, stone well. The gray, curving walls reminded Brie of a medieval fortress. They started up the winding iron stairs, and Ben continued his story, his voice echoing down to Scott and George, who were bringing up the rear.

"Harold grew up on this island. In fact, his ancestors were some of the original settlers on Sentinel Island. As a young man, he had a falling out with some fellow on the island. It was over a girl, of course. I guess it was one of the reasons he left the island. Anyway, he joined the Navy—became a career Navy man, like me. Years ago we were stationed together in Connecticut and got to be good friends, and even though our paths diverged after that, we always stayed in touch—kept the friendship going."

As they climbed, Brie paused at each of the small windows to enjoy the sea vista from behind the thick lighthouse walls. The world was in motion out there, but no sound carried through the stone walls, thus creating the odd illusion that she was viewing a diorama of a seascape rather than the actual thing. *This would be really cool in a storm,* she thought. Maybe they'd get a good blow, and she'd have a chance to come up here and look out. She tuned back in as Ben continued his story.

"Harold never returned to the island. After his parents died, he rented the keeper's house to a young couple. He gave it to them at a great price, and they agreed to do the upkeep on the property. About two-and-a-half years ago they moved on, and Harold decided he'd come back out here and see how he liked it. He was pretty reclusive, and the setting appealed to him."

"John told me about what happened with the fall," Brie said.

"Tragic," Ben said, shaking his head. "I guess he'd come up here during a storm. Must have gone out on the gallery and gotten his feet wet. He slipped on the stairs. I suppose John told you he died from head trauma."

"Yes," Brie said. "It's a common cause of death. The human head is much more fragile than people realize." The comment had slipped out the way things do when they're second nature, but Brie immediately regretted saying it.

Ben paused and turned around on the stair to look at her. "John told me that you're a homicide detective on leave from your job this summer."

Brie suddenly felt trapped and uncomfortable. "Yes, I was —or am, I mean." She studied the gray stone wall to her right.

"Looks like we're here," John said, coming to her rescue. "I can't wait to see this view."

Ben turned and led them up the last couple steps into the lantern room. "This is a second order Fresnel lens," he said, gesturing toward the light. "When it was operational, these prisms would capture the light from the lamp and bend it back toward the bull's-eye center of the lens, where it was focused and sent forth. The light could be seen by mariners up to twenty miles away."

The giant lens was as much a work of art as of science. Dozens of thick prismatic slats, arranged in ladder-like fashion, bent and separated the incoming light, creating a play of color, a magical space, in which the air itself seemed to pulsate. The lens sat like a great mesmerizing jewel on its clockwork of polished brass. Ben reached out and gave it a small push. It rotated silently, effortlessly, on its bed of liquid mercury, giving the illusion of complete weightlessness.

"Beautiful," Brie whispered.

Ben opened the door to the gallery, and they stepped out onto the catwalk. The sounds of the island came back to them —the splitting of waves against cliffs, the haunting calls of the gulls. Far below, the sea lay like a wrinkled blue quilt, here and there dotted by miniature boats rising and falling among its folds. Brie took a turn around the iron gallery, surveying the lay of the land. A short ways up the eastern side of the island a rocky point jutted out. On it sat a handsome log cottage.

"That's Amanda Whitcombe's cottage," Ben said, pointing to it. "She's the only other one out at this end of the island. She's our resident artist and sculptor." He handed Brie a pair of binoculars he kept in the lantern room. "Here, you can get a better look through these. The promontory her house sits on is called Puffin Point. They say puffins nested there before the island was populated."

Brie scanned the eastern shore, stopping to study the artist's cottage before moving on again. Five or six lobsterboats plied the waters off the eastern side of the island. Through the binoculars she watched them pause here and there among a flotilla of brightly colored buoys and haul up a pair of traps at each stop. She moved the glasses farther north, hoping to catch a glimpse of the village, but it was hidden behind the forest.

She handed the binoculars back to Ben and walked around to the ocean side of the lighthouse, thinking how amazing it would be to own this place, to come up here and observe the world from this vantage point, like master of the kingdom. *A view to die for.* As soon as the thought crossed her mind, she felt guilty, remembering about Harold and the fall. She was glad she hadn't spoken the words aloud. She cleared the image of the accident from her mind and turned to Ben. "This is an amazing place. You're a lucky man."

"I am, indeed," he replied.

Chapter 3

The keeper's house wasn't nearly as spectacular as the lighthouse. But what it lacked in drama, it made up for in charm. The five of them climbed the granite block steps and clustered onto a small covered stoop that formed the right-hand corner of the house. When they stepped into the entry hall, the smell of paint and sawdust greeted them. A staircase with a curving wood banister rose to a small landing that was graced by a tall window with lace curtains. The pine-floored hallway walked through to the kitchen, and under the stairs a homey alcove held an antique drop-front desk. A small, stained glass lamp atop the desk cast a yellow glow around the little nook.

They stepped through an archway on their left into the living room. It was a warm, inviting space. The walls were freshly painted in a pale golden-yellow, and the sun streaming in the front window set the room aglow. On the wall opposite the archway, an elaborate system of bookcases framed a west-facing window. A cozy window seat had been cleverly constructed as part of the library unit. It was a perfect spot to watch the sunset over the ocean.

"Did you build these bookcases?" John asked.

"Spent most of May on them," Ben said.

"Nice work." John stepped across the room and ran a hand over the smooth dark wood.

"Those shipwright skills come in mighty handy," Ben said.

Brie looked around the room. The large window on the front wall faced south, giving an unobstructed ocean view. Under the window sat a long coffee table strewn with *Down East* and *National Geographic* magazines, and books on construction and furniture building. A big comfortable sofa with worn, brown-velvet upholstery sat behind the table and faced out the window. A black iron woodstove filled the left corner of the living room. Two wooden rockers sat before it, promising refuge on cold Maine days. The beautiful heart-pine floor glowed with freshly applied varnish, and a large hooked rug in multicolored hues filled the center of the room

"It looks like you've been busy the past few months," Scott said.

"It's felt really good to work with wood and tools again," Ben said. "I feel calmer than I have in years."

"Did you redo the floors?" George asked.

"Yup," Ben said. "Rented a sander from the hardware store in Barnacle Bay. It was a big job."

"There's a lot of beauty in this old wood," George said. He squatted down and ran his hand over the polished floorboards.

George had a love for things antique. This love, of course, encompassed all historical aspects of the *Maine Wind*, foremost among these being his treasured cast-iron woodstove in the galley, which he affectionately referred to as Old Faithful. But his passion for antiques extended far beyond the *Maine Wind*. Over the past couple months, whenever they had had a day or two in port, George had dragged Brie to yard sales and flea markets. There he hovered over antique cookware and kerosene lamps, handmade quilts, and musty books by obscure authors. Brie was fascinated by the process, but equally disturbed by the thought of collecting a lot of stuff just because it was old. She wasn't sure if her feelings came from growing up in Minnesota with too many thrifty Scandinavian friends, or if the problem stemmed from her parents' penchant for relentless stockpiling. She suspected it was the latter.

Edna and Tom Beaumont were always on the lookout for a good deal. Whether it was something useful, like paper towels or something nearly useless, like left-handed scissors for a right-handed family, their philosophy was buy twelve, not one. Eventually their modest home fairly strained at the seams from excess stuff, and Brie had ended up with something akin to an allergic reaction to the material world. When she had set up her own apartment, an adamant minimalism ruled her choices. Well, most of them, anyway. There *were* her books—the one exception to the rule. These rose in precarious stacks around her apartment because she never seemed to find time to purchase bookcases. She had occasionally wondered if she took some subconscious comfort in those piles; if, in fact, some small part of her were not ruled by the Beaumont chaos gene.

At any rate, she allowed George to drag her to sales and wrote it off to her desire to form closer bonds with her shipmates. But, to her surprise, she'd begun affectionately fingering embroidered pillowcases and looking for rare pieces of cranberry glass. So far she'd refrained from actually buying them, but she took note of her affinity for them and thought it curious. She added it to the growing list of shifts and changes in herself since the tragic incident over a year ago.

They had moved into the small dining room, which was empty except for a drop-leaf table, placed against the side wall under the window, and six chairs that were lined up sentry-like along the back wall. A collection of kerosene lamps covered the tabletop. The rest of the room was filled with extra lumber, tarps, paint cans, and tools.

The kitchen was a deconstruction zone. Cabinets were either missing their doors or in the process of being dismantled. In a couple of spots the linoleum had been ripped up, revealing the original wood, so gouged and stained Brie doubted anything of beauty could ever rise from its ashes. Part of the lath and plaster had been ripped off the back wall. A door on the same wall led to a good-sized pantry beyond.

"Are you taking down this wall?" Brie asked.

"That's the plan," Ben said. He stroked his chin as if an imaginary beard grew there.

Scott stuck his head around the corner to see the pantry. "This'll add some good space to the kitchen," he said.

A bank of cabinets filled the entire back wall of the pantry. The upper cabinets had glass doors, and the bottom of the unit contained a bank of drawers and bins for flour, sugar, and potatoes.

"You gonna save these nice old cabinets?" Scott asked.

"Sure am," Ben said. "I've got my hands full with projects this summer, but next summer I plan to strip and refinish them."

"Well, don't forget to kick back a little," John said. "Leave some time for your birding."

"Plenty of time to relax when I'm dead," Ben shot back. There was gruffness in his voice that brought Brie's head up. She glanced at John.

"You're right about that," John said, deferring to Ben, and dropped the subject of bird watching for the time being.

Brie tried to reconcile Ben's comment with the "haven't felt this calm in years" remark of a few minutes ago. Maybe this was just his stern side that Scott had mentioned earlier, but Ben did seem driven. She wondered if his wife's illness and death had contributed to this tendency. Her mom had always told her, "Men are fixers. It's hard for them when they encounter something they can't fix."

Having finished most of the tour, Ben pulled a tray full of steaks out of the old Kelvinator refrigerator that looked to be from the 1950s. "We're eating alfresco tonight," he announced. "The baked potatoes are already on the grill. They should be nearly done by now. Hope you're all hungry."

"Scott and I made some cookies this afternoon and brought them in case you needed a dessert," George said. He opened the small rucksack he had slung on his back and took out a plastic container.

"Great," Ben said. "Somehow, I never get to the dessert." The gruffness had vanished. He opened a drawer next to the sink and took out a frilly pink apron that must have belonged to his wife. Without a second thought, he placed it over his head and tied it in the back. The apron coupled with Ben's muscular arms and military straightness formed an incongruous picture. He offered no explanations, but picked up the tray of steaks and headed out the back door. Brie and the others stowed their packs in a corner of the kitchen and followed him.

A few yards from the door, a large kettle-grill smoked away, and a picnic table stood at the ready, its red-and-white-checked tablecloth held in place against the wind by a good-sized rock on each corner. Ben lifted the top off the grill and added some more briquettes. He tested the foil-wrapped potatoes nested among the coals, moved them to a cooler spot on the grill rack, and put the top back on the cooker. "We'll give those coals a few minutes," he said. "Let's grab a cold drink and sit down. I've got beer and soda."

He opened the top of a cooler that sat on the ground beside the picnic table. Everyone opted for the beer, and Ben extracted five frosty bottles, popped off the tops, and handed them around. They walked over to a group of six Adirondack chairs, of various ages and colors, that were placed in an arc around a stone fire pit and faced out to sea.

"I borrowed a few chairs from my neighbor Amanda, so we could all sit around and enjoy a few campfires—weather permitting."

"You should have had Amanda join us tonight," John said.

"No reason for that," Ben said. "We're just neighbors who occasionally help each other out."

Brie noticed that Ben seemed flustered. He shifted in his chair as if to turn away from the subject of Amanda. "So, how do you like the *Maine Wind*, Brie?" he asked.

"Well, I have to pinch myself every day to make sure all this is really happening. Working aboard the *Maine Wind* has brought real joy back into my life."

"John's told me a little of your story," Ben said. "You deserve every bit of that joy. But I've been admonished not to ask too many prying questions about your police work."

"I'll admit it hasn't been my favorite topic in the past year," Brie said. "But I'm learning I can't completely hide from the job that's been the focus of my entire adult life. I need to somehow make peace with the fact that my partner is gone, and that certain things about me have changed."

Ben's voice became surprisingly gentle. "You know, Brie, I have a close friend who's an officer with the Maine State Police. He was shot a number of years back. He says it turns everything in your life upside down—changes everything you thought you knew about yourself." He studied Brie for a moment before continuing. "I really believe when you brush that close to death and survive, there's a very good reason. Something you've yet to do—maybe in your case, a life you've yet to save."

"I wonder," was all Brie said, but she was touched by the understanding in Ben's voice. She knew he must be all too familiar with the battle against mortality. He had watched his wife wage and lose that battle, and so had become part of the brotherhood of those who are forced to stand helplessly by.

"You know, Ben, as a cop, you somehow manage to convince yourself that it will never happen to you. But really, it's a numbers game, and the longer you play, the greater the odds you'll end up in the wrong place at the wrong time. That night, we were in the wrong place. My partner's number came up, and mine nearly did too." She looked toward the ocean for a moment, but then turned back to him, wanting to finish, knowing he would understand what she was about to say. "I've spent the last fifteen months alternately wishing it had been me that died and wondering why it wasn't. I've felt real guilt over surviving, and only recently has that guilt begun to turn to gratitude. And to come back to where we started, being here this summer—well, I'm thankful for it. And I'm thankful for the *Maine Wind* and these three great guys." She glanced shyly at her shipmates. "But enough about me."

Ben reached over and patted her knee. "Fair enough. But I reserve the right to get to know more about you later. And as for these three great guys, I'll bet they'd be grateful for a steak and a baked potato. So, what say we eat?"

Ben put the steaks on the grill, and Brie and George went back in the house for plates and silverware. John cracked open some more beers, and Scott went inside to get the salad and dressing out of the refrigerator. Within fifteen minutes they were all gathered around the picnic table enjoying dinner. The July sun warmed them with its intensity, even as it crept steadily toward the western horizon. The cloud bank in the distance seemed to have halted, and a gentle breeze brought the freshness of the ocean to them. Sitting between George and John, Brie felt the added warmth of friendship, good food, and drink.

Ben told a funny story about bargaining with one of the islanders, named Hooky Wilson, for the old Ford pickup truck that sat on the gravel drive behind the lighthouse.

"Hooky claimed the price he'd set had a lot to do with the vehicle's sentimental value," Ben said. "He'd earned the money for that truck, which he named *Rover*, working stern on a lobsterboat the summers he was fifteen and sixteen." Ben gestured toward the vehicle. "He insisted on regaling me with his escapades aboard the dilapidated conveyance. Said adventures occurred during his last two years of high school and earned him his moniker, Hooky. I told him no one was going to pay what he was asking, and maybe he should keep the truck—have it bronzed or something.

"Well, we finally struck a deal. He asked if I'd vacate the grounds here one evening, leaving the lighthouse open, so he could bring his girlfriend up to the top for a picnic. He said he wanted to propose to her up there. Now, how could I say no to that? The guy obviously has a romantic streak. Anyway, it worked out for both of us. He got the girl, and I got the truck."

Primed with this tale, Scott suggested they "start the lantern swinging," which meant telling their most exciting—in other words, most harrowing—sea stories.

John and Ben were flipping a bottle cap to see who'd go first when Scott pointed toward the woods. "Someone's coming."

They turned to see what looked like a teenage girl, just beyond the edge of the forest, heading toward them. As she got closer, Ben said, "That's Wendy McLeod, one of the young people from the island." He got up and went to greet her, and Brie, curious about the girl and what she was doing here this late in the evening, decided to follow.

Wendy was tall and slim, with chestnut hair that hung to just above her waist. It swayed gracefully from side to side as she approached in long strides. As they closed the gap, Ben hailed her. "Hello, Wendy."

"Hi, Mr. Rutledge," she called back.

She came to a stop before them and looked at Brie with large, questioning eyes the shape and color of roasted almonds.

"I have friends visiting," Ben said. "They sailed in this evening on the schooner *Maine Wind*. This is Brie Beaumont. She works on the ship."

"Hi, Wendy," Brie said, extending her hand.

A shy smile raised one corner of Wendy's mouth as she took Brie's hand. "Nice to meet you," she said. She looked back at Ben. "I came over to see if you might have seen Amanda. I was supposed to have a music lesson with her this evening. I waited around for quite awhile, and when she didn't come back, I thought she might be over here." The brown eyes turned back to Brie. "She forgets sometimes or loses track of the time," the girl explained. "Then I heard laughter as I came through the woods, and I thought she must be here." Wendy looked hopefully past them toward the picnic table.

"I'm sorry, Wendy, I haven't seen Amanda since this morning. When I went into the village earlier today for groceries, I stopped by her place to see if she wanted anything. On the way home, I dropped off a bottle of milk and a newspaper for her. Maybe she went off island or, as you say, just forgot about your lesson."

"Sometimes, when she's busy with her art, she does forget about things," Wendy admitted. She bit the corner of her lip, and her eyes slid sideways. She worked nervously at removing something real or imagined from beneath her left thumbnail.

It was obvious to Brie that Amanda was, somehow, very important to the girl and that the connection between them ran deeper than that of just student and teacher.

"I'm sure you'll catch up with her tomorrow," Ben reassured Wendy. "I'll give you a ride back to your house. It's getting dark, and it's a long walk."

"That's okay, Mr. Rutledge. You don't need to."

"But I want to, Wendy," Ben said, closing the discussion. "Brie, why don't you ride along? You can see where the village is."

"I'd love to," Brie said, smiling at Wendy.

Ben walked over to where the other three still sat at the picnic table and told them he and Brie were taking Wendy home.

"We'll clean up," John said.

"Why don't you start a fire in the fire pit?" Ben said. "When Brie and I get back, we'll all sit out for awhile and have some coffee."

Ben went into the house to get his keys. He brought out a Coleman lantern and gave it to John to light. Then he, Brie, and Wendy headed for the truck.

There was still plenty of light on the point where the lighthouse stood, but as soon as they headed into the forest, darkness descended. Ben switched on the headlights as they proceeded along the gravel road. Wendy sat in the middle of the seat with Brie next to the passenger side door. The window on her side was rolled down, and the cool, pine-scented air and night sounds of the forest filled the truck's cab.

They hadn't gone far when Wendy pointed off to the right. "That's where Amanda lives."

Up a short spur of road marked Puffin Point, a log house sat all by itself on a jutting point of land. Its west-facing windows reflected the last rosy remnants of sunset. Brie realized it was the same house she'd seen earlier from her vantage point atop the lighthouse, and supposed the isolated setting would appeal to an artist.

Not far past Amanda's house an intersecting road headed west toward the other side of the island. "Wendy lives down this side," Ben said, pointing straight ahead, "but we may as well take the long way around so you can see how the roads run on the island." With that he turned left and followed the road across the middle of the island. Where it intersected with West Island Road, they turned right and headed north toward the village of Barnacle Bay.

They had driven on in silence for a little ways when Brie turned to Wendy. "You said you take music lessons from Amanda. What instrument do you play?"

"Oh, it's just piano lessons," Wendy said. "I'm not very good, though—it's just for fun."

"Well, the best way to get good at something is to have fun doing it," Brie said. Wendy was unusually pretty, but Brie sensed the girl's self-esteem could use a boost.

"That's what Amanda says," Wendy replied, her voice brightening a bit as she mentioned her teacher. "I take art lessons, too. I'm better at art," she said quietly, dipping her head slightly toward Brie and lowering her voice, as if she'd just admitted something that needed to be kept secret.

"Do you draw or paint?" Brie asked.

"I make a sketch first, and then I do the painting from that. I'm learning to do watercolor. But it's hard." Wendy lowered her head, working on the thumb nail again. "My mom was good at watercolors," she said.

There was something wistful in Wendy's tone of voice that gave Brie the impression the girl's mother had died. That would explain the importance of Amanda in her life, she thought.

Near the end of the island, the road made a sharp right and ran along behind several gray shake-sided Capes that varied little in appearance. The pickup bumped down a hill, and at the bottom the gravel road turned to blacktop, indicating that they had officially entered the village of Barnacle Bay. They had passed a few houses, a hardware store with a jumble of merchandise in the front window, and a general store that had a tiny post office built onto one side of it, when they saw three men walking together a short ways down the road.

"There's my brother," Wendy said, pointing to them.

Ben stopped the truck just behind the men and rolled down his window.

"Doug!" Wendy called out.

The three turned, and Brie got a look at them in the headlights. They were an incongruous trio—young and handsome, tall and distinguished, and in the middle...hmmm—how to describe the third? Short was all that came to Brie initially. The men came over to Ben's window and leaned down so all three of their heads were framed in the opening. Ben switched on the light inside the truck so they could all see each other. The young, handsome head had dark-blond hair, cropped close. The tall, distinguished head sported a close-clipped beard that looked out of balance beneath a thick shock of unruly gray hair. It almost seemed like he and the young guy should swap hair. The short head, while not that old, had seen some weather and was handsome in a rough-hewn sort of way, with green eyes and wavy dark brown hair secured in a short ponytail at the back of the neck.

"Wendy, why aren't you home by now?" asked the young guy. "I thought you'd gone to your music lesson. What do you think you're doing?"

"I went to Amanda's for my lesson, but she wasn't there," Wendy explained. "So I waited around awhile and then walked to the lighthouse to see if she might be out there. But she wasn't, and Mr. Rutledge wanted to drive me home."

"Sorry for the inconvenience, Ben," the young man said. As he spoke, his blue eyes moved from Ben to Brie and settled there.

"No inconvenience," Ben said. "I didn't think Wendy should walk back in the dark. That's all."

The young man reached a hand in the window past Ben and Wendy. "I'm Doug McLeod," he said, eyes still on Brie.

Brie took his hand, meeting his gaze. "Brie Beaumont," she said. There was confidence in the gaze and in the handshake. Brie guessed both were a byproduct of his excessive good looks.

"I've got friends visiting up at the lighthouse," Ben said in way of explanation. "They sailed in on the *Maine Wind* this afternoon. My friend, John DuLac, is captain of the *Maine Wind*, and Brie here is part of his crew." Ben proceeded to introduce the other two men to Brie. "This is Bob Weatherby," he said, indicating the ponytailed head. "He runs the bait business down on the wharf. And this is Spencer Holloman. He's the town manager here on Sentinel Island."

The tall, distinguished head gave a nod. "Pleased to meet you, Brie," he said in a deep, resonant voice that sounded like it should sing bass in an a cappella group.

"Nice to meet you, too," Brie responded.

"You haven't seen Amanda around the village, have you?" Wendy asked, not directing the question to any one of them in particular.

"I'm sure she's around somewhere," Doug said. "You know she forgets your lesson sometimes, Wendy. You can catch up with her tomorrow. Now, hop out of the truck. I'm on my way to the Scuttlebutt for a poker game with the boys, but I'll walk you home first."

Ben opened the truck door and stepped out, and Wendy slid under the wheel and hopped out.

Doug leaned back down and spoke to Brie. "I'll see you around, Brie," he said with an affirmative tone that made it sound as if their next meeting were assured.

Ben got back in the truck, and they continued on through the village and out the other end. They swung south and picked up East Island Road.

"I get the impression Wendy's mother is dead," Brie said.

"Not just her mother," Ben said. "Both her parents drowned in a bad squall on the way back from the mainland one night three years ago. The next day a lobsterman found the McLeods' lobsterboat adrift with no one aboard a few miles east of the island. The Coast Guard never recovered the bodies, but it was thought Sarah may have been washed overboard, and Evan may have gone in to save her and didn't make it. Apparently, Sarah couldn't swim, so if she went overboard without a life jacket, in those seas, there wouldn't have been much hope for her. But Evan was a strong swimmer, so his death's more of a mystery."

In the dim light Brie saw Ben stroke his chin, worrying his imaginary beard. "Amanda—you know, the artist—she told me the McLeods had been having marital problems," Ben continued. "She'd known the family for a couple of years before the accident occurred. She was never convinced that it *was* an accident. It came out afterward that Evan had battled depression for years."

"So, is it just Wendy and her brother left?" Brie asked.

"That's right. Doug became her guardian. She was only thirteen when the parents died." Ben glanced over at Brie. "How old would you say young Doug is?"

"Hmmm," said Brie, "about thirty-three, I'd guess."

"It's amazing how that kind of responsibility matures a person. Actually, he's only twenty-seven," Ben said.

"He's protective of Wendy; that's obvious."

"He's done a great job with her, but it hasn't left him much time for his own life. He sure seemed interested in you, though, Brie. I wouldn't be surprised if he comes courting," Ben joked.

"He's a little young for me, wouldn't you say?"

"I'm not so sure he saw it that way. Truth be told, I've known quite a few forty-year-olds who couldn't hold a candle to that young man. I'll tell you one thing, John won't be happy if he comes calling."

Brie turned and gazed out the window at the blackness of the forest. If Ben was fishing, she wasn't taking the bait. No doubt John had told him something, but right now she had nothing to add to that something, especially since she wasn't all that certain herself what was going on between her and John. She changed the subject.

"So, have the islanders befriended you?" she asked.

"So far there's been no rush to send out the welcome wagon. But that's typical for year-round residents on these islands. They don't roll out the welcome mat all that easily. I think you kind of have to earn their trust." He stopped the truck suddenly as a deer bounded into the headlights. "Also, I'm in my own little world out at the end of the island, so I don't see the rest of them all that much. Amanda's been nice, but she's a warm person by nature. I can't imagine her ostracizing anyone."

As they pulled out of the forest, the last vestiges of daylight illuminated the end of the island. A ghostly presence in the fleeting light, the white stone tower seemed both taller and more austere than it had in the warmth of the afternoon sun. Beyond the keeper's house, flames danced above the fire pit, and flurries of glowing sparks rose skyward on the warm currents. John, Scott, and George lounged in the Adirondack chairs, silhouettes against the brightness of the blaze.

Ben parked the truck, and he and Brie went to join them. George had made coffee, and Scott had foraged some marshmallow sticks. They fell to the business of roasting marshmallows and planning the next day's activities. The men planned to take down the wall in the kitchen, and since four men needed no help tearing down one small wall, Brie volunteered to finish painting some of the trim on the outside of the house—a job that Ben had started but not completed.

They sat visiting by the fire for another hour, but Brie was beginning to feel all in. "What's the plan for sleeping arrangements?" she asked, letting out a yawn. "Do you want any of us to go back to the ship, John?"

"It's really up to Ben," John said. "We set a second anchor, so I don't think we have to worry. Even if we get a blow from the south in the night, the ship is protected in the cove."

"I've got plenty of room here. There are beds in all three bedrooms upstairs, although a couple of the mattresses aren't the best. Brie, I thought you could have the back bedroom over the kitchen. There are two beds in the front bedroom if you want to sleep in there with me, John. That leaves the third bedroom, which has a single bed, and the sofa in the living room."

"I'd be happy to cook breakfast for everyone," George said.

"George, your reputation precedes you," Ben said. "I'd never want to impose, but it'd sure be a nice way to start the day."

"No problem," George said, suddenly way too perky for the hour. "I noticed your larder and fridge are pretty well stocked. I think I can come up with something. I'll sleep on the sofa in the living room if no one minds," he said, as if nocturnal proximity to the kitchen assured a truly fine breakfast.

Brie could tell from his expression that he was already evolving an elaborate culinary plan, and it gave her a warm, cozy feeling. A day of hard work would be almost tolerable if it could start with breakfast by George. She stretched her arms overhead. "Well, guys, I'm all in, so I'll see you in the morning.

George, as soon as I smell the coffee, I'll come down and give you a hand. Thanks for dinner, Ben—it was delicious."

"The electricity's shut off, Brie, because of tearing out the wall, but there are some oil lamps and matches on the table in the dining room. You can light one and bring it up to your room with you."

"I'll feel right at home," Brie said, "since oil lamps 'R' us aboard the *Maine Wind*."

Ben pointed over to the picnic table where the Coleman lantern threw out a large circle of light. "Take the lantern in with you, so you can see what you're doing."

As Brie headed toward the picnic table, John stood up. "You staying up for awhile, Ben?" he asked.

"I think I'll sit out here a bit longer," Ben replied.

"Great, I'll grab a little more coffee and keep you company."

"Me too," Scott said, and started to get up.

John took his cup. "I'll get you a refill. How 'bout you, George? Want some more coffee?"

"No, I'm good," George said happily, obviously invigorated enough by his breakfast plans to forego more caffeine.

"Ben? Coffee?" John asked.

"No, I'm good. Any more and I'll be up all night."

Brie had started for the house, and John caught up with her. "I'll show you to your room, Brie."

"Okay," she said, suppressing a smile. *Not too hard to find the back room over the kitchen,* she thought, *especially for a homicide detective. Hmmm,* she wondered, *do I detect an ulterior motive? One can always hope.*

They stepped into the kitchen, and John set the two cups on the stove. Brie picked up the small backpack she'd left in the corner, and they walked into the dining room to collect an oil lamp. John automatically selected the prettiest one from the bunch. The lamp had a tall, slender chimney that sat on top of a pink, etched glass base.

"I think this one suits you, Brie," he said. Striking a match, he lifted the chimney and lit the wick. With John carrying the lamp, they made their way through the living room and climbed the stairs, which came out in a narrow hall at the top. On the left, a door to the front bedroom stood slightly open. Straight ahead across the hall, the lamp illuminated a small bathroom with an old claw-foot tub and a black-and-white tile floor. Down the hall to the right were two more doors to the back bedrooms.

John opened the one on the right and they stepped into a small square room with a bed tucked into the corner. An antique dresser sat catty-corner from the foot of the bed. A window next to the dresser looked north toward the blackness of the forest. Another window in the same corner faced east, where it would let in the sunrise. The ceiling sloped to accommodate the eaves of the house, giving the room a nestled-away coziness. The light from the lamp cast shadows about the room, dimly illuminating a few pictures on the wall of a family that must have tended the light at one time. From their clothes Brie guessed the photos were from the 1920s.

She stepped over to open the east-facing window, but the sash stuck. John stepped up behind her and gave the window a blow with the butt of both his hands. He reached down and lifted the sash. "There you go," he said. His voice created a pleasant vibration in the air just above her right ear.

She felt the heat from his body engulf her and fill the tiny corner they occupied at the end of the bed. "Thanks, John," she said, turning slowly around.

He held his ground and, placing one hand above her shoulder, leaned against the window frame and looked directly into her eyes. "I'm looking forward to these next few days," he said in a husky voice. He reached up with his other hand and gently traced the line of her jaw.

They had waited two months to be together again like this, and Brie felt a warm current course through her body. She reached out and slipped her arms around his waist, and that was all it took. His arm came down off the window and circled around her neck. He kissed her gently several times before pulling her against him and giving her a kiss so deep and sexy she thought the floor might ignite underfoot and send them straight down into the kitchen.

"Wow," Brie whispered when they parted lips for a moment. "That was worth waiting for."

"Wow, yourself," John said. "And by the way, I'm not quite finished." He kissed her again, and then with his free hand gathered her long hair together at the back of her neck. He pulled on it gently so her chin came up, and he had just placed his head down into her neck to kiss it when they heard the screen door to the kitchen bang shut.

They immediately stepped apart like two teenagers caught misbehaving. "I think we'd better call it a night," Brie said. "Sounds like Scott got tired of waiting for his coffee."

"I'll see you in the morning," John whispered. He reached out and stroked her upper arm with his knuckles, giving her a look that, while fleeting, went to her very core. He turned and left the room, shutting the door quietly behind him. A few moments later, she heard movement below in the kitchen and the sound of the back door opening and closing again.

She walked over and pulled back the covers on the bed. The patchwork quilt and cotton sheets had the worn softness of many washings. Sitting down on the bed, she bounced up and down a couple of times, testing the mattress. A little on the soft side, but it would do. She wondered for a moment how it might hold up with two on board, and unconsciously lifted her hand to touch the side of her face that John had stroked.

After a moment or two, she picked up the oil lamp and her backpack and went into the bathroom to wash up before bed. When she returned a few minutes later, she tried one of the windows on the back wall. It opened, and she stood for a few moments staring out into the darkness, feeling the cool night air on her bare arms. She could hear the ocean working relentlessly on the cliff beneath the lighthouse and, in counterpoint to that, the night sounds of the forest—crickets, toads, and the occasional hooting of an owl.

With a yawn, Brie stepped away from the window and turned down the wick on the oil lamp. In the fading lamplight, she took off her deck shoes and slipped out of her khakis. Tossing them over the metal footboard of the bed, she crawled under the covers. The sheets felt cool on her bare legs, and she rolled up in a ball to get warm. A wave of drowsiness washed over her, but she fought to stay abreast of it. She wanted to relive those few passionate moments with John, and as she did, her mind went to work and spun out a wonderful *what if* scenario. She was enjoying variations of that theme when she finally slipped into unconsciousness.

Chapter 4

T he killer maneuvered Amanda's stiffened body out of the base of the casting onto the tarp he had spread out. He noticed the marks on her neck had turned a deep, hideous purple. He tried not to look at them as he folded the tarp over. A strong smell of burned coffee filled the room. He wished he had noticed the coffee maker on when he was here earlier. Outside, lightning strobed. When thunder rattled the windows, he glanced nervously about him, unable to shake the feeling that someone was watching.

Calm down. Focus on what you're doing, the voice in his head admonished. He hated that voice. It reminded him of a woman, always nagging at him.

He ran a loop of rope through the grommets of the tarp and pulled it tight to form a closure, so it resembled a gigantic coin pouch. He felt his hands sweating under the rubber gloves as he tipped the casting back up. "Now, for that boat ride I promised you this afternoon, Amanda. It's too bad you're going to be lost at sea in this storm. You should have thought twice about crossing in this kind of weather." He smiled, momentarily calmed by his own twisted humor.

He dragged the tarp over to the back door and snapped off the light. He wrestled the awkward bundle through the door and down the two steps that led to the path. The lightning came so frequently he didn't need the flashlight he'd carried in his rain slicker.

The perfect storm. He chuckled at the thought. "It couldn't have worked out better if I'd ordered it. Everyone knows how careless you are, Mandy. They'll write this off as another one of your bad decisions."

Just keep moving, the voice in his head admonished. *You're not done yet. You could still screw it up.*

"Shut up!" the killer shouted, stopping in his tracks. "You shut up." He looked around him, momentarily disoriented. Applying his anger to the task at hand, he pulled his grim bundle the rest of the way down to a small cove and wrestled Amanda's body into the large inflatable boat pulled up on the beach. He pushed off into the dark water beyond and motored toward the lobsterboat anchored a little ways offshore.

The earsplitting thunderclap woke Brie with a jolt. The air reverberated around her body. She felt as if she were falling, and the imagined odor of stale cigarettes and body sweat played tricks with her mind, pulling her back to the night she'd been shot—to the darkness of that house, the smell, the deafening sound of the gun firing. She sat up and swung her legs over the edge of the bed, but it took a moment to orient herself. Her skin felt clammy, and her breath came in short, shallow gulps. She fought back the familiar wave of nausea that always accompanied these flashbacks. When the lightning came again, she glanced around the room, trying to ground herself in her current reality.

She rose to shut the windows as thunder rocked the walls of the small room. Her hands shook as she pushed the sash down on the first window. She moved over to the window at the foot of the bed. The rain was blowing in hard, dampening the sill and the floor where she stood. She tried to push the window down, but it stuck. She'd just given it a blow with both hands, as John had done, when something caught her attention. She stopped and squinted through the rain. She could just barely make out a faint light through the forest to the northeast of her. *That would be*

51

Amanda's house. She must have gotten home. Brie supposed the artist was up, also closing windows against the storm. As she stood peering into the darkness, the light suddenly went out.

On her third attempt Brie managed to get the window down. The dampness of her skin coupled with the wind and rain blowing in had chilled her, and she shivered in the darkness. She felt around for her backpack and, in the next flash of lightning, pulled out a pair of soft knit pajama bottoms she'd stuck into her pack, just in case. She put them on and climbed back under the covers to warm up.

Wendy will be happy Amanda's back, Brie thought, and was glad of it, too, for the girl's sake. Wendy seemed a bit lost. Brie had encountered enough young runaways in her work to know how important a mother was to a girl Wendy's age—even if it was a surrogate mother. Brie had a soft spot for the lost and troubled ones. As she lay in the dark listening to the rain, the faces of girls she'd mentored over the past ten years drifted in and out of her mind, and she felt the same thing she always felt—gratitude for her family and her childhood. Gratitude that she'd been spared from a life of abuse, and what that life might have turned her into.

The lightning and thunder were moving off, but the wind still whistled around the eaves of the house. *No whistling at sea. You'll whistle up a storm.* The old maritime superstition lingered a moment in her mind, along with a fleeting image of a woman— she was out at sea in the storm, and she was whistling. The odd thought disturbed Brie. After a moment she shook her head to clear the image and snuggled deeper into her covers. Before long, the comforting weight of the patchwork quilt and the rhythmic thrumming of the rain on the roof overhead, coaxed her back to sleep.

The smell of George's rich, dark coffee put a smile on Brie's face before she even got her eyes open. She lay there and inhaled deeply. *George is in the kitchen. All's right with the world.* It was a dark, drizzly morning. *There'll be no trim painting today,* she thought, and decided that, after breakfast, she'd take a walk down the road to Puffin Point, introduce herself to Amanda, and let her know Wendy was worried about her.

She crawled out from under the covers and found her toiletries in her backpack. George's coffee was about the only thing that could have motivated her on a day like this. She went down the hall to the bathroom and washed up. Back in her room, she put on a pair of well-worn jeans and a pale pink tee shirt. Against the chill of the morning, she pulled a gray v-neck cotton sweater over her head and strapped on her watch. It read 7:30 a.m. Brie was of the old school. She liked a watch. Even though cell phones were allowed on the *Maine Wind,* she had no need for one. There was no one she wanted to call. She had sent letters to her mother and her friend Ariel, letting them know where she was, but had no real desire to talk to anyone about her choices. Living on the *Maine Wind,* she had entered into an anachronistic lifestyle to which she felt oddly suited, and so the phone had remained at the bottom of her sea bag since she had boarded the ship in May.

She walked over to the window next to the dresser and looked toward the forest, where she'd seen the lights during the night. She remembered the strange image her mind had conjured up of a woman at sea in the storm. Brie didn't like to dwell on such things, but she had learned not to ignore them either. She turned from the window and headed downstairs to help George with the breakfast.

George was laying out bacon on a sheet pan and sprinkling it with ground black pepper and brown sugar in preparation for placing it in the oven. Flour, milk, eggs, and a bowl of frozen blueberries sat on the small kitchen table.

"Hey, George. I see you're giving the bacon your four-star treatment."

"Only the best for you, Brie. I know it's your favorite."

This was true. Brie had never tasted anything quite as good as George's bacon. When they were at sea, she loved smelling that bacon cooking as they went about their morning duties on the deck of the *Maine Wind*. Mopping the deck was actually a pleasure with those wonderful aromas wafting from the big stovepipe above the galley.

"So, what can I do to help?" she asked.

"Why don't you mix up the pancake batter while I finish the bacon?"

"I think everyone will be down before long. The smell of that coffee will bring 'em around."

"That was my plan."

Brie walked over to the table and started measuring out the flour. She knew George's pancake recipe by heart. She sometimes helped him down in the galley in the morning, since they were sailing without a mess-mate this season. In the short amount of time she'd spent on the *Maine Wind*, George and Scott had come to feel like brothers and the ship like her home. After all, they shared a common goal of keeping the ship running smoothly, much as a family keeps a household running. She had lived alone for so many years that being part of such a close-knit group, while foreign at first, now offered great comfort to her.

"Once we start tearing out that wall, I suppose cooking will cease in the kitchen for awhile," Brie said.

"I think I can make something in the oven for dinner. Ben has enough ingredients for a stew. I'm going to brown the meat after breakfast and cut up the veggies. I'll put the whole thing in a casserole so it can go in the oven later."

"Mmmm, that sounds delicious, George. I'll help with the chopping after breakfast."

"Are you two already planning dinner?" John asked as he walked into the kitchen and headed for the coffee pot. "This is your chance for a break, George. I don't want you feeling like you have to cook the whole time we're here. We can always go into Barnacle Bay and forage for food."

"Oh, I don't mind, Captain," George replied. "It's just lucky Ben's stove runs on propane, though, or we'd be out of luck."

Brie had decided over the past two months that George lived to cook. It was his form of self-expression, and like any artist, his happiness was rooted in practicing his craft.

Footsteps on the stairs announced the arrival of Scott and Ben. "Why don't we set up the table in the dining room," Ben said, seeing George preparing to pour the first pancakes onto the griddle. "There are dishes and silverware in the pantry. Come on, Scott." He and Scott disappeared into the pantry, and Brie followed John into the dining room.

There were three oil lamps still on the table, and Brie set them on the floor in the corner. As they moved the table out from the wall and placed five chairs around it, she cast a few furtive glances at John, noticing how his chest muscles moved under the snug gray tee shirt he wore. She spread a green woven cloth on the table, feeling his eyes on her as well. She wished they could continue where they'd left off last night, but Ben and Scott arrived in the dining room with plates and silverware, putting an end to her brief fantasy. They laid five place settings, and within ten minutes, everyone was gathered around the table enjoying sweet bacon and savory blueberry pancakes topped off with some of Maine's best, pale amber maple syrup.

"That was quite a storm last night," John said. He looked across the table at Brie. "I hope it didn't keep you awake."

Brie saw the concern in his eyes. She had told him that thunderstorms often triggered the flashbacks she'd had since the shooting. "It woke me up," she said. "I got up to shut the windows, and I could swear I saw light through the forest in the direction of Amanda's house."

"She must have gotten back from wherever she went," Ben said.

"I thought I'd take a walk over there this morning after breakfast and say hello," Brie said. "It's too wet outside to paint, and I figure you won't be needing me in here. After all, how many sailors can it take to tear down a kitchen wall?"

"Probably one to swing the hammer and two or three to shout orders," Scott quipped.

"See, that's what I'm talking about," Brie said, grateful for Scott's sunny humor on such a dreary morning. "If it clears off later on, I'll get going on the trim outside."

"You can take the truck if you want," Ben said.

"You know what? I'd like to stretch my legs. I'll wear my rain slicker." She looked out the window. A light drizzle was falling, but she didn't mind that. There was no shortage of rainy or foggy days in Maine, and aboard ship she'd quickly gotten used to working in damp weather.

They finished up breakfast and cleared the dishes. George and Brie did the prep for the beef stew that would go in the oven later, and John and Scott washed the dishes. Ben cleared the kitchen area in front of the wall that was about to be demolished and taped cardboard over the cabinets in the pantry to protect the glass doors. He and the other men hung heavy plastic over the kitchen doorways to keep the plaster dust from infiltrating the rest of the house. By the time Brie had slipped into her rain slicker and hiking boots and stepped out the front door, the four men had donned dust masks and were already taking turns with two sledgehammers, tearing into the kitchen wall.

The whole end of the island was wrapped in a soft, moist blanket of fog. She could hear the ocean raising a ruckus at the base of the cliffs. She walked past the lighthouse and out toward the edge of the bluff. The thrill of being constantly near the sea, and all its moods, had not diminished one bit since she'd come to the coast of Maine in April. In fact, the wilder the sea got, the happier she seemed to be, as if all that external drama somehow kept her internal drama at bay. She stood for a few minutes watching a pair of gulls dip in and out of the fog bank. She heard the reports of waves crashing in far below, but any view of them was arrested by the earthbound cloud. After a few minutes, she turned reluctantly and headed toward the narrow road that wound into the forest.

The spruce trees grew so densely at this end of the island that after a few minutes of hiking down the road, the sounds of the sea were nearly eradicated, and her olfactory sense became the dominant one. Smells of wet earth, plant mold, and pine finally brought her to a standstill. She closed her eyes for a moment and breathed in the heady forest bouquet. Certain smells triggered her most sensual yearnings, and the damp, moist smells of the forest raised an ache in her that had become a frequent companion over the past two months. She stood rooted to her spot on the road, her mind steeped in the memory of John's scent and of their encounter last night. *You can't do this, Brie,* she thought to herself. *You can't go down this road till you've made some decisions.*

"I'm already down this road," she said aloud. "Partway, at least. And you know what?" she added defiantly. "I like it." She was tired of trying to reason her way through human relationships, as if they were crime scenes to be dissected and analyzed. What had that gotten her but a lot of loneliness? She had learned in the hardest way possible how short life can be. She had lain down with death and, by some fortuitous twist of fate, been allowed to get up again, and that had changed her. There was something in the resurrected Brie that made her want to hurl, not throw, caution to the wind. She didn't want to make the same mistake with John she'd made with other men; namely, keep him at arm's length till she'd figured everything out. But she didn't want to hurt him either—or herself, for that matter. At the age of thirty-six, she wanted her emotional investments to pay bigger dividends.

She started along the road again. Two very divergent paths lay before her, and by the middle of October she'd have to pick one of them. Either stay in Maine and take a chance with John, which, of course, meant giving up her job at the Minneapolis Police Department; or return to her job and the career she had built over twelve years, which meant giving up John.

She spotted an unusual rock formation a few yards away in a clearing and decided to check it out. As she made her way into the forest, she felt the thick carpet of pine needles underfoot, and she heard the silence. A pine forest is an exceptionally quiet place. Brie wanted to wrap herself in that quiet—use it to still her restless mind. She sat down on a large, flat rock in the clearing. When she took stock of her own flaws, over-thinking was always paramount among them. But how, in her personal life, could she divorce herself from the quality she most needed in her work? That was the problem. As a homicide detective, she dwelt in an analytical realm, constantly weighing people's actions and measuring their motivations; constantly looking back and projecting forward.

Since being shot, she had embarked on a desperate search for the key with which she could turn her mind off at will. Her oldest friend, whom Brie loved but considered weird, had suggested meditation. "You need to learn to live in the Zen of each moment, Brie," Ariel had said. Dear Ariel—the least earthbound person Brie had ever known. Oddly, though, it was the act of being at sea, of working on the *Maine Wind*, that had brought meaning to Ariel's words. For the first time Brie had experienced the freedom of living each day solely to fulfill the needs of that day. What was more, the sights, sounds, and smells of the sea were so all-engrossing that they had awakened the purely sensory part of her. And at the center of the whole experience was the man who had made it all possible for her—the captain of the *Maine Wind*.

Realizing her circuitous thinking had brought her full circle, right back to her yearning for John, Brie threw her arms up in disgust. "See where all that thinking gets you? Exactly nowhere." She stood up and made her way back to the road. A short ways ahead, she came to the sign for Puffin Point and turned right up the narrow gravel road that led to Amanda's house.

Brie came to the top of the rise in the road and stopped. Amanda's house was wrapped in soft, gray batting. On its fog-bound point the house looked even more removed from the world than it had the night before. She stepped up on the porch and knocked on the door. As she did so, she realized that it was still quite early. Sailors run on a different clock, with days usually starting about 6:00 a.m., or 0600 hours. Sleeping in till seven o'clock this morning had been a guilty pleasure. Brie had known a few artists, and as a group, they tended to be late risers. She checked her watch—9:15—not that early. She knocked again, louder this time. The third knock was both longer and louder— *no way Amanda could sleep through that*, she thought. She stood on the porch for a few moments deciding what to do next. It seemed too early for Amanda to be up and gone already.

The porch ran along the front of the cottage, and she noticed a window open to her right. She walked over and peered in. A massive, fieldstone fireplace dominated the room, and a half-log stairway led up to a loft. The room pulsed with color on this dreary morning. The log interior glowed golden in the light from the roof windows. Handmade quilts decorated the walls of the great room. The furniture grouped around the fireplace was covered in fabric with bold Native American designs, and sat on a large rug of deep orange and brown tones.

The kitchen was tucked back under the loft, and a bank of cabinets with a stone countertop formed a peninsula that separated it from the great room, without closing it off completely. In front of the peninsula sat a round pedestal table covered with a red woven tablecloth and surrounded by four Windsor chairs. A pair of windows alongside the table looked east toward the sea, which was currently hidden in fog.

It hadn't seemed odd that this front window, sheltered by the porch, was open, but Brie noticed the two windows near the table were also open. And from her vantage point she thought she could see moisture on the pine floorboards. She knocked again on the window frame and, leaning down, called in the window. "Amanda? Hello. Is anybody home?"

Brie stepped off the porch and walked around the back of the house. A bank of tall windows let light from the north into a large room that ran the length of the house. Amanda used the space as a studio. The room had a vaulted ceiling and an over-sized, barn-style sliding door to allow for easy removal of large pieces of work. There was a heavily built work table in the center of the room that could be accessed from all sides. Two clay sculptures—works in progress—were covered with heavy plastic. Another table along the side wall held sheets of copper and an array of tools—tin snips, hammers, pliers, and two acetylene torches.

Brie noticed a work in progress in the back corner of the studio. It was a large copper sculpture, an underwater scene. Long, slender strips of copper were fashioned into sea kelp through which swam a variety of stylized, copper fish with un-usual colorations. She wondered if the unusual colors and patterns had been created by firing the copper with one of the torches. She'd read about a similar technique in a gallery she had visited in Minneapolis.

She moved around to the east side of the cottage—past a door that led into the kitchen—to where she'd seen the open windows. The ground here was high enough for her to look in and size up the situation. The windowsills and floor were damp from the rain last night. But she'd seen lights on here in the middle of the night. Why wouldn't Amanda have closed these windows against the rain? An uneasy feeling had been develop-ing in the pit of Brie's stomach, and now her detective's antenna was up and receiving. Something felt wrong here, and Brie had learned never to ignore that feeling.

She went back around to the front porch and tried the door. It was unlocked. She stuck her head in and called out loudly, "Amanda? You home?" No response. She stepped in the front door onto a small rug and stood surveying the room. She was looking for anything that seemed odd, and of course, as a homicide detective, she was looking for any signs of intrusion or a struggle. For a minute or two she studied the room—walls, floor, furniture. Finally, she slipped off her boots and rain slicker, left them on the entry rug, and walked forward into the room. Questions filled her mind as they always did in such a situation. *If Amanda wasn't here last night, who was? And why? If Amanda was here last night, why didn't she close the windows? And where has she gone so early in the morning?*

A number of sculptures and castings were placed around the great room. Brie assumed they were Amanda's work. Picking up a bronze casting, she turned it over and saw Whitcombe on its base, which confirmed what she was thinking. Most of the works were abstract in nature, but in the far corner of the great room, a large casting of a sailing ship, bow up, with two masts sinking in an angry sea, was so realistic she expected to hear the cries of frightened sailors.

Brie walked over to it and ran a hand over the pearly silver surface. The casting was wrought from aluminum, and there was a visual coldness about the piece that seemed appropriate to its subject matter. Beneath the bowsprit of the sinking schooner was a figurehead of a mermaid. She had a look of fevered anticipation, as if she'd been waiting a very long time to return to her watery kingdom beneath the waves. Brie stared at the mermaid, mesmerized by her expression, knowing exactly how it felt to be out of one's element—to long to return to a life that had been taken from you.

After a few moments she turned back around. At the opposite end of the room, a baby grand piano sat with its top up. Bookcases filled the wall behind it. Two bronze castings on one of the bookcases caught Brie's attention, and she walked over to look at them. They were bathed in light from one of the skylights. She studied the first. It was a small piece, no more than twelve or fourteen inches tall, and while abstract, it was still

61

easily identified as a pair of lovers entwined. The movement of the piece suggested unbridled joy, and Brie felt a small ache in her chest as she rotated it in a 360-degree circle. She hadn't made love to John, but somehow, she instinctively knew, in the way women often do, that it would be like this. She drew in a slow, deep breath that escaped as an unintended sigh.

She forced herself to turn her attention to the companion piece. It was almost identical in size and of the same abstract style. But the mood of this piece was very different. It depicted a mother cradling a young child. There was something strangely moving and intensely personal about the piece, as if in creating it, Amanda had briefly opened a door to a most desperate long-ing. Brie wondered if the theme of the piece had something to do with Amanda's relationship to her own mother, or if the feel-ing it conveyed was more universal—if it touched on the long-ing for motherhood that crescendos in those years when the biological clock is winding down. Years when the possibility of motherhood still burns in the heart, but like a beautiful, dying sunset. At thirty-six, Brie had begun to feel those flames licking at the gate of her consciousness, threatening to scorch yet an-other piece of her psyche. She pushed the thought out of her mind and headed up the stairs to the loft.

Amanda used the loft as her bedroom. Brie hadn't seen any bedrooms downstairs and wondered whether Amanda's studio, at the back of the house, might at one time have housed a couple of bedrooms. The pine floor of the loft was covered with a vi-brant red rug that ran under the queen-size bed. Mission-style bedroom furniture and some bookshelves filled the rest of the space. The lightweight down quilt on the bed had been hastily pulled up to meet the pillows. Brie slid a hand under the covers to feel for any residual warmth, but the bed was cold.

She walked down the stairs and into the kitchen and looked around for the coffee maker. She lifted the carafe off the hotplate. The coffee had boiled away as the carafe sat on the warmer, leaving the bottom of the glass pot coated with a burned-on residue. The carafe and the warming plate were cold, but the acrid odor of burned coffee was still present when she held the pot to her nose. This must have happened yesterday, Brie thought. Amanda must have gone out, leaving the coffee maker on, and come back later to a burned pot. Nothing else seemed out of order in the kitchen.

Brie was just leaving the kitchen when there was a knock on the front door. She headed toward the door, feeling awkward about her presence in the house. Being a homicide detective, and feeling that something might be amiss about Amanda's absence, she hadn't thought twice about stepping through the unlocked door and looking around. But she knew it would seem like a bold and intrusive act to anyone who lived on the island. She was relieved to see Wendy standing there when she opened the door.

At first Wendy was a bit startled to see Brie, but her surprise quickly turned to shyness. "Is Amanda here?" she asked, shifting her eyes to the right so as not to look directly at Brie. "I was hoping she'd be back."

"I was hoping that too," Brie said. "Come in, Wendy." She moved aside and let the girl in. Wendy stepped onto the entryway rug, slipped off her damp canvas sneakers, and walked into the room.

After a few moments of consideration, Brie decided to tell her what she'd seen last night. "I got up in the middle of the night to shut a window. The back of Ben's house faces this direction, and I could have sworn I saw a light through the trees. I figured maybe Amanda had returned, so I walked over here this morning to say hello. I guess I felt a little concerned when I couldn't raise her, so I tried the door."

"Amanda never locks her door," Wendy said. "Most people on the island don't." She smoothed her hair behind her ears and glanced at Brie. "She wouldn't mind you coming in."

"Who else lives along this side of the island?" Brie asked.

"The Sanders family lives a little ways down the shore from here," Wendy said. "Maybe you saw their lights."

"Maybe..." Brie mused, wondering if that were possible with the thickness of the forest. Maybe she had been mistaken. If Amanda *hadn't* actually returned home, that would explain why the windows were never closed. But, just in case, she decided to press Wendy for a little more information. "If by chance Amanda did return last night, do you know where she might have gone this morning?"

Wendy thought for a minute. "She sometimes teaches a class at the school on Herring Island. It's about a twenty-minute boat ride from here. But today's Sunday, so she wouldn't be doing that."

"Might she have gone into the village? Does anything happen there on Sunday morning?" Brie thought maybe a church service, although, from the little she'd gleaned about Amanda, it didn't seem like a fit.

"People like to gather at the Scuttlebutt Café on Sunday mornings," Wendy said. "Frannie Lempke makes her fresh caramel rolls. It's only on Sundays she makes 'em, so the place really fills up. Amanda never goes, though. She's all into her health food—likes to bake things for others but won't eat them herself." For the first time since she'd stepped in the door, Wendy looked directly at Brie, as if the chance to be of some help gave a boost to her self-confidence.

Since Wendy seemed to have warmed to her questions, Brie decided to go for a little more information. "I've been looking at Amanda's sculptures—some of them are amazing."

"They are," Wendy said affirmatively. She turned and glanced around the room, and Brie could see the admiration in her eyes. "Would you like to see something?" she suddenly asked Brie.

"Sure."

Wendy led the way through a door at the back of the great room into Amanda's studio. She walked over to a draped sculpture and lifted the plastic off. Beneath the drape was a clay sculpture of a pair of puffins, easily recognized by their distinctive parrot-like beaks. One was standing, and the other nestled down as if sitting on an egg.

"Ah, it's wonderful," Brie said. "Did you do this, Wendy?" she asked, but she already knew the answer.

Wendy nodded, and her eyes shone with pride. "Amanda's teaching me." She turned and pointed to a shelf that held two carved wooden puffins. "I used those as models."

What impressed Brie was that Wendy hadn't tried to exactly capture the models, but had brought her own interpretation to the work. "What do you like about doing this, Wendy?"

Wendy's eyes slid sideways, and she began to work on that imaginary something under her thumbnail, just as she had the night before. Brie was thinking this might have been too personal a question, when Wendy answered. "I like spending time with Amanda," she said, her voice barely audible. "And, well… it makes me feel calm, working with my hands."

Brie raised an eyebrow. It was uncommon for a girl of Wendy's age to have this kind of self-awareness—awareness that extended beyond outward appearances to inner needs. Seeing the girl's anxiousness, she wondered if Amanda hadn't used working with the clay as a kind of therapy. If that were the case, Brie felt oddly grateful to the artist for her caring. But that gratitude only deepened her concern about where Amanda was.

Wendy placed the plastic back over her sculpture and picked up a book that was sitting on the work table. She walked back out to the great room and over to the wall that held the bookcases. As she replaced the book, Brie scanned some of the titles. The art books were all in one area, and there were lots of them—biographies of artists, books on art theory and art history, and large volumes depicting the works of famous artists and sculptors.

Brie noticed that the adjoining bookcase held an equal number of books on archeology. The collection included books on famous archeological digs in Egypt, the Middle East, and South America. There were also books on marine or undersea archeology. Finally, there were biographies of and autobiographies by famous archeologists.

"Amanda must be interested in archeology," Brie said.

"Oh, those were her mother's books. Amanda's mother was a pretty famous archeologist. See, here's a book she wrote."

Brie read the name on the spine of the book—Eva Whitcombe.

"After her mother died, Amanda brought her archeology books here."

"How long ago did her mother die?" Brie asked.

"I'm not really sure. A few years ago, I think. She's had most of those books for as long as I've known her." Wendy gathered her glossy brown hair together at the back of her neck and brought it over her shoulder, where it hung nearly to her waist.

"You have beautiful hair, Wendy," Brie said.

This flustered Wendy so badly that she had to work on her thumbnail some more.

"Thank you," she said without looking up, and after a pause added, "I've thought about getting it cut, but somehow I just can't."

"Do you want to get it cut?"

"Well, no, but my girlfriends tell me I should try it."

It was the first mention of friends, and Brie was glad to hear that Wendy actually had some, but she decided to say what was on her mind anyway. "I wouldn't be too hasty, Wendy. You know, there are long-hair girls and short-hair girls, and never the twain shall meet."

Wendy looked at her quizzically.

"That means the two groups don't see things the same—at least when it comes to hair. I was always a long-hair girl—still am. At one time my hair was almost as long as yours."

"Blonde hair is so pretty," Wendy said, and to Brie's surprise she reached out and touched a lock of pale hair that was draped over Brie's shoulder. "Did *your* friends tell you to cut it?"

"Some did. Now, some of those friends had good intentions, and some were just jealous, which of course meant they might not have been my friends at all."

Wendy smiled—the first real smile Brie had seen from her—as she considered what Brie had said. "I think I'll keep my long hair," she finally said. "I like it."

"You know, I'm going to be here a few days, and I'm pretty good at French braids. If you'd like, I could do one for you."

"Really?" Wendy said.

"Really."

Wendy turned away suddenly, but not before Brie saw the tears in her eyes. "My mom used to braid my hair," she said quietly.

Brie wasn't sure why she'd made the offer, and her little voice was telling her not to get too involved. But here was this girl who'd already lost her mother, and Brie had that bad feeling—the one that was almost never wrong—beginning to percolate in her gut. She thought about the strange image that had come to her in the night, of the woman out at sea in the storm, whistling.

As if reading her thoughts, Wendy turned back to her. "I think I'll go back to the village and see if anyone's seen Amanda, and check if her boat is in the harbor."

"Sounds like a good plan," Brie said, trying to be as upbeat as possible. "I have to get back to the lighthouse, but I might come down to the village later."

Wendy was already at the door pulling her sneakers on. "I'll see you later, Brie," she said, straightening up, and was out the door in a flash.

"See ya," Brie called after her.

She took a deep breath and tried to refocus on what she'd been doing before Wendy's arrival. She walked back to the kitchen, where she'd been when Wendy knocked on the door.

She looked around; other than the burned coffee pot, there was nothing else of note here. She rolled some paper towels off the dispenser, walked around the peninsula, and stooped down to wipe up the moisture under the windows near the table. She closed the windows, threw the towels away in the kitchen, and walked back to the table.

There was a copy of the *Portland Press Herald* sitting folded on the table along with a partially-consumed cup of coffee. It was Friday's paper, but she knew Amanda had been here yesterday. Ben said he had stopped by and dropped off milk and a newspaper. Brie was glad she had that information—it gave her some kind of timeline. She lifted the paper to look more closely at the picture on the front and noticed something underneath. It was a contact lens case with one blue-tinted lens still inside. Brie glanced around the table and the floor to see if she might have dislodged the lens when she picked up the paper. When she found nothing, she looked again, more methodically, first unfolding and shaking the newspaper, then feeling around the table, and finally scouring the floor on her hands and knees. *Who goes out with only one contact?*

When she found nothing on the floor, she got back up and headed for the bathroom she'd seen next to the kitchen. There was a pedestal sink with nothing on top but a container of liquid soap and a hairbrush. Brie picked up the brush and extracted a couple of long, wavy red hairs. *Amanda's a redhead*, she thought, dropping the hairs in the wastebasket. She opened the medicine cabinet above the sink and looked through it. No contact cases.

She left the bathroom and headed up to the loft, feeling more and more disturbed by that lone contact lens. The same question kept ticker-taping through her mind. *Who goes out with only one contact?* To a homicide detective the answer, of course, seemed obvious—a dead person. Brie pushed that thought out of her mind and began searching the bedroom for evidence of a second pair of lenses, but found nothing.

On the right side of the bedroom, a door to an adjoining bathroom stood open. This bathroom had a vanity-style sink with a cabinet below. Brie scanned the top first, since it held all of Amanda's everyday toiletries—toothbrush, toothpaste, mouthwash, several containers of face cream, hand cream, and a tube of sunscreen. Next, she searched the three drawers in the cabinet. Nothing of interest in the first two, but in the third drawer, under the same pile of junk everyone keeps in the bottom drawer, she found another contact case, which she guessed contained an old forgotten pair of lenses. She looked inside—the lenses were there. She put it back, closed the drawer, and stood up. Suddenly, she remembered something she had seen on the kitchen counter. She headed down the stairs and around to the kitchen. There, on the back of the counter, near the sink, was an eyeglasses case. She opened it—the glasses were inside. She took them out and held them up to her eyes. "Whew—totally nearsighted," she said aloud.

Something didn't add up here. There were incongruities everywhere. First, the light she'd seen last night—Brie was pretty sure it had come from this house. She suddenly remembered Ben's story of Amanda finding Harold the day after he died, and how she'd come over that morning after noticing his lights on all night. Brie again focused her thoughts on Amanda's great room. If Amanda *had* been here last night, surely she would have closed the windows. Brie looked around. This home was loved. It had been put together with thought and care. *Not the kind of place you'd let rain come pouring in,* she thought.

And then there was the coffee pot. How could Amanda have had fresh coffee in her cup if the pot had a burned-on residue? She would have had to clean the pot in order to make herself coffee. That pot had burned after Amanda left yesterday. So, if Amanda hadn't come back, then who had turned off the coffee maker? *Obviously, whoever was here in the middle of the night,* Brie thought. She wondered how long it would take for a pot of coffee to cook down to nothing.

Finally, there was that missing contact lens. Even if one lens had somehow mysteriously disappeared into the ethers, someone as nearsighted as Amanda would have had to wear her glasses when she went out. Brie walked back to the table. What was more, she couldn't have been reading the newspaper. Not with only one lens. In spite of her attempts to push it away, a picture had begun to form in Brie's mind, and it sent a chill all the way down her spine. Amanda had made coffee and had sat down to put her contacts in so she could read the paper, but she was interrupted by something...or someone.

Brie walked to the front door. She put on her boots and slicker and stepped out the door, closing it silently behind her. She headed back down the long driveway and at the bottom turned left toward the lighthouse. She didn't know how or why, and she had no definitive proof, but still she knew—call it a sixth sense homicide detectives develop—she knew, deep down in her gut, Amanda was dead.

Chapter 5

Prematurely aged by plaster dust, a white-haired John DuLac sat on the back stoop, wondering what was keeping Brie. *She must have hit it off with Amanda,* he thought. He stretched his long legs out and leaned back on his elbows, looking up at the sky. A light drizzle was falling, and droplets of water freckled his dust-covered jeans, but the sky was beginning to lighten up. He had persuaded Ben to go out for a sail if the weather cleared. It was the only way he could think of to pry him away from his obsessive renovation schedule. *Why does he drive himself the way he does?*

John hadn't said anything to the others, but he had been shocked at Ben's appearance when they'd arrived the day before. Ben had lost weight, and there was a hollowness about his eyes, as if something haunted him. John could only guess at what it was about. Maybe it was Harold's death and how he had died, or maybe the fact that Ben would never get to share this place with his beloved Libby. Whatever was going on, John thought that getting Ben out on the *Maine Wind* might help, even if only temporarily. After all, she *had* been his ship, as well as his livelihood, for years before John had taken her over.

He looked toward the road where it ran into the forest, hoping to conjure up Brie. Deep as his concern ran for Ben, and much as he had wanted to spend time with him, he also wanted these few days to be about Brie. He could feel the summer slipping away, and with it, his chance to form a bond with her that might be strong enough to keep her here in Maine. But, somehow, he felt as if he wasn't trying hard enough—as if some invisible force were holding him back from his goal. He had to wonder if maybe he was a little afraid of Brie deciding to stay. But why? He knew he was in love with her, even though he couldn't imagine telling her so. So why would he hold back?

Feeling disgusted with himself, he got up from the stoop and brushed himself off. Trying to think about this kind of stuff gave him a headache, and he could never figure it out, anyway. Maybe that's why Ben drove himself so hard—so he wouldn't have to deal with his emotions. John opened the door and went back to the demolition.

Brie walked back toward the lighthouse at a brisk pace. The wind had picked up a bit and turned to the north. The fog was lifting, but a light rain had begun to fall. She pulled up the hood of her slicker. In spite of the rain, she had a feeling it was going to clear. She wished she hadn't gone to Amanda's. She could feel herself being pulled into this situation, and suddenly, painting the trim on Ben's house seemed very appealing. She wanted to immerse herself in home repair and forget about what she had just seen. But she knew it was too late for that. As a homicide detective, she was honor bound to pursue this.

John would flip. She slowed her pace, dreading the thought of telling him she suspected some kind of foul play had taken place. After what had happened on Granite Island in May, he'd probably think she was some kind of human lodestone attracting murder and mayhem wherever she went. She thought about contacting the Maine State Police, but she didn't have a shred of evidence. Even if they labeled it a missing person's case, they might do nothing for a couple of days. By then the trail would go cold. Brie knew the first forth-eight hours after a crime were critical. She knew she couldn't sit by and do nothing. She was going to have to investigate the situation, and she was going to have to keep her nosing around on the down low as much as possible. Not only was she an off-islander, she was from "away" — a curious Maine-ism used to refer to all who were not native to the state.

She was glad she had formed a kind of bond with Wendy. Nor had she been oblivious to the eyes Doug McLeod, Wendy's brother, had cast on her the night before when they'd driven Wendy into town. She had always been adamantly against using her looks to gain information, but maybe in this situation she'd have to reconsider that. After all, she was on leave. Maybe she could persuade herself to relax her ironclad protocols a bit.

Brie rounded a slight curve in the road and came out of the forest so suddenly it was a bit startling. The dense spruce trees formed an absolute line of demarcation beyond which very little vegetation grew. The lighthouse and keeper's quarters sat on a nearly barren granite promontory. In a long swinging stride she headed toward the house and soon stepped through the door into the cozy entryway. She hung her rain slicker on one of the hooks behind the front door. The banging of sledgehammers had been replaced with a chorus of crowbars, creaking out high and low notes as they pried lath from the stud wall beneath. She poked her head through the plastic and spoke to the demolition team.

"Hey, guys, what's up? Or should I say down?" They had made serious inroads into the kitchen wall. From the look of it, she guessed they'd be done long before dinner.

"We're ahead of schedule," John said, temporarily leaning on his crowbar as if it were a cane. His pose, coupled with his plaster-aged hair, gave Brie a glimpse of the future. *He's gonna look hot even as an old geezer*, she thought.

"I've convinced Ben we should take the *Maine Wind* out for a sail if we get done early."

Ben was busy sizing up the other side of the wall, deciding on their next plan of attack. He stuck his head around the corner when he heard his name and gave her a little wave.

"Sounds great," said Brie.

73

"It's a full moon tonight," Scott said. "If we stay out long enough, we'll get to see it rise." He sat on the floor, his back against the wall, drinking a can of Coke and looking like he'd just come through a blizzard.

"Hey, John, can I talk to you for a couple minutes?"

"Sure." John set his crowbar down, brushed himself off, and followed Brie through the entryway and out the front door.

"Wanna take a little walk?"

"Sure," John said. "Just let me tell the others I'll be gone for a bit. Maybe we can walk down and check on the *Maine Wind*."

"That's fine," Brie said. "I'll wait for you outside." She grabbed her lightweight jacket from the hook where it hung next to her rain slicker and headed out the front door. She dreaded having to share her suspicions about Amanda with John, and thought if they were walking, maybe it would go better. She paced back and forth, feeling anxious, unable to stand still. It was only a ten minute hike down to the ship, but it would serve to dispel some of her nerves.

Within a couple of minutes John emerged. He had brushed the plaster dust from his hair, cleaned up his face and arms, and changed his clothes. *Oh dear*, she thought, *if he only knew that this was the farthest thing from a romantic little walk.*

They set off at a brisk pace along the path they'd followed the evening before. They had walked on in silence for a couple of minutes before Brie got up the courage to speak. "I think something might be wrong," she said.

John looked at her. "What do you mean, Brie?"

"Well, you know, Amanda, the artist—Ben's neighbor?"

"Yes?"

"Well, I think she's dead."

John stopped in his tracks. "What do you mean—dead?"

"Dead, John, as in deceased—or more specifically, murdered, I'm afraid."

"But—why?"

"I have no idea why," she said, exasperated. "We just got here."

"No, I mean why do you think that?"

"Because things aren't right at her house. Because I saw lights in that direction in the middle of the night, but I don't think Amanda was there. I guess because I'm a homicide detective, and sometimes I just get a gut feeling."

"But you could be wrong, couldn't you? There *could* be an explanation for the lights, couldn't there?" he asked. There was a pleading tone to his voice that told her he wanted to make the whole subject go away.

"I could be wrong, John. But that gut feeling I mentioned — well, it's almost never wrong."

John was silent for a moment, digesting what she'd said. The path skirted the edge of the forest now. As it descended toward the cove, they had to go single file.

"Do you think you should notify the police? Ben said he knows someone on the force — maybe we should call him."

"There's just no hard evidence," Brie said. "No blood. No signs of a struggle. Add to that the fact that, apparently, Amanda is a bit flighty — known to leave the island without notice; forget about plans she's made with people — things like that. Wendy came by while I was there this morning. She went back to the village to check and see if Amanda's boat is in the harbor."

"Isn't it possible she just left the island without telling anyone?" John asked. They had arrived at the cove where the *Maine Wind* was anchored, and everything looked fine.

"Let's sit for a minute," Brie said. They climbed into the little dory they'd rowed to shore the day before and sat on two of the thwarts facing each other. Brie explained the details of the crime scene, admonishing John that they had to be kept secret. She told him about the coffee pot, the missing contact, and the eyeglasses in the kitchen, and she explained the implications of each discovery.

"It's all circumstantial," she said. "The police may wait a few days before filing a missing persons report. And assuming her boat *is* missing, they'd say she's gone off island and could be anywhere up or down the coast. Now, if her boat is here, that's a different matter."

"That would be proof something's happened to her, right?" John asked.

"It's really only proof that she's not at her house and hasn't left the island in *her* boat. There are lots of other possibilities. She could be with someone on the island—a lover, say—or she could have left the island on someone else's boat. So, you begin to see what we're dealing with. That's how the police will see it, and probably wait forty-eight to seventy-two hours before they begin to look for her. The trail can go mighty cold by that time."

"So what should we do?" John asked earnestly. He reached out and took her hand.

She looked at the bottom of the dory. "I thought you might be upset. You know, maybe think I have some weird magnetic attraction to murder scenes."

"I think you can't help who you are, Brie. If there's trouble here, I know you can't look the other way any more than I could if there were trouble on the *Maine Wind*."

Brie looked up at him feeling more hopeful. "We should head back," she said.

They climbed out of the dory and headed back up the path, single-file. When they reached the top of the bluff, they went on together hand in hand. Even after their encounter the night before in the bedroom, it seemed odd to share this casual closeness. Their relationship so far had been nothing but fits and starts, and sometimes Brie didn't know what to think about the whole thing. She checked her watch as they approached the lighthouse. It was nearing ten-thirty.

"I'm going into the village and talk to some of the town folk—see if I can pick up a vibe of some kind. Maybe find out who's seen Amanda the past couple of days. Wendy said people like to gather at the Scuttlebutt Café on Sunday mornings. Apparently, Frannie Lempke's caramel rolls are the closest thing to a religious experience to be had here on the island."

John chuckled. "Listen, why don't I come with you? I'm not an islander, but I *am* a Mainer. It might help break the ice. I sail around lots of the islands out here, and frequently drop anchor—it's possible I might even know someone here on Sentinel Island."

Brie mulled it over for a few moments. She preferred doing this sort of prospecting on her own, but John was probably right. If the islanders closed ranks and decided not to talk to her, she'd be out of luck. "Well, okay," she said. "If Ben can spare you, you're on."

"Good," John said. "We'll take the truck." They headed into the house to talk to Ben and get the keys.

Chapter 6

J ohn and Brie bumped along the gravel road in Ben's old
pickup truck. At the junction just north of Puffin Point, Brie
told John to turn left. "We'll go this way and up the west
side of the island, so you can get the lay of the land," she said.
John nodded and hung a left. They traversed the island and
headed north, and within ten minutes were descending the hill
into the village.

The clouds had finally burned off, and sunlight sparkled on
the ocean out beyond the harbor. In the light of day, Brie took in
the little hamlet more completely than she had the night before.
Barnacle Bay was a typical Maine fishing village. Gray wharves
and fish houses formed the interface between sea and shore. On
the outskirts of the village, they passed a number of red and
white clapboard buildings before coming to the hardware store,
whose front window was filled with a collection of clap-trap
that looked like it had been there for several decades. Farther
along, they passed the general store with its tiny attached post
office and came to a little white steeple church that sat in the
center of the village. A sign on the door read "Town Meeting
Next Wednesday." Beyond the church, a short spur of road bent
off to the right and curved up to the village library that sat on a
small rise behind a lush patch of lawn.

As they approached the far end of the village, John pointed
off to the left. The Scuttlebutt Bar and Café huddled next to the
small harbor. The weathered structure looked like it had at one

time been an unassuming two-story building. Seaward, a bank of windows provided a view of the harbor, where six or eight lobsterboats bobbed aimlessly at their moorings. A deck that looked newer than the rest of the establishment had been added to provide an outdoor dining area during the summer. Weathered fishing nets and floats suspended beneath the deck railings added atmosphere and suggested the presence of seafood within.

John pulled the truck into the gravel parking lot on the side of the building, and they got out. Through the windows Brie could see people gathered around the tables with coffee mugs in hand. She and John climbed the wooden stairs and stepped inside. Heads turned and necks craned as the door closed behind them, and a soft murmur of speculation as to who they were went round the room. Brie spotted Wendy and her brother in the far corner of the room and waved to them. The aroma of freshly brewed coffee mingled with the smell of cinnamon, convincing Brie that it was just about time for her second breakfast.

Light coming through the bank of north-facing windows illuminated the interior of the establishment. To their right, the bar—crafted of rich, dark mahogany and polished to a high gloss—ran almost the full length of the wall. Behind the bar, in two tiers, liquor bottles of every conceivable shape and size stood before a heavily framed and beveled mirror. But what riveted Brie's attention was the bright red shell of an enormous lobster mounted atop a piece of fishing net and hung above the bar. She estimated its length, from the tips of its claws to the end of its tail, at around four feet, and the span between the gigantic claws was nearly equal to its overall length. She assumed it had been caught many years ago, since the current lobster fishing laws prohibited the taking of any lobster whose carapace was over five inches.

As a child, she had once seen a very large lobster in an aquarium in Oregon, but it paled next to this behemoth. She wondered if lobsters this size still patrolled the ocean floor any-

Danger Sector

where. She wanted to think they did. The idea of such creatures, while a bit scary, was enormously compelling to her.

She and John had stood by the door no more than a few seconds when a burly fellow, carrying a tray of coffee mugs and caramel rolls, came through the doorway at the far end of the bar and spotted them.

"Welcome aboard, mates," he growled. "Anchor yourselves wherever ye please."

Brie smiled. Ben had told them to expect a character in Fudge Lempke, but he hadn't elaborated. Fudge had a big head and a burly walk. His left eye opened wider than the right and wandered slightly, giving him a bit of a carp-like appearance. Brie decided a lazy eye might not be such a bad thing in Fudge's line of work. He could keep one eye on the door, and with the other, tend the beer taps at the bar.

She and John had started across the room toward an empty table next to the far wall when Wendy McLeod called to them. "Come sit with us, Brie."

Brie was glad for the invite, since it announced to the other villagers in the café that she wasn't a complete stranger. *Anything to break the ice*, she thought as she steered John toward the McLeods' table.

As they approached, Doug stood up and pulled out the chair next to him. "Nice to see you again, Brie," he said, his blue eyes fixed intently on her as she circled around the table.

As she sat down, she caught the confused look on John's face. "I met Doug last night when Ben drove Wendy back to the village." She made the introductions. John shook hands with Doug and said hello to Wendy. They had just settled in when Fudge lumbered over.

"What'll it be, mates? Coffee and rolls or a menu?" he asked.

"Two coffees," John said, "and a plate of Frannie's famous caramel rolls."

Fudge beamed with pride. "Ye be off-islanders, and yet, ye know of my Frannie."

"We're here visiting Ben up at the lighthouse," John said. He introduced himself and told Fudge they'd sailed in on the *Maine Wind*—one of the schooners in the windjammer fleet. "I'm the captain, and this is Brie, my... second mate."

Brie noted the pause and wondered if he'd been about to say "girlfriend." She smiled to herself. *He probably decided that'd go over like a lead balloon.*

Fudge smiled a broad, gap-toothed smile, as if he'd just struck gold, and fixed his stationary eye on Brie. "Servin' before the mast, are ye?"

Brie decided to join in the fun. "Aye," she answered in her hardiest sailor's voice. Her eyes wandered from Fudge back to the giant crustacean over the bar, and she suppressed a smile. *You're not in Kansas anymore, Dorothy*, she thought to herself.

Fudge hurried off toward the kitchen doorway, above which was affixed a brass nameplate engraved with the word "Galley." As he entered the kitchen, Brie heard him call out, "Order of sticky buns for the salty dogs from the *Maine Wind*, Frannie."

Brie was half expecting a hardy "*Arrrr*" to finish it off. If anyone in the place was still uninformed as to who they were—which she doubted, this being an island—Fudge had just rectified the situation. She noticed John was staring intently out the window, trying hard not to laugh. She slipped out of her jacket and hung it on the back of her chair.

"In case you haven't guessed, Fudge thinks he's a pirate," Wendy said, by way of explanation.

"I kinda picked up on that," Brie said. "He seems pretty entrenched in the role."

"That's just it," Doug said. "It's a little hard to know if it *is* just a role." He glanced toward the kitchen door to make sure Fudge wasn't on his way back to the table. "You see, old Fudge used to be a lobsterman. One day he was out hauling his traps, and apparently he slipped and hit his head real bad on the gunwale of his boat. One of the guys from the island found him out there, unconscious. He was never quite right after that." Doug shifted his glance from Brie to John. "Soon thereafter he took on his pirate persona. And now, with those pirate movies coming out and being so popular, it's just made matters worse."

"Well, I'll tell you one thing," Brie said, "what with the giant lobster up there and Fudge being a pirate and all—it sure makes for some pretty good local color."

"That's for sure," Doug said. "Sometimes I think people come in here just to see what kind of a wild story Fudge'll come up with."

Wendy leaned forward, and the crooked Mona Lisa smile raised one corner of her mouth. "Lately he's been telling people about buried treasure," she said in a confidential tone.

"Ah," Brie said, lifting her eyebrows. "Buried treasure, eh?" She gave Wendy a knowing wink. She was glad to see Wendy in a less anxious state, but her own mind kept wandering back to Amanda's cottage and the incongruities she had found there.

Over the girl's shoulder, Brie noticed a bearded man heading toward them.

"Well, if it isn't 'salty dog' John DuLac," the bearded fellow said as he arrived at the table. He had a mellow voice, smooth as aged cognac, which made the listener want to hear more. He clapped John on the shoulder, and John stood up and shook his hand.

"Adam Blake. So this is where you disappeared to." John introduced the man, explaining that Adam had been a captain in the windjammer fleet for a number of years.

With that voice of his, Brie could imagine him spinning a good yarn in the warm belly of a ship on a stormy night. She guessed Blake was in his mid to late forties. He had wavy dark hair, almost shoulder length, neatly combed and tucked behind his ears, and a carefully trimmed beard, beginning to show some gray. Reckless good looks was the thought that came to her—something in the dark eyes immediately labeled him a risk-taker.

"I'd heard you bought a small schooner and moved out to one of the islands," John said. "So what do you do out here to keep yourself honest?"

Adam laughed but didn't seem all that entertained by the comment. "What everyone else does on an island like this," he said. "Lobstering. My wife's family is from out here, so I was able to get a territory." Blake shifted his weight uneasily, as if he'd already run out of things to say.

"Well, maybe I'll stop by and see that schooner of yours."

"It's nothing fancy," he said with a shrug, as if trying to diminish its importance. "Come by, though, if you like. We're over on the east side of the island. Just follow the road here, out the far end of the village and around." He gave Brie and the McLeods a nod. "Nice seeing you again, John," he said, and with that, he turned and headed back to his table.

Brie noticed that he didn't say exactly where the house was. "Did you know him very well?" she asked John as he sat back down.

"Not that well, but there's usually a certain camaraderie with other windjammer captains, whether active or retired from the trade."

"Do you think you'll go visit him?"

"I don't know. He didn't seem all that welcoming, now did he?"

"Well, I wouldn't read too much into it," Doug said. "Islanders tend to be hermits. And I'll admit, we can be a little suspicious of outsiders, but that doesn't mean we won't come to like you." As he said it, he gave Brie a meaningful look, one that was uncomfortably flirtatious.

Brie heard John shift in his chair and knew without looking that he was glaring at Doug. She gave him an *oh-grow-up* kick under the table.

Fudge backed through the swinging kitchen doors and headed toward them with a tray full of *unburied* treasures. He set down two sturdy mugs full of coffee and a plate of four steaming rolls. Buttery caramel and pecans glistened the tops and slid down the sides of the delicate pastries. The aroma rising from the plate could only be described as unabashedly comforting. Brie offered the rolls to Wendy and Doug first, but they declined, saying they'd already eaten. So she and John each took a roll and waded right in.

Fudge, who had lingered next to their table, suddenly motioned toward the door. "Avast there, Charlie!" he called out. "Once again, ye have forgotten to pay."

All eyes shifted to a tall, lanky man with unkempt hair who had one hand on the door. He turned and shuffled lazily toward the register as Fudge bustled over. Fudge appeared not in the least upset, which led Brie to conclude that this might be a frequent occurrence with said Charlie.

"Sorry, Fudge," he apologized. "Guess I just forgot, man."

"Son, you'd forget your head if it warn't lashed on." There was a hint of concern in Fudge's voice.

Charlie set his grimy baseball cap on the bar and pulled a tattered wallet, held together with duct tape, from his back pocket. He extracted a bill from the wallet and handed it to Fudge. Fudge gave him the change, which Charlie started to stuff into his jeans pocket. Fudge stopped him. "Stow that proper, now, Charlie, or you'll lose it fer sure." Charlie obediently pulled the money back out and stuffed it into his wallet, which received a nod of approval from Fudge. He methodically placed the baseball cap on his head and shuffled out the door.

Brie and John went back to their sticky buns and coffee. After a minute or two, during which they were singularly focused on the marvelous confections, Wendy broke the silence.

"I forgot to tell you, Brie, Amanda's boat is gone from the harbor. So she must have gone to the mainland and just forgot to tell me. Her best friend lives in Rockland. Maybe she went to visit her." Wendy pulled one knee up under her chin, propping her foot on the edge of the chair. She hugged her leg, looking at Brie for a moment, until Doug leaned over and moved the foot off the chair, quietly telling her, "Feet on the floor, Wendy."

Wendy's comment brought Brie back to the stark reality of what she, herself, believed had happened to Amanda. She didn't know how she was going to tell the girl about her suspicions, or if she was going to share them with her at all, for that matter. She took a swallow of her coffee, and it tasted bitter in her mouth. She looked around the Scuttlebutt Café, suddenly taking in the people gathered there through different eyes—the eyes of a homicide detective.

Shortly after Charlie left, the door to the establishment opened, and Spencer Holloman, the town manager, came in with a woman. Brie recognized him from their encounter on the road the night before, but in the light of day, she took him in more definitively. At around six foot four, everything about him seemed exaggerated, from the shock of gray hair on his head right down to his feet, which were encased in a pair of very white, very large athletic shoes, and which turned out duck-like when he walked. He moved across the café toward the opposite corner, creating a drafting effect, so that paper napkins atop the tables lifted in his wake.

Brie turned to Doug. "Is that Spencer's wife?" she asked.

"Yup, that's Birdie. She's our town librarian."

Birdie seemed the antithesis of Spencer in every way. Short and petite, she looked her name. Her straight gray hair was styled in a boyish cut. She nodded shyly to her neighbors as she passed and took a seat at the table closest to the wall. She crossed her blue-jean-clad legs and hugged her arms to her chest as if folding in on herself like a delicate piece of origami.

As Brie was studying the pair, one of Wendy's friends appeared at the table. Brie had noticed the girl sitting with her parents across the room.

"Wendy, you *have* to come over. I downloaded some new music. We can listen to it." Wendy turned to Doug for permission, and he waved her on, telling her to be home by four o'clock so they could make dinner.

Brie was actually glad to see Wendy leave, since it kept at bay any further speculation about Amanda. But once the girl was safely out the door, she turned to Doug. "I suppose it would be pretty hard on Wendy if anything were to happen to Amanda," she said, testing the waters.

Doug rocked back in his chair and looked at Brie. He was silent for a moment as if deciding what he wanted to say. "Our parents died three years ago in a boating accident," he began. "Since then, Wendy's become pretty attached to Amanda, it's true. But nothing's going to happen to Amanda. She's just gone off island, that's all. She's flighty like that. Picks up and leaves at a moment's notice." He must have sensed something in Brie's demeanor, though, because he brought his chair back down and looked from her to John and back again. "Is there some kind of a problem?" he asked.

Brie felt John give her a warning nudge under the table. "No, I'm sure it's nothing," she said.

"What's nothing?" Doug asked, in a tone that indicated he wanted an answer.

"Just, well, I went by her house this morning to say 'hi,' and her door was unlocked." Brie knew the comment was a cop-out, but she had decided she wasn't going any farther down this road till she had more information.

Doug responded exactly as she knew he would. "Oh, that's nothing, Brie. Everybody leaves their doors open on an island. It doesn't mean anything, trust me."

John stood up at this point, saying they should get back — that he needed to help Ben with the kitchen wiring.

"I'd like to walk around the village a bit," Brie said, holding his gaze for a moment, trying to silently convey her intentions. "Maybe talk to Birdie; see if she'll give me a tour of the library."

It was something to say to put Doug off the scent, but also, Brie was genuinely fascinated by the tiny libraries that graced many of the small towns in Maine. A lover of books, she was naturally drawn to these compact little islands of knowledge.

"How will you get back?" John asked. "I'm not sure we'll hear the phone, with all the construction we've got going on."

Doug jumped in. "I'll be glad to drive you back. Just come up to the house when you're done. It's right up the road from the Scuttlebutt here. You'll see a dark red house on your left, just around the first bend. That's us." He stood up. "I need to go, too. I promised a friend I'd help him with a repair on his pickup today. So I'll see ya later, Brie. Okay?"

"It's a deal," she said.

John and Doug walked to the register and paid Fudge, and then headed out the door together. After they were gone, Brie picked up her coffee, pulled her jacket off the back of her chair, and made her way over to Spencer and Birdie's table. Since he was the town manager, she had decided he'd be the logical one to express her concerns to about Amanda.

As she approached, Spencer stood up. "Well, hello, young lady," he said formally, but there was a twinkle in his blue eyes.

"Hello again," Brie said. She turned and introduced herself to Birdie, telling her they'd run into Spencer when they drove Wendy home the night before.

"Spencer told me all about it. Pull up a chair and join us," Birdie said, gesturing to the place on her right.

"Thanks, I'd love to," Brie said, taking her seat. Birdie seemed genuinely welcoming, but Brie's immediate sense of her was that she was lonely or maybe depressed. Brie wondered if this was yet another marriage that had gone on forever, kept in motion by the sheer force of inertia. At least Birdie was making an attempt to be friendly and hospitable.

Spencer's friendliness felt politically motivated—the what-can-you-do-for-me kind of friendliness. He shifted in his chair to face the kitchen doorway, and as soon as Fudge appeared, he signaled him with his coffee cup. Fudge hustled behind the bar for the pot and came over and refilled their cups.

Brie took a sip of her coffee and exchanged a few pleasantries about their visit at the lighthouse before moving to the topic of Amanda. "I've been getting to know Wendy McLeod," she said. "And this morning I walked over to Amanda's place to see if she was home. Wendy was looking for her last night, which is how we ended up driving her home."

Spencer shifted in his chair as if wondering where this was going, and Brie hoped she didn't sound like she was babbling.

"But Amanda still wasn't there. Here's the odd thing, though; I got up in the middle of the night during the storm and saw lights through the trees. They had to be coming from Amanda's cottage."

"So, what's the problem?" Spencer asked, sounding mildly irritated. "She obviously came home at some point last night and went out again before you got there this morning."

"It's possible. Wendy said her boat's missing from the harbor this morning."

"See—there. She's gone off island is all," Spencer said, but he was looking at Brie more carefully now, sizing her up.

"I'm not so sure. Amanda's door was unlocked this morning, so I stepped in and called to her, thinking maybe she didn't hear me knocking. And, well…certain things just didn't seem right about the place." If pressed, Brie planned to reveal some, but not all of the details.

Spencer's brows knit together as he considered what she'd said, and Birdie's gentle smile melted, replaced by a look of alarm.

"Since you're the town manager, I just thought I should tell you," Brie said. "Maybe someone saw her leave on her boat this morning. If so, there's no need for alarm. If not, maybe we need to figure out when she was last seen by someone on the island."

"Tell you what," Spencer said; "I'll ask around the village. Why don't you stop down at the town dock? Bob's got the bait business down there. You met him last night—remember? He might have seen her this morning. You could ask Charlie, too. He lives on his boat down in the harbor. Bob'll point it out to you."

Brie wondered if this was the same Charlie who'd forgotten to pay his bill a little while ago. "Well, it's a place to start," she said, trying to sound enthusiastic. "Ben told me about Wendy and Doug's parents and, well, I guess I feel bad for the girl, and hate to see her worried about Amanda." She refrained from telling Spencer that Wendy now seemed assured that Amanda had left the island aboard her boat. Brie thought about the half-truths she had also told Wendy, and took it as a sign that her devious detective gene was slowly reactivating. She wasn't sure how she felt about that.

"Well, my dear, care to take a stroll around the village with me?" Spencer stood up and stepped around to pull out Birdie's chair—a gesture Brie wrote off to keeping up appearances, since he hadn't pulled the chair out for her when they came in.

"Birdie, Doug told me you're the town librarian," Brie said. "I'd love to see the library. I'm a bit of a bibliophile." *An understatement if ever there was one,* she thought, reflecting on the piles of books stacked everywhere in her apartment back home.

Birdie seemed to visibly relax, as if she'd received an infusion of warmth from Brie's words. Clearly, her library was where she felt at ease. "You come right on over to the library after you're done talking to Bob. I've got some work to do—just got a shipment of new books. I'll show you around. You can even take out a book if you're going to be here a few days."

"Great," Brie said. "I'll definitely stop by."

Spencer and Birdie left. The café had nearly emptied out, but at the next table over, a man sat looking directly at Brie. He would have been considered handsome, but he had mean eyes, the color of algae on the surface of a pond. Brie wondered what swam beneath. She gave him a brief smile as she stood up and put on her jacket. Whoever he was, she had no interest in making his acquaintance right now. She knew an unwelcoming vibe when she felt one.

Fudge was puttering around behind the bar, dusting off the tiers of liquor bottles with a blue feather duster. Brie picked up her empty coffee cup and headed over to talk to him. "Hey, Fudge," she said.

He turned around and fixed her with his good eye and, seeing her cup, asked, "Be ya wantin' some more coffee, lassie?"

"That'd be great. I just wanted to tell you how good everything was."

"Thank ye kindly, miss," he said, giving her a formal little bow.

"Name's Brie," she said, extending her hand.

Fudge wiped his hand back and forth on his apron before shaking with her, as if she might be royalty or something. She'd taken a liking to him almost as soon as they had stepped into the Scuttlebutt Café. Being the town barkeep, she figured him for a fountain of information on the island folk. Of course, the pirate persona was a bit worrisome, but there was always Frannie. She had high hopes of making a good connection with Frannie, and so told Fudge, "I'd love to meet your wife if she isn't too busy. I just want to tell her how good the caramel rolls were."

Fudge beamed with pride. "Ye just wait here a minute, lassie, I'll go fetch her."

As soon as Fudge walked off, Brie saw the mean-eyed guy get up from his table and head toward her. She made him for late forties or early fifties. He was a big guy—six-two or three—and his hair was buzzed short. He would have looked like a drill sergeant, except that he slouched. He came right up to her and, leaning his forearm on the bar, stared her directly in the eyes. "We don't like folks from 'away' showin' up askin' a lot of questions," he said in a husky voice, loud enough to be menacing but not loud enough for Fudge to hear.

"And who might you be?" Brie said, straightening up and giving him her best you-don't-intimidate-me-one-bit look.

"See, that's what I mean about the questions. It's none of your dang business who I am. We don't take to strangers here, so maybe you should take your questions off island."

Fudge had come through the kitchen doorway in time to hear this last remark. "No need bein' rude to the pretty lassie there, Wade," he protested.

"Stay out of this, peg-leg. Ain't none o' your business."

"Arrrre too my business," Fudge said, advancing toward him menacingly. "This here be my tavern. Thou'll not be abusin' the clientele. Savvy?"

The mean guy let out a snort of disgust, pulled a couple of bills out of his pocket, slammed them down on the bar, and marched toward the door.

"Ain't got no peg leg, neither," Fudge shouted after him as the door banged.

Brie tried not to laugh. Here was Fudge, her pirate in shining armor. An unlikely protector if ever she'd seen one.

"That's right, lassie," Fudge said, seeing her expression. "Pay him no heed."

"Who *was* that?" Brie asked.

"That there's Wade Sanders. He's a lobsterman hereabouts." Fudge nodded toward the corner table by the windows, where she and John had been sitting with Doug and Wendy. "Young Master McLeod used to work stern on his lobsterboat when he was a lad—still does sometimes."

Good, thought Brie. At least if she needed to know more about this Wade character, she could ask Doug.

Just then, Frannie came through the kitchen doorway smoothing her apron. She was short and tubby with a round pudding face, bright red from the heat of the kitchen. Her coppery-brown hair was so tightly curled on her head it reminded Brie of a scouring pad. She hustled over to where Fudge stood.

"Hi, Frannie, I'm Brie."

Frannie reached across the bar and shook Brie's extended hand. "Pleased to meet you, Brie, and welcome to the island."

The rotund little woman exuded a warmth that had nothing to do with the climate in the kitchen, and her smile showed a mouthful of perfect teeth—so perfect, in fact, that when placed side by side with her less fortunate physical attributes, they seemed to even the score.

Brie liked her immediately, and mentally added her to her list of people who fell under the heading "breath-of-fresh-air." "I wanted to tell you how delicious the sticky buns were," she said.

"Well, thank you. Aren't you a sweet thing to say so? Isn't she, Fudge?"

"Aye," Fudge agreed with gusto. "A sweet lassie."

"I learned that recipe from my grandmother when I was just a girl," Frannie said, smoothing her apron again. "Cold winter days on the island, there was never much to do. I'd go over to grandma's and we'd bake up a storm. When Fudge and I decided to give this place a go, those sticky buns were one of the first things we tried. And they've been good to us ever since."

"No point tampering with perfection," Brie said.

"That's my Frannie," Fudge said, giving her a squeeze. "Perrr-fection itself."

Frannie face got even redder, and she smoothed her apron again, saying, "Now Fudge, perfect I'm not."

"Arrre too," Fudge growled affectionately, and planted a kiss on Frannie's cheek for good measure.

Brie observed this simple display of love a bit wistfully. She'd often wondered why finding such a love had been so difficult for her. She wondered if Fudge and Frannie knew how truly blessed they were to have one another. When she had tried to picture herself and John with this kind of happiness, she was plagued by the question of what the cost might be. Her next thought was always, *If you have to ask what it costs, you probably can't afford it.*

"I see ye know young master McLeod and his sister," Fudge said.

This was a perfect opportunity, and Brie jumped on it. "Actually, I met Wendy just last night. She was supposed to have a music lesson with Amanda Whitcombe, and when she didn't find her at home, she walked over to the lighthouse looking for her."

"Oh, now, Amanda, she's a hard one to figure," Frannie said. "So full of life, being an artist and all. Always busy it seems — comes and goes a lot, what with all her art projects. Loves this island like nobody's business, though. Always encouraging folks in the village here to make improvements, try new things." Frannie paused and smoothed her apron. "Still and all, there's something about her. Seems a bit lost, somehow."

"In what way?" Brie asked, feeling the irony of Frannie's words and thinking again of her dream the previous night.

"Oh, I couldn't say—couldn't say." Frannie was looking down now, smoothing the apron some more.

Brie wondered if she "couldn't say" as in didn't know, or *wouldn't* say, due to island protocol. She suspected it was the latter.

"If you'll be excusin' me, I need to swab the decks." Fudge gave Brie his funny little bow and disappeared into the kitchen for his mop and bucket.

Brie turned back to Frannie, hoping to glean a little more information. "Wendy seemed so upset when she couldn't find Amanda last night or this morning, I told her I'd ask around — see if anyone knows when she left the island."

"Ah, young Wendy…well, she's a lonely little thing, for sure," Frannie said tenderly. "I wish I could be of help, but I haven't seen Amanda for a few days." She paused for a moment, reflecting. "They're a pair, all right—Wendy and Miss Amanda —a motherless child and a…" Frannie stopped mid-sentence as if casting around in her mind. "Well, and a good, caring woman, is all," she said, nodding and smoothing her apron. "But I should be getting back to the kitchen now," Frannie said. "It's kind of you to help Wendy. You're always welcome here at the Scuttle-butt."

"Thanks, Frannie." Brie hopped off the stool and looked around the café. Fudge was still busy mopping up. She called a good-bye to him and headed for the door.

"Beware of scallywags, lassie," he called out. "There be sunken treasure out thar."

Oh, my, thought Brie, *now it's sunken treasure*. She could see that Fudge lived in a shifting reality—lucid one moment; the next, not. She turned and gave him a little salute. "Don't worry, Fudge, I'll keep a weather eye."

Outside the door Brie noticed a pair of brass-fitted lan-terns—one green, one red—affixed on either side of the door. Upon entering the bar, the red light would be to the right. Brie smiled—*Red on the right returning*—a sailor's adage for entering a harbor safely by keeping the red buoy or light to the right or starboard side of the vessel. Fudge and Frannie had certainly managed to make their little establishment feel like a safe harbor for the villagers. Brie crossed the parking lot and headed down the road toward the heart of the village to find Bob's bait shop and to talk to Charlie.

Chapter 7

Brie walked back down the road toward the red clapboard building she'd seen next to the wharf. A rough sign painted on a board and affixed to the side of the building read "Bob's Bait." Brie knocked on the wooden screen door and stepped inside. The shop smelled like a small indoor ocean. Large rubber-lined tanks, filled with fish of various sizes, bubbled away. Along the side wall, beneath a bank of windows that looked out on the harbor, sat a row of coolers and an extra large tank that held lobsters.

The sound of the screen door closing brought Bob from the back room. He was carrying a broom. He stopped behind the counter that held his cash register. Next to the register stood a wire rack with candy bars, gum, playing cards, and batteries. Another rack held outdoor magazines. Bob Weatherby was slightly shorter than Brie's five-foot-seven, but taller than he had appeared on the road the night before in the company of Doug McLeod and Spencer Holloman. She placed him in his early thirties and thought he had an air of excess testosterone about him that frequently accompanied shorter men. From the surprise on his face, Brie figured whoever he was expecting to see, it wasn't her.

"Hello," he said. "Welcome to my fishy world." His voice had a surprising modulation. There was a hint of refinement to it that didn't seem to match his swarthy pony-tailed appearance. Brie tried to remember if he'd spoken the night before on the road, but for some reason all she could remember were Doug's eyes, and how they had studied her with particular intensity.

"It's Brie, isn't it?" he asked.

"That's right," Brie said. "Good memory."

"It's never hard to remember names attached to pretty faces," Bob said. It would have sounded like a come-on if he hadn't said it in such a matter-of-fact way.

Brie chose to ignore the compliment, but gave him points for not coming out with some sorry line or other, especially considering the excess testosterone.

"Let's see, last night Ben said you were visiting at the lighthouse. Are you planning a fishing trip?" he asked, obviously trying to figure out what she was doing in his store. "I run a small charter business, taking folks out fishing, if you're interested."

"Well, no thanks," Brie said. "But I am fishing in a way."

The beginning of a smile lit Bob's green eyes. "Is that so?" he said. There was curiosity in his voice now.

"It's nothing, really. I'm just trying to help Wendy McLeod figure out when Amanda—you know, the artist—might have left the island."

"So you know the McLeods?" He began slowly sweeping the floor behind the register as if mulling this fact.

"Yes I do," Brie said without elaboration. "Wendy's been eager for me to meet Amanda." She was fabricating again, but saw no other way to get information. "Apparently she left the island unexpectedly, some time yesterday, and I just thought she might have mentioned to someone down here where she was going or when she might be back."

Bob studied her with a slight smile, as if he found her somehow amusing. Brie was prepared for some more don't-ask-questions-on-our-island antagonism, like the kind she'd gotten from Wade Sanders up at the Scuttlebutt. But when Bob spoke, there was no trace of hostility.

"People assume I see all the comings and goings down here, just 'cause I'm so close to the harbor. Fact is, I'm in my back room a fair amount." He set the broom down and came around the counter. "Now, Amanda's one to stop in and visit. Doesn't seem to mind the fishy smell the way most gals do. I like that about her." He leaned back against the counter. "How about you?" he asked. "You mind the smell?"

"Doesn't bother me," Brie said. "It's an okay smell, actually." She could think of smells that did bother her—ones she could never fully erase from her mind. Drug house smells. Smells of rotting food, and human and animal urine. Bob's shop was redolent with the clean scent of the sea. It was a far cry from the smell of human weakness and failure.

"Did you talk to Amanda yesterday?" she asked.

"Nope. And as to her boat, all I know is it was in the harbor when I came back from dinner. I always eat up at the Scuttlebutt on the early side, so I can get back here by six. Catch anyone going out for evening fishing."

Bob turned and walked into his back room. He came back out with a string mop and headed across the store. "Amanda's not one to check in with anybody. She comes and goes a lot. Wendy should know that." There was water on the floor in front of one of the tanks, and he swabbed it up.

"I think Wendy's turned Amanda into a kind of mother figure. And you know how it is with kids; they may not like Mom to interfere, but they like to know where she is."

Bob chuckled. "Amanda? Motherly? I don't think so."

Brie searched for a hint of sarcasm in the remark, but there was none—just another matter-of-fact statement like his one about names and pretty faces. *He sees the world black and white,* she thought. *No surprise in that; lots of guys do.* Still, she wondered what he based his remarks on, and knew she needed to learn more about Amanda Whitcombe.

"Well, she's certainly spent a lot of time with Wendy," Brie said.

"I doubt that'll last. Most things don't with Amanda."

"Why do you say that?"

"Because it's the truth. She's just not big on long-term commitments."

Brie studied him for a moment, aware of the irony in his remark. "I thought you said you liked her."

Bob swirled the mop across the floor once more. "I'm just sayin' the McLeod kid shouldn't get too attached. Amanda has a way of changing her mind a lot about things."

Brie's silence must have struck him, because he decided to qualify his remarks. "Hey, she's an artist. You'd expect her to be like that, wouldn't you? It's not a bad thing. Nobody's judging."

Brie smiled to herself. *Kinda sounds like judging to me*, she thought.

Just then Bob's phone rang. He sauntered toward the back room, in no apparent rush to catch it.

"I'll be off then," Brie said. He raised a hand in acknowledgement, but said no more. As she headed for the door, she glanced into the back room and saw a work table awash with clutter. Bob reached in among the junk and produced a mobile phone. She heard him say, "Bait Shop," and then she was out the door and down the steps.

"Yup, black and white thinking *and* stereotyping," she said under her breath. "Amazing how often the two go together." She gazed at the harbor for a few moments, thinking about what Bob had said. His remarks almost sounded like those of a jilted lover, but based on what she knew so far about Amanda, she thought he would be way too young for her. Maybe Amanda went through boyfriends. If that were the case, it could lead to a number of suspects in her disappearance. But why would Bob Weatherby care, except for the fact that people in small villages tended to mind each others' business.

Brie realized she needed to learn a lot more about Amanda, starting with her age. She decided to ask Ben some questions when she got back to the lighthouse. Maybe he could help her flesh out a picture of the artist. Until she had a better sense of who Amanda was, there would be little hope of figuring out what might have happened to her.

As she studied the harbor, she remembered that Spencer had told her to talk to Charlie, who lived aboard one of the boats down here, so she headed out the town dock to inquire as to which lobsterboat was his. A man about Ben's age was just rowing up in a small skiff. Brie bent down and asked him if he knew which boat was Charlie's.

"Charlie Cappy?" the man asked. He looked at her quizzically, as if wondering what connection she could possibly have with the likes of Charlie. She didn't volunteer any information, so after an expectant moment, the man pointed out a good-sized lobsterboat moored a short distance out in the harbor. It was a nice craft—what would have been referred to as a lobster yacht—and it appeared to have a cabin below deck.

"You can borrow my skiff if you like," the man said, as if reading her mind.

"Thanks," Brie said. "I'll just be a few minutes."

"No problem. Just tie it up down there when you're done," he said, pointing to the other end of the dock, where a whole little flotilla of skiffs was secured. The man tied the painter to a rung of the ladder and climbed up to the dock.

Brie climbed down the ladder and boarded the skiff. She untied the painter, dropped it into the bow, climbed back to the center thwart, and pushed off. "Thanks again," she said as she swung the oars into position. She rowed across the harbor toward Charlie's boat, thinking as she went that it was an awfully nice craft to be owned by such a lackadaisical fellow—or at least that had been her impression of him in the café.

As she approached the boat, a familiar odor wafted out to her. She'd dealt with enough pot-smoking teenagers over the years to know exactly what she smelled. Now *this* picture definitely fit with her assessment of Charlie.

Brie shipped the oars as she came alongside Charlie's boat and called out, "Ahoy there, Charlie. Are you aboard?"

After a few moments, a bewildered and clearly stoned Charlie stuck his head out of the companionway. His hair was thinning, and he looked awfully haggard for what Brie guessed to be a man in his thirties. He wore a sheepish look on his narrow face, which probably had a lot to do with his current activity below deck. "Wha's up?" he asked, attempting to focus on Brie.

Brie had a strong urge to turn the skiff around and head back to the dock. She doubted if Charlie would notice the *QE II* steaming into Barnacle Bay, and had to wonder why Spencer would have sent her on such a wild goose chase. But there was a remote chance Charlie might have seen Amanda, so she decided to press on with a few questions.

"My name's Brie, Charlie. I was at the Scuttlebutt Café a little while ago."

A lazy smile of recognition crept onto his face. "Oh, yeah. You're from the windjammer. I saw you sailing in yesterday. She's a beauty, that ship."

"She's all of that," Brie said.

"I remember now," Charlie said, the fog continuing to lift. "You were with the McLeods. So, what's up?"

Brie decided to keep the explanations to a minimum. The condition Charlie was in, she doubted anything would seem strange to him. "We're just trying to find out when Amanda left the harbor yesterday," she said. "Spencer thought you might have seen her leave on her boat."

"I turned in kinda early last night," Charlie said, which Brie translated into, *I was getting stoned.*

"What time did you…turn in?" she asked, playing along.

"Maybe about eight." But then he shook his head. "No, that ain't right. It woulda been about nine. Amanda's boat was still there"—he turned and pointed off the starboard side—"when I turned in."

"Did you hear anything after that?" Brie asked.

"Naa," he said, sounding a bit like a goat. He looked at her in a pleading way, like he wanted this to end. Then suddenly his expression changed, as if a dim light had been turned on in his brain. "You know what, man? I heard a boat start up late last night. Least I think it was late. That musta been when she left."

"No idea what time it was, I suppose?" Brie asked, already resigned to the fact that he wouldn't know.

Charlie just shook his head.

"Does it seem odd she would have left the harbor that late?"

"Can't say, man," Charlie shrugged. "Amanda marches to her own drum. She's cool that way."

"What kind of boat does she have?" Brie asked.

"It's a Newman 32." Even through the haze Charlie could see this didn't register with Brie. "It's just a mid-size lobsterboat," he explained.

"Well, thanks, Charlie, and good meeting you. Awful nice boat you got here. You must catch a lot of lobsters." When he didn't respond, she put her port-side oar back in its lock. "I'll let you get back to whatever," she said. She had an urge to give him a knowing wink, but wasn't sure how that might be received, and she didn't want to burn any bridges just yet. She pushed the skiff off.

"Hey, peace," he called after her.

She flashed him the peace sign.

Disturbed by what she'd heard, Brie rowed slowly back to the dock. She didn't think for a minute that Amanda had taken her boat out in the middle of the night with a storm coming. Maybe Amanda was eccentric and unpredictable, but she wasn't crazy.

Taking that boat out of the harbor would have been a bold and potentially careless move by the killer. *Why not just leave Amanda's body at her cottage?* Brie wondered. Obviously, it was worth the risk to the killer to make her death or disappearance seem accidental. She knew, of course, that in an ideal world this was what most killers would have preferred, but few were brazen or cunning enough to pull it off.

Brie tied the skiff up at the dock and headed back up the road toward the library. She had told Birdie she would stop in, and she wanted to catch the librarian before she finished her work and locked up. If she was lucky, maybe she could elicit Birdie's impressions of Amanda. Anything to begin to flesh out a picture of the artist's life here on the island. Without that picture it would be impossible to come up with any suspects or motives.

Brie climbed the three wooden steps that led to the library's door. She gave a courtesy knock on the door and stepped inside. The familiar and comforting smell of books engulfed Brie as she closed the door. The overhead lights were off, but plenty of natural light filtered through the windows on the front and side walls of what looked, at first glance, to be a one-room library. The checkout desk was an L-shaped affair, about six feet long across the front. It sat directly opposite the door. Behind the desk Birdie was busy emptying a box of books.

"Hello, Brie," she said, in a quiet but not unwelcoming tone. "I'd almost given up on you."

"Sorry," Brie said. "I'm glad I caught you, though. I'd love to take out a book since we'll be here a few days." In reality, if things were unfolding as she suspected, Brie doubted she'd have much time for reading, but it seemed a good way to break the ice.

"Do you have a favorite author?" Birdie asked.

"Well, I guess I probably have a few of them," Brie said. "Now, if we're talking old masters, then I'd have to say Thomas Hardy."

"Ah," Birdie said reflectively. "His novels—so tragic, so fatalistic." It was spoken almost with a sigh.

"But life is tragic," Brie said, unequivocally. "So there's truth in his stories."

Birdie regarded her with interest. "You're so young to hold such an opinion."

Brie realized she should have been more careful in what she had said. She certainly wasn't about to tell Birdie that her stock and trade was homicide. She was sure, if it were known she was a homicide detective, the entire village would clam up, and she'd learn nothing about Amanda.

"My dad died when I was twenty," she said. "It left us in a bad way, emotionally and financially. I think his death colored the way I think in some ways. It was just at that time that I was reading Hardy, and I got very caught up in his tragic characters. I guess I identified with them." All this was true, of course, and Brie was relieved to have a viable explanation for her feelings—one unrelated to her work.

"I'm sorry to hear that," Birdie said. "I guess it's as they say, 'art imitates life.' " She came out from behind the desk. "Would you like a tour of my little library?" she asked.

Brie noted the use of the possessive. It didn't surprise her. She suspected this was where Birdie, in a sense, nested—where she felt most at home.

They walked among the stacks with Birdie pointing out this and that section. When they came to the back wall, Brie was surprised to see a wide doorway that opened into another whole room. This room looked like it had been added onto the structure sometime recently, and the earth tones of the carpet and walls gave it a warm and inviting feel. The room held juvenile and children's books and computer stations for doing research. Another section of the room held racks of magazines and newspapers. Comfortable chairs covered in green and gold fabric were tucked into cozy corners. It would have been a great spot on a rainy afternoon. Brie was actually surprised to find such a well-appointed library in this small village.

They walked back out into the main room, and Birdie led her to the opposite side of the library and down a stairway to the lower level. Here there was a room with microfiche and a machine for reading the files, as well as several more computers of varying ages, each sitting on its own small desk. Next there was a meeting room that held a large table surrounded by about a dozen folding chairs. A little farther down the hall Brie noticed a closed door that said *Storage Room*.

"Would you like a cup of tea?" Birdie asked. "I made a pot about fifteen minutes ago, thinking you might be by."

"I'd love some tea," Brie said. Birdie's offer would give her an opportunity to ask some questions about Amanda in a less interrogatory mode.

Birdie walked into the meeting room and over to the side wall, where there was a counter with a small sink and a cabinet underneath. On top of the counter was a coffee maker, a cookie jar shaped like the Gorton's Fisherman, a hotplate with a tea kettle, and a dark blue teapot sitting on a cork trivet. Birdie poured out two cups of tea, and they sat down at one end of the table. "So, how long are you here for?" she asked.

"Just four days," Brie said. "I'm here with Captain DuLac and the other two members of his crew. We're helping Ben do some repairs to the keeper's quarters out at the lighthouse. John and Ben are old friends. Well, actually, they have something more like a father – son relationship, I guess you'd say." Brie realized she was doing all the talking so far, but that was okay. Hopefully, it would encourage Birdie to open up a little on the topic of Amanda.

"I don't think any of us has gotten to know Ben very well yet. He keeps to himself a lot out there."

This gave Brie the perfect opening. "I think he's gotten to know Amanda a little since she's his closest neighbor." Brie took a sip of her tea. "I know she brings him food and baked goods on occasion. Apparently, she used to do the same for Harold, the previous owner of the lighthouse."

At the mention of Harold, Birdie's eyes dropped to her teacup, and she shifted ever so slightly in her chair. Brie had marked her as a sensitive soul and guessed that the mention of Amanda and Harold in the same breath had upset her, since

Harold's unfortunate fate was known, and now Amanda's whereabouts were in question.

"Did you learn anything about Amanda?" Birdie asked. "Had Bob or Charlie seen her this morning?"

"No, I'm sorry, they hadn't," Brie said. "Charlie said her boat was in the harbor yesterday evening, but in the middle of the night he thought he heard the engine start up, and then the boat was gone this morning." Brie looked at Birdie. "Do you think Amanda would leave like that in the middle of the night on her boat? Does that sound right to you?"

Birdie's face darkened. "No, that doesn't sound like her at all. She told me once that she didn't like to be out on the water after dark. She's known for doing things on the spur of the moment, but I don't think that would be one of them."

"Do you think she might have gone if there was someone with her? Someone she trusted? A boyfriend maybe?"

Again, Birdie looked uncomfortable, but Brie pressed her, saying, "I think we need to try and figure out where Amanda is."

"Do you really think something could have happened to her?" There was concern that verged on alarm in Birdie's tone.

"It's just that certain things don't add up. Her boat missing—lights on in the middle of the night—and there was water on her floor from the rain. If she was there, why didn't she close those windows?"

Birdie looked at her guardedly. "You're not one of those private investigators, are you? You talk like one."

"Heavens, no," Brie said with a laugh she hoped was convincing. "I guess I just have a soft spot for motherless girls, and Wendy seemed so worried last night."

Birdie let out a sigh, as if resigned to an unpleasant task. "Amanda has no trouble attracting men. She fascinates them, in fact. Even men much younger than herself."

"How old is Amanda?" Brie asked.

"I believe she's around fifty," Birdie said. She took a sip of her tea to fortify herself. "Amanda's independent, unpredictable, some would say wild. She's kept company with more than one man here on the island; that's all I can say. I'm not going to name any names. It doesn't seem right."

"Doesn't sound like she'd be a very good influence on Wendy," Brie said. "That must concern her brother, Doug."

"Oh, you're wrong there. Amanda loves that girl, and I'm sure Doug knows it." Birdie looked down at her teacup for a moment. "In some ways Amanda's at odds with herself—with her own nature, it almost seems. I think she longs for things that have always eluded her. But she loves this island—has told me more than once she'll never leave it, and she loves that girl like a daughter."

Reflecting on Birdie's remarks, Brie remembered the two bronze statues Amanda had created—the lovers entwined and the mother and child—and the strong feelings each had evoked. They had conveyed a sense of joy, but also one of unmistakable loneliness. She suddenly felt an affinity for the artist—this woman she'd never known. If there was one thing Brie understood, one thing the past fifteen months had taught her, it was the meaning of loneliness.

Birdie stood up. "I should finish my work upstairs," she said.

"And I'd still like to look for a book, if it's okay?" Brie knew this would give her an excuse to come back if she had more questions.

"Go right ahead," said Birdie. She picked up the teacups, walked over to the counter, and put them in the sink. She and Brie walked back upstairs. Brie went to look for a book, and Birdie went back to the front desk.

Brie had been browsing the shelves for a few minutes when she heard the front door open. She was three aisles back from the desk, but peeking over the books, she saw it was Spencer. Birdie got up from her chair, but before she could say anything,

Spencer announced, "I'm calling a meeting of the group, here, at three-thirty."

Brie saw Birdie bring her finger to her lips, and then saw the look of alarm on Spencer's face. Brie quickly ducked out the end of the aisle and into the children's room, where she took a seat in the back corner in one of the chairs that faced out a window and opened one of the two volumes she'd been carrying. She drew in a breath to calm herself, and sure enough, within a few seconds Spencer appeared alongside her. She looked up, hoping her feigned expression of surprise was convincing. "Spencer! Hi. I didn't know you were here."

He looked at her for a moment, assessing. "I just came in," he said.

"I guess Birdie sent you to find me and tell me it's time to leave," Brie said lightly. "I was just trying to decide between these two books."

Spencer picked up the book on the floor next to her and read the spine. "This is a history of Maine." He seemed surprised for whatever reason.

"I'm not from around here," Brie said. "Just trying to learn more about the state." She immediately regretted sharing even this ambiguous fact about herself, and before he could ask where she was from, she stood up and said, "I talked to Bob and Charlie, as you suggested. Charlie thought he heard Amanda's boat leave the harbor sometime in the night. He couldn't say when, though."

Spencer's brows knit together, as if what she'd just said didn't make any sense. "Well, I wouldn't worry myself about it if I were you. I'm sure there's a perfectly good explanation. And, knowing Amanda, I'm sure it's a colorful one. I'll make a few calls—see if I can track her down."

"Great," Brie said, as if the subject was closed. "I should be getting out of Birdie's way and back to the lighthouse. I promised Ben I'd help with some painting." She hoped to convey the impression she was bowing out. She took the book from Spencer.

"I'll put this one back before I leave." She turned and walked out of the room without any further ado.

Brie checked out one of the books, entitled *Islands of Maine: Where America Really Began*, by Bill Caldwell. She thanked Birdie for the tea and the tour of the library, and told her she'd bring the book back before they left the island. She headed out the door, down the steps, and up the road to find the McLeods' house.

Spencer's words replayed in her head—*I'm calling a meeting of the group*. And that subtle gesture by Birdie—the finger coming to the lips to silence Spencer. Obviously, whatever *the group* was, as well as the fact of its meeting, were things Birdie and Spencer preferred to keep secret. And Brie knew that missing persons and dead bodies were things often connected to secrets. She decided she'd be attending that meeting—unbeknownst to *the group*, of course.

Chapter 8

Brie headed toward the east end of town, mulling over her encounters with the villagers. After she passed the Scuttlebutt Café, the road wound up a hill and swung east toward the ocean. She had decided to walk back to the lighthouse to get a sense of who lived up this side of the island and where they were situated in relation to Amanda's cottage. But she needed to stop at the McLeods' first and tell Doug she wouldn't need a ride back to Ben's place.

Any remnants of last night's storm had cleared almost completely. High brushstrokes of cloud streaked the canvas of blue Atlantic sky. The wind had freshened into the north, but the sun warmed the island, pushing the temperature toward 70 degrees. Doug had said to look for a dark red house, and Brie came upon it just after the road bent south. The house sat on a rise up a short driveway. It had been freshly painted, and against the backdrop of azure sea and sky, it blazed in the noonday sun. Grass grew all around the house, here and there punctuated by a granite outcropping, a clump of bush roses or a bed of black-eyed Susans. It was a pretty spot, and Brie stopped to take it in before heading up the driveway. Obviously, Doug took first-rate care of the homestead. Brie was glad Wendy had the comfort of a nice home. She'd lost so much, and now, Brie feared she would have to deal with the loss of Amanda as well.

There was a pickup truck at the far end of the driveway, and Brie could hear men's voices under the raised hood. "Hello," she called as she approached.

Doug stuck his head around the side of the hood. "Hi, Brie. I've been waiting for you." He picked up a rag and came toward her, wiping his hands. "Come on up to the house. I'll show you around." When they got to the truck, he said, "This is my friend, Hooky Wilson."

Hooky had a broad face and a ready smile, and he greeted Brie enthusiastically when introduced. He was a good-sized guy, but built like a fireplug. His head sat directly on his shoulders, and his arms, possibly because they were so brawny, seemed too short for his body. Somehow Brie had pictured him differently— more like Casanova in a pickup—after hearing Ben's tale about buying his truck. Hooky was older than Doug, but with his bumpkin demeanor, came across as younger. Doug, on the other hand, had a smoothness of manner and carriage that would have put him in good stead in any urban setting.

The McLeods' house had the look of a two-story Victorian cottage. They climbed a set of wide stairs and stepped onto a covered porch that ran the full width of the house. Gingerbread trim framed a stunning view of the ocean. At the far end, a large swing with yellow-and-white-striped cushions hung from the bead board ceiling. Painted wood rockers and rattan chairs were placed in a grouping that spoke of friends, lazy afternoons, and iced tea. Brie would have loved to sit down for a visit, but knew she had to get back to the lighthouse. John would be wondering about her by now.

"I wanted to thank you for the offer to drive me back," she said, turning to face Doug. "I think I'd like to walk, though. Kind of get the lay of the land and do a little thinking as I go."

Doug looked disappointed but didn't press her. Over-eagerness didn't jibe with his natural confidence. "Did you find anything out about Amanda?" he asked.

"Just that her boat was in the harbor yesterday evening and gone this morning."

Doug looked out to sea as if conjuring up Amanda's whereabouts. Brie was good at picking up on vibes, and right now his spoke volumes.

After a few moments he turned back to her, as if he had divined the future. "Something's very wrong, isn't it?" he asked.

"I'm afraid that may be," Brie said. "And if it is the case, I feel just terrible for Wendy."

"I'm not going to pry, Brie, but somehow you know more than you're telling us, don't you?"

Brie remained silent, but was having an internal battle with herself. She wanted to take someone on the island into her confidence—tell them they needed to work fast or they might never find out what had happened to Amanda. But she knew that was impossible, because anyone on this island could be the killer. Even Ben, much as she hated to think about it, was not beyond suspicion. She had seen uneasiness in him each time Amanda had been mentioned. If she could venture a guess, it would be that he was attracted to the artist and felt embarrassed about it, possibly because of the difference in their ages. There was something between them, though. Her gut had told her so last night, before Wendy even showed up.

Doug had been studying her as she stood silent. "I don't know what your story is or why you're crewing on that ship, but there's more to you than meets the eye," he said. There was no hostility in the remark, just a statement of fact. Doug was no dummy—he had her number.

"There's more to everyone than meets the eye, wouldn't you say?" she responded.

"Well, I suppose there is. *Touché.*"

"I should get going." There was nothing else she was at liberty to say. She pointed south. "Does this road run all the way to the lighthouse? When we drove back last night, it took a couple of turns. I don't want to get lost."

"It takes a jog inland for a ways. There's a deep gorge that cuts into the island and forms the northern boundary of Amanda's property. At high tide the ocean makes quite a racket when it rushes up that split. Once you're around that, the road swings back toward the shore and runs all the way to the end of the island."

They walked off the porch. Along the back of the house, where it would be sheltered from the wind and catch the afternoon sun, grew a lovely bed of cultivated roses. Brie stopped to admire them.

"They were my mother's pride and joy," Doug said. "She fussed over those roses as much as she did over us." He pulled out his pocket knife and cut a long red stem that was just beginning to open and handed it to Brie.

"What a beauty," Brie said.

"Just what I was thinking."

Brie looked up. He was gazing straight into her eyes. She looked away, feeling awkward yet flattered. It bothered her that she was attracted to him. John was the one she cared about, so what was *this* about? Just random attraction, she told herself— what they call chemistry. Maybe she could use it to glean some information about people on the island; find out who Amanda was close to—who might have had a motive to kill her. She thought about asking him about *the group*, but decided against it. For all she knew, he could be involved. No, she'd have to do some old-fashioned sleuthing at the library later on to see what she could learn on that score.

"Hey, Earth to Brie."

"Sorry," she said. "Just thinking."

"I can see that," Doug said. "Anything I can help with?"

"Not right now," she said. "But I'll let you know if there is. I should be going," she said for the second time. "The others will be wondering what's keeping me. Thanks for the rose," she said, meeting his eyes briefly.

"If I learn anything new, I'll come up to the lighthouse."

"Thanks," Brie said. She headed down the driveway, wondering how John would react if Doug showed up at the lighthouse and continued his flirting with her. She had seen John's jealous side when he got all steamed up over her calls to Garrett at the department, during the unpleasantness on Granite Island. And that was nothing. Garrett was 1500 miles away, sitting at a desk at the Minneapolis Police Department. A little jealousy was flattering, but she hoped John knew how to keep it in check. She thought about the previous night; about him pressed against her in that tiny corner of the bedroom, and the proximity of the old brass bed into which they so easily could have fallen. The memory of it put a sharp ache between her legs. She quickened her pace, suddenly wanting to get back.

Along the road she passed a number of modest Cape Cod-style houses—houses most likely belonging to the lobstermen who kept their boats down in the village harbor. One sign bore the name *Weatherby*—she figured it belonged to Bob, the bait shop guy. Farther along she came to a sign that read *Blake*. Remembering the former windjammer captain from the café, Brie craned her neck and tried to look down the driveway. Something about their encounter with him at the Scuttlebutt had seemed strained. She planned to encourage John to drop in for a visit, thinking she'd tag along. The next house bore the name *Sanders*—same name as the mean guy who had accosted her in the café. The memory of Fudge coming to her defense brought a smile to her face. She remembered Wendy telling her that the Sanders' house was just down the shore from Amanda's.

Beyond the Sanders' driveway, the road bent toward the center of the island and skirted the steep, narrow gorge Doug had described. Brie walked off the road and made her way to the edge of the gorge. Looking down, she could see the high tide mark. The rocky gash was about fifteen to twenty feet wide and thirty to forty feet deep. She imagined the thunderous noise of the surf pounding in here during a nor'easter. The road hugged the edge of the gorge for about an eighth of a mile, swung around the end, and traveled east again toward the shore. When it turned right, Brie realized she must be at the northwest corner of Amanda's property. Here, the lip of the gorge swung seaward to form the promontory known as Puffin Point. It separated Amanda's property from the others north of her, thereby affording her cottage a fair degree of isolation. The killer had, no doubt, used that isolation to his advantage.

Brie decided she would stop at Amanda's and take another look around—see if maybe she had missed anything. As she approached the driveway to Puffin Point, she noticed a pickup truck pulled off the road at the base of the drive. *Someone is up at the cottage.* She made her way cautiously up the driveway, staying off to the side and clear of the sightlines from any of the windows. She crept along the back of the house, crouching down, staying below the windows, and peeked carefully into Amanda's studio. No one there.

She moved around to the east side of the cottage, but as she crossed the path that led up to the kitchen door, she stopped. Small shreds of black material lay here and there along the path. She picked up a few of the fragments, and after examining them, removed a tissue from her jacket pocket, carefully folded them into it, and put the tissue back in her pocket.

She moved to the windows near the kitchen and carefully looked in. From here, she had a view across the great room. On the opposite wall, next to the bookcases, stood an antique secretary desk. Adam Blake was rifling through it, looking for something. Brie had been watching him for a minute or two when there was a knock on the front door. He started at the sound, closed the drawer he was searching, and walked over to the door. Brie crept along the side of the house and peeked around the corner. Wendy was standing on the porch, and she jumped back, startled, when Adam opened the door.

"Oh, hi, Mr. Blake. Is Amanda here?"

"She's not back yet," Adam said. "I was just looking for her appointment book, since there seems to be some concern as to her whereabouts."

Brie knew, hands down, it was a lie. There was a desperate air to his search that in her opinion, had nothing to do with an appointment book. But she gave him points for quick thinking —it was a viable excuse. What interested her, though, was that Wendy didn't seem all that surprised to find him there. Brie wondered why.

"Can I come in and help you?" Wendy asked.

"No, that's not necessary," Blake said. "Actually, I was just leaving. I'll walk down the road with you." He closed the door behind him and steered her off the porch.

Brie listened for the sound of the truck's engine. She heard Adam Blake pull up the driveway just enough to back up and reverse his course. After he drove away, she stepped onto the porch and slipped in the door. She knew he'd be back, but probably not for a little while. Maybe she could find what he was looking for. She had a lot more experience at such things than he did.

She slipped off her shoes, laid the rose next to them, and headed straight for the stairs that led to the loft where Amanda slept. She guessed whatever he was seeking might be up there. Blake had probably already done some searching on the first floor, obviously unsuccessfully. Since he was rifling through the desk, she already knew he was looking for something he thought would be in a desk. That meant some kind of written document—a diary or maybe some kind of record book or ledger. Or letters—possibly letters that someone wouldn't want found. *Ah, the benefits of being a detective*, she thought.

She surveyed the room, deciding where to start. There was a large dresser, two nightstands, and the bed. On one side wall there were low bookcases, and on the other, louvered doors hid a long, narrow closet. Brie checked the easy spots first—under the mattress and in the nightstand drawers. Next, she moved on to the dresser and worked her way carefully through it from top to bottom.

As she searched, she thought about finding Adam Blake in the house and what his presence implied. Two things were immediately obvious—that he had some connection to Amanda, and that she had something he wanted, or maybe something he didn't want anyone else to see because it could compromise or even incriminate him. Brie started a mental list of suspects. It began with "A" for Adam Blake. Word had already spread around the island that Amanda was missing. The game was afoot, but what the killer didn't know was that a pro had joined the field.

Brie opened the doors to Amanda's closet. The floor was covered with racks of shoes, and above the hanging clothes were shelves that held an array of folded sweaters in colors that ran to reds, yellows, and greens—shades that would compliment a redhead. There was a wood chair in one corner of the room. Brie moved it over to the closet and climbed up on it. She worked her way along the shelves, sliding her hands underneath and between the sweaters. "There's a lot of cashmere here," she said to herself. "The art business must be good." Brie didn't worry a lot about clothes or fashion, but cashmere was one thing she had a weakness for. Unlike wool, you could wear it right next to your skin. Soft as a puppy's ears, it offered the ultimate cozy comfort on frigid winter days.

Brie had come to the end of the shelves. All that remained were several boxes. Taking them down, one by one, she found they all contained photographs. The envelopes of pictures had dates written on them. The earliest ones went back to the 70s—a time when Amanda would have been in high school. Brie found a packet with a fairly recent date and took the prints out. She shuffled through them until she came to a photo she knew must be Amanda. The artist was sitting atop a large boulder wearing jeans, a dark green sweater, and hiking boots. A halo of wavy red hair fell to her shoulders and framed a pixie-like face—a face that looked way too youthful to belong to someone fifty years old. She was a beauty.

Brie remembered Birdie's comment—*Amanda has no trouble attracting men. She fascinates them. Even men much younger than herself.* Brie thought about the men she'd met so far on the island. There were a number of them she could conceivably picture with Amanda, but it was all conjecture. She'd have to do some more digging to find out Amanda's lovers. Whoever they were, they'd go straight to the top of the suspect list. Sadly, that's how it was with lovers when significant others mysteriously disappeared.

She put the photos back in their envelope. While there might be something among the more recent ones that could offer a clue to Amanda's disappearance, Brie had no time to look through them right now. She checked her watch. It was nearly two o'clock. She needed to get back to the lighthouse and talk to John—let him know about the meeting and her plans to spy on the proceedings. He'd try to talk her out of it, of course, and she'd tell him not to worry, that she knew what she was doing, and he'd let her do her thing. She liked that about him—she liked it a lot. She could never be with a guy who threw up blockades—got in her way. She'd spent too many years in a dangerous job to be hovered over in that way. When it came to anything relating to her work, she needed lots of space, and he gave her that.

Brie put the boxes back on the shelf, set the chair in the corner, closed the closet doors, and headed downstairs. Sunlight was coming through the roof windows, hitting the wood floor. Halfway down the stairs she stopped, noticing something about the floor near the dining table. She came down the rest of the way, squatted down, and looked sideways at the floorboards. A thin coating of dust covered the floor, but running toward the corner of the room that held the large casting of the sinking schooner were two dust-free lines, each about two to three inches wide. She recognized the pattern at once. It was a drag pattern.

She'd seen it any number of times at crime scenes where some-one had moved a body across a floor or the ground outside. Like fog before a strong wind, the last vestiges of doubt evaporated from her mind, as a grim picture took shape.

She walked over to the sculpture and circled it carefully. She remembered she'd seen an LED flashlight in the drawer of Amanda's nightstand, and she ran back upstairs to retrieve it. On the way down she grabbed a cushion from the sofa and laid it on the floor behind the sculpture. She shone the flashlight over the surface of the casting from several different angles, looking for fingerprints. It was clean—the killer must have worn gloves.

She debated about tipping the casting over—disturbing what might be a crime scene. But if this was indeed a crime scene, it had already been compromised by everyone tramping around in the cottage, so she decided to go ahead. She needed to convince herself that her theory was correct. She carefully tipped the piece over backwards. It was fairly light for its size, being made of aluminum. She laid the top of the casting so it rested on the sofa cushion, walked around to the front of it, and knelt on the floor.

The first thing she noticed were scuffs in the finish of the floorboards—marks that had been covered when the casting was upright. She ran her fingers over them. With something heavy in its base—say a body—the casting could have skidded backwards while being turned upright and created these marks. She leaned forward and studied the base of the casting and its hollow interior. A long red hair lay along the lip of the base, as if glued there. She ran her fingers along the lip and felt a slightly sticky residue there. She peered inside the casting, a disturbing picture now in her mind—a picture of Amanda's dead body stuffed inside, her eyes staring blankly from the womb of her own creation.

The killer had probably covered the base with some kind of plastic, knowing he wouldn't be back for hours. Maybe he wor-ried the body would give off an odor, and that someone might come by the cottage looking for Amanda before he returned. All of it spelled premeditation. Something had been awfully urgent or threatening for the killer to risk attacking Amanda in broad daylight—not to wait for cover of darkness. Anyone could have caught him in the act. Brie shuddered involuntarily, thinking how often Wendy visited the cottage, and what might have happened to her had she appeared at the wrong time yesterday.

Brie decided the killer was almost certainly male. The body had to have been taken from the cottage down to the shore. She thought about the black fragments she had found on the path. The killer must have wrapped the body in something in order to drag it down the path. From the beach he would have loaded it into a skiff or inflatable boat, taken it out to Amanda's boat, and wrestled it aboard. With the storm blowing the night before, that skiff would have been rocking pretty good. Even if the artist was as petite as she looked in the picture upstairs, few women would have had the strength to get her body from A to B.

The body would have been in the throes of rigor mortis when he came back for it in the middle of the night. Brie wondered if he had thought about that before stuffing her into the base of the sculpture. "I hope you put up a good fight, girl," she said aloud. "I hope he had the devil's own job getting you out of here. Stupid bastard. Whoever you are, you picked the wrong week to commit this heinous crime." Her voice became menacing as a sudden squall. "I'm gonna track you down, you SOB."

She looked around the cottage, saddened by the loss of such talent—the loss of all that possibility. The void Amanda's death had left. Brie couldn't help grieving for what might have been. She tipped the sculpture upright again and stepped around the front to look at it. There was the mermaid, her expression altered somehow, as if the imminent return to her watery world were now tinged with doubt. *Interesting,* Brie thought. *Interesting how our moods color our perceptions.*

She took one more look around her before walking to the door and slipping on her shoes. She picked up the rose Doug had given her and let herself out. As she walked down the long driveway and turned left toward the lighthouse, she reflected on the synchronicity of her arrival at the island on the day Amanda was murdered. Maybe it was a sign—Brie believed in signs. Maybe it was a sign the world needed her to stay a detective—a sign her work made a difference. The wind stirred the forest, strumming the spruce into a gentle susurrus. As she walked the road toward the lighthouse, she emptied her mind of everything but that hypnotic sound.

Chapter 9

The killer fidgeted with the cards, shuffling them again and again. Splitting the deck, he flexed the corners and let the stacks slip through his thumbs so the corners collated perfectly. He arched the two halves in the opposite direction and saw the cards magically riffle together into a single deck. It always calmed him, this simple repetitive movement. Occasionally, he stopped to fan them out on the table with a large sweeping motion, only to scoop them up again and recommence the shuffling.

Just my luck some outsider shows up and starts snooping around. Relax, she can't prove anything. Even so, there might have to be an accident. A fall, maybe. Strangers should be more careful about their footing on unfamiliar terrain.

He smiled, feeling calmer, now—more confident. Bolstered by his plan, he fanned the cards again. *Or maybe a fire. All that construction going on—faulty wiring to blame. Too bad that lighthouse is so far from the village. By the time the volunteers get there, it'll be too late. Such a sad loss—the second pretend lightkeeper to die in two years. And all his friends, too. Tsk, tsk, the place must be cursed.*

Brie arrived back at the lighthouse just after 2:30 and stuck her head into the kitchen. The men were so busy removing the stud wall that they had exposed with saws, pry bars, and sledges, they didn't even notice her. She withdrew her head and went quietly upstairs. She laid the rose on the dresser and carefully extracted the tissue with the black fragments from her pocket. She tucked it into a zippered pouch in her backpack, took off her jacket, and tossed it on the bed.

There was an empty glass on the dresser. She went to the bathroom and filled it with water. Back in her room, she retrieved her sailor's knife from her pack, cut a few inches off the rose stem, and put it in the glass. She set it on the dresser, went over to the bed, and lay down with her hands locked behind her head. She closed her eyes and took a few deep breaths to relax herself and clear her mind.

After a few minutes she opened her eyes, reached over, and picked a length of thin braided line off the bedside table, where she had tossed it that morning. Tucking a pillow behind her, she sat up with her back against the headboard and folded her legs Indian style. She tied a carrick bend, undid it, and tied another. She skillfully worked the line into a number of intricate knots— a figure eight loop, a butterfly loop, a Tarbuck knot. The more she tied, the more she relaxed, as if physically tying those knots somehow magically undid corresponding emotional ones inside her. She was working the line into a lover's loop and thinking about John when there was a soft knock on the bedroom door.

Brie undid the knot in case he might recognize it. "Come in," she said.

John opened the door and leaned against the jamb. "I saw you stick your head into the kitchen, but you left before I could say anything."

"You guys looked pretty entrenched. I didn't want to disturb you."

"So, where'd the rose come from?" John asked, staring across at the dresser.

Something in his tone told Brie he knew exactly where it had come from. "Doug cut that for me from the rose garden behind his house." She tried to sound nonchalant about it. "The roses were his mom's hobby before she died. I stopped at the

McLeods' place to tell Doug I wouldn't need a ride—that I'd decided to walk back to the lighthouse."

"So, he decided to give you a rose in lieu of a ride, eh?"

"Guess so," Brie said in her best we're-done-with-this-discussion inflection. To her way of thinking, this single gesture wasn't grounds enough for jealousy.

John must have caught her drift, because he moved on. "How'd the information gathering go? Any luck turning up Amanda?"

"Afraid not. She won't be coming back, John. I went back to her cottage and caught Adam Blake ransacking her desk in search of something. Wendy showed up and he told her he was looking for Amanda's appointment book, which I didn't believe for a minute. But I think Wendy bought it. After they both left, I looked around the cottage again. I'm not going to go into the details, but to my way of thinking, there are unmistakable signs of foul play."

"You found Adam Blake there?" John asked, surprise in his voice. "You think he's got something to do with all this?"

"I don't know, but on another front, while I was at the library I overheard Spencer Holloman talking to Birdie. He said he was calling a meeting of *the group* at 3:30 p.m. today, at the library."

John glanced at his watch. "The group, eh? Sounds mysterious."

"And just a little sinister, don't you think? I mean, right on the heels of Amanda disappearing. And then I go to her cottage and find Adam rifling through her desk. I don't know what to think." She wound up the piece of rope she'd been fiddling with, stuffed it in her jeans pocket, and swung her legs over the edge of the bed. "I'll tell you one thing, though, there's going to be an invisible presence at that meeting."

"Brie... I don't like the sound of that. You have no idea what's going on here."

"That's why I'm going to go and be a fly on the wall."

John sighed. "I know there's no point in trying to stop you. But at least let me come along."

"Actually, I was going to see if you'd drive me in there. That way I can stay out of sight. No one will see me come into town. I'll hop out near the library. Maybe you can stop at the hardware store and kill some time, and we'll set a time to rendezvous outside the village somewhere."

"Sounds like a plan."

"I'm thinking of asking Ben to contact his friend at the Maine State Police. But since Amanda's been missing less than twenty-four hours, and there's no hard evidence, I doubt they'll get involved this soon. Maybe I'll wait till I find out what's going on at this meeting."

"What time do you want to leave?"

"Pretty quick. My guess is they'll have their meeting in the basement conference room. When Birdie gave me the tour, I noticed a storage room down there. When I left the library, I walked around back to where the storage room's located, and the window was open a bit. It'll give me easy access."

As Brie was describing her plan, a dark cloud of anxiety began to gather on John's face. "I don't like the sound of all this," he said. "It's kind of cloak and dagger, isn't it?"

"Sometimes you have to do what you have to do. Don't worry, John. I'll be like a cat. They'll never know I was there."

"I wish you'd make like a cat and find a little time to curl up with me the next few days." He gave her that long, steady look of his—the one that always made her heart race.

Brie got off the bed and slipped her arms around his waist. "I promise we will."

"I like the sound of that," he whispered. "Now, I guess we should get going. We need to talk to Ben first, though, and tell him what you think is going on."

"Right." Brie said. "Let's go find him and fill him in."

They headed downstairs and through the kitchen. There was a to-die-for aroma coming from the oven—George's beef stew cooking away. It made Brie think of cozy nights in the galley of the *Maine Wind*. Nights when it was raining, and all the passengers and crew would eat below deck at the big varnished table, tucked in the bow of the ship. They'd be rocking at anchor just enough to get the lanterns swinging a bit. The big old wood stove would be puffing out warmth, and they'd sit shoulder to shoulder savoring one of George's soul-warming concoctions.

Brie and John went out the back door and found Ben, Scott, and George lounged in the Adirondack chairs, enjoying a round of beer.

"Should we ask Scott and George to step away?" John asked.

"No need for that," Brie said. "I trust them like I trust you, John."

They sat down with the others, and Brie told Ben what she felt had happened. Without giving certain details of the crime scene, she filled him in as best she could, all the time carefully taking in his demeanor and reaction to what she was saying. At first he was incredulous at what she was suggesting. But she reminded him that she'd dealt with many crime scenes. "At a point you develop a sixth sense, Ben. And, sadly, it's almost never wrong."

"I believe you, Brie. My friend with the Maine State Police has said the same thing. I did sense some kind of a strain in Amanda, almost like she was trying to be two different people at the same time. Sometimes she would be warm and open—other times removed and almost secretive about what she was doing." He looked toward the ocean, and Brie saw a wave of sadness engulf him. She felt its undertow, felt it tug at her own heart. One more person senselessly gone. She wondered again what Ben's relationship with Amanda had been.

She turned to the others, searching her mind for something to say, so Ben would have a moment to process what he was feeling. "That sixth sense I was talking about—that gut feeling—

it's actually something we try to teach the public to trust. When someone gets the sense they're in danger, quite often they are."

She noticed she had George's rapt attention.

"That's good advice, Brie. I'll remember that the next time I'm in New York City."

"Things happen everywhere, George—not just big cities. It's an awareness you should carry with you at all times. It can save your life."

George nodded, impressed by the seriousness of what she was saying.

She looked at Ben again. "Have you ever gotten the sense there's anything odd going on on the island?" she asked.

"What do you mean?"

"I'm not sure what I mean," she said. "Just wondering if maybe anything here has seemed off to you?"

Ben grew silent, mulling the question. "All I know is there hasn't been a real warm reception for me here. Except for Amanda and a couple others, people haven't been very welcoming. I guess I wrote it off to their *islandness*—you know, the fact that outsiders aren't always that welcome when they invade these island communities."

"Hmmm," was all Brie said, but she was thinking about his response.

"Brie, we should probably go," John said, tapping his watch.

"Right," she said.

John asked if they could use the truck again, and Ben told him to stop asking—that the truck was his to use whenever he wanted.

"Thanks," John said. "We'll be back before too long. Anything you need from the hardware store while we're there?"

"I think we're good," Ben said.

"George, how about you?"

"I can't think of anything right now," George said.

Brie could tell he meant that literally. He was still processing what she'd told them about Amanda. George was a status quo kind of guy. Change wasn't something he took to easily—he preferred the predictable. Maybe that's why she liked him so much. He was like a rock. She knew what to expect from him, and that had been a great comfort to her since she'd shipped aboard the *Maine Wind*. She still felt too close to the chaos she'd gone through a year ago, and George's personality, along with his homespun cooking, was like balm for her troubled spirit.

Brie and John headed for the truck. By way of the road she had just traveled on foot, the library was only a few minutes' ride. She'd be able to slip quietly in the basement window and hide in the storage room before everyone gathered for the meeting at 3:30 p.m. She checked her watch as they climbed into the truck—3:05. They'd be near the library in less than ten minutes. Plenty of time to get into position.

There was a wooded area that ran from the road to within ten yards of the back of the library. At Brie's request, John dropped her off on the road, so she could cut through the woods and approach the building from behind. When she got to the edge of the woods, she looked around carefully to be sure no one would see her heading for the library. The window was still open. She ran across the small patch of lawn and knelt down on the ground. She peeked through the window to make sure nobody was inside.

She pushed the sash up, and in one smooth movement, swung her legs through the window, turned onto her stomach, and lowered herself into the storage room. She went across to the door and tried it. It was unlocked, and she opened it a crack and peeked out into the hallway. The door to the conference room was on the same side of the hall, near the foot of the stairs. Once everyone had arrived, she'd be able to work her way along the wall without being seen, and get close enough to hear what was going on.

Within a few minutes she heard the door begin to open and close upstairs, and a growing murmur of voices filtered down the stairwell. She could pick out Spencer's deep, resonant voice. It carried down through the floor like a horn through fog. The talking continued as *the group* descended the stairs, so she slid the door open a tiny slit. She heard Amanda's name mentioned a few times. Whatever this group was about, Brie decided Amanda must have been part of it.

Everyone was too preoccupied to notice the storage room door, and Brie, through the slim crack, was able to note each of the players pass into the conference room. Spencer and Birdie were first, followed by Adam Blake—the sea captain; Wade Sanders—the mean guy; Bob Weatherby—the bait guy; and Charlie Cappy—the stoned guy. From her years of homicide work, Brie had developed the habit of labeling suspects, usually based on their relationship to the victim, but she hadn't learned enough to do that with this group yet. Her heart sank as the last person descended the stairs. It was Doug McLeod. She had a bad feeling about the reason for *the group's* existence, and for Wendy's sake, she wished Doug were not a part of it.

Brie could hear the seven of them milling around in the conference room, but before long, Spencer called things to order. "Let's get down to business," he said. After the sound of chairs being pulled out had ceased, Brie slipped silently from the storage room and made her way down the hall with her back pressed against the wall, until she was a couple inches from the conference room door.

"Let's get right down to it," Spencer began. "There's some concern that Amanda's missing. Do any of you know where she is?"

There was silence from the group.

"Adam, how about you? When's the last time you saw her?"

Brie wondered why Adam had been singled out, and what his connection to Amanda might be. She thought about him ransacking the desk at her cottage.

"I don't know any more than the rest of you." Brie recognized Adam's voice from their meeting in the café earlier. He sounded defensive. "I haven't seen her since the night before last."

Brie wondered about the implication of his words. The night before last could have referred to an innocent encounter at someplace like the general store, say, or it could imply a totally different relationship—one that the members of *the group* were privy to. If Adam was indeed Amanda's lover, he had just become a suspect, since the *other woman* had now gone missing.

Spencer was talking again. "I was supposed to meet with Amanda yesterday afternoon, but she never showed up. She called me Friday and said we had to talk. Something about a member of the group. She didn't say who. Something about a problem that had developed. That's all she said. When she didn't show, I figured it was nothing. Just Amanda being dramatic—you know how she can be. But maybe I was wrong."

It was killing Brie that she couldn't see the faces of *the group*, couldn't note the emotional responses of the members to what Spencer was saying.

She heard Charlie speaking now, his speech slightly slurred. "Her boat was in the harbor last night, man. I seen it there around eleven, right before I turned in."

"Amanda would never have gone out on her boat after dark. She was afraid of the ocean at night." Birdie's voice had a tremor in it. A buzz went round *the group*, and in the midst of it, Brie heard sobbing and knew it was Birdie.

"That's enough, Birdie." Spencer's voice was like a cold draft on Brie's skin, and she felt momentarily sorry for his wife. She thought about her first impression of Birdie, and the thick aura of loneliness that seemed to surround her. As the cloak of marriage wears thin, a coldness creeps in, along with its companion, loneliness. Brie had seen it too often. She had seen it in her own parents' marriage.

"What about the records? She's got all the records. We need to find that shit fast." Brie snapped back to attention. She recognized the voice. It belonged to Wade Sanders, the mean guy. There was panic in Sanders' coarse voice.

"Take it easy, Sanders," Adam Blake interjected. "We don't even know if anything's wrong here."

"Yeah, like you'd give a damn if there was, Blake. You'll just pack up your little ship and move on to the next port of call. Maybe that hot little blonde that just blew ashore."

Brie was wondering if he could be referring to her—she'd never considered herself "hot," and at five foot seven she'd also never considered herself little, but compared to the gorilla-like Wade—when she heard a chair fly backwards and hit the wall.

"Shut up, Sanders."

Brie edged her way up to the doorway and peeked in. Adam Blake was on his feet glaring at someone across the table. She knew it must be Wade Sanders. The rest were staring at Blake, waiting to see what he'd do.

"Everyone calm down, right now," Spencer ordered. "That means you, Adam. Get a grip on yourself and sit down. And that's enough out of you, too, Wade. There's no doubt that if Amanda *has* disappeared, it would jeopardize our whole operation. She plays things close to her vest, and she's never let me know who her contacts are. Without that ledger and the information it contains, our operation grinds to a halt."

Maybe that's what Blake was looking for, Brie thought. It sounded to her like Amanda had fairly limited trust in some or all of the members of *the group*. If that were the case, she never would have kept said ledger where any of them could easily lay hands on it.

"So, where do we go from here?" she heard Adam ask.

"You take care of the business at hand," Spencer said. "I'll deal with the rest."

What business at hand? Brie thought. *And why was he address-ing Adam? What was Adam supposed to do?* She wished somebody would say something to give her an inkling of what was going on.

"Charlie, you were the last to see her boat. What else do you know? Did you see her yesterday?" It was Bob Weatherby talking now. Brie recognized his voice from her bait shop visit.

"I don't know nothin', Weather." The slur was gone, and Charlie's voice rang with irritation. "I went to the mainland yes-terday morning and didn't get back till last night. I ain't seen Amanda in a few days."

If that's the case, Charlie has an alibi, Brie thought. She'd found him pretty approachable. If his story checked out, maybe she could elicit a little more information from him. She had de-termined two things from her fly-in-the-hall vantage point. One, Amanda was the lynchpin in some unknown operation this group was involved in; and two, her killer was most assuredly sitting in that room right now. If Amanda had called Spencer about a problem within *the group* and then disappeared before she could meet with him, that pretty much put a cap on it. Right now, Brie was most interested in the outburst between Wade Sanders and Adam Blake. There were intense feelings there— anger, maybe jealousy—and Brie knew one thing: intense feel-ings lead to murder.

At the sound of chairs moving, she skittered back down the hall, still clinging to the wall, slipped back into the storage room, and closed the door silently after her. Climbing onto a box under the window, she pushed the sash up, hoisted herself through the opening, and lowered the window again from the other side, being careful to leave it in the exact position she'd found it. Be-fore any of the others had left the library she was already at the edge of the woods, making her way back toward the road to meet John.

She hung back from the side of the road just far enough that she could duck behind a tree if anyone came along. While she waited for John, Brie mulled over what she felt she knew about Amanda, as well as the information she had gained from her spying mission at the library, to try and assemble some picture of what might be going on, and who might have had a reason to harm the artist. She pulled out the length of line she'd stuffed in her pocket back at the house and mechanically tied a bowline as she ran down her list of facts.

Amanda Whitcombe, artist, redheaded, beautiful, somewhere around fifty years old, daughter of an archeologist. Lived alone in her cottage on Puffin Point. Had extended friendship and possibly more to Harold and Ben up at the lighthouse. Had taken Wendy McLeod, motherless girl, under her wing—hence was kind and caring. Had no trouble attracting men—possibly involved with more than one of them at a time. Loved her home and loved the island—hence her strongest ties would be here. Was the ringleader of some kind of operation—probably illegal —that *the group* was involved in. Had exclusive knowledge of certain parts of *the group's* operation that she refused to share with the others. *Why?* The single word lingered in Brie's mind like an itch that needed to be scratched.

She sat down on the ground near a spruce tree and folded her legs. She worked the line into a Portuguese bowline, undid it and moved on to a Spanish bowline with its twin forked loop. *Why would Amanda keep certain facts from the group? To shift the balance of power in her direction? To protect the identity of her contacts? Or maybe just to make sure "the group" couldn't operate without her?* Hmmm, there was an interesting thought. *Was she afraid of being edged out?* After all, except for her and Birdie, who didn't seem to have much of a voice in anything when Spencer was on the scene, *the group* was pretty much a boys' club.

Brie guessed whatever the killer's motive was, it might not relate to the activities of *the group*, per se. Doing away with Amanda would be like killing the goose with the golden egg, since she apparently held the purse strings to their operation. But she had supposedly scheduled a meeting with Spencer. A meeting she'd never lived to see. "Something about a member of *the group*, and a problem that had developed." Brie recalled Spencer's words and wondered if Amanda had been afraid of someone in the group. *Had she been threatened? Was she being blackmailed? Or was this a crime of passion?* she wondered, recalling the outburst that had just occurred between Adam Blake and Wade Sanders.

The questions rolled through Brie's detective mind—a mind used to weighing and measuring all the possibilities. *Had Amanda even scheduled that meeting with Spencer, or had he made the whole thing up?* Brie wondered if there might have been a power struggle going on between the two of them, since Spencer had already stepped up to take the reigns of an operation that Amanda had controlled. But, as the town manager, Spencer was used to that role—of course he'd take charge. No, what she sensed here were layers of things going on—layers of information to be peeled away like the leaves of an artichoke, before she would find the bitter truth at the center of it all.

She decided she needed to find out who Amanda was closest to on the island. Even though the artist seemed a bit of a loner, Brie was hoping there might be a good friend—someone who could flesh out the details of her existence here. But who to turn to for information? There was Ben, and of course, Wendy. Maybe Frannie Lempke could be of help, and possibly even Doug, if she could determine that he didn't himself have a motive. She had uncovered the basic strands of Amanda's life. But now they lay before her like the warp threads on a loom, waiting for the weft—waiting for the threads of color and texture that would reveal the design of the artist's life.

Brie practiced her one-handed bowline a couple times before stuffing the line back in her pocket. It occurred to her that she would need to conduct a very different kind of investigation than she was used to. Without the authority of her badge and her official connection to the law, she would have to go about her information gathering indirectly. *Tricky*, she thought, *like a one-handed bowline*. She couldn't just march up to the likes of Spencer or Wade Sanders and say, "I need to question you since you were connected to Amanda, and now she's missing."

She realized she would have to operate like a private investigator—working from the outer edges and slowly moving toward the middle. It was not unlike processing a crime scene—picking up clues on the periphery that might explain what had unfolded at the center. She was already beginning to develop a respect for the difficulties PIs—a group she had previously looked on with some degree of disdain—faced.

She checked her watch. What was keeping John? The question was no more than framed in her mind when she heard the crunch of tires on the gravel. She scrambled up and stepped behind the tree until Ben's truck came into view. She headed out to the road and hopped in.

"Hey, you. Any bad guys on your trail? I was hoping I gave you enough time."

"Plenty," Brie said. She related the details of the meeting and who was in *the group*. "I have no idea what they're up to, John."

"Any obvious motives?"

"Not so's you'd notice," Brie said. She couldn't help taking note of John's question. Clearly, he'd already learned a bit about police procedure from the events on Granite Island. She was glad she had someone to verbally hash out the details with.

"So, where to now?" he asked.

"I'm thinking a sandwich and coffee from the Scuttlebutt might hit the spot."

"Ah. I wonder if hunger has anything to do with it, or if it's just plan scuttlebutt you're after?"

Brie gave him a wink. "Fudge and Frannie seem like neutral territory. Maybe I can find out who Amanda was close to—who she might have confided in."

"It's worth a try." John did a U-turn in the road and headed back toward the village.

Chapter 10

Brie and John parked in the lot behind the Scuttlebutt Café next to a rusty red jeep, circa mid-1980s. Since it was the only other vehicle in the lot, Brie knew it must belong to Fudge and Frannie. She and John climbed the three wooden stairs and stepped through the door. The place was empty except for Fudge, who was behind the bar swabbing out coffee cups in a tiny sink and singing a sea chantey under his breath. He looked up when they entered and fixed them with his stationary eye.

"Well, if it isn't my two swabbies—or beggin' your pardon, one captain and one swabbie." He gave Brie a wink.

Brie and John sat down on two of the high stools in front of the bar near where Fudge was working. He had resumed his dish detail and was washing and stacking the cups in time with his sea ditty. Suddenly, his face went serious, as if he'd just remembered something. He looked around cautiously before leaning across the bar toward them. "There's trouble in the wind today. Mark my words," he said in a low voice. Brie wasn't quite sure what to make of Fudge and his predictions. She was momentarily put in mind of the old prophet in *Moby Dick* and his warnings to Ishmael to steer clear of the *Pequod*.

"We had to make a run into the hardware store," John said. "The breakfast was so good, we thought we'd stop in and grab a sandwich."

Fudge dried his hands on his apron and slapped a pair of menus in front of them. "Be ye wantin' coffee, mates?" he asked.

"You bet," John said. "How about you, Brie?"

"Sure." She knew she should cut back, but the excessive coffee habit had always gone hand in hand with being a cop.

Fudge deposited two of the thick diner-ware mugs in front of them and filled them with coffee. They studied the menu for a couple of minutes and decided on the half sandwich and cup of soup combo. John went for the ham and cheese, and Brie decided on the toasted BLT. The soup today was clam chowder—a sure bet anywhere in Maine. They gave Fudge their order.

He lumbered to the end of the bar and rounded the corner. They heard him call into the kitchen. "The sailors are back, Frannie. They can't get enough of your cooking." He delivered their soup and sandwich order and then headed out into the café to wipe off tables.

Brie racked her brain for a question she could ask him. It seemed like a golden opportunity to gather some information, but nothing occurred to her. She was hoping Frannie would deliver the lunches, so she could ask her if she knew who Amanda was close to on the island.

Fortunately, within five minutes, Frannie rounded the corner of the bar, carrying the lunches. She set them down in front of Brie and John and smiled warmly at them. "Hello, you two. Didn't think we'd be seeing you again so soon." She smoothed her apron twice and hesitated for a moment before asking if they'd had any luck finding Amanda.

This gave Brie the perfect opportunity. "Not yet," she said. "I wonder if you might know who Amanda is close to on the island, Frannie? Someone who might know where she's gone?"

"Well, there's old Miss Harriet up the other side of the island."

"Miss Harriet?" Brie repeated.

Frannie smoothed her apron again. "Harriet Patterson. She's kind of the island matriarch—also the island historian.

She's eighty-eight years old and has lived here longer than anyone else. She was a friend of Amanda's parents, God rest their souls. She's always been close to Amanda, almost in a motherly kind of way. If there's anyone on this island Amanda would have confided in, it would be Harriet."

"You say she's up the other side of the island?" Brie asked.

"Just go through the village and take the road up the west side of the island. You'll see her name on a board when you get to her driveway."

"Thanks, Frannie. We'll stop up there as soon as we finish our sandwiches."

Frannie bustled back to her kitchen, and John and Brie polished off their lunch. Fudge was running a string mop along the floor behind the bar and glancing shyly in their direction from time to time to see how they were liking their lunches. As they finished the last of their soup, John said, "Fudge, that's some award-winning chowder."

Fudge beamed with pleasure, and nodding his head, said, "Thank ye kindly, Captain." John stood up, took his wallet out of his back pocket, and walked over to the register at the end of the bar. Brie hopped off her stool and followed behind. Fudge put down his mop, came to the end of the bar, and settled up with John. He kept his stationary eye on the register as he deposited the money.

"See you again soon, Fudge," Brie said as they headed out the door.

"Aye, mateys," Fudge growled back at them with a friendly nod.

They backed the truck around and took a right out of the parking lot and headed toward the west end of the village. "Do we have time to do this before we head back?" Brie asked.

"I don't know why not," John said. "We've wrapped up work for the day, and George said dinner won't be till six or six-thirty. So we've got time to kill."

"We still planning on that moonlight sail with Ben?"

"Yup. He's looking forward to it, and we should have a perfect night. Ben had the weather on this afternoon, and they're predicting fifteen-to twenty-knot winds on through tonight."

"Perfect night sailing," Brie said. "What time we heading out?"

"Right after dinner. George said he'll be serving dessert on board." John chuckled. "He goes through withdrawal, you know, if he's away from his galley for too long."

"I know," said Brie. "We're a lucky bunch of swabbies to have George."

John smiled and reached for her hand. "Beggin' your pardon—one captain, one swabbie." He gave her a wink. "And a pretty swabbie to boot."

Brie looked out her window and smiled. In her previous life, she would have considered John's little comments corny, but somehow they were just what she needed now. It was great to feel like a girl again. It helped her to forget all the ugliness she had been party to so short a time ago.

"There," John said. He pointed ahead on the right. A weathered, gray shingle bore the name Patterson. He turned the truck into the driveway.

The cottage was like so many others that graced Maine's coastline—a modest Cape Cod with its signature gray shakes. A few yards behind the cottage, a large granite outcropping, nearly as wide as the cottage itself, loomed out of the ground. Surrounding the house, what looked like it might once have been a small lawn was rapidly returning to forest habitat, and young spruce trees sprouted everywhere. The driveway ended alongside the house. To the right of the driveway a large woodpile— approximately two cords in size—was split and partially stacked.

John switched off the truck and they got out. There was a back door, but they decided to try around front. Outside the door, a small stoop ran along the front of the house. It held two white painted rocking chairs and a good-sized firewood box with a hinged lid. Brie wondered if Harriet still came out here to sit and take in the air. A large picture window looked toward the ocean. At one time it would have offered an unobstructed view of the sea, but the new growth of spruce had now largely blocked that view.

They walked up a pair of steps onto the small porch and knocked on the door. Within a couple of minutes they heard the tap of a cane approaching, and an elderly woman opened the door. She hunched slightly over her cane, but her appearance was quite tidy. Her silver-gray hair was slicked back into a bun at the nape of her neck. She wore a long wool skirt and a soft pink cardigan sweater, buttoned up all the way.

A look of surprise crossed her face, as if she might have been expecting someone else. "Can I help you?" she asked cautiously. Brie introduced herself and John, telling her about their connection to the *Maine Wind* and to Ben at the lighthouse, and then using the *we're friends of Wendy and Doug McLeod* story. At this, Harriet seemed to relax a bit and asked if they would like to come in.

"If we wouldn't be intruding," Brie said politely.

"Oh, Lordy," Harriet said, "it's been a long time since you could have intruded on anything here." Her blue eyes were surprisingly clear for a woman of her age, and when she spoke, they took on a twinkle. She looked shyly up at John, as if it had been a long time since a handsome man had come calling.

They stepped in the door and followed Harriet into a cozy living room on the right. Although it was summer, a fire blazed in the hearth. Harriet moved over to the pile of logs on the hearth and started to lift one.

"Here, allow me," John said, stepping quickly to her side. He took the log and added it to the grate.

"Well, thank you, young man," Harriet said. "I'm used to handling the fire, though. My husband's been gone a long time." She settled into a high-backed chair to the right of the fireplace and motioned Brie and John toward the sofa across from her. It had a faded, floral slipcover, and when they sat down, it welcomed them with a broken-in comfort that told Brie life had not always been so solitary for Harriet.

"So, what brings you here to visit an old woman?"

"Well, actually, Frannie down at the Scuttlebutt Café told us you're a friend of Amanda Whitcombe. And, well, Wendy has been looking for her since yesterday. There seems to be some question about where's she's gone. Apparently her boat has been missing from the harbor since last night." Brie saw no sign that Harriet was alarmed, so she went on. "Frannie said you're quite close to Amanda, and she thought you might have an idea where she is."

"Amanda and I are close," Harriet said. "I've known her since she was a little girl. I was friends with her parents." Harriet shifted in her chair, as if not quite comfortable with this little tableau. But she continued. "Amanda was supposed to stop by yesterday afternoon. She comes by almost every day to check on me and bring wood in."

Brie looked over at the dwindling pile of logs, and as she did, John stood up. "Let me get some firewood for you, Mrs. Patterson," he said. He headed for the door before Harriet could refuse his offer. Brie wondered if John hadn't picked up that Harriet seemed a bit uncomfortable talking to them. Maybe he thought it would go better if he left her alone with Harriet.

After John was out the door, Brie said, "Wendy was so upset at not being able to locate Amanda that I've been asking around a little. Do you know if she was planning to go off island?"

Harriet stared into the fire. "Little Wendy's made a mother figure out of Amanda. It's been good for both of them. I think it's filled a hole in both their lives." Harriet smoothed her hair with her right hand even though it was in perfect order. "I can't tell you where Amanda is, though. I was a little surprised she didn't come by yesterday. Folks will say she can be flighty, but she never forgets about me. I don't like anyone fussing over me, but I have to admit, at my age, it's nice to know someone is looking out for you a little."

Brie could hear John filling the wood box on the porch. She guessed he would take his time so she wouldn't be interrupted in her information gathering with Harriet. She wasn't sure quite how to begin, so she was happy when Harriet addressed her first. "I can hear by your speech that you're not from around here, Miss Beaumont," she said matter-of-factly.

"No," said Brie, impressed that Harriet had so easily recalled her name. "I'm actually from Minnesota." She hoped Harriet wouldn't ask about her connection with the McLeods. She hated being devious, but she was learning that this *on the down low* kind of investigating required it.

"My, you're quite a ways from home, aren't you?" Harriet was studying her with those clear blue eyes, and Brie found it mildly unsettling. You couldn't lie to someone with eyes like that—they acted on you almost like a truth serum.

"Well, I'm afraid a series of unfortunate events led me to come to Maine," Brie said, "but I'm happy to say that life has gotten better since I've been here."

"Sometimes the good Lord picks us up and puts us in a whole new picture," Harriet said. "A picture we fit into perfectly even though we may not know why."

There it was again, Brie thought, that simple faith in the rightness of things. A faith that seemed to come so easily to some people. She sat for a moment, looking at her hands.

"You don't believe that, do you?" Harriet asked.

Brie glanced up. Harriet was watching her with those discerning eyes. "I'd like to," she said. "Somehow, it's always been hard for me." How could she tell Harriet that many of the things she had seen as a police officer and a detective hadn't bolstered her faith in a philosophy that affirmed the rightness of all things?

Brie knew she needed to move the conversation back toward center. "Frannie Lempke told me how much Amanda loves this island," she said, being careful to keep her verbs in

142

present tense, even though she was sure Amanda now belonged to the past tense. "Has she lived here her entire adult life?" This seemed to Brie like a safe place to start, but one that might also lead to some helpful information about Amanda.

"The cottage Amanda lives in used to be the Whitcombes' summer home. She inherited it after her mother passed away. Amanda's mother was an archeologist with something of a worldwide reputation. She was part of a team of archeologists who discovered the Mayan cities and pyramids back in the nineteen fifties and sixties." Harriet paused and stared into the fire before continuing. "The family always summered here. Amanda had the soul of an artist even as a child. I think island life was a catalyst for her imagination and creativity. She loved roaming the forest and exploring the rocky beaches and tidal pools. I think the island fueled an independent streak that was always part of her."

"So, she was here every summer from childhood to adulthood?" Brie asked.

Harriet turned back to Brie. "Well, no, she went to school in France for her art education. Left Maine at eighteen and stayed in France for seven or eight years."

Brie heard the sudden tightness in Harriet's voice and noted how she looked down at her hands. It was enough to tell her that all had not gone well in France. She knew she'd have to tread lightly here to gain any information. "But, sadly, things went awry while she was there." Brie said it in a sympathetic but declarative manner to give Harriet the impression she already knew the story.

"It's amazing how island life is immune to secrets," Harriet said with a resigned sigh. "In a big city you can hide things, remain anonymous. Not on an island, though. You'd almost think the very trees and waves have some power to know all and whisper the truth to anyone willing to hear."

Brie stood up and put a log on the fire, hoping Harriet would continue.

"Amanda was lucky her mother had an international reputation as an archeologist. She had connections in the art world
and learned just in time what Amanda had become involved in.
Fortunately, she was able to get her out of the country in time."

Brie knew it was time to venture a guess and hope her detective instincts had led her down the right path. "The black
market art world and the men who frequented it must have
held a dangerous allure for such a young woman," she said. She
knew her die was cast. Despite her age, Harriet was sharp as a
tack, and if Brie was wrong in her guess, it would undoubtedly
be the end of her visit.

"The man had been one of Amanda's teachers at the École
des Beaux-Arts in Paris," Harriet said. "Over a number of years
he had drawn her more and more into his circle, which Eva,
Amanda's mother, later learned included art thieves, forgers,
and fences. Eva managed to extricate Amanda just before Jean
Paul—that was his name—was arrested, along with his band of
crooks." Harriet shifted in her chair as if she'd just become
aware that they'd been talking for awhile.

"Amanda's lucky she got away," Brie said. "Had she been
arrested, it would probably have been impossible to get her out
of France."

"And then, two years ago, he showed up here on the island. Can you imagine—after twenty-some years?"

"You mean Jean Paul?" Brie asked.

"Yes," said Harriet. "I didn't think convicted criminals
could even get passports. Fortunately, he didn't stay long. I
guess by the age of forty-eight, Amanda had finally come to her
senses." Harriet shifted to look toward the front door. "My, that
young man of yours is certainly taking his time, isn't he?"

"Let me go see what he's up to," Brie said, standing up and
walking toward the door. She felt like she was making progress.
Not only had she discovered some of Amanda's history, she had
learned the artist could be drawn into illicit activities. *Once a person goes down that road, it's always possible they'll revisit it.* She

found John out by the woodpile stacking the split logs that had been heaped up there. "It's safe to bring in the wood now, John."

"I didn't want to intrude. Thought you might get further with Harriet if I stayed out here."

"Well, you were right," Brie said. "I got some interesting information, but I'm not sure how it might connect to Amanda's disappearance."

"I filled the wood box on the porch," John said. "I'll bring some in the house now."

He made several trips carrying armloads of wood in and stacking them in the built-in niche for firewood next to the fireplace. He pulled all the driest wood out and put it on top so Harriet could use it first. While he was busy, Brie asked Harriet if there was anything she could do, and was given the job of replacing two light bulbs that had blown out the day before. They were both in ceiling fixtures, so Brie brought the kitchen ladder out and climbed up to replace them. She assured Harriet that if Amanda wasn't back by tomorrow, she'd stop by and check on her.

The old woman was clearly touched by the gesture. She took Brie's hand in hers and patted it gently. "You're a very nice young lady," she said. With that, John and Brie took their leave. As they walked toward the truck, Harriet lingered at the open door for a few seconds before retreating back to the warmth of her house.

Chapter 11

J ohn and Brie pulled the truck up behind the keeper's quarters and climbed out. Over on the far side of the house, Ben
and Scott lounged in the Adirondack chairs, laughing and
talking together. George was nowhere in sight, but Brie guessed
he was in the kitchen embroiled in some phase of beef stew concoction.

"Hey, you two," Ben called as they approached. "We were
getting ready to send out the sheriff. I didn't know you could
get lost on an island with only three roads."

Brie wasn't about to divulge the details of her spy mission at
the library, and thankfully, John came to the rescue. "We drove
too close to the Scuttlebutt, and the aroma of clam chowder way-
laid us," he said.

"You'd best not let George hear that," Ben said.

"See, that's what you don't get, though, Ben," John said.
"George's fun is in the cooking. Sure, he appreciates it when
people praise his fare, but he doesn't seek that out. And he'd
never be hurt if someone turned down a meal."

"For George, it really is about the joy of cooking," Brie added. She turned to Ben. "Is the lighthouse open?" she asked. "I
thought I'd take a hike up to the top and hang out for awhile."

"Help yourself, Brie. Door's unlocked."

"Great." Brie turned to go.

"Mind if I tag along?" John asked.

"Of course not," Brie replied. She turned and headed toward the tower, and John followed. She couldn't very well say "no," but she *had* looked forward to being up there by herself. She wanted to think, and it was that time of the day when she liked to carve out a little alone time. She had developed the habit on the ship, where the close quarters left little chance for solitude. It was another change she had noted in herself over the past couple of months. Before the *Maine Wind*, solitude had seemed like the enemy—something to be avoided at all costs. After the shooting, she had found ways to work even more hours than the compulsive schedule she had kept before that.

But she had learned the sea was conducive to emptying one's mind, and she had come to look forward to that time in the late afternoon when she would climb out on the bowsprit and roost on the small wood seat formed by the planks of the pulpit. Passengers generally wouldn't venture out there, at least not without the captain's permission. John, being a man of the sea, was fully aware of its healing capabilities. She wondered now if that wasn't one of the reasons he had wanted her to join the crew.

He must have been reading her thoughts, because he suddenly stopped as if something had just occurred to him. "Maybe you'd prefer to be alone, Brie," he said.

"No, don't be silly. Come along," she encouraged. She knew he had looked forward to spending extra time with her out here, and so, despite her desire to escape for a little while, she took his hand and pulled him along.

They opened the door and stepped into the cool silence of the lighthouse. The iron stairs wound upward, and Brie paused to stare up into the dizzying spiral. Like Mohamed going to the mountain, she knew the vantage from up there could only be conducive to enlightenment. Right now, she needed some of that. She knew Amanda was dead, and she knew something sinister was going on here on the island, but she had no clue what or why.

Two-thirds of the way up, she paused to look out one of the small, oblong windows toward the ocean. She felt John step carefully up behind her, so they shared the same step. She could feel his body pressed against her in that tiny precarious place, and somehow the danger of it, and the solitude and romance of the old lighthouse got to her. She slowly turned around, pivoting on her left foot, and carefully slid her hands up onto his shoulders. To steady himself, John reached over her head for the vertical iron pole—one of many that ran upward, supporting the structure. His free arm went around her waist. He pulled her even closer and stared silently down into her eyes. They stood like that, barely breathing, suspended in the silence and passion of the moment, hesitant to break it, even for the kiss they both knew was coming.

"I'm glad I came along," was all he said as his mouth closed over hers. Her arms went around his neck as the kiss deepened, and she felt his arm tighten around her waist as he lifted her against him. Her toes barely touched the iron stair step, and she hung suspended in the smooth, strong fabric of his kiss. Some wild part of her wanted to fly away with him to a secret place where they'd never stop making love.

He finally eased her back down to terra firma, and they spent a few delightful moments planting kisses on each other's faces, until he pulled her close again and placed his lips on her neck. She let her head fall back, surrendering to the moment as he grazed down the side of her neck. She opened her eyes in delicious anticipation of what might come next. She was actually wondering how many clothes they could remove while standing on this precarious perch when her eyes lit on something.

"John."

"Hmmm," came a delirious sound that vibrated against her shoulder as he slid the tee shirt off of it and placed his lips there.

"John. Look up there." He slowly raised his head. "Do you see that?" she asked.

"I don't think I want to see anything right now. Well, I'll take that back, I can think of a couple things," he said, looking down at her breasts.

"Really, John. What is that? It looks like something is hidden under that step up there." And just like that, the detective in her edged the woman right out of the picture. John held her captive for a moment, which felt terribly sexy, but she could see in his eyes that he knew the battle was lost.

"Rain check?" he whispered in her ear and held her tight till he got his response.

Brie slid her hands to his face. "Rain check," she replied, kissing his lips gently. Then she added, "And I hope next time it's a really long dry spell."

"Well, maybe not completely dry," he whispered mischievously. Brie felt herself blush. John played with a strand of her hair. "It's so cute when you do that," he said. "You make me feel like a teenager."

"Ah, shucks," Brie said, pushing him away gently. "Now let's see what that is." They carefully disengaged from one another, and John stepped down one step so she could turn and head upward.

They climbed the spiral of black iron until John said, "Brie, let me go by. I think I can reach it from here."

Brie could see the object clearly now. It was a black container a little bigger than a cigar box, affixed in some manner to the underside of the step. It would only have been visible to someone who had paused partway up the stairs, and looked upwards long enough to notice something there. And even then, most wouldn't have seen it. But Brie was trained to notice subtle, nearly invisible details.

John felt around the edge of the box, and before she knew it, pulled out a pair of what looked like thin books covered with black leather. Brie felt her curiosity shoot up like a thermometer in boiling water. John turned the books over and opened the cover of the top one.

"What are they, John?" she asked, climbing to the step below him.

"They look like journals."

"Do you suppose they belonged to Harold?"

"I have no idea," he said. "I think we need to let Ben see them first, though."

Brie knew he was right, but all the same, it was killing her not to be able to look at them immediately. "I suppose you're right," she said, "but why do you suppose anyone would have hidden them up here?"

"Maybe they weren't hidden so much as just stored here," John said. "Maybe this was someone's favorite thinking spot— you know, like the bowsprit on the ship might be for someone else." He paused and winked at her. "So, whoever it was, maybe they just liked to come up here and write in their journal."

"Yeah, and maybe lobsters will sprout wings and fly away. Believe me, John, I know something hidden when I see it."

"Well, we've got to give these to Ben. I'm sure he'll let us know what they are, and whether we can see them."

"I know," said Brie, wishing she had come up here alone. Maybe she would have found the journals, and being not quite as noble as John, she suspected she would have taken a good long look inside. But then she thought about the close encounter that had just taken place on the narrow step a ways below them, and she decided that was a really stupid wish.

"Well, shall we continue on up to the top?" John asked.

"That's okay, John. I think it might be anticlimactic after what just happened down there." So they headed back down the iron stairs with Brie leading the way, and she could swear she still felt passion, thick as honey, hanging around that one step opposite the small window. She glanced at her watch as they descended the rest of the way. It was nearing six o'clock. Where had the day gone? She decided she'd go in and help George with some of the final dinner prep when they got back to the house.

They walked around the keeper's house, and John headed toward Ben with the journals. Brie opened the screen door and stepped into the kitchen. The smell of freshly baked blueberry cobbler added a much needed hominess to the deconstruction zone. George was busy at a big mixing bowl, and Brie already knew what he was making—parsley dumplings to go on top of the beef stew.

"So, what can I help with, George? Are we doing a salad?"

"Well, Ben doesn't have much on hand for a salad, but there's a nice head of lettuce in the fridge. I thought I'd cut it into wedges and make up some of my homemade French dressing to go with it."

"Sounds great. Maybe I can make the dressing?"

"Sure. Grab a bowl, and I'll tell you how to proceed."

Brie found a small, steep-sided mixing bowl and set it on the makeshift work table George had created out of a piece of wood and two sawhorses. She rummaged through the utensil drawer next to the stove and found a whisk. "Okay, George, ready for action."

"You'll need a lemon, an onion, and the ketchup from the fridge, and there's some apple cider vinegar, sugar, and oil in that cabinet back there in the pantry." He motioned across the kitchen with a doughy wooden spoon. "And, while you're in there, take a look for some paprika."

Brie collected all the ingredients and put them on the work table. She measured them into the bowl as George recited the amounts. She drizzled in the oil last, whisking briskly as she poured it in. When the dressing was done, she found a crockery cream pitcher and poured about two thirds of the mixture into it. She put the remainder into a jar large enough to hold what would be left after dinner.

She got out the lettuce, washed it, and cut it into five wedges. She placed them in a bowl, covered it with plastic wrap, and put it back in the fridge. She went over to the dish cabinet and got out salad plates and bowls for the stew, and asked George where the checkered tablecloth was that they had used for dinner the night before. He sent her into the dining room to get it. With the tablecloth over one arm, Brie picked up the stack of plates and bowls and headed out the back door. When Scott and John saw her coming, they hopped up to help. Ben stayed in his chair, and Brie could see that he was already absorbed in reading one of the journals.

She got the table set with help from the guys, and went back to the house to see how close George was to being done. He was just dropping dollops of dumpling dough onto the bubbling stew, and the aroma coming from the pot on the stove took her right back to the last time George had made his beef stew.

That night was memorable for two reasons. One, it had been unusually cold, even for June in the north Atlantic, and the warm savory stew had been wonderfully comforting. And, two, they were sailing overnight. Brie had awakened before her watch and gone forward to have a mug of coffee. It was her first overnight sail, and she remembered the galley that night as a charmed place. One oil lamp had been left burning low, and it cast a dim glow illuminating the cozy space. She had crawled onto one of the benches behind the table. In the bow of the ship you feel the motion of the sea more than anywhere else aboard, and that night George's pots and pans, hung above the wood stove in the galley, swung gently on their hooks like strange cookware pendulums counting the moments till dawn. Their quiet timpani, coupled with the creaking of the decks and the rise and fall of the ship's hull, created a lovely sea melody. Brie sat in that still space and realized she dwelt in a different element now, where motion was universal, a constant, where life simply adapted and moved on. That was the night it really came home to her that the change of life she had undergone couldn't have been much greater had she moved to a distant planet. Yet, oddly, it felt like the home she had always waited for.

George was about ready to transport his big pot of stew out to the picnic table. Brie debated about grabbing a jacket—the air was already cooling as the sun dropped lower—but she decided the warm stew would probably do the trick. Seeing George preparing to lift the heavy pot, she went to the fridge for the bowl of lettuce wedges and the dressing and backed out the screen door, holding it open for him.

They gathered around the picnic table, and George served up the stew and dumplings. Brie placed a lettuce wedge onto each plate and passed them down the table along with the pitcher of dressing. They all got down to business, and there followed the usual reign of silence that George's cooking was likely to effect. After a few minutes, though, a space for conversation reopened, and they talked about the night sail they were planning, as well as the logistics of anchoring the *Maine Wind* when they would be returning after dark. They decided to leave a couple of lanterns on the beach to mark the cove, and since the weather was forecast to be fair, they resolved on anchoring the ship along the shore outside of the cove.

As soon as dinner was finished, they cleaned up and gathered jackets, caps, and the lanterns. George carefully wedged the baking dish with the cobbler into the bottom of his rucksack. "Once we're aboard, I'll fire up the stove and make coffee," he said.

Along with the lanterns for the cove, they took several flashlights so they could easily find their way up the trail when they returned. Brie noticed Ben slip the two journals into the small pack he was carrying. She decided whatever was in them must be interesting. By seven o'clock, the five of them were winding along the top of the bluff, heading for the *Maine Wind*.

Chapter 12

They hiked down the narrow path to the rocky beach where the dory waited. John told Brie and Scott he'd row them out to the ship first so they could start unlashing the sails. They carried the dory to the water's edge. Brie tossed their packs in the bow and climbed in, moving to the seat in the stern. John got in next, took the middle seat, and placed the oars in the oarlocks. Scott pushed them off, hopping in at the last second with one graceful movement as the dory floated free of the beach.

John rowed them up to the starboard side of the ship. He reached up with an oar and coaxed the rope and slat ladder off the starboard rail so it hung down the side of the ship. Brie and Scott scrambled up it, climbed aboard the *Maine Wind,* and got busy on deck with the sails. John pushed off to go back for the others. By the time he got back to the beach, Ben had lit the two lanterns and placed them in a secure spot on the beach so they'd serve as a homing beacon. Ben climbed to the stern of the dory, and George pushed off.

"So, I see you already took a look at the journals," John said to Ben. "What's the story with them?" He thought he'd better broach the topic since he knew Brie was itching to know what was in them.

"They're Harold's," Ben said. "He must have started keeping them when he came back to the island. So far, it's pretty typical journal stuff—reflections on the island and his thoughts about being back here."

"I told Brie you needed to look at them first, but if it's okay, when you're done, she'd like to have a look at them. This situation with Amanda is tough. If Brie suspects foul play, she feels honor bound to investigate. She really believes Harold had those journals hidden up there in the lighthouse, and she thinks they may contain something important." They were drifting up to the side of the *Maine Wind* now, and John shipped the oars and reached out to grab the ladder.

"She's perfectly welcome to look through them if there's any chance they might shed light on Amanda's disappearance."

"Great. I'll let her know, Ben. And thanks."

"No thanks to me, John. It's already clear, from what I've read, that Harold liked Amanda. He'd want Brie to look through these," he said, patting his knapsack.

John and Ben climbed up the ladder and over the side of the *Maine Wind*. John told George to row the dory around to the other side of the ship, so Scott and Brie could haul it up onto the portside davits where it hung when not in use.

Brie was feeling a little guilty about going out on the ship when there was a crime to investigate, but she had done about all she could for today. Maybe if she could read through the journals, they'd point her in some direction, because right now all she had were disjointed bits of information. There was a game afoot, and she knew who the players were, but had only the vaguest sense of what the game itself was about.

As for Amanda's disappearance, her suspect list was short, but at least she had one. There was bad blood between Wade Sanders and Adam Blake, as evidenced by the outburst at the meeting she had spied on. That bad blood centered on Amanda. It wasn't much, but it was a place to start. If, by chance, both men could be romantically linked to her, that made them prime suspects in her disappearance. In homicide cases, spouses and lovers always topped the suspect list.

John called everyone to the stern, and they lined up to port and starboard to lower the yawl boat. The wind was coming out of the north, and the *Maine Wind* had swung at anchor to face north and out of the cove. Once they had the yawl boat down, it would be an easy maneuver to push the *Maine Wind* free of the cove and west of the island, where they would raise sail. Getting the yawl boat down with only a crew of five was a tall order. With its wooden hull and diesel engine, the yawl was no birch bark canoe, but with the system of blocks attached to the stern davits, the job was doable.

The captain put George, Brie and Ben over on the port side halyard, and he and Scott, being the two strongest, took the starboard halyard. They released the lines, and leaning their collective weight against the force, slowly lowered the yawl boat down to the water. Scott climbed over the stern and down to the yawl. He turned the engine over and brought the yawl boat around in a circle to butt up against the stern of the *Maine Wind*. A giant Turk's head knot worked around the bow stem formed a bumper or cushion between the two craft. Brie and George got busy cranking up the anchor, and once it was clear of the water, Ben helped them secure it to the starboard rail. Scott opened up the engine on the yawl, and the *Maine Wind* started to make headway.

John steered to the northwest. When they were clear of the cove, he headed the ship due west of the island, and when they were far enough off the island, he steered the ship up into the wind for raising sail. He signaled Scott to cut the engine on the yawl boat. Scott tied the yawl off to the stern, where it would be towed behind the ship while they were under sail. He climbed back aboard and went forward to help Brie raise the foresail. Then all hands lined up again to port and starboard to get the mainsail up. When the main was sheeted off, Brie asked Ben if he'd like to help her with the headsails. They went forward to the bow of the ship to raise the jib and the staysail.

By eight o'clock they were fully under sail, on a heading south-southeast around the end of the island where the lighthouse was situated. They had decided to sail due east of the island. With the wind out of the north, they could put the *Maine Wind* on a beam reach and enjoy that wonderfully smooth point of sail as they waited for the moon to rise off their bow.

As soon as his duties were done above decks, George had headed down to his galley and already had the woodstove burning. Brie could hear him clanking pots around down there, and the comforting sound of it warmed her heart. Before long, she knew he would have water boiling on the stove, and not long thereafter, they'd be enjoying hot coffee and blueberry cobbler.

She walked across the deck to the windward side of the ship, and standing at the port rail, reached up and took hold of the ratlines to steady herself. Even though they'd been ashore just a little over twenty-four hours, she had already started to lose her sea legs. She leaned into the wind to compensate for the angle of the deck, and felt the wind on her face and the silent power of the ship as it sliced forward in the fresh eighteen-knot breeze. This was how life should be—free, beautiful, uncomplicated. How had she ever gotten so lucky? She thought about the pain of the shooting, the pain of losing her partner, Phil, and the fact that, without that occurrence, she would never have come to Maine. And she thought about Harriet's words. "Sometimes the good Lord picks us up and puts us in a whole new picture." She had to wonder, *Could there really be truth in that*?

The last year of her life had become food for a kind of thought process that was new to her. She was used to thinking about cause and effect in relation to her police work, but not so much with regard to her own life. But she couldn't deny that this place of peace and happiness—her life aboard the *Maine Wind*—was the direct result of a set of diametrically opposed circumstances. Her struggles with PTSD hadn't ended, but hope—absent from her life for over a year—had returned.

Brie turned and looked back toward the island. She could see Amanda's cottage perched on the end of Puffin Point. She wondered whether Amanda would be found, and if in the few days they had left here, she'd be able to sort out the arcane goings-on on the island. She looked back out to sea and reflected on the fact that, in this beautiful place, she was once again being confronted with the ugliness of humanity run amok. She really hoped that somewhere there was a place, a reality—call it hea-ven—where the coin always came up heads; where there was no dark or tarnished side.

She was suddenly aware of John standing behind her, and she automatically turned to see who was at the helm. There was Ben with a rare smile on his face—a look of deep contentment, unlike anything she had seen in him since they had arrived at the island. "This is good for him," she said.

"Sure is," John replied. "I need to find a way to get him aboard more often. He's in his element here."

"We all are, John. Birds of a feather, or maybe something more oceany. Fish of a scale?"

John smiled at the image. "Ben's turned the journals over for you to go through." He held them in his left hand. "I talked to him, and he said if there's a chance anything in these can lend a clue to what's happened to Amanda, he wants you to go through them right away."

"Thanks, John," she said, taking them and folding them in-to the crook of her left arm. "There's still good light, so I think I'll sit on the cabin top and start into them until it gets dark."

"It'd be nice if you'd just enjoy the sail and let those wait till we get back tonight."

Brie turned her head and looked off the stern of the ship. "John, there's trouble on that island. I'm not sure why or what it's about, but I know one thing—trouble breeds trouble. If there are any answers in these journals, I need to find them." She laid a hand on his shoulder briefly before she walked away.

John watched her go. He turned and gazed out to sea for a few moments. The north wind on his face was a reminder that fall was only two months away. He turned from the rail, walked aft, and stood silently next to Ben at the wheel.

"You know, John, sometimes you just have to step back and let things take their course."

"I guess," John said, noncommittally.

"I learned about powerlessness when Libby died of cancer. Do you know I still sometimes run through that heart-sickening list of would of's, could of's, and should of's?"

"Is that why you drive yourself the way you do?" John asked.

Ben smiled. "You noticed, eh?"

"Just a bit," John said.

"It's the only way I've ever found to escape my demons. Maybe I should take up drinking."

"Living up on that cliff, I'm not sure that'd be the best plan," John said with a smile.

He looked toward Brie. She had climbed onto the cabin top amidships and was staring off into the distance. "Brie's a woman who needs meaning in her life. Look at the work she's done. I'm just worried she won't find that aboard the *Maine Wind*. At least not enough to keep her here."

"You can't hold her too closely, John. She's the kind of woman who'll get skittish if you do. She's lived an independent life for a long time and worked in a job where she's had to be strong."

"You're right, Ben."

"You know, there's a saying: 'The more you let someone go, the more they'll come back to you.' "

"I'll try to remember that, Ben."

"It's good to be here on the *Maine Wind* again, together," Ben said.

"Like old times," John said.

Brie propped her feet against the grabrail that ran along the edge of the cabin top and leaned back on her hands. High, fair-weather clouds like puffy down quilts were scattered in clumps across the tranquil evening sky. She wished she could curl up in one of those clouds for a long nap. *John probably thinks I'm more interested in the unfolding case than in him.* Little did he know how often these days she had to force herself to take on what she considered her responsibilities. So unlike the Brie of the past was she that sometimes she could barely recognize herself. What had once been an intense drive to clear cases had, in the past year and a half, been replaced by a kind of apathy against which she struggled. Even worse was the overwhelming, crushing feeling of fatigue that had accompanied her cases in the months after she was shot.

She knew it was all part of the post-traumatic stress, and she knew there was no magic cure. She had learned that this fatigue, this feeling of being overwhelmed, was part of the disorder. Every time she could recognize it for what it was, she took away a little of its power. Life aboard the *Maine Wind*, with its simple, uncomplicated, immediately gratifying tasks, had been immensely healing. And so for right now, and for the foreseeable future, this was the only place she could imagine herself being.

She opened the cover on the first journal and stepped back into Harold McCann's life on the island. The pages were not large, nor were the entries for each date extensive. Each new entry was assigned its own page. According to the journal, Harold had moved back to the island approximately two years and three months ago. Brie recalled Ben saying that Harold had grown up on Sentinel Island, and immediately the journal began to reveal this childhood connection to the island.

April 14

I've come home finally. Finally home after so many years. I've traveled the world, been to many ports of call. So strange to be back here. So familiar in a way and yet so different. So much smaller than the kingdom I perceived as a boy and as a teen.

April 17

Today I walked all the roads on the island deciding where my course would be for running. The roads on the western side of the island are in better shape, probably because that side is more sheltered from the bad gales. I should be able to get in a good three mile run and have plotted a couple different routes so it won't get boring. The island folk haven't been all that friendly, but I have a nice neighbor in Amanda Whitcombe. She is lovely and bears a striking resemblance to her mother, Eva, whom I remember as the island beauty when I was a teenager.

April 25

I love to come up to the top of the light. It's my favorite place on the island, and a special kind of drama unfolds when a storm is approaching. I love to watch the thunder clouds advancing ominously from the south, swords of lightning flashing. And the gales from the northeast with winds strong enough to rock the walls of my stone fortress.

Brie read on through a couple of months of entries. Harold became borderline poetic when he wrote about the lighthouse and what transpired when he was at the top. It became clear that he had spent more and more time up there in the solitude of his airy kingdom. Aside from Amanda, whom Harold clearly admired, this first journal contained few mentions of the other islanders. But interestingly, starting some time in June, Bob, the bait shop guy, appeared regularly in the journal. Apparently, he and Harold had formed an unlikely friendship, which Harold seemed both surprised and somewhat delighted by. Entries revealed that they fished together from Bob's boat, and also that they spent time together out at the lighthouse.

Old Harriet Patterson also began appearing midway through the journal. The entries revealed that she and her husband had been friends of Harold's parents when he was a boy on the island. Brie guessed that Harriet would have been a touchstone to Harold's past here, but also with her warmth and wisdom, a comfort to him in the present. Harriet was independent and reclusive, qualities Harold would have liked. The journal revealed that he had formed the habit of checking on her a couple of times every week to see if anything needed doing around her place. Brie made a mental note to ask Harriet some things about Harold when she stopped by her cottage the next day.

Brie set the journal down on the cabin top and stretched her arms above her head. Due to the reflective nature of water, daylight lingers on the ocean longer than ashore. So, even though they hadn't gotten under way until eight o'clock, she had had more than an hour of light to sit and peruse the first journal and had nearly finished reading it. But now the sun was preparing to dip behind Sentinel Island, which they were sailing due east of. The undersides of the high clouds blushed pale pink and lavender. That palette of colors would soon give way to more intense golds, oranges, and reds. They were going to be treated to a full-spectrum Maine sunset tonight. Brie had never witnessed anything that could rival the beauty of sunsets on the ocean, where sky and water became frenzied with color, and in counterpoint, the islands and the hills of the mainland retreated into smoky gray silhouettes, hunkering down for a peaceful night's sleep.

Scott had just come up from the galley carrying a large tray that held stoneware bowls, coffee mugs, and two carafes of coffee. He was followed up the ladder by George, who bore a baking dish filled with cobbler, heated through on the woodstove and wafting aromas of warm dough, blueberries, and cinnamon. In the crook of his other arm George held a crockery bowl, and Brie knew it was filled with freshly whipped cream for the cobbler.

She hopped off the cabin top and stowed the journals in the small cuddy, tucked under the aft cabin top, diagonally across from the wheel. The cuddy held the radar and GPS displays and was also the repository for rolled-up charts, sunscreen, and binoculars.

John had been visiting with Ben and now offered to take the helm. "You and Brie go forward and have dessert," he said.

"If you don't mind, John, I'd rather stay at the wheel," Ben said. "I'm really enjoying sailing the ship."

"Fine by me," John said.

"I'd love a cup of hot coffee, though."

"I'll bring you one," Brie said.

She and John headed forward. George was starting to plate up the cobbler. "I'll have a double on the whipped cream," Brie said.

"Ditto that for me, George," Scott chimed in.

Brie poured out a cup of hot coffee and brought it back to Ben. Then she and the others took their desserts and coffee and sat on the cabin top facing west to watch the sunset. The blueberries in the cobbler were liquidy, and the whipped cream, melting into the berries, created a little bit of heaven in a bowl. They lounged on the cabin top as the sky turned to pure gold, then flame orange, and at last fiery red. When the last color was seeping away, Brie and George collected the plates and silverware and headed down to the galley. Brie offered to wash things up, but George shooed her back up the ladder.

Scott had gone for his guitar and was sitting near the stern playing blues. John was all the way forward in the bow of the ship, looking through the binoculars at a schooner quite a distance ahead of them, sailing on the same heading. Brie walked forward and stood beside him.

"What's so interesting there, Captain?" she said as she approached.

"Just checking out yon schooner. I don't think I've seen it before."

"And do you know all the schooners hereabouts, Captain?" she asked. She realized it sounded like ribbing, but actually she was curious to know the answer.

"Anyone who gets around the Gulf of Maine as much as I do has seen most of them," John replied. "Each one has its own unique lines. You can often tell who's who even from quite a distance."

"May I?" Brie asked. John handed her the glasses, and she brought them up to her eyes and adjusted the focus. "*Deep Blue,*" she said aloud, reading the name on the back of the schooner.

"I wonder if that could be Adam Blake's boat, since he's sailing due east of the island?" John conjectured.

There was a man at the wheel, but that was all Brie could divine through the glasses. "Maybe he's on the trail of a full moon, same as us."

"Maybe. Speaking of which, look there."

Brie lowered the glasses.

"Moonrise, bearing zero-three-zero."

"Ohhhh, look at that!"

There, 30 degrees off the starboard bow, a golden arc appeared just above the horizon. She turned to call to the others, and by the time she looked back, it had already doubled in size. The old moon slipped silently, effortlessly from the deep like an ancient, burnished coin, eternally beckoning mariners. It cast its path of gold across the water—a benevolent force field, drawing ship and crew toward it. Resistance was futile.

Scott and George had come forward to witness the spectacle, and the four of them stood transfixed in the bow of the ship. An experience of such beauty bonds those who share it. Brie felt the power of that bond very strongly as she stood with her shipmates on the deck that night. They and the ship had become her world, closer to her than she could have imagined possible.

After the death of her father there had been such chaos, such struggle in her family, and they had never been the same afterward. His death had come at a time when she and her brothers were just getting ready to spread their wings, and it had soured a part of each of their lives that should have been filled with adventure. Occurring as it had, when Brie was on the cusp of adulthood, it had left her feeling as if she'd lost not only her father, but her entire family. Over the few years that followed, she and her brothers had gone their separate ways, and until this summer aboard the *Maine Wind*, she had never again felt that kind of closeness.

She thought maybe she understood, for the first time, how heartbreaking it must be for parents when their children leave. The breaking up of the family unit—the end of an era. Her mother had borne it all heroically, as she did everything. The problem with that kind of heroism is that it can fool those around you, especially the young and selfish, into thinking you're just fine. A tear rolled silently down Brie's face as she realized how little she had understood her mother's pain.

She felt John's arm around her shoulder. "Hey, you okay?" he asked.

"It's very beautiful out here tonight," was all she said. She knew John sensed things about her and the process she was going through. There was no need to say more. He understood.

Brie raised the glasses again to look at the schooner ahead of them. *Deep Blue* had changed course and was heading south-southwest. *Obviously out to enjoy the moonrise*, Brie thought, *and now the sailor or sailors are headed back toward the mainland.*

Darkness was setting in, and John ordered everyone to don their PFDs. Coast Guard regulations stipulated that anyone on deck after dark when the vessel was underway must be wearing a lifejacket with flashlight or beacon attached. Brie always felt a little like the Pillsbury Doughboy in hers, but rules were rules. She needed to invest in a good inflatable vest that wouldn't be so cumbersome when working on deck. She decided she'd acquire one when they got back to the mainland before the next cruise.

She joined Scott on the bow watch, and they sailed east on their same heading for another twenty minutes. The moon rose higher and bathed the deck in silvery light. Brie turned and looked up. The gentle roll of the ship had set the tops of the masts in motion, and they traced arcs among the stars overhead. Standing in the port bow she had a perfect view of the sky to the northeast. With the full moon, some of the stars of lesser magnitudes were invisible, but the big guns could still be seen. Deneb, Vega and Altair—each the alpha star in its own constellation—formed the Summer Triangle. Brie walked over to starboard and looked to the southwest. There sitting low in the west was Spica, alpha star in the constellation of Virgo, and above it halfway to the zenith, Arcturus, alpha star in the kite-shaped constellation of Boötes.

Ben stayed at the helm, where he had been the whole time, and John hung back there with him, talking and reminiscing about their days together on the *Maine Wind*. When it was time to come about, they turned up into the wind, and Brie and Scott released the jib and made it off on the port side of the ship. They made their heading south-southwest toward the southern end of the island.

The lighthouse on nearby Drake Island cast a fixed red light on the water—a *Danger sector*, or *Red sector*, as it would be called on a nautical chart—warning mariners of submerged shoals. It got Brie thinking about Sentinel Island and what lay beneath the surface of the seemingly peaceful island habitat. Amanda had somehow strayed into dangerous waters, and if there had been warning signs that she was in peril, she had chosen to ignore them. But it was far too beautiful out here to think of such things, and Brie turned her gaze back toward the heavens.

"Hey there, space cadet," Scott said, seeing her fixated on the sky overhead.

"Guilty as charged," Brie said. "I'm a sucker for a starry sky."

"So educate me, Brie. You're the astronomy buff. I know my constellations, but beyond that, not so much."

In the moonlight, Brie could almost see Scott's green eyes twinkling with interest. Intellectual curiosity ran deep in him. "Sadly, I've forgotten a lot of what I used to know. But some of the important stuff has stuck, I guess."

"So, fill me in about the stars. All I know is that they're basically like our sun."

"Well, I guess that's a good place to start." She swept a hand across the night sky. "Each star is burning. They're composed mostly of hydrogen, and the light we see coming from them is energy created by nuclear fusion at their cores. But there are lots of different kinds of stars of various ages and sizes that astronomers have to classify."

"And she says she doesn't remember much," Scott said.

"Believe me, Scott, in the realm of astronomy, that's about as basic as it gets."

"Okay, professor, keep going then."

"Well, let's see. Stars are classified by what's called spectral type."

"Spectral type, eh? I hope I have a ghost of a chance of understanding this."

"Oh, very funny," Brie said, smiling.

"But, keep on."

"Well, spectral type just means where on the visible spectrum—from the blue end to the red end—light coming from a particular star falls."

"So, based on my high school physics, I'd guess shorter wavelengths of light fall at the blue end and longer wavelengths at the red end."

"Exactly right," Brie said.

"And that tells us what?" Scott asked.

"It tells us how hot a star is burning and, hence, how old it is."

"Hence, eh?" Scott ribbed her. "Now we are sounding like the professor."

"Well, you're the one who got me going, so hence on you." Brie gave him a friendly shove.

"Just kidding. Keep on, professor."

"Well, another system of classifying stars, called luminosity class, groups them by size."

"But doesn't luminosity mean how bright they are?"

"Well, see, that ties in. For example, take a very bright star whose light falls at the red end of the spectrum; that star is burning at a much lower temperature. So, how can it be so bright? Well, that star must be extremely large. In other words, the biggest stars—what are called giants and supergiants—whether they are old or young, will always appear among the brightest stars in the sky. So brightness is a factor of size."

"Very interesting," Scott said.

By the tone of his voice, Brie could tell he meant it. "It can be, if you have a really good teacher. I was lucky enough to have a great one.

"There's this little mnemonic we learned in astronomy class for memorizing the spectral types of stars from hottest to coolest or bluest to reddest," she said. "You'd think they'd classify them alphabetically, but they don't. The types are O-B-A-F-G-K-M. So the mnemonic went, "Oh, Be A Fine Girl, Kiss Me.""

"Great," Scott laughed. "And when the captain hears me saying that to you, I'll just tell him I'm memorizing the star classifications."

Brie smiled at that.

"Speaking of the captain, if you ever get tired of that guy…"

Scott didn't finish the sentence, but Brie didn't need him to. She knew Scott admired her, and stranger things had been imagined, even if she was older than he.

"There's nothing quite like a really smart girl, you know." Scott put his arm around her waist and gave her a little brotherly hug. At least that's how she chose to see it. "I'm headed down to the galley for a mug of coffee. You want one, professor?"

"Why not?" Brie said.

While Scott was down in the galley rustling up coffee, John made his way to the bow of the ship to talk to her. "Hey, there, starry eyes," he said.

"Oop, sorry," Brie said. "You just missed the big lecture. You'll have to borrow someone's notebook."

"Or maybe I could schedule a private session."

"Now, Captain, I'm on bow-watch. This is no time for that kind of talk."

John chuckled. "Well, maybe there'll be another opportunity. Ben has asked if he can sleep aboard the *Maine Wind* tonight. He doesn't get that many chances any more. He's a little worried about leaving things up at the house, though, so I told him a couple of us can go back up there for the night. Actually, I was thinking maybe you and I…"

His words trailed off, and Brie turned and looked at him, trying to divine exactly what he was thinking.

"I was just down and talked to Scott and George. They said they would stay aboard with Ben. George wants to cook breakfast on board in the morning. He thinks Ben will like that. We can come back down to the ship in the morning and have breakfast with the others."

Brie agreed to the plan, but as John walked aft, she felt a little tenuous about it. She knew she could only keep him at bay for so long, and the truth was that her resolve was getting weaker and weaker. In fact, their encounter that afternoon on the spiral stairs in the lighthouse had just about rubbed it out. As that resolve weakened, though, so it seemed did her hold on her former life, and that scared her—a lot. What was more, she had to try to find out what had happened to Amanda. These forty-eight hours were critical. Ironically, in the days before a missing person's report might be filed, the trail could go very cold, and key evidence could be destroyed. And despite what one saw in the movies and on TV, being in love was not all that compatible with the kind of critical thinking a detective needed to employ.

But Brie's train of thought suddenly screeched to a halt. Had she really just said those words in her mind—"being in love"? They had snuck up on her, unawares, and the thought had flowed right out, as natural as breath—"being in love"—as if she and it were already inextricably linked. The genie had been let out of the bottle, and the revelation of what already *was* rushed through her, an uninvited tempest of panic and passion.

The next hour was an uncomfortable one for Brie. As they sailed back to the island, there was nothing required of her but to stand watch. And so, she was left to grapple with her own unsought realization—one that thrilled and terrified her in equal parts. How could she have so thoroughly hidden from what had already taken place within her? She was in love with him. Sometime in the last two months this shift, this change of heart, had silently occurred, like fog in the night, and now she woke to find herself in a strange, uncharted place. A place of greater vulnerability—or so it seemed at this moment—than she had faced in all her years as a policewoman.

Chapter 13

By the time they had anchored the *Maine Wind* outside the cove, the wind had moved into the west. It was just past midnight when Brie and John rowed ashore from the ship and secured the dory on the beach. Brie was unusually silent as they hiked up the trail to the keeper's house. Here and there they went hand-in-hand, but the trail was narrow and winding, making progress along it mostly a single-file affair.

If John noticed her taciturn mood, he didn't say anything. Brie wasn't in the mood to talk. She was focused on what was going on inside herself. She didn't know what to think of her unexpected realization about being in love with John. She didn't doubt or question the fact of it. Like her friend Ariel always said, "You'll know the truth when you meet up with it." And the calm way the thought had arrived in her mind—as an already well-rooted fact—told her there was no point in wasting energy denying it.

What gave her pause was the thought of grappling with all the attendant emotions that accompanied *being in love*. She was just getting to a better place with her PTSD—a place of acceptance more than anything else; a place of realizing that while the flashbacks and nightmares might never go away completely, they didn't have to immobilize her the way they had the year after the shooting.

She had finally found some serenity aboard the *Maine Wind* this summer, after what had been a year and a half of chaos. So,

171

the thought of another highly charged emotional situation, even a positive one, made her hesitate. And then there was her track record, and the fact that relationships just didn't seem to work out for her. She had always chalked this up to the fact that police work, especially homicide work, took a toll, progressively filling up more and more space on her emotional hard drive.

She took a breath and tried to clear her mind of all the objections, remembering what Ariel had always said to her— "Ground yourself in the moment, and then the past has no power over you." She turned briefly and looked back at John in the lantern light. She knew herself, and she knew once they had sealed the deal, she would find it very hard to leave him and go back to her life in Minnesota. Of course, when she had fled her home state she hadn't paused, even briefly, to reflect on the law of unintended consequences, the universal nature of which she encountered daily in her dealings with criminals, yet often failed to consider in relation to her own choices. When she took that leap, she had opened the door to a whole new set of possibilities and circumstances. The question now was, would she leave that door open? She didn't know the answer.

"You're awfully quiet up there," John said.

"I know. Sorry."

"You thinking about Amanda and what you're going to do?"

"Ah, not really," Brie said. "I suppose I should be."

"No, you shouldn't, or I'd rather you didn't is what I mean."

"Well, you're in luck then, because I wasn't. I'm hoping I'll find something significant in Harold's diaries."

"Anything so far?"

"Not really, but there must be some reason he had them hidden. I'm going to read some more tonight."

There was a moment of silence from John, and then, "I'm not so sure about that."

Now it was Brie's turn to be silent.

John reached for her hand and stopped her. She turned and looked at him. They had come to the last part of the trail that ran along the high bluffs. She could see his strong features outlined by the same moonlight that silvered the ocean far beneath them. He set his lantern down, reached for her lantern and placed it next to his, and pulled her into his arms. It was one of the few times they had ever been truly alone, and the beauty of the night and the island spun its spell. How long they stood there enfolded in each other, kissing and caressing, was unclear to Brie. Time had slipped away, leaving only the overwhelming sensation of John wanting her. It was intoxicating. Finally, she whispered, "We should keep going."

"You're right," John said. "We'll continue this up at the house." He handed her one of the lanterns, picked up the other one, and took the lead up the rest of the trail.

Brie hung back a bit, struggling with herself, knowing she wasn't ready for what was coming, but not wanting to hurt John or make him think she didn't care. She knew if she said "no" it could change everything between them. Of course, there was an alternative. They could be lovers, and she could stay in Maine—give up her job with the Minneapolis Police Department. But she wasn't ready to make that choice yet. She'd invested lots of years of her life earning the place she held in the Homicide Division, and she wasn't ready to throw it all aside.

The light tower and keeper's house were fully illuminated by moonlight as they approached, but they kept their lanterns burning so they'd have light when they entered the house. They stepped through the screen door and into the kitchen. They had left the house door open to allow some fresh air into the space after the day's construction work. Brie couldn't get over the fact that folks in these island communities didn't lock their doors. She knew it was the same throughout small town America, but from a police perspective, she found it hard to get used to.

"We going to leave that door open all night?" she asked John.

"May as well. It's not gonna be very cold tonight."

Brie smiled to herself—*as if cold's the only reason to close and lock a door*.

In the center of the kitchen was a heap of stuff from the day's deconstruction. Old lath and dimension lumber, along with chunks of plaster, pieces of old linoleum, a couple stacks of newspapers and magazines, and some other miscellaneous debris that Ben had had stored in the pantry area. John pulled the plastic aside that covered the door and affixed it to the frame with a long piece of duct tape that had been placed there for that purpose. They had cleaned up thoroughly after the day's work, so he wasn't worried about dust migrating into the rest of the house.

He and Brie proceeded into the front hallway, where he extinguished his lantern. He had obviously decided they'd only need one. Brie placed her lantern on a small table next to the stairs, walked into the living room, and stood looking out the big picture window. The moonlit ocean lay like a sheet of hammered silver, stretching away to the horizon.

They sat down on the sofa together and propped their feet up on the old coffee table. For a few moments they looked silently out on the beauty of the night. Brie was aware that this was a point of no return for them, and she guessed John knew the same thing. But surprisingly, he held back. She had expected him to pull her into his arms the minute they came through the door and carry her upstairs to bed. Instead here they sat, silently communing on the sofa, and she realized that her thoughts on the inner workings of John were maybe a bit too simplistic.

After a few moments, John reached for her hand and brought it to his lips. "Make love with me, Brie," he said, still gazing at the ocean.

Brie wondered if he was afraid to look at her, already sensing what the answer would be. But he needn't have been. Those simple words had gone straight to her heart. She brought her feet to the floor and stood up. Gracefully, methodically, she swung her leg across his and knelt astride him. Holding his eyes with hers, she peeled off her jacket and pulled her sweater and tee shirt over her head in one smooth movement. In the chill of the room she felt her nipples go hard; she felt his eyes on them and loved the thrill of that. She leaned in and kissed him with the kind of intention she was pretty sure she had never shown any man before.

He cupped her bottom and pressed her to him, and she gasped and arched her head back. As he kissed her throat, his hands slid up her back and skillfully unhooked her bra. Then in one surprisingly easy move, he brought her down onto the sofa beneath him. He held her hands captive above her head as he worked his way down to her breasts. "Beautiful," he murmured and paused to look up into her eyes so she knew he meant it.

Their kissing, touching, caressing, and undressing now moved to a smolderingly slow pace as they tenderly explored each others' bodies. But the further they went, the greater grew Brie's sense of panic. They were dangerously close to the point of no return when she stopped him. She actually had to call his name three times to get his attention.

He stopped what he was doing very suddenly and looked at her. "What is it, Brie?" And just like that, the mood was broken.

"I can't, John. I just can't do this."

She didn't know what she had expected—probably for him to plead or cajole. But there was none of that. He was on his feet before she could blink. She thought she heard him mutter *fine* as he gathered up his clothes. But before she could say anything else he was gone, and she heard his footsteps ascending the stairs.

Brie reached down to the floor for her sweater and clutched it to her chest. As she rolled into a ball, the tears came and she bit her lip to keep from sobbing. She was aware of a dull ache in her chest and a fathomless sense of fatigue.

John lay on his bed staring up at the ceiling, knowing he had acted like a child. He didn't blame Brie. She'd been through a lot. She was right to stop him. For God's sake, they didn't even have any protection. But he regretted how it had gone down—the fact that he'd stormed off and not even tried to talk to her. At the moment he had felt like she was toying with him, but he knew that wasn't true. Brie was too honest and clear-headed to act that way. Which only left one possibility—she had genuinely wanted him.

He wished he could tell her that everything about her made him lightheaded—that he was crazy in love with her. But the older he got, the harder it was to verbalize those things to a woman. He had fully intended to go back downstairs and talk to her. But, as he lay there framing up what he wanted to say, sleep overtook him.

Brie woke with a start, knowing she hadn't been asleep for long. She was chilled. She rolled over and felt around the floor for her tee shirt, bra, and jacket. She got herself dressed and walked out to the table in the hall, where she had dropped her pack and set the lantern down. She didn't feel sleepy and didn't want to lay in bed thinking about what an idiot she was. And anyway, she needed to read some more of Harold's journals. If there were any clues in them about what was going on on the island, she needed to find them. She also hoped the journals might reveal more of Harold's observations about the people here. She had already found mentions of Amanda, her mother Eva Whitcombe, and Harriet. And she had learned that Harold had formed a friendship with Bob, the bait shop guy. She still believed there had to be a reason the journals were hidden, and she hoped to stay awake long enough to find out what that was.

She carried her pack and the lantern back into the living room. She pulled a small table over to the end of the sofa and set the lantern where it would cast enough light for her to read by.

She went to collect a knitted afghan from the back of one of the rocking chairs that sat near the woodstove. She took the journals out of her pack and curled up in the corner of the old sofa. She opened the first one and looked for the spot where she had stopped reading aboard the *Maine Wind*.

She quickly found her place and read the entry for June 23, in which Harold talked about removing the shutters from the keeper's house and painting them cranberry red. The next few entries were a running chronicle of his work on the outside of the house and brought her uneventfully to the end of the first journal. She reached for the second journal and opened it. Harold had skipped a few days between entries.

June 28

Cold and rainy today. I was glad for a break from the painting. The gingerbread trim on the eaves is fussy, tedious work. Perfect cooking day, though. I made beef stew and oatmeal cookies and spent the afternoon by the fire reading from my maritime history of Maine. Tomorrow I have to go to Harriet's and fix a leaky faucet. I'll bring her some stew and cookies. Then I promised to mind the bait store for Bob while he goes to the mainland for supplies. If he gets back in time, I'll stop up at the library. Time to turn in now, but first some cookies and milk.

Brie decided Harold must have been a rainy day person, since his entries for stormy days were infused with an unmistakable enthusiasm.

June 30

Tommy and Taylor Sanders visited today. This time they brought their soccer ball and were flabbergasted when I joined their game. I'm sure they think I'm a hundred years old. They're nice little guys—nothing like their old man, who seems to have a large chunk of something permanently affixed to his shoulder. At noon their mom showed up looking for them. This time she brought a large picnic basket with potato salad and fried chicken—must have worked all morning fixing it. She's a sweet woman, but sad, I can tell. I'm not surprised with that bully for a husband. The boys talked me into going to the top of the lighthouse with our picnic. It turned out to be a good plan.

Brie stopped reading. This must be the family of Wade Sanders that Harold was writing about. From this entry she surmised that he had formed a friendship with the boys and more notably, their mother. She wondered if Wade—better known to her as *the mean guy*—had known about all this. She decided tomorrow she would pay a visit to the Sanders' homestead. Hopefully, Wade would be out on his lobsterboat, and she'd get a chance to talk to his wife.

Brie knew one thing for sure: if a murder can be thought of as a jigsaw puzzle, the people surrounding the victim, both suspects and non-suspects, are the pieces. The shape and color of each piece provides a clue to where it fits in. With human dynamics and crime solving, both logic and guesswork have to be applied, and various theories explored, like those pieces of the puzzle you try and set aside, looking for just the right fit. Each piece, correctly placed, narrows your sense of what else you are looking for, and piece by piece a picture begins to emerge. Figure out exactly how they fit together, and the solution will present itself. Brie knew she had to cover a lot of bases tomorrow—gather a lot of information. Without more knowledge of the players in this game, she was like a blind person trying to assemble the puzzle.

She laid the open journal down on the coffee table and stood up, stretched her arms over her head, and leaned slowly from side to side. The sofa had seen better days, and her body was slowly shaping itself into a mirror image of all those humps and hollows. She headed out to the kitchen for a glass of water. Nothing but the screen separated her from the darkness of the night. This open-door business bothered her, or maybe more correctly, bothered the policewoman in her. She walked out the door and stood in the cool night air. The moon was sinking toward the western horizon but still cast enough light to see by. The spruce forest stood like a dark, jagged fortress wall across the headland. She thought she glimpsed a light in the forest, but a moment later it was gone.

She headed around the house and stood in the ghostly moonlight, listening to the sea assaulting the granite cliffs. She wasn't sure what triggered the memory—the sound of the waves or the light she thought she had seen in the forest—but her mind suddenly rolled back to an October night on the north shore of Lake Superior.

She had rented a cottage near Grand Marais, Minnesota for a long weekend, to get out of the city and do some hiking. One night she'd gone out for a walk long after dark. She had headed down the dirt road that ran behind the cabins that fronted on the lake. It had been a moonless night, black as the inside of a coffin, but the air was warm for mid-October, and the wind whispered through the tall balsam forest that fringed the rocky shore. She had taken her flashlight to see her way along the road.

At a point she had felt the urge to turn and look behind her; it was the kind of feeling she always heeded—the kind that can save one's life. Behind her maybe fifty yards down the road, she saw the beam of a second flashlight. She instinctively snapped her light off. The other light clicked off a second later. She immediately stepped to the middle of the road, keeping her light extinguished, and ran on silent feet for about thirty yards. Then she had made her way into the blackness of the forest to take cover. A chilling stanza from *The Rime of the Ancient Mariner* played in her mind:

> *Like one, that on a lonesome road*
> *Doth walk in fear and dread,*
> *And having once turned round walks on*
> *And turns no more his head;*

Danger Sector

Because he knows a frightful fiend
Doth close behind him tread.

Memorized in school, years before, those lines had acquired new meaning when she had become a homicide detective.

Down the road the light switched on again and gradually came closer, scanning the fringes of the forest. Finally, Brie had seen the figure of a large man outlined in the backwash of the flashlight beam. He paused on the road, just north of where she had entered the forest and hidden. She crouched low in the undergrowth behind a screen of balsam fir, as he played the flashlight beam to left and right scanning the edges of the forest. The beam was too weak to penetrate far into the darkness—darkness which, that night, had been her friend.

Brie shivered and looked around her, trying to shake off the frightening memory. She walked back around the house and in the screen door. She closed the back door and tried to shoot the deadbolt, but much as she jockeyed the door, it wouldn't lock. She finally left it, not wanting to make a lot of noise and wake John. She padded back to the living room and curled up under the afghan with the second journal.

There were more entries on the painting of the house, and the Sanders boys, and on several dates, Harold had chronicled dinners with Amanda either at her cottage or the keeper's house. They seemed to enjoy sharing a bottle of wine when they got together, and Brie wondered if, possibly, they were sharing anything else. She recalled how flustered Ben had gotten when she had asked him about Amanda. It wasn't hard to imagine certain possibilities when wine, a beautiful woman, and a single or widowed man were combined.

About halfway through the second journal Brie came upon something that piqued her curiosity. From his vantage point atop the lighthouse Harold had started to record the comings and goings of various boats sailing east of the island. The dates, names of vessels, and times of departure and return were carefully chronicled, somewhat sporadically at first, starting in mid-

July, but as the entries progressed through July and August, Harold displayed a fixation with this process that seemed to be turning into a borderline obsession. Gone were any entries about the Sanders boys, Amanda, or Bob. She turned one page to find nothing on the next but a name in brackets—*SS Ulysses*. It looked as if Harold had planned to fill something in on that page but never did.

Brie thought about the hours he must have spent at the top of the lighthouse, and she had to wonder if all that solitude might possibly have caused Harold to slip his moorings. But, as she followed the entries, a pattern seemed to emerge, along with cryptic little notes and questions that Harold had posited to himself. Two boats seemed to be of particular interest—*Emily Ann* and *Deep Blue*.

She stopped reading. She was always struck by synchronicities, and here was an interesting one. The ship they had seen sailing before them on the same heading—the one she and John had checked out through the binoculars and speculated might belong to Adam Blake—bore the name *Deep Blue*. Also, the little voice in her head was suddenly reciting the directive that Spencer had given to Adam Blake during *the group's* meeting in the basement of the library. "You take care of business." Coupled with the information in Harold's journal, it had her thinking. Thinking she was going to have to find a reason to call on Adam Blake and see if the schooner *Deep Blue* belonged to him. And if that turned out to be the case, she might just have to get aboard said ship— probably not via formal invitation—and have a good look around.

Brie ran through the patchwork of information she had assembled relating to Amanda, her disappearance, and the islanders who constituted *the group*. There were big holes that she'd have to begin to fill in tomorrow, but conjectures, like those puzzle pieces, were starting to take shape in her detective's mind, and she hoped a pattern would emerge as she began fitting them together. She turned the next page of the journal and read the entry there.

September 7

Thoughts of Grace consume me. I must let them go. There is no future in it.

It was a single brief statement. There was nothing else on the page. Brie eagerly flipped to the next page, hoping to find another reference to this "Grace." She kept turning pages, skimming over the contents, searching for some other mention of her, but there was nothing.

She read on, wanting to reach the end of the second journal, but she was starting to get really sleepy. The endless chronicling of the forays of *Deep Blue* and *Emily Ann* was becoming boring to the point of madness. And the occasional entries about visits to Harriet's place were little better. Finally, she could go no further—sleep was overtaking her. She checked her watch. It was nearly two-thirty in the morning. She reached over and turned the knob on the Coleman lantern to extinguish the light. Like a moth in a flame, the mantle flared brightly for a moment, and then the lantern sputtered out. As she drifted off, Harold's poignant entry played hauntingly through her mind. *Thoughts of Grace consume me. I must let them go.*

The killer parked his truck at the edge of the woods. He had switched off the lights long before he got to the clearing at the end of the island. He eased out of the truck and stood shadow still as he observed the darkened keeper's house. The moon was nearly down, but he could make out the outline of the house, and over to the left, the light tower. After a few seconds he reached over to the floor on the passenger's side and withdrew the can of kerosene. A part of him wanted to retreat, and a faint voice in his head pled with him—*Don't do it!* But the louder voice was saying, *Do it. There's no going back now. She's a detective.*

She's caught the scent of something going on. Do you think she's just going to drop it?

The killer stepped back from the truck's door and soundlessly closed it. He hated the voice, but it was right. There was no going back. It had to be done. No one would be the wiser. Even if the authorities looked into it, they'd see Ben had been doing construction, and write the fire off to carelessness. Maybe, if it happened on the mainland, they might look a little deeper, but not out here. County and state policing of the islands was, at best, hit-or-miss.

He crept along the edge of the forest until he was directly behind the house. He was dressed in black like the night, and as he approached the house, his breathing came in shallow puffs. Even though the night was cool, sweat beaded his neck. At the back door, he paused and listened. He opened the screen door and gingerly tried the doorknob. *Not locked—good.* He opened the door a crack, testing for squeaks. It moved soundlessly. He stepped into the kitchen and removed a small flashlight from his pocket. The light was covered with a thick piece of cloth held in place with a rubber band. It gave off just enough light for him to survey the room.

The light immediately found the pile of debris in the middle of the room. The killer smiled. *Perfect. They couldn't have planned it better. Now get going*, the voice ordered. He unscrewed the cap on the kerosene and began pouring it, moving methodically in a circle around the pile. He was making his second pass when he stopped dead. He thought he heard a faint sound from the other room, like the frame squeaking on a piece of furniture. He held his breath and listened. The sound came again, coupled with a human sigh.

Pour the rest and get out of here. The voice was so loud the killer was sure whoever was in the next room would hear it. He poured a stream of kerosene directly onto some old foam cushions on the pile and trailed a path of the fuel toward the door. It was all he could do. He had to get out. The structure was old, though. He was sure it would be enough.

Weapons drawn, they slipped in the front door of the house on Upton Avenue. Phil was beside her. They probed the darkness with their guns. Brie saw red lights reflected in the front window. It must be more squads or the EMTs. How did they know Phil was going to die? How did they know she would be shot? The dream was wrong.

That's when Brie woke with a start. Something was wrong. A strange glow dimly lit the living room. She bolted to her feet and turned. She could see the fire burning in the kitchen. She smelled acrid smoke in the air, and in the glow she could see it snaking black and lethal along the hall ceiling and up the stairs. She didn't know how long the fire had been burning, but she knew it wouldn't take long for the smoke to fill the upstairs. She darted for the staircase, praying John was in the front room. She took a breath, and crouching low, took the stairs two at a time, her hands feeling for the treads as she climbed. She went to her hands and knees when she hit the upper hall and crawled into the front bedroom and over to the left.

"John!" she called. Staying low, she reached up and felt for him, shook him. Nothing. In a fire it isn't the flames that kill people; it's the carbon monoxide and the super-heated smoke. They're dead long before the fire reaches them. Brie took a breath, and holding it, knelt up, reached across John's body, and rolled him towards her. She gripped his shoulders, pulled him off the bed onto the floor, and turned him over. The room was getting unbearably hot.

She scuttled back, found the edge of the door, and kicked it shut. She felt around the floor for something hard and heavy—a shoe, a boot, anything. Her hands touched a pile of books on the floor. She took a second to orient herself in the blackness of the room, and then hurled one of the books in the direction of the windows on the front wall of the house. It thudded against the wall and dropped to the floor. She hurled the next one. No luck.

And a third. On the fourth try she heard glass shatter, and a whooshing sound as the smoke rushed out the window.

She crawled back to John and started CPR. Her eyes stung from the smoke and tears streamed down her face—tears of regret. What if he died? He'd never know how she felt about him. They'd never make love—never make children. She pumped his chest. "C'mon, John. Come back to me." A sob escaped as she pumped his heart. "I love you. You have to come back." She knew she was running out of time. "Please, John, please. Please, God, don't let this happen."

She bent and blew the next breath into his mouth. Nothing. But then something. She felt a twitch, and then suddenly he was coughing and choking. She rolled him onto his side, and he struggled for breath and consciousness. "That's it, John. Come on. Wake up." She knew they had to get out of the house.

"Brie," he gagged. "What's happening?"

"The house is burning, John. We have to get out of here. We have to go out the window." He was gagging again. "Can you crawl? I'll help you. We have to get to the window."

She knew he was disoriented and dizzy, but he somehow struggled onto his knees and they crawled toward the window. Brie felt for the casement, stood up, and kicked the rest of the glass from the frame. "We're going out onto the roof over the front stoop." She helped him to his feet and steadied him for a second.

"Okay," he rasped.

"It's small, John. Be careful. Once you're out, slide down to the edge and jump to the ground. I'll be right behind you."

John slid down the roof, and Brie was already partway out the window when he jumped. Her mind was on the fire extinguishers. The men had placed them behind the house under a tarp to make room in the kitchen for the demolition. There were six or eight of them, and they were large.

By the time John got to his feet, she had jumped to the ground. "Come on, John. We have to get to the fire extinguishers." They ran around the house and threw the tarp aside. They each grabbed two tanks and headed for the kitchen door. The smoke was pouring up the living room stairwell. A slight breeze blowing in the kitchen door pushed the smoke toward the front of the house. Why was that door open? She had closed it. The thought came and went in a microsecond.

The kitchen was ablaze. The pile of old lumber and materials in the center of the room was now a huge bonfire, and the wall adjoining the living room and the ceiling of the kitchen were burning. Fortunately, the old asphalt tile on the floor had kept it from igniting. Were it not for that, the fire would have been well beyond their control.

John went in first, his fire extinguisher spitting out pressurized foam in the face of the beast, creating a safe path for himself. Brie was right behind him. They attacked the ceiling first, concentrating the foam in the center and moving slowly apart as they eradicated the flames overhead. They grabbed the next two tanks, and Brie began knocking down flames on the pile of burning material in the center of the kitchen. John moved to the burning wall to attack on that front. Brie went for two more canisters and joined John in beating down the last of the fire, as they worked from opposite ends of the wall and finally met in the center.

They moved into the dining room and then the living room, making sure nothing was burning there.

"I'm going for the ladder," John said. "We have to break the upstairs windows on the back of the house." They headed out the back door, and Brie helped him maneuver the extension ladder up against the house, beneath her bedroom window. John went up the ladder with a crowbar and broke the glass. Smoke poured out but thankfully no flames. They wrestled the ladder over to the other window on the back of the house, and John went up and broke the glass there. He came down the ladder, and they stood for a moment in the pitch dark in a state of shock. No more than fifteen minutes had elapsed since Brie had awakened on the living room sofa, but she felt like she had waged the battle of a lifetime.

"You saved my life, Brie."

It was a statement of fact, and she heard a mixture of gratitude and wonder in it. "It's okay, John. Now we're even."

"I'm so sorry about what happened earlier."

"Me too," she said. Too exhausted to say more, they stood close to one another in mute silence.

"How could this thing have started?" John asked.

Brie realized he wouldn't have read what, to her, was a blatant sign of arson—the strip of blackened floor leading from the pile in the center of the kitchen out the back door, where accelerant had been poured and lit. What amazed her was that the arsonist had been either half-hearted about what he or she was doing, or just plain ignorant. And she sent up a prayer of thanks that that had been the case, because otherwise, John would never have survived, and she might not have either.

"This wasn't an accident, John," was all she said. She could feel him staring at her in the darkness, too shocked to speak. "There's a flashlight just inside the door of the lighthouse. I'm going to get it."

"Not by yourself, you're not. Not after what you just said." He felt for her hand, and they walked around the corner of the house toward the tower. He opened the door; Brie felt for the flashlight to the left of the door, and finding it, turned it on. She scanned the area at the base of the tower with the light and then played it on the stairs, tracing the spiral all the way to the top with the beam of light. They closed the door and headed back to the house. The trauma of the fire had pushed their failed attempt at lovemaking so far into the background, it was almost like it had never happened, which was fine with Brie. Were it not for this near disaster, things would have been awkward between them, but that awkwardness had been replaced by something of far greater moment.

They did another sweep of the house, upstairs and down, to make sure the fire was really extinguished. They had retrieved two pieces of towel from a stack of rags Ben kept in a cabinet in the lighthouse for polishing the brass on the Fresnel lens. They used these as makeshift masks to cover nose and mouth as they moved about the house.

"Ben's going to have to get new mattresses," Brie said. "But maybe the hard surfaces can be washed and painted." Fortunately, the furniture in the house was sparse, and any upholstered pieces leaned toward early American Salvation Army. Replacing them wouldn't be a big deal, and Brie was sure Ben had insurance.

"Should we go back to the ship for the rest of the night?" John asked.

"It seems like a lot of work for a few hours' sleep, but the house is pretty smoky. Is there anywhere we could curl up and get a few hours' rest?"

"How about the lighthouse?" John suggested. "There are cushions on some of the outdoor furniture. We could gather those for padding."

"That sounds like a plan," Brie said. She was already heading toward the back door, eager to escape the smell in the house.

They foraged six cushions from various chairs and a swing near the fire pit and headed for the lighthouse. There was nothing to use as a blanket, but Brie figured they'd be huddled together, and inside the tower, they'd be protected from the wind. The lighthouse door had a bolt, and Brie shot it as soon as they were inside. "If people would lock their doors…" she grumbled.

"It's a Maine thing," John said, "or maybe more specifically an island thing."

"Well, it's foolishness," was all Brie said.

They arranged the cushions in a rectangular shape on the floor. Brie was so exhausted she decided it was better not to speak. Her mood right now was blacker than the inside of the tower, and what was bound to come out of her mouth wouldn't be pretty. They lay down, and John immediately reached over and pulled her against him. She felt the warmth of his body work on the tense muscles in her back, and it helped her to relax a little.

"Just sleep, Brie. We'll figure everything out in the morning," he said.

It was the permission she needed. "Okay," was all she said, and sleep came quickly.

Chapter 14

B rie opened her eyes to momentary disorientation. She stared at the stone wall of the tower, and slowly her gaze shifted upward. Shafts of sunlight, like arrows of recollection, came through the tiny lighthouse windows, reminding her of where she was and why. She rolled over and looked straight up at the magical play of prismatic light underway within the giant lens at the top of the tower. She turned her head to look at John and got a shock. His face and hands were covered with black smudges, and his tee shirt was filthy and ripped open under one arm. She could only imagine her own appearance and had to reflect on the irony of the two of them waking up together for the first time, looking like this. For some reason the whole thing suddenly struck her as hilarious, and she started to laugh. This was so typical of how things had unfolded over the past sixteen months, in what she was beginning to think of as her theatre-of-the-absurd life.

"I'm dying to know what can be so funny, considering…" John said, without opening his eyes.

"Just open your eyes—you'll get it."

He rolled over. "Well, well," he said, studying her, "you're looking a little Eliza Doolittle this morning."

Brie could see him trying to suppress a smile. She felt her face and brought away a soot-streaked hand. Her ponytail was thoroughly askew. Half the hair had escaped and fell around her face in what she was pretty sure were blackened strands matching the soot on her jacket.

"Is that how I look?" John asked.

"Pretty much."

"I wish I had a camera. I could send this to your friend Garrett back at the department to show him you're doing just fine."

"Very funny."

John leaned over and kissed the tip of her grimy nose and then her lips. "Nothing like a woman who can handle a little disaster and come up laughing."

"Yep, that's me, a regular Calamity Jane—disaster always only a blink away."

"It's never boring—I'll give you that."

Brie looked at her watch. It was seven-thirty. If only George were here with a mug of coffee. "I don't care how bad it stinks in the house—I'm getting a shower," she said.

"Why don't you let me go in first? I'll get the rest of the upstairs windows open and take a quick shower. That should drive some of the smell out of the bathroom. Then you can get cleaned up, and we'll go down to the ship. George said he'd have breakfast ready about eight-thirty."

They gathered up the cushions on the floor and headed toward the house. John helped put the cushions back where they belonged and then went in for his shower. Brie heard a few more windows being opened in the upstairs. Counting the ones they'd broken or opened after the fire was out, they had as much air exchange going up there as possible.

She walked back and forth behind the house looking for signs of footprints or tire tracks. It had gotten windy and warmed up yesterday—the ground was dry and hard with no signs of a visitor. She walked to the edge of the forest where the road emerged. There were tire tracks, but they looked like they'd been made by Ben's truck. Whoever had done this had probably parked back a ways on the road and walked. She headed back to the house.

John hadn't come out yet, so she walked around the front of the house and found a sunny patch of grass. She stood quietly for a moment in yoga mountain pose—hands in prayer position in front of her heart—and breathed slowly in and out several times before starting the sun salutation pose. She had learned this sequence of movements from her friend Ariel, the year after she had been shot. She had taken up the habit of doing the poses each morning for the past year or so. The slow, studied movements had often brought her comfort after the nightmares she endured, and so she had kept on with it.

She moved now with grace and ease through the sun salute, deepening her breathing as she flowed from one pose to the next. She gave quiet thanks for a strong body. Without it she never would have survived the shooting. She heard John come up behind her. He waited a few seconds until she finished, returning to mountain pose, hands together over the heart.

"Just watching that was kind of calming, Brie." She turned and regarded him. "I didn't know you did yoga."

"I do this on deck every morning," she said.

"I've never seen you."

"I like to wait till I'm alone. And I don't actually *do* yoga—just this one sequence that a friend taught me. I'm thinking maybe I'll learn more, though. It seems to have helped me. I did classical dance until I was twenty-two, and it feels good to move my body again in a studied way."

"You never told me you studied dance."

"I guess it never came up for discussion."

"I've always noticed a certain quality to your movements," he said. "A kind of grace coupled with strength."

"Thanks," Brie said, hoping she wouldn't have to talk about it right now. She just wanted to get cleaned up.

"Anyway, the shower's all yours. And the smell isn't too bad in the upstairs. Hold your breath going through the kitchen, though."

"Will do." She headed into the house and up the stairs to the back room to get her soap, shampoo, and clean clothes. She grabbed a towel from the very back of the linen cabinet in the hall, hoping it wouldn't smell too bad. She undressed and stepped into the old claw-foot tub. There was a shower curtain rigged up on an oval-shaped rod. The set-up made her feel a bit claustrophobic, but once the hot water was running over her head and down her back, she forgot about everything but the comforting herbal scent of her shampoo and the pleasure of scrubbing the grit off her body.

The anger that had been building inside her since the fire last night had subsided briefly during the sun salute, but now she could feel it ramping up again. If someone here was trying to kill her, it hadn't worked, although she did pause to ponder the fact that she'd been running through her nine lives at an inordinately rapid pace over the past two years. If the killer was just trying to scare her off, well, he'd picked the wrong girl.

She knew one thing: when she found Amanda's killer, she would also have their arsonist. And she knew one other thing: she was going to get to the bottom of whatever was going on here. She felt the old Brie rise up for a moment—the Brie whose arrival seven years back in the Minneapolis Police Department homicide division had heralded the beginning of a record-breaking era for clearing cases. Not that it had been singly due to her presence, of course—"no I in team"—but clearly she had added some crucial element.

She was out of the shower within ten minutes. She applied some moisturizer and stepped into a clean pair of jeans. She pulled a long-sleeved, black tee shirt over her head, brushed her teeth, and slicked her wet hair up into a ponytail. She went back to the bedroom and stuffed her clothes from yesterday into her small backpack. They reeked of smoke. She'd air them out when they got back to the ship. She knew they would be staying on the *Maine Wind* for the rest of the time they were here, and that was good. Aboard ship, she felt a sense of security that existed nowhere else. For her, the *Maine Wind* had become a floating haven in what seemed a mad mad world.

She headed downstairs, collected Harold's journals from the living room, tucked them in the outside pocket of her pack, and went out the back door, where John was waiting for her. He was stretched out in one of the Adirondack chairs, eyes closed and face tilted up to catch the sun. She paused a moment to take him in, and a slight shiver went through her as she realized how different this morning might have been, and for that matter, that it might not have been at all, had the Fates stacked the deck a bit differently. As she approached, John opened his eyes and stood up.

"I don't know about you, but I'm famished. All that fire-fighting really takes it out of you."

"I'm having a hard time feeling jolly about all this," Brie said. "I guarantee you it wouldn't have happened if I hadn't been sniffing around asking questions about Amanda."

"First of all, Brie, it could have ended so much worse. And second, you're a cop. If someone on this island has killed Amanda, asking you to not investigate would be like asking the tide not to come in. Fire or not, Ben would want you to get to the bottom of her disappearance."

Brie had no response to that. "Let's head for the ship," was all she said. "We have to tell Ben what's happened, and I guess I need to eat. It's going to be a long day."

They headed toward the edge of the bluff to pick up the trail. "Ben may need to hire some help now," John said, "but he can afford that, and we'll see how much we can recoup in the couple of days we've got left."

"You know what the hardest part of all this is, John?"

"What?"

"After reading the journals, I think Harold was onto some-thing—something that's still going on here. And I think it got him killed."

"But his death was an accident. He fell."

"It was ruled an accident, John, because they couldn't prove differently, but those are two very different things. At any rate, I don't want Ben to know my thinking on that if you don't mind."

"I won't say anything."

"I just want to wait and see how this all shakes out. If it turns out Harold *was* murdered, how will Ben ever be able to feel good about living here?"

"Then what do we tell him about the fire?"

"We tell him the truth, but also that it's about me and not him."

"Look, Brie, there's a bad apple here on the island—for that matter, there may be several—but there are lots of good people here, too. Ben's the kind of guy who can figure that out. He's also the kind of guy who'll stand his ground."

"I hope so," Brie said.

They continued on in silence. A light wind out of the south carried the ocean to them. That smell of the sea, fresh as a morning's promise, had laid quite a claim on Brie's heart over the past two months. This morning, she wanted nothing more than to up anchor and escape into it. Such moments left her wondering if she'd ever go home.

The past two months on the ocean had brought her to a better understanding of her father, and how—having grown up on the coast of Maine—he must have missed the sea. Landlocked in Minnesota, there was Lake Superior, but grand and beautiful as it was to her, it wasn't the sea. No briny smell, no rise and fall of the tides—that breathing in and out of the great liquid realm. Tom Beaumont must have missed the sea terribly, and this realization had softened Brie a little toward some of the familial heartache his choices about boats and sailing had led to. It was too late, of course; he had been gone for many years. But to understand is to find peace, and she was grateful for that.

As they came around the final bend in the trail and started down toward the shore, she could see the ship lying peacefully at anchor just outside the small cove. They carried the dory down to the water, and Brie climbed into the stern. John pushed off, took his seat in the middle, set the oars in the locks, and started rowing.

As they got closer to the ship, wonderful aromas drifted in their direction—first wood smoke, sharp and pungent, then coffee with its dark robust notes, and finally the sweetness of bacon with maple overtones. Brie could almost hear it sizzling in the cast iron skillet atop Old Faithful. "Thank you, George," was the only thought running through her mind.

Scott saw them approaching and lowered the boarding ladder. They tied the dory off to the ladder and climbed aboard, with Brie going first. Ben was sitting on the cabin top with a mug of coffee, and he hailed them as they came aboard. Brie wished they didn't have to ruin such a perfect morning, but there was no way around it.

"George has pulled out all the stops," Ben said as the three of them headed aft in his direction. "Wait till you see what he's concocting..." Ben stopped abruptly and studied John's face. "Something's wrong," he said.

"There was an incident last night," John said.

"What incident?" Scott beat Ben to the punch.

"There's been a fire," Brie said.

"My God. Are you two all right?"

"We're fine, Ben," Brie assured him.

"I knew we weren't being careful enough with our clean-ups," Ben said.

"The good news is, we got it put out and managed to re-strict most of the damage to the kitchen," John said.

"The bad news is it wasn't caused by carelessness," Brie said. "Someone set it."

"What? Why?" Ben's words were sharp projectiles propelled by anger.

"I'm certain Amanda's disappearance is not an accident," Brie said. "The setting of the fire confirms that I'm getting too close to the truth for someone's comfort."

"I sent you two up there last night. You could have been killed."

"But we weren't, Ben. What's more, we were able to save the house."

"Maybe it's time to call the Maine State Police," Scott suggested.

"You need to call them, because there are clear signs of arson," Brie said. "The police will notify the fire marshal. The cause of the fire will have to be established for insurance purposes. As to the situation with Amanda, I'm pressing on. Harold's journals have confirmed some thoughts of mine and revealed some vital bits of information."

"I don't know, Brie. This has turned dangerous. And you've had enough adversity lately," Ben said.

"On the other hand, Brie's a pro at this, Ben, and she's caught the scent. I think we should let her run with it," John said. "I'm not going to let anything happen to her. What's that cop phrase? 'I've got your back.' Well, don't worry; I've got her back."

Brie could tell that Ben wasn't convinced, but he said no more. For her part, she was going ahead full-bore with her investigation, as soon as she ate breakfast.

Just then the ship's bell rang, and they turned to see George, sleeves rolled up, apron in place, looking happy and in his element. "It's nice up here this morning," he said. "Should we eat on deck?"

"Let's do that," said John. "But no need to bring everything up. We'll come down to the galley and dish up."

"I'll bring the coffee and the mugs up on deck," George said.

They all went below to line up, and as she passed John, he grabbed her and steered her in front of him. "Detective second mates, who happen to be ladies, first," he said.

Brie smiled and focused in on the feel of John's hands on her waist. Their moment had come last night, and she'd pretty much blown it. Their relationship so far had been nothing but fits and starts. She wondered if it would ever be more. She wondered if she wanted it to be. John must have picked up her thoughts, because he removed his hands from her waist and turned to talk to Scott about the day they had ahead of them.

The top of Old Faithful was brimming with food—oven-roasted potatoes with mushrooms, onions and peppers, a plate piled high with maple bacon, scrambled eggs with dollops of cream cheese melted in, and a steaming platter of pancakes filled with tiny, wild Maine blueberries. One by one they filled their plates with the savory breakfast and headed up the companionway ladder. Brie set her plate next to the coffee tray and poured out five mugs of coffee, which she handed to her shipmates as they came up on deck. Scott and George asked her to come and sit with them. The three of them climbed on the cabin top, and Brie nestled in between her crew mates, taking comfort, as she always did, in their camaraderie. There was silence as everyone dug into the hearty breakfast.

The food was delicious as always, but Brie's mind was on the day ahead. She planned to pay Harriet a visit this morning to see if the elderly woman needed any help, but also to ask her some questions. She hoped Harriet might be able to shed light on some of Harold's cryptic notations in his journal. First, though, she planned to stop by Spencer and Birdie Holloman's house. Their property was adjacent to Harriet's. She hoped to catch Birdie at home since the library didn't open until noon. So far, Brie had had pretty good luck with the island women. She wasn't exactly sure what she hoped to learn from Birdie, but on two occasions, she had witnessed Birdie's distress at the thought of Amanda's disappearance—once at the Scuttlebutt Café the previous morning, and again when she spied on the meeting at the library. Even though Birdie was part of *the group*, she might be of two minds about whatever they were up to. It didn't hurt to try.

Brie knew one thing from her police work, and that was that information is often gleaned from the strangest places.

Every mystery is a locked door. Right now, she felt she had precious little to go on, but she knew how quickly the pieces can fall into place once the key to that door is discovered. She had often seen the domino effect play out in investigations. Find the catalyst that sets a chain of events in motion, and like the game of Mouse Trap, the cage will eventually fall on the culprit. Her arrival on the island the same day as Amanda's disappearance had been the catalyst. The chain of events was now in motion. The fire last night was proof of that.

"Is everything okay, Brie?" George asked.

Brie realized she was staring off across the ocean, her breakfast half uneaten. "Things are definitely not okay on this island, George."

"I meant with your breakfast."

"Oh, sorry. It's delicious, as always, George. I'm just a bit preoccupied."

"You haven't heard about the fire yet," Scott told George.

"Fire! What fire?" George said, aghast.

Brie knew George did not like surprises. "There was an incident up at the house last night," was all she said. "I'll let Scott fill you in." She dug back into her breakfast. She had the feeling she was going to need the sustenance for the day ahead of her.

Scott filled George in on the details that he'd heard from Brie and John when they'd come aboard. As the story unfolded, George clucked like a mother hen, repeatedly casting concerned glances at Brie.

Brie decided she needed to make her exit before she became embroiled in George's concern. She slid off the cabin top, thanked George for breakfast, and took her dishes down to the galley. She had a long day ahead of her, and she needed to get to it. After cleaning up her dishes, she headed for her cabin in the aft compartment. With no passengers on board this week, she had the option of sleeping in one of the cabins, which gave her a little more space and also a bit of privacy. The wind had come up, so she grabbed a clean jacket—one that didn't smell like smoke. She went through her pack to see if there was anything in it she needed. She stuffed her lucky rope in her pocket, along with a small notebook and pen, and headed topside. She asked John to row her to shore.

By nine-thirty she was hiking up the trail. Since last night, the wind had moved into the south as it continued its march around the compass. Storm clouds, far off on the horizon, signaled that they were in for some heavy weather by the end of the day. Brie quickened her pace, eager to get on with the investigation.

Chapter 15

Brie crossed the top of the bluff, heading for the keeper's house. She stepped in the back door, and her nose curled up at the smell. She took a quick look through the house to be sure everything was okay. The guys would be up here soon enough to assess what needed to be done. She found the keys to the truck on the desk under the stairs. Ben had encouraged her to take the truck after she told him her plans for the day's investigation. She promised him she would stop back at the lighthouse around noon to see if he needed to use it. She headed out the back door. No time to waste today. As she climbed into the truck and started it up, she reflected on the fact that they had arrived at the island just two days ago. It felt more like two weeks to her. "Boy, time sure creeps when you're not having any fun," she said to herself.

She put the truck in gear and headed for her first stop. Just beyond the driveway for Puffin Point, Brie turned left and headed for the other side of the island. At the junction with West Island Road, she turned right and almost immediately spotted the sign for the Holloman's. She took a left and followed the winding gravel driveway toward a large cottage that sat on the shore. This side of the island was high and rocky, and she could already tell they had a spectacular view.

She couldn't get over houses this size being called cottages. Back in Minnesota a cottage was usually a lake cabin of very modest size, often no bigger than two or three small rooms.

Many of the so-called "cottages" in Maine, and along the East Coast, were very large houses, even what might be called mansions. Small lake and seaside residences were referred to as camps, and were not unlike what she would call a cottage back home.

At the end of the driveway, Brie pulled the truck up next to a large shed that had an ample supply of split firewood stacked alongside and covered with a tarp to keep it dry. As she got out of the car, a large crow that had been sitting atop the pile took flight, passing just above her head and scaring her half to death. He had blended so completely with the tarp and the dark siding on the shed that she hadn't even noticed him. "Get a grip, Brie," she told herself. After what had happened the night before, she figured today might be full of unsettling occurrences. She'd just hoped they wouldn't start quite so early.

She walked up the flagstone path to the back door and knocked. Within a few seconds Birdie Holloman opened the door. She was wearing a pale pink sweatshirt and sweatpants, and with her boyish haircut and delicate features, she reminded Brie of an elf in a sweat suit. She had a faraway look on her face, as if she had just returned from a mythical land. Brie had seen that look before on people who lived in a world of books. But Birdie's expression quickly morphed into a look of concern.

"Miss Beaumont, this is a surprise."

"Good morning, Birdie, and please, call me Brie."

"Well, all right then, Brie." She hesitated a moment and then asked, "Would you like to come in?"

"I would, thank you. I hope I'm not stopping by too early."

"Oh, heavens no." Birdie waved that off with a delicate gesture and stepped aside to let Brie in.

Brie stepped through the door into a large welcoming kitchen. The room had a beautiful pine floor of variegated hues. A rectangular table with six ladder-back chairs sat atop a red India print rug and filled the center of the room. Her eyes were immediately drawn to the cottage-pane windows and the ocean beyond. "I thought I might catch Spencer at home and see if there's any word of Amanda."

At the mention of Amanda, Birdie seemed to shrink visibly, and she hugged herself as if a sudden draft had passed through the room. "I'm afraid Spencer has already gone out. I don't believe there's any word of Amanda yet, though." Birdie looked away, but her distress was evident. "I know you're a friend of Wendy McLeod," she continued. "The poor girl must be beside herself. She's so close to Amanda."

The use of the present tense caught Brie's attention and told her that, as yet, Birdie hadn't decided on a worst case scenario, nor did she seem to have knowledge that Amanda would not be returning.

Birdie was talking again. "It's kind of you to help Wendy. She seems a little lost at times. Amanda has been so good to her."

"I've heard that from other people on the island. It seems Amanda has filled a place in Wendy's life since her mother died," Brie said. "Wendy's a good kid. She deserves that."

"A girl that age needs a mother."

"Yes, that's true," was all Brie said. She had decided not to mention the fire because she knew once she did, the news would travel around the island like another fire, and she was hoping for a surprised reaction from someone at seeing her alive. She suspected, however, that the arsonist had hidden nearby the night before to see how the whole thing played out—behavior not unusual for arsonists, who often like to blend into their surroundings and watch their work.

"But where are my manners?" Birdie suddenly asked. "Can I offer you something? Coffee or tea?"

Brie noticed a full pot of coffee on the warmer, and despite being stuffed to the gills, she accepted the offer, hoping it would keep Birdie talking. Birdie poured out two mugs of coffee, handed one to Brie, and led her into the dining room. Brie could see that the house sat out on a slight promontory. Every window in the downstairs had a different view of the ocean. *My kind of place,* she thought.

She walked over to the triple set of windows on the front wall of the dining room and looked out momentarily. She turned and surveyed the living room, which, along with the dining room, was painted the softest gold. Area rugs added warmth to the rooms, but left plenty of the pumpkin pine floor uncovered and open to admiration. The house had a colonial-style central hallway. Beyond it, the living room ran lengthwise along the southern wall of the house. A large stone fireplace flanked by an assortment of comfortable-looking sofas and chairs anchored the room. A wood-inlayed card table and four chairs occupied the bay window on the front wall of the living room. But what really caught her eye was the antique desk that sat in front of a window to the right of the fireplace. Brie had a thing for old desks with their roll-tops and drop fronts that always hid intriguing little drawers and pigeonholes. She thought if she ever got together the money, she'd like to buy a really cool old desk.

Birdie saw her looking at it. "That was my mother's writing desk," she said.

They walked into the living room and over to where it stood. Brie reached out and ran a hand over the soft leather top. "It's lovely," she said.

"Back in her day, people still sat and wrote letters to one another on beautiful parchment and vellum," Birdie commented. "Now it's all electronic. Generations to come will never know the pleasure of poring over a stack of letters from a loved one, long gone."

Brie had no such letters, so she guessed it was a pleasure she would never experience. She took a swallow from her mug of coffee. It was a dark, robust French roast, so unlike the timid Birdie that its presence in the cup surprised her. They walked back to the dining room. She didn't want to launch right into the topic of Amanda, having seen how Birdie reacted to any mention of her, so she decided to tread on safer ground and ask about Harold and the lighthouse, and hope it would lead back around to his relationship with Amanda.

"You and Spencer live so close to the lighthouse; you must have known Harold." This got no response, so Brie pressed on. "His death must have been a terrible shock. He had been back on the island for such a short time."

Birdie walked over to the window and looked out toward the sea. "Harold took risks."

It was said in such a cryptic way. *What is she implying?* Brie wondered. *What does she know?* Brie waited for Birdie to explain, but she said no more. Brie was aware that an island is like a small town—everyone knows everything that goes on. Had Harold gotten too close to the truth about what *the group* was up to? Or had he gotten too close to a woman—either Amanda or the Sanders woman?

"What do you mean, 'He took risks,' Birdie?" There was a pause, during which Brie got the impression Birdie was making some sort of decision. She wished she could see her face, read what was there, but she remained turned toward the window.

"He shouldn't have gone to the top of the lighthouse during a thunderstorm. It was a dangerous thing to do."

Brie was certain the risks Birdie was referring to had nothing to do with that thunderstorm, but before she could pry anything else out of the diminutive librarian, she heard the back door open.

At the sound of the door, Birdie literally jumped. Brie had her pegged for the nervous type, but there was something more here. Birdie had the demeanor of one who knew too much. Knowledge, Brie guessed, she had acquired sitting as the silent observer during meetings of *the group*.

Birdie headed toward the kitchen with Brie in tow. "Did you forget something, dear?"

Spencer Holloman's deep voice filled the room. "I think I forgot to give you a kiss…." He turned from the coffee pot and stopped mid-sentence. "Miss Beaumont! What brings you here?"

"Hello, Mr. Holloman. I stopped by to see if there was word of Amanda."

Spencer looked at Birdie for confirmation and seemed satisfied with what he saw there. "I'm sorry, but there isn't. I hate to have to say it, but folks are starting to worry."

Birdie went to his side, and he put an arm around her. "I wish she would get back so we can put our minds to rest. I'm so distressed about this."

"I know, dear," Spencer said with surprising gentleness. "But there's nothing for it but to wait."

The tenderness in his voice took Brie by surprise. In the privacy of their home Spencer treated Birdie differently—the bombast and sharpness replaced with what seemed like genuine caring. She thought back on the shortness with which he had addressed Birdie in the café the day before and again during the meeting of *the group*. She had encountered such men and women, ones who demeaned their wives or husbands in front of others, as if such behavior made them look in some way superior, when really just the opposite was true. For Birdie's sake, she was glad to see Spencer had another side.

She decided it was time to make her exit. "Thank you for the coffee, Birdie, but I should be moving along. I need to stop by Harriet's to see if she needs anything."

"That's most decent of you, Miss Beaumont."

She was about to tell him to call her "Brie," but somehow she wasn't quite on a first name basis with him, so she let it ride. "It's the least I can do," she said. She headed for the back door. "Thanks again, Birdie."

Birdie got off a quick "You're welcome," just as Brie closed the door behind herself.

Once outside, she mulled over the possibilities. She was more convinced than ever that Harold had been murdered. Birdie's loaded words, "Harold took risks," played through her mind. Something lay hidden behind those words; that was for sure. She didn't know how his death might be related to Amanda's, but she knew one thing—in such a small community, five'll get you ten they were somehow connected.

Brie knew from reading Harold's journals that he had formed some kind of relationship with both Amanda and Wade Sanders' wife, whose name she had yet to learn—she reminded herself to ask Harriet about that. There were men who easily attracted women. Maybe Harold had been one of those. If so, that could have spelled trouble.

She thought about Wade Sanders. *Mean* was all that came to mind. She wondered if he was mean enough to kill someone. She thought about her spy mission at the library the day before, and remembered the confrontation between Wade Sanders and Adam Blake over the subject of Amanda. From that scene, Brie had gleaned that Wade had, at one time, been involved with Amanda, and that Adam Blake's arrival on the island had ended their relationship. Had Wade found out that Harold was shining around his wife? Was that the final straw? Did he snap and kill Harold, or get in a fight that caused Harold's fall? But why would he kill Amanda? What was his motive?

Brie opened the truck door and climbed in. As far as she was concerned, Adam Blake was the one with that motive. He was a married guy having an affair with Amanda. Those things have a way of getting messy. She thought about how she had found him ransacking Amanda's desk the day before. How did he know she was missing? True, there had already been speculation going around yesterday morning as to Amanda's whereabouts, but still, his actions were suspicious. As usual, there were too many questions, and each one led to several more. Such was the nature of investigation. It was like descending into a labyrinth, and God help you if you forgot your ball of thread.

The clues definitely pointed toward the other side of the island, but Brie had to go to Harriet's first. She wanted to check on her, but also hoped that Harriet might shed some light on the cryptic notations in Harold's journals—mentions of *Deep Blue, Emily Ann, SS Ulysses* and, of course, "Grace." Brie turned on the truck, headed back toward the road, and turned left at the end of the Hollomans' driveway.

Chapter 16

Harriet Patterson's property immediately adjoined the Hollomans', so Brie was no more than on the road when Harriet's driveway appeared. She eased the truck down the gravel drive, dodging several large potholes. She parked alongside the wood pile that John had stacked the day before and climbed out. She took her jacket off, tossed it back in the truck, and went around to the front door. She knocked three times and waited a few moments, knowing Harriet wouldn't be all that quick to answer. Another minute passed and Brie knocked again, harder this time. She put her ear to the door, and now she could hear the tap of Harriet's cane on the floor as she approached.

The door opened tentatively, as it had yesterday. When Harriet saw Brie, she brightened a bit. "Miss Beaumont. Back so soon?" She stepped back and opened the door for Brie.

Harriet was wearing an outfit just like the one she had had on the day before, but today her long, wool skirt was navy blue, and the button-up sweater was the color of a robin's egg. It set off Harriet's clear blue eyes. "I promised I'd stop by today, Harriet. I hope it's not too early."

"Oh, lordy, my dear, it would be hard to be too early. Old people don't sleep all that much, you know. When the clock is ticking down, there are lots of better things to do than lay in bed."

They walked into the living room. There was a chill in the air. The temperature overnight had dipped near the forties.

"Would you like me to lay a fire?" Brie asked. "It's a bit chilly in here."

"Oh, I don't want to put you to any trouble, Miss Beaumont."

"It's no trouble, Harriet. As for Miss Beaumont—well, I'm not sure I know who that person would be. I'm really more of a 'Brie.'"

"Well...Brie," she hesitated as if the lack of formality were a bit of a strain, "a fire would be nice, I guess. It *is* a bit chilly."

"No problem," Brie said. She walked over to the fireplace and knelt down.

"I was making tea in the kitchen when you arrived. Would you like some?"

"I'd love some, Harriet. I'll get the fire going and then come out to the kitchen."

Brie had laid lots of fires in her life. Growing up in Minnesota, camping was a right of passage, and her family had also had a fireplace in their old house on Cherry Street in east St. Paul. From a basket on the hearth she took two large curls of birch bark and placed them on the grate as tinder. She cross-hatched the kindling wood in three layers, and atop that she placed two pieces of split log with two more of the same cross-hatched above. She checked the damper to be sure it was open, twisted a piece of newspaper into a torch, and lit it with a match. Squatting down, she held the torch above the fire to create a draft and then tucked it under the fire bed, next to the birch bark. A thin thread of smoke rose, and the bark ignited effortlessly. Brie shuddered, thinking about the fire the night before. After a moment, she stood up and went to find Harriet.

In the kitchen Harriet had the cups, saucers, and napkins laid out on a wood tray, and she was pouring steaming water into the teapot. There was a tin filled with small scones, and Brie wondered if she would be able to make room for one, considering George's ample breakfast. She carried the tray into the living room, where the fire was now blazing, and set it on the coffee table in front of the sofa.

She pulled the table over nearer the chairs where she and Harriet would be sitting. Once Harriet was settled in her chair, Brie poured her a cup of tea and handed it to her, along with a soft linen napkin, the color of aged parchment. Brie turned her chair a bit so she and Harriet could talk. She poured herself a cup of tea and sat down. She was glad Harriet hadn't asked about Amanda, because she had no idea what to tell her. Until Amanda's boat turned up, it was best to leave that topic alone.

"So, where's your young man this morning?" Harriet asked.

It took a moment before Brie realized she was referring to John. She guessed he might seem like a young man from Harriet's perspective. "Well, he's not really *my* young man. Actually, I'm part of his crew aboard his ship." Brie reached over and took a scone from the tin and bit into it. A subtle explosion of flavor — orange, vanilla, and cream — filled her mouth, and she actually let out a little moan.

"I wouldn't be too afraid to take the next step with your sea captain, dear. It's clear he's quite fond of you."

Brie's heart sank a little. She'd had that chance the night before and had let it pass. "You're right, Harriet. I'm not sure what I'm waiting for."

"If you know where all the roads lead before you get on them, you'll never have an adventure, dear."

"I know," Brie said. "You're right, of course." How could she tell Harriet the last year and a half of her life had been one long, bad adventure into some scary psychological territory?

Harriet's blue eyes shown with wisdom. "Life is short, and one thing is for sure — fear will never let you get anywhere near love." Brie's head came up at that, and she studied Harriet with interest. She had always considered herself brave. Over the years, her job had called for bravery on many occasions. But as she listened to Harriet, she had to wonder if there was a kind of courage she lacked.

The old woman was talking again. "Love is a leap into the unknown, and fear will never let you get close enough to the edge to take that leap."

"How did you get so wise, Harriet?"

"Well, I read a lot, and of course I raised my children, and that helps make you wise. So many chances to learn from your mistakes."

Brie smiled at that. "What do you read, Harriet?"

"Oh, mostly history and biographies. I like to read about real people and real events." Harriet smoothed her hair and held Brie's eyes for a moment. "Most of us miss so many opportunities, and then, before we know it, life is over."

Brie sat silently for a moment. This wasn't why she had come to Harriet's this morning, but she was learning to take all things at face value and realized these were words she needed to hear. She had wondered lately whether everyone isn't pretty much bumbling around in the dark most of the time, just waiting for one of their fellow humans to turn on a light. Here was Harriet, a torch bearer. Brie knew to listen to her.

As if she sensed the lesson had sunk in, Harriet moved on. "How is the work going up at the lighthouse?" she asked.

This was the opening Brie needed, and she jumped in before it could close up on her. "It's going pretty well." It was the truth if you didn't consider the past eight hours, and the fact that the house had nearly burned to the ground. "Ben is redoing the kitchen, so the guys have been busy taking down walls and such."

"Men like that kind of work," Harriet said.

"I noticed," Brie said. "They all seemed to be in an extremely good mood yesterday. Covered with plaster dust, but in an extremely good mood." She took a sip of her tea. "It's been interesting learning a little about Harold's time here, as well. John and

I found some journals he had left in the lighthouse. You are mentioned quite fondly in them, Harriet."

"Harold was a dear. He was always stopping by to chat or to see what needed doing around here. It's just so sad what happened to him out there. Especially when he had come home after so many years."

Brie filled Harriet's cup and let her talk.

"Harold's forebears were some of the original settlers on this island going back to the sixteen-hundreds. His family owned the cottage next door."

"You mean where Spencer and Birdie live now?" Brie asked.

"That's right, dear. Harold's parents eventually sold the house and moved off island. Harold's mother, Elizabeth, had terrible arthritis by the time she was in her sixties. The dampness of the island and the cold Maine winters were finally too much for her. They moved to the mainland and starting wintering in Arizona. Harold was an only child, and I know they would have left the house to him, but he'd become a career Navy man, and they didn't want to rent the house out and be responsible for it."

"Still, I wonder how Harold felt about that," Brie said.

"I'm sure he wouldn't have minded. After all, he and Spencer had grown up together. They were boyhood friends." Harriet stared into her teacup, looking back in time. "Oh, those two competed over everything, as boys will, but they balanced each other, somehow, Harold being from a wealthy family, and Spencer, the son of a poor lobsterman. They might never have been friends were it not for growing up together on a small island. But that's the nature of island life; it's a great melting pot. Spencer worked hard to build his lobstering business—make it a success. He's been a great advocate for the island. And Harold, well, he had less to prove, and as it turned out, his life lay elsewhere."

"But Harold's parents, the McCanns, still owned the lighthouse?"

"Well, yes. Harold's father had bought that property when it came up for auction in the nineteen sixties. Mostly for sentimental reasons, I think. A branch of the McCann family had been the lightkeepers here on the island for several generations." Harriet smoothed a hand over her hair and patted her bun. "It was good to have Harold back on the island. But I'm afraid he felt like an outsider after being away for so many years."

"That's sad, considering his heritage here," Brie said.

Harriet played with a button on her sweater. "Well, maybe it's true what they say. One can never go back."

Brie realized this comment might just as easily relate to Amanda. She thought about what Harriet had told her the day before about Amanda living in France, and she realized she had never learned how long the artist had been away from the island. "Did Amanda find happiness when she returned to the island?" she asked.

Harriet gazed into the fire. "It's hard to say. There's a tendency, maybe a danger, when one returns to a place after many years to try and pick up where one left off. But life moves on, of course. It's never possible."

Brie mulled on this for a moment, trying to read between the lines of what Harriet had just said. She wondered if Harriet might be referring to a love connection that Amanda had once had on the island. From her detective work she knew this was a situation humans often fell into—one that seldom ended well and occasionally ended disastrously. She chose her words carefully. "The promise of a love, once lost, being regained can be terribly compelling."

"Yes…yes, it's true," was all Harriet said, but there was a lifetime of sadness in those words.

"Is that what happened to Amanda?" Brie asked gently.

"I don't know that she would want me to talk about it, Miss Beaumont." Harriet paused and studied her frail hands as if they might offer guidance. Then she did the most extraordinary thing. She looked straight at Brie with her probing blue eyes and said, "But she's not coming back, is she?"

Brie was unprepared for this. She turned and looked at the fire, gathering her words carefully around her, wanting to pick the right ones. She realized now that Harriet was both too wise and too intuitive not to have figured out that Amanda was gone.

"I'm so sorry, Harriet, but I'm afraid that may be the case."

Harriet just nodded slowly, acceptance already woven into of the fabric of her thinking—the kind of acceptance that is decades in the mastering; the kind that Harriet would have spent a lifetime learning.

"I've had a strong feeling, you know—the kind that's almost never wrong."

"I understand," Brie said.

"I believe you do, Miss Beaumont. I believe you've had the same feeling. Am I right?"

Brie realized it was time to tell her own story. If she didn't, Harriet would sense that she was being less than forthcoming, and then the trust she had worked so hard to establish would be compromised. "Yes, Harriet, I have, and I'm so sorry to have to say that. And I think I now need to share more of my own story with you." She looked at Harriet hesitantly, but the old woman just nodded at her, her keen blue eyes never leaving Brie's.

"My place on Captain DuLac's crew—well, I've only been with him for two months. I came to Maine to work out some problems related to my work at home. As I told you yesterday, home for me is Minnesota. I am a homicide detective with the Minneapolis Police Department."

"Oh, my," was all Harriet said, but Brie could see that she had her rapt attention.

"I don't want you to think I've been keeping the truth from you, Harriet. I'd been hoping I might be wrong in my feeling that something had happened to Amanda. I didn't want to alarm you unnecessarily."

215

"I understand," Harriet said. "Please continue. I want to know your thoughts on what has happened."

"Well, the night we arrived at the island, we were having dinner with Ben, and around nine o'clock Wendy showed up out at the lighthouse. She was looking for Amanda and was hoping Ben might know where she was. We gave her a ride home in Ben's truck." Brie looked at Harriet to see if all this was making sense.

"Yes, go on," Harriet said.

"Well, that night there was a storm. I woke up in the middle of it. Sometimes storms..." Brie thought about explaining a bit more about her problems, but decided to just stick to the point. "Anyway, I went to shut the window and noticed a light through the trees. I decided Amanda must have returned home sometime late in the evening. The next morning I decided to walk over to her cottage and introduce myself since she was a friend of Ben's. But there was no one home, and the more I looked around, the more convinced I became that something was terribly wrong. When you've been in my line of work for a while, you develop a kind of a sixth sense about these things." Brie's gaze had drifted to the fire as she spoke, but now she looked back at Harriet and found the old woman studying her hands. "I am so sorry to have to tell you this, Harriet."

"That's all right, my dear. None of this is your fault. You just have the unfortunate job of bearing bad tidings." She looked into the fire for a few moments before framing her next question. "Do you believe Amanda has met with an accident?" she asked. "Or are you implying something much worse?"

"I won't lie to you, Harriet. I'm afraid Amanda may have been the victim of foul play." Brie immediately regretted her rather clinical description when she saw Harriet's eyes cloud with tears. She rose from her chair, squatted at the old woman's side, and gently took her hand.

Harriet removed a handkerchief from her skirt pocket and dabbed at her eyes. "It's all right, Miss Beaumont... Brie. I would want you to be honest with me. Amanda would have liked you, and I think she would be glad of your instincts and your concern."

Harriet hugged herself as if suddenly cold, and Brie went to get an afghan from the back of the sofa. She wrapped it around the old woman's shoulders and poured her another cup of tea. "Here, drink this, Harriet. It will warm you." She stepped over and placed another log on the fire she was very glad she had built. She went back to her chair and studied Harriet for a moment, deciding whether she should go on or not. But her sense was that Harriet would want her to find the truth.

"Harriet, I'd like to talk a little more about Amanda, but if you want to be alone…" She didn't finish the sentence, hoping Harriet would give her a cue.

"No, please go on," Harriet said. "I want to help in any way I can."

"Well, can you tell me a little more about Amanda's early years here? It might help. Did she, in fact, leave someone she loved behind when she left the island as a young woman?" Brie waited, hoping Harriet would confide in her—hoping that she had formed a strong enough connection with the old woman to be trusted.

Harriet set her teacup down. She gathered the afghan around her and patted the neat silver bun at the nape of her neck. Brie could see that these adjustments gave her the few moments she needed to make her decision, and when Harriet turned to look at her, Brie knew the old woman had decided to tell Amanda's story.

"It was the summer Amanda was seventeen," Harriet began. "The Whitcombes had arrived in June, as they always did. Amanda had become such a beauty, and even at that young age she was beginning to realize what power resided in that beauty." Harriet picked up her cup and seemed to settle into both her chair and the story. "She was a headstrong girl, but then what intelligent and beautiful girl isn't at that age? I know I was."

"Me, too," Brie nodded.

Harriet's eyes twinkled for a moment as she regarded Brie. "Yes, I believe you would have been," she said, thereby admitting Brie to the sisterhood of headstrong women. "At any rate, Amanda seemed to delight in upsetting her parents—particularly her mother. There was a young man on the island that summer. Oh, he'd always been here; I just don't think Amanda had ever noticed him. But he'd grown several inches between that summer and the one before, and he'd filled out. Probably from working stern on his father's lobsterboat. It's hard work, you know."

"I do know," Brie said with authority.

Harriet looked like she wanted to ask how Brie knew that, but instead decided to continue her story. "I think at first Amanda was just looking for fun and maybe a way to irritate her parents. But surprisingly, those two young people became inseparable. They would come visit me sometimes. I think as Amanda realized she was falling in love, she genuinely wanted someone's approval. And there was no doubt the two of them were in love. It was young love, but real love, nonetheless."

Harriet paused and looked toward the fire. "I don't know when people started thinking teenagers can't truly be in love or that they don't know what they're doing. I've often thought Amanda's life might have been happier had she just married that boy and lived on the island. But it wasn't my place to comment, and I could certainly understand that the Whitcombes wanted Amanda to go to college and experience the world a bit more."

Brie reached for her teacup and took a sip, hoping Harriet would keep going. She didn't know yet how this story would help her catch a killer, but what she did know was that any investigation is, in itself, an unfolding story, where everything relates in some way to everything else. "So, what happened?" Brie asked.

"In the middle of August that summer, the Whitcombes packed up quite suddenly and left the island, and of course, took Amanda with them."

"Was that normal?" Brie asked.

"Heavens, no," Harriet said. "They always stayed till Labor Day. The village of Barnacle Bay holds a big celebration on that weekend, with a bonfire and a lobster feast. Everyone goes— islanders and summer folk alike. In those years, the Whitcombes always helped organize the celebration. It wasn't like them to just up and leave."

"Do you know why they did?"

Harriet looked down at the teacup in her lap, but Brie could see her eyes and the way they shifted from side to side, as if the old woman felt suddenly trapped. "I don't know," was all she said.

Brie studied Harriet, uncertain if she was holding something back, but feeling the boundaries of respect both for Amanda and for Harriet's relationship with the dead artist pressing on her, stopping her from any more prying. She decided instead to return to what had been said the day before. "Harriet, you told me yesterday that Amanda returned from France when she was in her mid-twenties. Did she come back to the island then?"

"She never came back here," Harriet said. "Not until the summer after her mother died, five years ago. She hadn't been back here in almost thirty years."

"Didn't that seem strange to you, considering how much she loved the island?"

Again Harriet was noncommittal. "I don't know," she said. "After the trouble in France, Amanda moved to New York City and became part of the art scene there. Her mother always came to the island in the summer even after Mr. Whitcombe died. Maybe that's why Amanda never returned. I'm not sure she ever really forgave her mother for what happened the summer she was seventeen." Harriet paused and gazed at the fire.

"Mothers and daughters—why is it so hard for them to get along? Don't they understand how much we love them?"

Brie noticed tears fill the old woman's eyes, and while it wasn't clear whether Harriet was referring to her mother or her daughter, she guessed it was the latter. Brie was at a loss for words. Harriet's last comment had caught her off guard and made her think of her own mother, and how hard that relationship had sometimes been. "I don't know why, Harriet, but daughters seem to be tenaciously and often unjustifiably critical of their mothers. And sometimes, by the time our hearts soften enough to realize how foolish we've been, it's too late."

Harriet remained silent, as if all the talk had drained her. Brie hoped to gather a little more information but didn't want to cause Harriet any stress. "Should we stop, Harriet?" she asked. "Are you too tired to talk more?"

"No, it's all right. I'm not sure how much more help I can be, though."

"Do you think you could tell me who Amanda's young man was that summer on the island?"

"Well, that's not much of a secret. Everyone that grew up here knew about it, so I don't think I'm revealing anything that shouldn't be revealed. It was Wade Sanders."

"Wade Sanders," Brie said, dumbstruck. She tried to conjure up some picture of the "mean guy" from her encounter at the Scuttlebutt Café that could possibly mesh with the touching story of the two teenagers so desperately in love. She wondered what the young Wade must have been like, and how the loss of Amanda might have forever changed him. Her heart actually softened a bit toward him, and the scene between him and Adam Blake at the meeting of *the group* the day before suddenly took on a whole new meaning. The revelation made Brie even more eager to meet Sanders' wife, whom Harold had mentioned in his journals.

"Harold mentioned Wade's wife and sons in his journal. Apparently she and the boys used to visit him out at the lighthouse. Her name isn't, by chance, 'Grace,' is it?"

Harriet seemed puzzled by the question. "Why, no," she said. "Her name is Summer Dawn. Summer Dawn Sanders." She fingered her teacup. "Harold liked those little boys. He talked about them a lot."

"Do you know anyone one the island named Grace?"

Harriet thought for a moment. "I can't say I do. Is it important?"

"It's nothing," Brie said. "Don't worry your mind about it." She wondered if *Grace* hadn't been Harold's little code that he used in his journal for a woman whose name he didn't want to write there. She was also beginning to wonder if Harold hadn't just liked the drama of being cryptic. But she pressed on, hoping to learn something about the boats he had mentioned.

"Harold had a couple of curious notations in his journal," Brie said. "And by the way, Harriet, I read the journals with Ben's permission, after Amanda went missing. I was hoping they would help me better understand the people here." She didn't want to tell Harriet her other reason—her suspicions that Harold might have been murdered. One blow was enough for the old woman.

"I understand," Harriet said. "What were these notations you mentioned?"

"Well, he seemed to be keeping track of the comings and goings of two boats—*Emily Ann* and *Deep Blue*. And there was a notation about an *SS Ulysses*, which sounds like the name of a ship, and also a notation about someone named 'Grace.' Do any of those names ring a bell, Harriet?"

"Well, let me think here," Harriet said. She set her teacup on the table next to her and smoothed a hand over her hair. "I think *Emily Ann* is Wade's boat, but I don't know about the other one —what was it, *Blue* something?"

221

"*Deep Blue*," Brie offered. She got up and rearranged the fire bed to give Harriet time to think. There was a nice bed of embers now, and she added another log.

"That name doesn't ring a bell," Harriet said, "but, you know, so many vessels have come and gone in these waters, even in my lifetime."

"And I imagine some of them have been lost over time, as well."

"Oh yes," Harriet said. "The Maine coast is quite a graveyard for ships. And of course, if you go back to the late seventeen and early eighteen hundreds, before many of the lighthouses were built, there's quite a colorful history of wreckers along these shores. In fact, there are families still on this very island whose ancestors were wreckers."

"Who were these 'wreckers,' Harriet? I've never heard that term before. What did they do?"

"Oh, my, the things they did were terrible. The wreckers were like pirates in a way, but they operated from land." Harriet shifted in her chair to look at Brie. "Before the days of lighthouses, they would build signal fires on the shores along the coast and on the islands, to fool ships and lure them toward shore or confuse them as to where they were. Many of these islands are surrounded by shoals and so are particularly treacherous for ships. When a ship wrecked on the rocks, it would be a free-for-all, with islanders killing any survivors that made it to shore and making off with the ship's cargo."

"That's terrible."

"The odd part is, people all along the New England coast felt a kind of entitlement about this activity. Many villages depended on a good wreck or two just to get through the harsh winter. Believe it or not, many of them thought it was a perfectly fine and honorable occupation. There was quite an uproar from those folks when all the lighthouses began to be built. After all, generations of people had made their living as wreckers."

"Amazing," Brie said. "What an absolutely amazing story."

"No story, though. All true," Harriet said, her blue eyes alive from the telling of it.

"How far people can stray from their moral compasses." Brie paused for a moment to digest Harriet's tale. "And you say there are families still here whose ancestors were wreckers?"

"There are many families on these islands whose ancestors go back to the sixteen hundreds, and yes, some of them were wreckers."

"I've been reading about Maine's history, and I've learned that the first ships from Europe fished these waters back in the fifteen hundreds."

"That's right, dear. Long before the *Mayflower* landed at Plymouth Rock, explorers and fishermen had frequented these islands. These have always been the richest fishing grounds in the world. My heavens, history has it that in those early days these waters were so thick with cod you could practically walk from island to island. The largest of them could weigh two hundred pounds. Now the cod are all but gone. That fishery has completely collapsed."

Brie was silent for a moment as she absorbed all this. She felt like she was slowly becoming versed in all things Maine-like. Today it was the history of the wreckers and the disappearance of cod.

As if Harriet suddenly realized she had strayed from the topic, she said, "But you mentioned the name of another ship."

"Yes," Brie said, coming back to the present, setting aside the heavy weight of all that history. "The *SS Ulysses*. Do you have any idea why Harold might have made a note about it in his diary?"

"If my memory serves me, I believe there have been many stories passed down about a ship by that name and its ill-fated voyage."

"Tell me about it," Brie said, settling back in her chair.

Harriet adjusted the afghan and picked up her teacup before starting into the story. "At the end of the Civil War many speculators sailed from New York and Boston harbors bound for the South, which had been decimated by the war. There were fortunes to be made there. The *SS Ulysses* was such a ship—a side-wheel steamer loaded with gold and speculators, headed for the South. It sailed from Boston in August of eighteen sixty-five unaware of the dangerous storm that was bearing down on New England. The ship was caught in a violent hurricane and blown north, all the way to the Gulf of Maine, where it sank supposedly somewhere in these waters. A number of the survivors made it to this island in one of the lifeboats, but most of the others perished in the storm."

"And the shipwreck has never been located?" Brie asked.

"Not to my knowledge, although stories abound, of course. Late in her career, Amanda's mother, Eva Whitcombe, became quite interested in marine archeology. She even put together a team to search for the *Ulysses,* based on the stories that had always circulated on the island. But I don't believe they ever found anything. A hundred forty-five years is a long time in the ocean."

"All that gold," Brie said. "It would have to be worth millions."

Harriet yawned, and Brie realized she had been here for over an hour, and that Harriet had probably had enough questions. She had gathered a wealth of information, and some thoughts were percolating on how all this might relate to Amanda's disappearance. She was eager to get to the other side of the island, and hopefully talk to Summer Dawn Sanders.

"I hope some of this helps," Harriet said.

"It does, Harriet, a lot. And thank you. I should be going, though. I have some people I want to visit on the other side of the island. But if there's any news about Amanda, I'll be sure to let you know."

"Thank you, Miss Beaumont, and thank you for the fire."

"Is there anything else I can do for you before I leave?"

"No. I'm fine. I think I'll just doze in my chair a bit."

Before leaving. Brie placed several logs on the fire, so the room would stay warm for awhile. Then she said good-bye to Harriet and let herself out the front door, being sure to lock it. As she headed for the pickup truck, her head was filled with images of wreckers and ships in hurricanes, and of a young couple so much in love all those years ago.

Chapter 17

As Brie drove toward the other side of the island, she sifted through everything she had learned from Harriet. Some of it was factual information, and some of it just flat out wisdom. So wise was the old woman that a discerning person could continue mining gold from her words for a long time — possibly a lifetime. But right now, Brie was focused on the factual pieces that related to both the island and Amanda's life. As often happened with homicides, Brie had a sense of things buried just below the surface of these peoples' lives. She just had to keep digging.

Harriet's story about the *SS Ulysses* intrigued her. Had Amanda continued the search for the ship based on her mother's research? Had she, along with the help of the others — *the group* — found the ship? Were they salvaging the treasure and using Amanda's former black market connections to sell it off? If this were true, Amanda would have played a key role in the operation, which made Brie wonder if the motive for her murder didn't lie elsewhere, and if it wasn't linked in some way to Harold's death. On the other hand, if Harold was onto what they were doing, it could have put him in jeopardy. But she was getting ahead of herself. She knew there were gaps to be filled in, questions to be answered, and motives to be uncovered.

Summer Dawn Sanders was first, and Brie was most curious to make her acquaintance, but Adam Blake was also foremost in her mind. She planned to visit him and get a good look at this schooner of his to see if it bore the name *Deep Blue*, one of the names Harold had recorded in his journal. She thought about meeting him at the Scuttlebutt Café the day before when he'd come over to their table to talk to John. After the initial "hellos," he had seemed ill at ease, as if he was genuinely glad to see John but guarded about reopening their acquaintance. It had struck Brie as strange at the time, but after some of her discoveries about *the group* and their covert goings on, the encounter had made more sense. However, when there was a crime afoot, she always focused on people whose behavior seemed off in any way.

When she reached the intersection with East Island Road, she turned left and followed it as it swung west around the gorge. She knew the Sanders' place would be the first driveway on the right. She tried to conjure up an image of Summer Dawn Sanders but, sadly, the name suggested conflicting images of dewy sunrises and over-scented air freshener. She wondered if possibly Harold had thought "Grace" a better moniker.

Brie saw a sign coming up and knew this would be the Sanders' driveway. She turned into it and followed the narrow track. Dense spruce crowded a rutted gravel driveway sorely in need of repair. Near the end of the driveway the spruce opened into a kind of yard behind a small Cape Cod-style house that could have used some TLC. The paint around the windows was peeling, exposing badly weathered wood. The back yard was overrun by tall grass and weeds, and a large portion of it was stacked with unused lobster traps and buoys. There were a few old tires and several bikes that had seen better days. Brie pulled the truck up to the end of the driveway. As she did so, she caught a glimpse of a slender woman hanging out laundry over on the south side of the house. She climbed out of the truck and headed in her direction.

As Brie came out from behind the house, the wind and sun hit her. White sheets snapped on the clothesline against a field of deep blue that was the Atlantic Ocean. She was once again reminded that on an island such as this, the ocean is everywhere present. An island is like the sun; the ocean its blue solar system, and the boats that come and go mere planets in its orbit. Brie took a deep breath as her eyes rested on the Atlantic. This was a more pleasant scene than the one behind the house, and she paused a moment to take it and the woman in.

Summer Dawn was wearing a loose sundress with a tattered cardigan sweater over the top. A pair of old lace-up sneakers that had once been white, but now bore the color of too much housework, covered her bare feet. The dress billowed around a figure so slim Brie was amazed it remained upright in the strong wind. Two twin boys, who looked to be about age ten, tore in and out among the laundry, brandishing plastic swords in a frantic game of thrust and parry. Occasionally, one of them would become entangled in a bath towel or an oversized man's shirt, and while trying to extricate himself, would receive a potentially fatal stab from the other. Then the wounded one would fall to the ground, taking the piece of clean laundry with him. The woman would turn briefly, hands on hips, and shake her head before retrieving the fallen item. She seemed utterly unflappable, or maybe just resigned, as if the boys' antics barely registered on her time-to-get-angry scale. Even from this distance Brie had the sense of a faded woman, threadbare from life's demands; a woman struggling to keep body and soul together.

It was one of the boys who spotted Brie. He stopped dead in his tracks and stared at her for a brief moment before going to his mother. "Mom, there's someone here," he said, tugging at her misshapen sweater. She turned to look, clothespins still in her mouth.

"Mrs. Sanders?" Brie called as she approached.

Summer Dawn set the shirt and pins back in the basket and smoothed her dark, shoulder length hair, which refused to cooperate in the strong wind. "Yes, I'm Mrs. Sanders," she said hesitantly.

Brie held out her hand as she got close, and it was received with exactly the grip she had expected.

"You must be Wendy's friend from out at the lighthouse," the woman said.

Brie was delighted to have this opening, but curious nonetheless. "Yes, I am, but how would you know that?"

"Wendy mentioned you when she came to watch the boys this morning. She keeps an eye on them while I go for groceries every Monday. She described you perfectly—tall; long blonde hair. When I saw you standing there I knew right away who you were. I'm Summer Sanders, and these are my boys, Tom and Taylor."

Mrs. Sanders was younger than Brie had expected. She placed her between thirty-five and forty years old. Her voice also came as a surprise to Brie. It was soothing, like water over rocks, but there was strength in it, too, like the current in a river, and Brie thought maybe it suggested a kind of fortitude, as if deep inside her, trying to bubble to the surface, was another woman, untouched by the drubbing life had given her—possibly the woman Summer had once been.

"I'm Brie Beaumont. I wonder if I could have a few minutes of your time?"

Before Summer could respond one on the boys piped up. "We're hungry, Mom. What's for lunch?"

"It's not time for lunch yet," Summer said. "You and your brother go inside and let me talk to Miss Beaumont."

Brie now had to add refinement to her assessment of Summer, and while she had never known Amanda, she had to wonder if there weren't similarities between her and this woman. Similarities that Wade had found comforting.

Summer turned back to Brie, but as she spoke, her gaze traveled beyond her to rest on the ocean. "Wendy's very worried about Amanda," she said. "Of course, we all are." But her voice had gone flat as she said this, belying the truth of the statement.

Brie was trying to think of some way to work the discussion back around to Harold and the journals. She decided the chatty approach might work. "We just arrived at the lighthouse to visit Ben on Saturday evening. Ben was a close friend of Harold McCann, and I've been told Harold willed the property to Ben." Brie watched Summer's reaction closely, and noticed that, at the mention of Harold, her jaw had gone tight, as if she might be clenching her teeth. "Ben loves the place, but I know he feels bad about the circumstances that led to his owning it."

Summer lowered her head to stare at the ground, but not before Brie noticed the tears in her eyes. "Summer," Brie said gently, "the reason I'm here is that Harold left some journals behind. We found them in the lighthouse yesterday, and Ben gave me permission to read them." At this, Summer's gaze shifted back and forth and, while she held her ground, Brie could see she felt trapped. She pressed on before Summer decided to escape. "From the journals it sounds like you were a friend of Harold's, and I hope you won't think I'm prying, but I found some curious notations in them, and I thought you might be able to help."

A sudden and violent sob escaped from Summer, and Brie noticed her fists had turned to tight balls inside the pockets of her cardigan. That sob held the entirety of what Brie had suspected. Whether spoken or not, whether acted on or not, there had been love for Harold in Summer's heart. Brie had no way of knowing if the feelings had been requited or if she might be the mysterious "Grace." She reached out and gently took hold of Summer's arm. "I'm so sorry," she said.

There was silence for a few moments, during which Summer seemed to be gathering her courage. She finally lifted her eyes to Brie. "Harold was the dearest man. So kind and so generous."

"I got that sense of him from his journals and from everything Ben and Harriet Patterson have said. Did you notice, in the last couple months before he died, if he seemed different? Like something might be bothering him?"

Summer looked toward the ocean again, possibly seeking solace there. "He did seem preoccupied those last few weeks. I even asked him about it, but he just said he was grappling with some decisions about his life. I think there was something else, though."

"I found mentions of the *Emily Ann* in Harold's journal. That's Wade's boat, isn't it?"

"That's right."

"It seems Harold liked to watch the comings and goings of boats from the top of the lighthouse. Did he ever mention anything about it to you?"

"You know, it's funny you mention that, because Harold asked me if Wade had a new lobstering territory—said he'd seen the *Emily Ann* traveling east of the island a lot."

"And did he?"

"I don't think so, but Wade doesn't talk much about his work, except to let me know when the catch is bad."

"Summer, just one more question about Harold if you wouldn't mind. Did he, by chance, ever call you Grace? You know, in the way people make up names for those they're fond of."

Summer shook her head. "No…well, except for one time, he said I was a lovely, graceful woman, but that was on a day I was feeling pretty down. I think he could tell and said that to cheer me up." The tears returned to her eyes. "Sometimes I wish we had never become friends."

"Why would you wish that?" Brie asked, although she thought she knew the answer.

Summer studied the ground. "I just do." She raised her eyes to look at Brie. "I have to go in now and fix lunch for the boys."

"Thank you for talking to me," Brie said. As she walked back to the truck, she reflected on Summer's apparent guilt over her friendship with Harold, innocent though it may have been.

Brie had spent her career reading between the lines, and one thing was clear; Summer believed Harold might be alive had they not become friends. Had the anger boiling inside her husband morphed into violence directed at Harold? Brie thought about the two young boys darting about the clotheslines and hoped, for their sake, it wasn't the case. The tunnel of spruce crowded in on her as she steered the truck back toward the road. Sometimes her work left a lot to be desired. She suddenly longed to escape back to sea. She took it as a sign she was getting closer.

Chapter 18

Adam Blake, the schooner captain—or as Brie liked to think of him, the suspect most likely to be the "perp"—was next on her list. *Always look to the lover first, especially if he also has a wife.* She was thinking alternately about John and a big bowl of egg noodles when a marker with the name Blake on it sailed past her passenger-side window. She stepped hard on the brakes and backed up. As she turned into the driveway on her right, she was again mulling over their encounter with Blake at the Scuttlebutt the day before. Her initial impression of him, aside from his rakish good looks that reminded her a little of Johnny Depp plus a beard, was that he had seemed skittish—equal parts glad to see John and horrified that he was on the island. Maybe he had realized that John would want to see his schooner, and maybe that presented a problem.

The driveway wound up a small hill, and as she came over the crest, the house appeared. Another gray shake-sided cottage, this one was both larger and better tended than the Sanders' house she had just left. Most striking were the window boxes, overflowing with impatiens, petunias, and sweet alyssum, and the lovely gardens, laced in and out among clumps of cedar trees.

Brie was surprised that Blake would have his schooner anchored here and not in the town harbor, but as the driveway swung right to skirt a giant boulder, she saw why. The curve of the land created a small, natural harbor, to which a breakwater had been added to give more protection to the east. *Took some moola to build that,* Brie thought. Within that sheltered arm a double-masted schooner lay at anchor. Brie judged its length at the waterline to be approximately 50 feet—not as large as the *Maine Wind,* but impressive nonetheless.

All in all, the place spelled money, and she couldn't help but wonder whose money it was—Blake's or his wife's. She remembered him mentioning that his wife's family was from out here on the island, and that that was how he had gotten a lobstering territory. One thing she knew—money and who owned it factored greatly when it came to motives for murder. But she temporarily set these thoughts aside so as to approach Blake with an unbiased demeanor.

She parked Ben's dumpy pickup next to a brand new GMC truck. She hopped out and headed for the back door of the house, where she knocked three times. Within a few seconds Adam Blake opened the door. His eyebrows went up at seeing her, yet he didn't seem all that surprised, and she wondered why. Brie introduced herself, reminding him of her connection to John and the *Maine Wind.* "Would you mind if I came in for a few minutes?"

"I guess not," he said half-heartedly.

"I'm glad to find you home," she said, stepping through the door. "I thought you might be out hauling your traps. You said yesterday you lobster for a living."

"I hire a couple young guys to work my traps. We split the take."

"Hmmm," was all Brie said. It sounded more and more to her like he had money, and maybe didn't like to work too hard. "I suppose you're wondering why I'm here," Brie said.

"Actually, I know exactly why you're here." Thinly veiled antagonism percolated in his words. "Charlie Cappy went to the mainland yesterday for some supplies and ran into a lobsterman he knows from Granite Island—name of Paulie Tillman—who told him about this homicide detective sailing on the

Maine Wind who helped solve a murder out there in May. Sound familiar?"

Brie stared at the floor. She'd been expecting this, knowing what a tight-knit group the lobstermen were and how quickly gossip got around. She thought about her options and decided on the spit-in-your-eye approach. She stared him straight in the face and said, "So... I guess I arrived at just about the right time, since you seem to have a person who's gone missing."

That pretty much took the wind out of Blake's sails. His eyes iced over momentarily as he realized he couldn't intimidate her. "Believe me, the whole island knows by now. You won't be getting any warm receptions."

Brie didn't miss a beat. "I guess that makes us even, since the whole island also knows you were Amanda's lover, which makes you chief suspect in her murder."

Now his gaze went truly arctic. "What do you mean, murder?" he snapped. "Amanda and her boat are missing. That doesn't mean she was murdered."

"Let's just say, based on my former occupation, that I know what I'm talking about. What's more, I saw you ransacking the desk in her cottage yesterday morning, long before the meeting of your little cabal in the library. That would suggest prior knowledge of her disappearance."

Adam's face turned a shade of red that suggested simmering rage nearing the boil-over point. He actually took a step toward her, but must have thought better of that because he quickly stepped back.

"Listen, Detective Beaumont," he spat at her, "if you want Amanda's killer, you need to find the person who killed Harold McCann, the former lighthouse owner."

Brie tried to mask her surprise, but was too late. She knew she had just lost a bit of her advantage. "What makes you think he was murdered?" she asked, trying to sound dismissive.

"I'll tell you what makes me think it. Amanda told me she was sure Harold was murdered. What's more, she said she knew who did it. She told me the night he died she'd gone over to his place with a coffee cake she had baked for him. She was always taking him things—don't ask me why. Anyway, she didn't find him at the house, so she was heading toward the lighthouse when she heard shouting. Apparently, Harold and someone else were on the catwalk at the top of the lighthouse. She said she wasn't about to interfere. There was a storm moving in fast, and she wanted to get back home before it started to rain. The next morning she went back over there. Amanda was the one who found Harold at the base of the lighthouse staircase. She was really shaken by it, and absolutely sure he'd been murdered."

"Why didn't she tell her story to the police? They would have investigated more thoroughly. All the coroner had to go on was the head trauma, which could have been sustained from a fall down those stairs."

"I told her she needed to tell the cops her story, but she said 'no.' I asked who she had seen, but she wouldn't tell me. Mandy was funny that way. She liked to acquire information that... well, let's just say she could use as leverage. She played things close to her vest, and I'd guess she was hanging onto that information as a kind of ace in the hole to use down the line, to gain some kind of advantage for herself."

"Let's talk plain here," Brie said. "What you're telling me is that she was into blackmail."

"That's a pretty strong word for it, I'd say."

"Is it? Knowledge you're using against someone that may get you killed. I'm pretty sure that classifies as blackmail."

"Whatever." He waved a hand, indicating he was done with the discussion. "There's no proof Amanda is dead. She may have taken her boat to see a friend and not told anyone. She's impulsive like that."

"I could almost buy that if her boat hadn't disappeared from the harbor in the middle of the night during a storm. Charlie Cappy's moored next to her, and he told me he heard her motor start up the night before last. He wasn't sure of the time, but he said it was late."

Blake laughed out loud. "That's your source—Charlie, the stoner? Half the time he doesn't even know what day it is."

"Well, I guess time will tell, won't it? Boats and bodies have a way of turning up, so we'll just have to wait. And, speaking of boats, what's the name of your schooner?"

"*Deep Blue.* Why?"

"Just wondering. You didn't tell me why you were going through Amanda's desk."

"I overheard you at the café talking to Spencer about Amanda, and, well, I thought I might find a note or her desk calendar so we could figure out where she was. Look, I love Amanda. I know you think that gives me a motive, since I'm married, but I'm telling you, I'd never hurt her."

"Really? Well then, if you're not guilty of anything, you have no reason to worry." Despite what he'd said, though, she got a guilty vibe from him. The question was, what was he guilty of? Taking part in some illegal operation, cheating on his wife, or something far worse?

"Before I leave, I'd like to meet your wife," Brie said. "Is she home?"

"I'm afraid that won't be possible. She's visiting a friend on the mainland. I'm going to get her this afternoon."

"How long has she been gone?"

"Since Friday. Not that it's any of your business."

Brie did the math. The wife had left the day before they arrived on the island—hence the day before Amanda was murdered. One more nail in Adam Blake's coffin. "Would you have a picture of her? I like to put a face with the people I'm inquiring about."

"Wait here," Blake ordered. He stalked out of the kitchen and in a few seconds returned with a framed photo. "This is Holly," he said, handing the picture to her.

It was a picture of the two of them. The woman wore a red turtleneck and blue denim jacket. She was slender, and her light brown hair was slicked back in a ponytail. She was pretty, but not beautiful. Amanda, on the other hand, even at fifty, had a rare beauty about her.

Brie handed the picture back, thanked Blake, and took her leave. She walked to her truck, got in, and turned the key. She planned to come back this afternoon, while he was off collecting his wife, and get aboard that schooner—see what was what.

She decided it was time to stop back at the lighthouse and see if the guys needed the truck, so at the foot of the driveway, she turned left onto East Island Road and headed toward the other end of the island. As she drove back, her mind was awash with bits of information and speculation. There was nothing to substantiate anything Blake had just said. For all she knew, he could have made it all up. And his explanation about being at her house looking for a note on her desk calendar. Bogus. He was ransacking that desk, trying to lay hands on something— possibly the ledger Spencer had mentioned at the meeting— before anyone else did.

But what he had said about Harold being murdered struck a chord with her, since her gut had told her the same thing. Brie knew Harold's death could relate to the fact that he was onto something taking place on the island—something *the group* was involved in—something she needed to find out about. But she guessed if he had been killed over that, they would have planned it differently. Certainly, whoever did the deed wouldn't have gotten into a heated argument with him at the top of the lighthouse. Sure, the place was secluded, but it was always possible someone could overhear such a fight—and apparently someone had. No, Harold's death didn't sound premeditated. It sounded like a crime of passion. And then there was the part about Amanda using the information as leverage. Brie reflected on this. There was a side of the artist that was all too comfortable operating outside the law. No wonder she had been drawn into the black market art world in France. The danger and excitement of living on the edge had held some kind of fascination for her, and Brie feared this fascination had finally turned deadly.

Chapter 19

As Brie drove south along the road, she noticed the forest was in motion. *Wind picking up,* she thought. *Storm moving in.* Within a few minutes she cleared the edge of the spruce and followed the curve of the road toward the keeper's house. She saw John and Ben standing behind the house with a third man she didn't recognize. She parked the truck east of the house and climbed out. As she approached the men, she heard Ben say, "Here comes Brie now. This is perfect timing."

She was already pretty sure who she was about to meet, and she assessed the visitor as she approached. She estimated his age at mid-forties, and his height just shy of six feet. There was no doubt he would hold his own in a fray. He had a thatch of medium brown hair, cut short, but still unruly in the strong wind. His attire—jeans and hiking boots—indicated an unofficial visit. He had on a navy-blue windbreaker that concealed the gun she was certain he wore.

"Brie," Ben called, "there's someone here I want you to meet." As she came up next to him, he introduced her to the visitor. "This is Detective Dent Fenton of the Maine State Police. Dent, this is Brie Beaumont, on leave from the Minneapolis Police Department and here in Maine for the summer."

Brie extended her hand. "Pleased to meet you, Detective," she said, looking directly at him. He had welcoming blue eyes like the sky after a long gray spell, and her attention rested there for a moment before either of them spoke. *Intelligent eyes,* she thought. A protruding brow bone dominated his facial features, and juxtaposed with the intelligent eyes, created the incongruous impression of a being somewhere between primitive forest dweller and Ivy Leaguer. It may have been the brow bone that gave Brie the sense of something untamed in him, but her sense of it was strong.

"Nice to meet you, Brie, and call me Dent—'Detective' is for those who work with me." The clipped, rolling cadence of his speech branded him a native Mainer, and as he regarded her, his eyes warmed with a casual friendliness. But there was that tendency toward wariness in him, which she recognized — the ingrained wariness of a cop that seldom eases completely. She could hear it in his voice.

"Ben tells me you're with the homicide division," Brie said.

"That's right. We call it the CID—Criminal Investigation Division. The Maine State Police has two CID units that cover the entire state."

"It's a lot of territory to cover," Brie said. "Coming from a big city PD, my work is focused in just one community—crime rates being what they are in a large city."

"Portland and Bangor have their own police departments for that same reason, and the Maine State Police and county sheriffs cover the greater Maine area. Logistics are different, but I imagine the investigative side of our work is much the same."

"I've no doubt of that," Brie said.

"I have to say I was already familiar with your name from the case you solved out on Granite Island. Unfortunately, I was gone from headquarters the day you stopped in to file your report on the details of the case."

"Yes, I spoke with a Detective Dupuis. I believe his first name was Martin." She recalled the short fellow with the healthy mustache and twinkle in his dark eyes, who looked for all the world like he belonged back in the seventeen hundreds in a Montreal canoe with the voyageurs.

"That's right. Marty Dupuis—good detective." Dent Fenton shifted to parade rest and pulled a small notebook and pen from his jacket pocket. "So, there's been some excitement out here. John here's related the details of the fire, and Ben's said there's another issue you may want to fill me in on."

Before Brie could get started Ben said, "We'll be getting back to work and leave you and Brie to talk. If you've got time, I hope you'll stay for dinner down on the *Maine Wind*. George puts out some mighty tasty fare."

"Thanks, Ben, but I have to get back to the mainland. But next time you're up near Old Town, you give me a call. We'll put some fresh trout on the grill and really catch up."

"Roger that, Dent." Ben put a hand on Fenton's shoulder. "Dent here's quite a fly fisherman. You want the best trout dinner in Maine, it'll be at his house."

In response Dent lowered his head and scuffed the ground, which told Brie he was a humble man.

"We'll be inside if you need us," Ben said, and with that, he and John headed back toward the kitchen door.

"I'm glad you're here, Detective Fenton." He looked up and started to correct her. "Sorry, you said to call you Dent," she interjected. "Guess I'm just used to protocol."

"I understand," Fenton said.

"Interesting name you've got. Short for Denton?" Brie managed to say it with a straight face and level voice. It was an awkward name, like tripping on a sidewalk crack, but somehow Dent Fenton fit his asymmetrical appearance.

"I can hear that laugh trying to get a toehold."

"Sorry," Brie smiled. "So what's the story?"

"My dad always fancied himself a poet of the rhyming persuasion. He somehow managed to convince my mom that Denton was the perfect accompaniment for Fenton. So, here I am, Denton Michael Fenton. I don't know why they didn't just go with 'Michael' and call it a day. You can imagine how many 'Dent' jokes I've had to endure in my lifetime."

"Well, it's not as bad as Moontune," Brie offered. "I had a childhood friend named Moontune. No kidding. Her parents were hippies—the genuine article. You know there had to be some really corny conception story behind that one."

"Moontune what? I'm afraid to ask."

"Monahan," Brie said. "Moontune Monahan. Sounds like a character from the funny paper, doesn't it?" That brought a smile, and Brie again glimpsed a bit of the inner Dent Fenton. His were the eyes of an honest man—calm and clear, like the light that shines in the northern latitudes during the shortest days of the year. She liked him, and she was glad, because she had the odd feeling they would be working together somewhere down the line.

"So, tell me what's going on out here," Dent said, coming back to the topic at hand.

"Well, last night certainly wasn't a dull one, as you can see." She motioned toward the kitchen doorway, now just an open portal since the door had been removed. As she did so, Scott emerged carrying a charred piece of sheetrock.

"It's clearly arson—a real amateur job."

"I agree," Brie said. "I'd say it was a kid—a maladjusted one, of course—except for the fact that there's a woman missing from the island. Based on past experience, I'd say all the signs point to murder."

"Evidence?"

"Circumstantial—no signs of outward struggle—and then there's the fact that her boat is missing, and she's known to be something of a free spirit. She's an artist. Lives alone, comes and goes on a whim; doesn't always say where she's off to."

"When was she last seen?" Dent asked.

"Saturday morning. So, it's been about forty-eight hours."

"I'll get the information into the NCIC system today. Unless there's some strong evidence of foul play though, we may wait another twenty-four hours before launching a search, to see if she turns up."

"There's no hard evidence. Just an odd combination of circumstances along with some troubling incongruities at the artist's cottage, and of course, that gut sense. You know the one I mean." It felt good not to have to explain herself.

"I do know," Dent said. "So, fill me in."

"Well, the previous owner of the lighthouse property died out here about fifteen months ago."

"Really? How?"

"Fell down the stairs in the lighthouse one rainy night."

"There would have been an autopsy."

"There was," Brie said. "The COD was blunt force trauma —perfectly plausible with that kind of fall."

"The coroner rule it an accident, then?"

"Yup. It was raining that night. The supposition was he slipped on the metal stairs and took a header."

"Hmmm." Dent was quiet for a moment. "I wouldn't think anything of it, but now there's this arson attempt. Makes one wonder."

"Yup," was all Brie said, "plus the missing artist, Amanda Whitcombe."

Dent didn't respond immediately; he was busy scribbling notes in his small notebook. "Well, the arson boys were out here this morning and documented everything. There's an accelerant trail on the floor traveling out the door. It's clear that's the point of origin."

"I'd like to show you what I found at the artist's cottage."

"Let's go," Dent said, without hesitation. He placed the notebook and pen back in his pocket.

They headed for the pickup truck. She had been hesitant about meeting Ben's cop friend, but that reticence was gone. Dent Fenton had the measured approach of a veteran detective. *Here was a man she could work with.* It was the second time in ten minutes she'd had the same thought, and the ease with which it recurred surprised her. She climbed into the truck and turned over the ignition. *Don't get ahead of yourself, Brie,* she thought.

John applied the crowbar to the sheetrock with more force than needed, sending a chunk of it rocketing across the kitchen. He had felt the old feelings rise up inside him as Brie's eyes rested on Dent Fenton for what he thought was a bit too long. He asked himself again for the umpteenth time—*Why? Why this jealousy?* But for all the years he had been asking the question, he'd never felt he had found the right answer, and he knew he needed to. This part of him had destroyed a number of relationships in his adult life, and he didn't want Brie to be another casualty of what he considered his darker, or at least, more insecure side.

Jealousy was like a poison that gnawed its way into every fiber of a person's being. John *had* decided one thing: that the cure had to lie in discovering the cause. But he wasn't one to believe in counseling. The thought of sitting in front of some stranger baring his soul made his skin crawl.

Since the advent of Brie, though, he had started the search in earnest. In his quiet moments he had begun thinking about his childhood and teen years—something that was exquisitely painful. It was like a house he'd boarded up long ago that he now had to reenter, clean, sort, and label the contents. He had started writing his thoughts on the job in a notebook he kept under the pad of his berth on the *Maine Wind*. The interesting part was that as time progressed, he found himself writing more and more questions. At first he thought this was confusing him, but he had since learned that the questions seemed to open doors of thought in his mind—blaze some kind of new pathways in his brain.

He had begun to think in earnest about his mother and about his father's death when he was sixteen. And, oddly, inexplicably, the old wrenching feeling of fear had returned as he revisited that time in his life. Fear that he was inadequate to take care of his mother, now gone these fifteen years. It had been a terrifying time that had left little space to grieve for his father. He

245

had left school, and his father's friend, Joe Dorsey, had gotten him a job at the Bath Iron Works—better known as *the yard*. Looking back he realized he shouldn't have been there. It was no place for a boy. But his mother was already showing the devastating symptoms of MS. He had had no choice. Then two years down the line he had met Ben, who must have seen his desperate need for support—for a father figure.

After that, things got better. He managed to finish the work for his high school diploma and even took an occasional course through the community college system. And he began to date, but right away there were problems. The more he liked the girl, the worse the jealousy would be, until it poisoned everything. Eventually, he chose women he didn't care so much about, just so he wouldn't have to fight the battle. But the advent of Brie had started the old war once again. Those boyhood feelings of inadequacy had come surging back, and with them the feeling that he would never be what she truly wanted—never be enough.

During long nights with his notebook, he had worked some of this out and ultimately decided that not only might his discoveries be the truth, but the root of his problems. Yet he seemed to struggle with selective memory, and when he needed that knowledge most, it would drain from his brain like oil escaping an engine, and once again he would find himself seized with jealousy.

"Something wrong, John?" Ben had stopped working and was regarding him with questioning eyes.

"No, everything's fine," John said, trying for a level tone. He picked up the slab of blackened sheetrock and stalked out the door. He was determined to conquer this erosive part of himself—to be the man Brie deserved.

As Brie and Dent approached the sign for Puffin Point, Brie saw Doug McLeod striding along the road in their direction. He was wearing deck shoes and baggy shorts. His shirt hung open, revealing that here, indeed, was a fine specimen of masculine beauty. He was carrying a large bouquet of wild daises she guessed were intended for her. It was hard not to be flattered. She bit her lip to hide the involuntary smile. *This certainly is different from back home,* she thought. There was an elemental quality to the men here—maybe it was their proximity to and connection with the sea, or possibly their distance from big city life. Whatever it was, it made her feel a bit like a girl again, and she had decided to enjoy it.

She brought the truck to a halt alongside Doug. He leaned down to look at her. "I was just coming to visit you—see how things are going at the lighthouse. I guess I picked the wrong time." His eyes traveled past her and rested on Dent momentarily.

"This is Detective Dent Fenton of the Maine State Police," Brie said.

His eyes darted back to hers, and she saw a flash of wariness mixed with apprehension. "Is this about Amanda?" he asked.

"Amanda and other things." She didn't specify what the other things were, but noted that some of the color had drained from Doug's face at the mention of them.

He straightened up. "Has Amanda been located?"

"Not that I know of," Brie replied.

"Wendy's worried sick. She's sure something's happened, and well, I guess we're all wondering at this point."

"I feel sorry for Wendy, but about all we can do is hope Amanda's boat turns up," Brie said. "Unfortunately, it's a waiting game. But right now, I should get going."

"Oh, right." He shifted awkwardly. "These are for you." He handed the bouquet of daises in the window. "I thought you might like them."

"Thanks, Doug. That's very nice," Brie said, but she was also thinking, *More flowers to explain to John.* She set the bouquet on the bench seat beside her. Dent was staring out his side of the car, trying to be discreet, but she caught the hint of a smile on his face and thought, *Great. This makes me look really professional.*

Doug headed back in the direction he had come, and Brie turned the truck into the driveway that led to Amanda's cottage. She filled Dent in a little on the McLeods, telling him how the parents had died, and that Wendy had formed a close connection with Amanda. Inside the cottage, she pointed out the things that had raised her suspicions of foul play—the coffee pot, the drag marks, the missing contact. And she told him about waking and seeing lights on the night before last and wondering why, if Amanda had been there, she hadn't shut the windows against the rain. Dent had little to say but scribbled notes as she talked. Occasionally, he would smile and nod, which told her he might have reached the same conclusion that she was positing. Several times, from the corner of her eye, she caught him assessing her, and it was clear that he was weighing and measuring her conclusions about the supposed crime scene, although he said nothing.

After Brie stopped talking, Fenton continued writing notes and surveying the room for a few minutes. Brie drifted back to the bookcases on the far side of the great room, drawn once again to the two bronze castings of Amanda's—the lovers, and the mother and child. They emanated beauty and sadness all at once. She wasn't sure why, but she was haunted by them.

Brie jumped when Dent came up behind her. "Sorry," he said. "Didn't mean to startle you."

"Oh, it's okay. I just startle a bit easier than I used to."

"Ben said you'd been through a rough patch the past year and a half." He must have sensed that she felt awkward talking about it because he quickly moved on. "The missing boat presents a problem. If she's found at sea, the Coast Guard will have to investigate. I'm with you; I believe something happened here, but with the boat missing and without a body…"

"I understand," Brie said.

They left the cottage and headed back toward the lighthouse. "I'm going to contact the Coast Guard and tell them to be on the lookout for her boat. In the meantime, I'd like you to continue looking into the situation out here—unofficially, of course."

"That's been my plan," Brie said. "I just couldn't ignore my feelings about Amanda's cottage."

"No good detective could. You know, Brie, should you decide to stay in Maine, you might consider working with the Maine State Police. I think we could find a spot for a detective with your experience."

"Thanks, Detective. I'll give that some thought."

He fished in his jacket and produced a business card. "Call me if anything else develops out here," he said, and handed her the card.

Back at the lighthouse, Dent visited with Ben for a few more minutes before they headed down to the cove together.

John had come out the back door, and he and Brie walked around to the front of the house and stood looking out at the ocean. The blazing blue sea that had so captivated Brie when she visited the Sanders' house had faded to a lackluster gray, reflecting the now overcast sky. Since morning, the wind had shifted to the southeast, and it was starting to build.

John broke the silence. "That might be a good connection for you, were you ever to stay in Maine."

Brie looked at him for a long moment. "Thanks, John. It's something to consider." As he looked out to sea, she continued studying him, sensing there had been some kind of shift in him that had nothing to do with her liaison with Dent Fenton, and yet, somehow, everything to do with it.

Chapter 20

B rie had taken time to sit outside and have a sandwich with John before continuing the investigation, and she was trying hard to focus on him as they shared a bowl of fresh strawberries. But her mind kept returning to Amanda's cottage and the weight of responsibility she always felt in these situations. The clock was ticking, and she needed to find answers. John must have sensed the urgency she was feeling, because unexpectedly, he stood up and pulled her to her feet. He held her close for a moment. "You need to press on," he said. "Don't worry, there'll be time for us when all this is resolved." His words lifted a burden of guilt she'd been feeling about how the past couple of days had spun out.

Now, as she steered the truck along East Island Road, she was thinking again of the bronze castings at Amanda's cottage and the feelings of sadness and longing they evoked. They had a story to tell. She wished she knew what it might be. Suddenly, something Frannie Lemke had said the day before at the Scuttlebutt Café flashed into her mind, and with it an *aha* moment. The comment had been about Wendy McLeod and her friendship with Amanda. She recalled Frannie's words—"a motherless child and…" Frannie had paused mid-sentence, but now Brie was pretty sure how that sentence *should* have ended— "…and a childless mother." Amanda had had a child. She had been pregnant with Wade's child that summer on the island so many years ago. That was why the Whitcombes had left so suddenly; she was sure of it. She didn't know how or even if this might be connected to Amanda's disappearance, but it was a missing piece in the history of the artist's life that could now be put into place. And Frannie knew something about it, if Brie could just get her to reveal what that was. She stepped harder on the accelerator, eager to reach the Scuttlebutt Café.

Within a few minutes she entered the outskirts of Barnacle Bay and turned into the small lot behind the Scuttlebutt. She climbed the wooden stairs, stepped through the door of the café, and glanced around. Fudge was humming a sad little dirge as he wiped the table tops. He looked up when she came in, fixed her with his good eye, and offered a glum forecast. "Mark my words, lassie, there be a storm a-brewin'."

"Hello, Fudge. Good to see you again," Brie said. "I think you're right. The wind seems to be doing a tour of the compass."

"Aye, she's a-gonna blow. You mark my words." He went back to his task, lost in his own world.

The place was empty. Whoever had been in for lunch was gone now, which suited Brie fine. Frannie wouldn't be busy. She was a bit surprised that Fudge hadn't asked what she wanted, but it gave her the chance to seek out Frannie on her own. She headed toward the kitchen doorway at the other end of the bar, sneaking a peek at Gargantuan, king of the lobsters, on the way.

She paused at the swinging doors into the kitchen. Frannie was sitting on a high stool next to a granite-topped work counter, sipping a tall glass of iced tea. Brie knocked on the door frame to get her attention. "Hello, Frannie."

"Well hello, dearie," she said, warm and welcoming as usual. Brie hadn't been sure what to expect now that word was out she was a detective. Apparently, Frannie was unphased by it all.

"Come over and sit down, and I'll get you an iced tea."

Brie couldn't have hoped for a better turn of events. "Thanks, Frannie. I'd love one," she said.

Frannie went to the refrigerator and took out a pitcher of tea. She poured out a tall glassful and brought it over to the counter. Brie pulled up another stool.

"There's sugar and lemon here," she said, sliding forward a small tray. She smoothed her apron and sat down, looking at Brie as if she wanted to say something.

Brie beat her to it. "I know word's gone round the island that I'm a detective, Frannie."

"Well, there's no problem I can see with that." Frannie smoothed her apron with authority. "Maybe a detective's not such a bad thing considering no one seems to know where poor Amanda is."

"Frannie, you said something yesterday, and, well, it's come back to me after visiting with Harriet and after wondering about a pair of sculptures at Amanda's cottage. I hope you won't think I'm prying unnecessarily. I'm just trying to get a picture of Amanda's life and her history here on the island."

"What was it I said?"

"Well, you were talking about Amanda's relationship with Wendy McLeod, and you referred to Wendy as 'a motherless child,' and then you paused, and referred to Amanda as 'a good and caring woman.' But I had the impression you meant to say something else—that you were comparing them, one to another. That maybe what you meant to say was, 'a motherless child and a childless mother.' "

Frannie looked down at her hands in her lap, but said nothing.

Brie could see her struggling with some kind of decision, and so she continued. "Harriet told me about the Whitcombes coming here when Amanda was young, and about how Amanda and Wade Sanders fell in love that last summer they came to the island. She also said the family left suddenly that summer, and that Amanda never returned to the island until many years later. When I visited Amanda's cottage, I saw two castings she had created—one of a pair of lovers, and one of a mother and child. I find them mysteriously haunting; they are beautiful and sad and seem to reach out to you as if they want to tell a story. I guess those castings got me thinking about Wade and Amanda all those years ago and wondering if she wasn't pregnant with his child. I don't know what all this might have to do with her disappearance, but in my line of work I've learned that the more you know about a person's background, the more likely you are to solve any mystery surrounding them."

"If I thought that anything I could tell you could help Amanda in any way, I wouldn't hesitate." She looked up at Brie now. "It's just that I made a promise many years ago."

"And you've kept it all these years, haven't you?"

Frannie nodded.

"You need to ask yourself if the reason for keeping that secret still exists," Brie said. She could see Frannie considering this.

"I'm not sure it does," Frannie said, and then her demeanor changed. She straightened up like a weight had been lifted off her. She took a couple sips of her tea, gathering her resolve, and then began to tell the story.

"Amanda and I were girlhood friends. She was a year older than me, but that didn't matter. We were very close during those teen years. I think our friendship was even stronger because we only saw each other in the summer. It was like we had to cram a whole year of being friends into three months. But that last summer, I barely saw Amanda. She was always with Wade. Oh my, but those two were in love. And then Amanda came to see me one day near the beginning of August. She was crying and frantic. She said she thought she was pregnant. I didn't know what to say, and I remember we just hugged. I asked her if Wade knew, and she said 'no.' She was terrified of what her father would do to him. And then, within a week, the Whitcombes were gone. Amanda never even said good-bye to me." Frannie's voice caught at this last remark.

"That following winter was a hard one on the island, unusually cold and snowy, and I guess my mood matched the bleakness. I thought about Amanda all the time and wondered about the baby. I wrote to her time after time, but got no letters in return. My mom never said anything, but I'm sure she knew what was wrong— somehow moms always know those things. Anyway, she started sending me over to Grandma's on the weekends—supposedly to help her with cleaning. But Grandma's house was always neat as a pin, and so we spent those days baking and talking. That's when I learned to love the kitchen and all the magic that happened in it. I mastered all Grandma's recipes that winter." Frannie paused and smoothed her apron. "But you're wondering what this had to do with Amanda."

Brie smiled. "Go on," she said. "I know it's connected."

"Well, Grandma lived next to the Weatherbys back then— over on the west side of the island." Brie was trying to place the name, but Frannie pressed on. "Mrs. Weatherby, Joan was her name, was pregnant that winter. I must have said something to Grandma, only because Mrs. Weatherby seemed so old to me. You know how it is when you're eighteen; anyone over thirty seems ancient. And Mrs. Weatherby was closer to forty. Well, it wasn't like Grandma to gossip, but she confided in me that she didn't think Joan was pregnant at all. 'If you can hide a pregnancy you can certainly fake one,' she had said. I remember asking why you'd fake something like that, but she didn't say anything.

"It didn't take me long to put two and two together, though. From summer on, there had been rumors that the Whitcombes had arranged for someone they knew to take the child. I also heard rumors that Amanda never went home to New York with her family, but that she went to live with her grandmother in upstate Maine until the baby was born. And, in fact, that's what happened. It's the reason she never got any of my letters; she told me so herself when she came back to the island a few years ago." Frannie paused for a sip of tea.

"As the months went on, the speculation kind of died down. There were a number of women on the island pregnant that winter. But I knew when Amanda's baby would have been due. And after Grandma's remarks I paid close attention to the Weatherbys. Back then we had a doctor and a midwife on the island. It was rare for a woman to go to the mainland to have her baby. But that's what Joan Weatherby did, and that clinched it for me, because it was right around the time I knew Amanda would have had the baby.

When they came back to the island with the child, I told Grandma what I thought. She said there was a good chance I was right, and then she got out her Bible and made me swear on it that I'd never tell anyone. She said it wasn't fair to the child. And I kept that promise till now. But I owe my first loyalty to Amanda, and if any of this will help you find out where she is, then I'm glad I've told you the story."

"Were the Weatherbys good to the child?"

"It's hard to say. They seemed like harsh parents to me, especially Mrs. Weatherby. I always wondered if she had been hoping for a girl. And, of course, there would be no brothers or sisters for poor little Bob. I think he was a lonely child. You know, the good Lord has reasons for things, and maybe those two just weren't meant to be parents, because they sure didn't seem to take to it."

"Did you say the child's name was Bob?" Brie asked.

"That's right," Frannie said.

"Bob Weatherby who owns the bait shop is Amanda's son?"

"Yes, he is."

Brie didn't know why she was stunned, but she was. This was a giant piece of information. "Does he know he's Amanda's son?" she asked.

"Yes, he does," Frannie said, smoothing her apron. "Amanda told him shortly after she moved back to the island. I questioned whether it was the right thing, but Amanda was set on it. She said she'd never have another child, and she was determined to know her son."

"Does he know who his father is?"

"Nooo. Amanda refused to tell him. I don't really know why, but that put a division between them right away. Maybe Amanda didn't want to cause problems for Wade's family."

"But she had an affair with Wade when she came back here. Seems that wouldn't be too good for his family." Brie wasn't one hundred percent sure of this, but decided ninety-nine percent was good enough, and so she put it out there.

"Yes, but she's also the one who ended it. She told me she couldn't do that to his little boys. I think she thought they deserved the father her son never had. It broke Wade's heart though—a second time. I don't think he'd ever stopped loving Amanda in all those years."

Brie thought about the situation, and surprisingly, her heart softened toward Wade Sanders. She wondered if that sense of lasting loss could, over time, morph into the kind of anger and meanness that seemed to define him. She also wondered if Amanda had been right in never telling him about their son.

"When I talked to Bob yesterday about Amanda, I sensed no warmth in him toward her. And he certainly never mentioned she was his mother. In fact, I thought he said some harsh things about her."

"Oh, he liked what Amanda could do for him. She set him up in that business. But he never showed her any affection as far as I could see, and I think that broke her heart."

"Are the Weatherbys still on the island?" Brie asked.

"Oh, no. Not for many years," Frannie said. "Mrs. Weatherby died about ten years ago, and Mr. Weatherby moved off island the year after that."

"Frannie, thank you for telling me all this."

"I don't know how it can help."

"Well, that remains to be seen," Brie said. "But I should be going. Thanks so much for the tea, Frannie."

A warm smile lit her round face. "You're welcome, dearie," she said.

Brie smiled. To Fudge and Frannie she had become "dearie" and "lassie." She had been told more than once that Maine islanders were standoffish, but she wasn't sure she believed it. Here was proof to the contrary, and Harriet seemed to negate that theory as well. What was more, she had found helpful people on Granite Island during the trouble there.

Frannie walked with her, back out into the café. Brie was saying good-bye to her and Fudge when the door burst open and Spencer Holloman stepped through. His face was serious and he wasted no time delivering the news. "Amanda's boat has been found adrift near Marshall Island with no one aboard." His voice caught on the last part, and he cleared his throat to try and collect himself. He stood for a moment looking from one to the other of them. "The Coast Guard is beginning a search of the area," he said. "I'm just trying to let folks know around the island." He didn't mention anything to Brie about her being a detective, although she was certain he would have heard about it. This news may have dwarfed any other concerns for the moment. Before she could say anything, he turned to leave. He mumbled something as he headed out the door, but Brie didn't hear it.

Brie turned to Frannie and Fudge. Frannie looked stricken. She had sat down at one of the tables and was staring at her hands in her lap. Fudge had come over to comfort her and stood next to her, an arm around her shoulder, gently patting her. Brie squatted down in front of her. "I'm so sorry, Frannie," she said.

"I think we all feared something like this," she said, almost in a whisper. "Something's just not right with it." She shook her head slowly. "We've all heard what Charlie said about her boat leaving in the middle of the night. Amanda would never do anything like that." A sob escaped from her, and she foraged in her pocket for a tissue as the tears started down her face.

"I'm going to do the best I can to find out what happened to her," Brie said.

"Thank you, lassie," Fudge said softly. He was more lucid than Brie had seen him—his pirate demeanor temporarily gone. He sat down next to Frannie, took her hand, and rubbed it gently. Brie had begun to feel like an intruder. She gave Frannie's other hand a pat, stood up, and left the café quietly. She was feeling sad too—sadness for a woman she had come to know, but now would never meet.

Chapter 21

B rie sat in the truck next to the Scuttlebutt Café for a few minutes. She pulled the small notebook and pen from her pocket and jotted down some of the key things Frannie had said, along with some of her own thoughts. Adam Blake had been her most likely suspect since he was Amanda's lover. Wade Sanders ran a distant second. She could easily imagine Wade having a motive to kill Harold, since something had developed between Harold and Summer Sanders, but it was nearly impossible for her to imagine him killing Amanda. Now there was this startling information about Bob—that he was Amanda and Wade's son. She tried to conjure up what resemblance the rather short, pony-tailed man had to either of them, and realized that he had the very same green eyes as Wade. And now that she reflected on it, there might also be a facial resemblance—the same carved jaw line and cleft chin. Amanda's most distinguishing feature was her voluminous, wavy red hair. Bob's hair, though dark, was wavy like hers.

She slowly accepted the information as truth, but still it came as a shock. She didn't know why she was surprised. People's lives held unexpected secrets. It reminded her of the crayon drawings she had made as a child, where she would color all kinds of bright colors on a sheet of paper and then cover the whole thing with black crayon. With her fingernail, she would scratch out a design. The colors would come blazing through that black layer, unexpectedly brilliant in contrast to it.

Detective work had always reminded her of those drawings. Scratch the surface of anyone's life, and you'll often be amazed at what jumps out.

Bob had unexpectedly moved to the top of Brie's suspect list, and she now considered what she had learned about him that would go to motive. Harold's journals had revealed that he and Bob had become good friends. Maybe Harold had confided in Bob—told him about the comings and goings of the two boats, *Deep Blue* and *Emily Ann*. Brie guessed Harold had done his research on the *SS Ulysses*, or maybe Amanda, in some offhand way, had inadvertently mentioned something about the sunken ship. Maybe she had even thought of bringing Harold into their circle. Maybe Bob had felt threatened by Harold's sniffing around the edges of whatever they were up to. Maybe they had gotten into a heated argument, and one thing had led to another. Maybe that was why Amanda wouldn't reveal who she had seen atop the lighthouse with Harold that stormy night. She was trying to protect her son. *Maybe, maybe, maybe.* Brie let out a sigh. She rolled down the driver's side window and propped her elbow on the frame. She was getting way ahead of herself. All this was wild conjecture until she had some solid proof of what *the group* was up to.

She focused on what she knew for sure. First, Harold had undoubtedly been murdered by whomever Amanda had seen arguing with him at the top of the lighthouse the night before he was found dead. Second, Amanda had refrained from passing this information on to the police, for whatever reason. Third, there was a small cabal of people on the island that Spencer Holloman had referred to as *the group*, and said *group* was up to something secretive—possibly illegal. Fourth, the name *SS Ulysses* was written in Harold's journal, and Brie had learned the story of the ill-fated ship from Harriet. And finally, Amanda had been murdered—of that Brie was certain.

She reflected on the other obvious aspect of Bob's motive. He hated Amanda. He hated her for abandoning him—maybe blamed her for an unhappy childhood. Amanda may have confronted him about killing Harold, and that could have been the final straw. *More conjecture.* She put her pen and notebook in her pocket and fired up the engine. She turned right out of the Scuttlebutt parking lot and headed for Bob's Bait Shop. An uneasy feeling clutched at her stomach. She took it as a sign she was closing in on the truth.

Down near the harbor she pulled into the small parking area next to the bait shop. To her right was a brand new Ford F150. It was polished to a black mirror finish, and custom-painted red flames licked the sides of the truck's bed. *That had to have cost plenty,* Brie thought, and she remembered Frannie's comment about Bob—"He liked what Amanda could do for him." She turned off the truck, and as she opened the door, a gust of wind caught it, jerking it from her hand. The leading edge of the approaching weather system had overtaken the island, and the heavy, dull sky had turned the ocean gunmetal gray. The wind was bullying its way into the northeast, and the seas were building, starting to roll. Fudge's prediction played in Brie's mind like a dissonant little melody: "She's a-gonna blow."

Brie climbed two wood steps, paused a moment to peer through the screen door, and then stepped into the bait shop. "Hello," she called out but got no answer. She walked across the shop to the windows that fronted on the harbor. Several lobsterboats rocked uneasily at their moorings, waiting for the approaching weather. A door banged in the back room, and she turned as Bob appeared in the doorway behind the register. He had a wary expression, which told her he'd heard the news about her being a cop. But she was more interested in whether he had heard about Amanda's boat being found and what his response would be. Before she could say anything he spoke.

"So, it seems you weren't completely forthcoming with me the other day."

"A quality I share with most of the rest of the human race, I'd say. Yes, back in my real life, I'm a cop—a homicide detective, to be more specific." As she said this, Brie watched him carefully for any signs of agitation or emotion. "And, yes, there was more to my first visit than just trying to help Wendy McLeod. I felt something bad had happened to Amanda. I still do."

Bob gave no response to that, but Brie sensed hostility mounting in him, threatening as the oncoming weather.

"Have you heard about Amanda's boat being found?"

Bob lowered his head. "I've heard," he said in a low voice, and even though she had walked across the store to get closer to him, it was hard to read his expression. "Something like this was bound to happen. She wasn't careful about what she did."

Brie wondered if he really believed that or knew a very different truth. She pressed on. "Do you have any reason to think this might not have been an accident?" she asked.

"You mean like someone planned it—someone killed her? Who would do that?"

Brie studied him with unswerving eyes, trying to divine whether the question was rhetorical or not.

"Oh, I get it. You think it was me." He stepped from behind the counter and his eyes flashed with anger. "You've been talking to people, so you know, don't you?"

"Know what?"

"You know *what!*" he shouted. He moved menacingly toward her, but Brie stood her ground. She had to see what he'd do next. If she appeared scared, it would change the dynamic. He stopped no more than six inches from her. "That she was my mother," he spat at her.

The shop fell unnaturally silent, as if all the air had been sucked out, and the two of them now resided in a vacuum—one with explosive potential. Bob glared at her for what felt like a small eternity, so charged was the space between them. Suddenly, he jerked away, as if breaking free from a strong magnetic field. He stalked to the side window that looked out at the harbor.

After a few moments, Brie turned toward him and spoke. "Yes, I know she was your mother. I'm sorry."

"What makes you think I care? And what makes you think she's dead? She could be alive. Maybe she fell overboard in the storm that night. She could have made it to shore."

Brie was interested in the fact that he had mentioned the storm that took place the night Amanda died. The killer would have been keenly aware of the storm—would have used it to his advantage.

"If she'd made it to shore, I think someone would have heard from her," Brie said.

"There are over six thousand islands in the Gulf of Maine—many of them with no inhabitants. It's possible she could be on one of them with no way to let anyone know."

"The Coast Guard has mounted a search," Brie said.

Bob turned away when she said this, so she couldn't see his expression, but he gave the sense of an extremely conflicted human being, almost as if there might be two people inside him, each vying for control. Either he had killed Amanda and was trying to hide his guilt or he was struggling with the loss of a woman—his mother—whom he had chosen to push away. Or, bizarre as it seemed, maybe both were true—ambivalence carried to the extreme. Brie had seen it all before. Whatever the truth was, she felt uneasy around him, and she took note of that uneasiness. As for his Gilligan's Island scenario—Amanda falling overboard and somehow making it to shore—Brie knew that hadn't happened, and she wondered if Bob Weatherby didn't know the exact same thing.

She studied the back of his head, the dark, wavy hair secured in a short ponytail. He'd be remaining at the top of her suspect list. The feeling of uneasiness had deepened. She knew this feeling. There was something she was missing, possibly something right in front of her. Sometimes the sensation left her feeling like she had swallowed glass, but Brie knew this gut instinct was her friend, her ally—more than once it had saved her life. Just once it had abandoned her—she would always wonder why. After the long, dark year she had just been through, she was learning to trust that instinct once again.

"I'm going to find out what happened to Amanda," she said.

Bob didn't turn around, and whether he took it as a warning or a promise, she had no way of knowing. Brie had nothing more to say to him, so she left the bait shop. There was only one thing she knew for sure—it was time to start watching her back.

Chapter 22

As Brie walked back to the truck, a chill ran through her. The wind off the sea was cold, but she knew this sensation—knew it wasn't caused by the weather. She opened the driver's door, grabbed her jacket, and pulled it on. As she backed out onto the road next to the bait shop, she looked toward the harbor. She spotted Adam Blake heading down the long dock where the skiffs were tied off. She pulled to the side of the road and watched him. He climbed into one of the skiffs, released the painter, and pushed off. He rowed out to one of the moored lobsterboats and climbed aboard. Brie knew he was heading for the mainland to pick up his wife. He would be gone for a few hours. This was the opportunity she'd been waiting for—a chance to get aboard his schooner and see what she could find.

She headed toward East Island Road, but as she passed the library she decided to pull in and check on something. She mounted the small flight of steps and entered the library. Birdie Holloman was at the big front desk, and she started as Brie stepped through the door.

"I'm sorry if I startled you," Brie said. She noticed Birdie's eyes were red and knew she would have gotten the news about Amanda.

"Oh, it's all right," she said. "I guess I was lost in my thoughts."

"I've heard the news of Amanda's boat. I know it's a hard day for everyone here who cared about her," Brie said. "I'm very sorry."

Birdie just nodded and dabbed her eyes with a tissue she had retrieved from her sweater pocket. Brie thought she looked exhausted.

"We'll be leaving the island tomorrow, and I just wanted to see how late the library will be open today. I need to return the book I borrowed."

Birdie looked surprised at Brie's statement, as if she expected her to stay, now that Amanda was officially missing. They had, in fact, been planning to stay one more day and sail back to the mainland on Wednesday, but the fire at the keeper's house had changed their plans.

"I guess I thought with all that's happened, you'd be staying longer." Birdie sounded almost disappointed.

"Well, I work for Captain DuLac, and he has a cruising schedule to maintain. When he and the *Maine Wind* leave, so do I."

"I guess I just thought..." Her voice trailed off, and she didn't finish her sentence.

"Now that Amanda has gone missing at sea, the Coast Guard will take over. They will need to determine what has happened to her."

"Of course," was all Birdie said. "Well, I'm always here late on Monday night. It's Spencer's poker night, and I like to work here while he's at the game."

"I thought the game might be cancelled tonight, what with the bad news," Brie said.

"It's always best to stick with routine at such times, I think. Don't you? Keeps your mind off the situation."

"I guess so," Brie said tentatively.

Birdie turned back to her work, as if continuing the discussion was just too much for her. Brie understood how she felt—she had been through enough months where just the thought of having to talk to people had drained her of her vital force. She thanked Birdie and left the library quietly. She hadn't wanted to linger, anyway, since this would be her only chance to check out Adam Blake's schooner. She climbed in and fired up the truck, eager to see what secrets *Deep Blue* might hold.

She followed the road out of Barnacle Bay. When she came to the McLeods' place, she craned her neck to see if there was any sign of Wendy. She knew she should stop and talk to the girl, but right now she was intent on taking advantage of Adam Blake's absence from the island. As she neared the drive to his place, she saw John on foot heading in her direction. She waved through the windshield and accelerated slightly to close the gap between them. She pulled up beside him and he climbed into the truck.

"Is something wrong, John?"

"No. We've just gone as far as we can. Ben has to wait for the insurance people at this point. I needed to stretch my legs, so I thought I'd walk into the village and see if I could find you." John was eyeing the bouquet of flowers on the seat next to Brie. "Dent Fenton feel the urge to pick flowers?"

Brie gave him the evil eye and the silent treatment. She had no intention of commenting on the flowers or how they'd gotten there. She set them down on the floor of the truck, where they would be less obvious, and told John the news about Amanda's boat being found and also about Bob being Amanda's son.

John shook his head. "This is getting more and more complicated."

"When I was in the village, I saw Adam Blake leaving the island. I was just heading for his place to check out *Deep Blue*."

"In that case, I found you just in time," he said. "I wouldn't want you doing that alone. Too dangerous with everything that's gone on here so far."

"I guess you're right," she said. She would have boarded the schooner by herself without thinking twice, but she was not averse to having John's help. Together, they'd be able to search the ship more quickly and have less the risk of being discovered. She put the truck in gear and continued along the road to Blake's driveway, where she turned left.

She approached the house cautiously in case anyone was there. The place looked abandoned, so they parked the truck behind the house and got out. Brie went to the door and knocked, just to be sure no one was watching the place while Blake was away.

"All clear," she said to John.

"Are you sure about this, Brie? I don't like boarding someone else's vessel like this."

"Here's the thing, John. Harold was onto something going on on the island that involved both Amanda and Blake's schooner *Deep Blue*. Now Harold and Amanda are both dead, and while their deaths may not relate to what Harold recorded in his journal, I think we have to find out as much as we can." Brie stopped and turned to face him. "After what I overheard at the meeting in the library, I'm thinking Blake may have been headed for some kind of rendezvous last night when we spotted him from the *Maine Wind*. If he was planning to deliver something, he didn't get the chance, which means it may still be aboard his ship."

"I guess if no one had died, it'd be different."

"Listen, John, I wouldn't give a hoot what they're up to out here, except for the fact that people are dying. And while their deaths may appear accidental to the casual onlooker, I know better." She turned and continued down to the shore and out a short dock, where a small skiff was tied off.

They climbed in and John set the oars and began to row toward the schooner. The low, gray canopy of sky hung ominously above them, and a petulant wind, building in the northeast, caused him to pull harder on his starboard oar. *Deep Blue* was a sleek-looking vessel with a bald-head rigging. Brie figured John might be feeling a pang of jealousy that Blake could own such a boat and not have to be involved in the commercial windjammer trade. She knew John loved the *Maine Wind*, but the life of a windjammer captain got tedious by the end of a season. The endless turnover of passengers, dealing with the inclement weather that was inevitable on the Maine coast, and trying to keep everyone aboard happy. Their eyes met and neither spoke, but Brie could pretty much read his thoughts.

"It'd be nice to just sail away, wouldn't it?" she said. "No having to be back to port every four to six days just to reload and head back out."

"Sure would, but who's got that kind of money?"

"Obviously Adam Blake does. The question is, where does he get it? And did the threat of losing it, maybe through divorce, turn him into a killer?"

"I guess we're about to get some answers." John shipped the oars and they floated up to the starboard side of *Deep Blue*. There was no ladder, but by standing on the seat of the skiff, John was able to boost himself over the gunwale. He found the boarding ladder and lowered it to Brie. She tied the skiff's painter to the ladder and climbed aboard *Deep Blue*.

They wasted no time above decks. Whatever they were looking for would be below. They descended the forward companionway and found themselves in a tidy galley complete with wood stove.

"I have a feeling whatever we're looking for is going to be stowed aft," John said. They climbed back on deck and headed for the stern of the ship, where a second companionway led below. At the foot of the ladder, on the starboard side, was a chart table and navigation center with a full array of instruments and a radio. Directly across from this was the ship's head. Beyond the navigation center was the saloon—the main area of the ship for gathering and socializing. *Deep Blue's* interior was fitted out with teak, which lent warmth and coziness to the space. The vessel was well built, and based on the careful appointing of the interior, obviously well loved.

Danger Sector

Brie and John began their search in all the obvious places, checking equipment lockers, cabinets, and storage areas under the settees in the saloon. As they searched, Brie related Harriet's story of the sinking of the *SS Ulysses* and its cargo of gold, originally bound for the South immediately after the Civil War. She also told him of Eva Whitcombe's involvement in marine archeology and her attempts to locate the sunken vessel. "I believe Amanda Whitcombe took up the search after her mother died. What's more, I think they found the *Ulysses*, John, and I think they're salvaging her cargo and selling it on the black market, using Amanda's former connections in France. The question is, why not do it on the up and up? Why all the cloak and dagger?"

"I don't know," John said, "but I'm guessing they didn't want to share the profits with the state or anyone else. There could also be insurance claims or descendents of the original passengers who could lay claim to the gold. I remember reading about this ship, the *SS Central America*, and how its treasure of gold coin and gold bars worth tens of millions was tied up in legal battles for ten years. Between the costs of bringing up the treasure and fighting for years in court to keep it, the company that discovered the shipwreck and salvaged the treasure actually thought they might lose money on the venture."

"Hmm," Brie said, mulling over what she had just heard. "That would be incentive enough for Amanda and her cronies to keep their operation on the down low."

"If the *Ulysses* sank in shallow enough water so they could dive on the wreck, and little by little recover the cargo…well, think of the profits." John was on his hands and knees now, trying the floorboards, seeing if he could find access to the hollow area beneath the cabin sole.

"I believe that's exactly how it played out, with Amanda putting together a hand-picked team of people she trusted—*the group*. We just need to find the proof. Then we'll know Harold wasn't crazy—that he was onto their comings and goings."

"More important, if we can find any of the treasure, we'll have evidence, and a concrete motive that could have led one of them to kill him," John said.

"Now you're thinking like a cop," Brie said. "If Harold was murdered, it shouldn't go unpunished. I'm still not sure why Amanda would have been murdered when she was the ringleader, but I know the two deaths have to be connected."

"I don't think there's anything here," John said, standing up.

Brie had walked aft and ducked into a stern cabin accessed from behind the navigation center on the starboard side of the ship. It contained a sleeping berth running abeam that was big enough to accommodate two people. The berth was covered with a colorful quilt, and brass-fitted portholes let light into the cabin. She heard John climb the companionway ladder, and a few moments later he called down to her.

"There's a lazarette behind the helm. I'm going to check it out."

Brie headed up the ladder just in time to see John disappear through a hole at the back of the ship. She walked aft, stepped around the hatch for the lazarette, knelt down, and peered into the shadowy space. The small hold was tucked between the decks of the ship, and except for where the hatch opened onto the deck, John had to stoop to move around in the confined area. Most of the windjammers had a similar space, usually used on voyages to store wood for the stove, but sometimes used as berth space for crew.

"See anything?" she asked.

"Not yet. Just letting my eyes get acclimated," John said.

Brie placed her hands on opposite sides of the opening and lowered herself into the hold. Just as she prepared to drop, John turned and caught her by the waist so she came down directly into his arms.

"Well, hi there," he said, holding her against him. "Nice of you to join me."

"I thought you needed company." Brie put her arms around his neck and kissed him gently on the lips.

"Sometimes I like the position your work puts us in." He pulled her closer, and they stood in the small space with their arms entwined for a few moments.

Brie smiled to herself because she felt the same way. Moments like this, that held an edge of danger, could be quite intoxicating when shared with John. What was more, being aboard *Deep Blue* reminded her that soon they'd be returning to their regular routine on the *Maine Wind*, and chances for romantic moments would be scarce.

A gust of wind swirled down the hatch, and they looked up at the sky. "We're in for a good blow before the night is over," John said.

Brie studied his neck, wanting to kiss it, but she knew this wasn't the time or place. "Let's see what's down here," she said, gently extricating herself from his arms.

The hold was partially filled with crates and boxes containing wood, tools, extra line, and canned goods, but nothing that resembled salvage from a hundred-and-fifty-year-old ship. John was moving things about, checking for openings in the floorboards, while Brie worked her way around the walls of the lazarette, tapping and prying at the boards, checking for anything that might indicate an opening or hidden space. Suddenly, she stopped and went back a few feet, tapping the wall, and then moved forward again. The sound had changed.

"John, over here! It sounds like there might be a hollow space behind this wall."

John moved over next to her and tapped on the wall. "I think you're right."

They tried moving the boards up and down to see if they could slip them free, but no luck. Brie was tracing her fingers along the seams between the boards, applying pressure, feeling for any irregularities, but came up empty. "This has to be it," she said, frustrated. She started going over the seams again, and sure enough, at the bottom of one of the boards, she felt something give. There was a faint click, and a panel, approximately twenty-four inches square, sprung open. Brie gave John a high five and then peered into the opening. The space was filled with small, sturdy wooden boxes, each about the size of a twelve-pack of beer. The lids were nailed on. Small handholds were cut on opposite sides of each box.

John reached in and lifted one of the boxes out of the space. "It's heavy," he said. He looked around the space for something to pry the lid off. In one of the boxes of tools he found a small crowbar. He worked it around the edge of the crate, and each nail protested with a loud squawk as it was pried from the wood. Brie sat expectantly on her haunches as John worked the lid free and removed it. They both peered in. The top of the box was filled with thin sheets of Styrofoam packing. Brie lifted them out and gasped at what she saw.

The box was filled with gold coins. Each one had been carefully cleaned and placed in a plastic sleeve to protect it. She picked one of them up and studied it. It was a twenty-dollar gold Liberty dated 1861. She checked more of them and found they all bore the same date. "These are in perfect condition," she said, astonished. "Probably never circulated. They could be worth thousands of dollars apiece." She looked up at John.

"More than enough to kill for, wouldn't you say?"

"Without a doubt. I wish I had my camera. We really need to get a picture of this."

"I saw a small digital camera in one of the cabinets when we were searching the saloon. There were a couple extra SD cards with it. What do you think?"

"I think you're a genius." She leaned over and kissed him.

"I'll be right back." John boosted himself out of the lazarette and went to retrieve the camera.

Brie hauled several more boxes out from behind the wall and began prying the tops off so they'd have a better representation of what was being salvaged from the *Ulysses*. John arrived back with the camera and helped her get the lids off the other boxes. Each of them contained gold coins identical to the ones in the first box.

"It looks like they're only salvaging the gold," Brie said. "The artifacts from the wreck would have to be worth a lot, too."

"Maybe they're saving those for last," John said. "Compared to the gold, their value would have to be minimal."

"They'd be rich in archeological importance, though," Brie said. "But maybe Amanda didn't care about that. After all, it was her mom who was the archeologist."

"That's the problem with lots of marine salvage operations. They don't care enough about the historic importance of what they damage or leave behind."

Brie didn't comment, but rather started moving the boxes together to snap some pictures. She was eager to get off the ship as soon as possible. When she was done, she removed the SD card from the camera and put it in her jacket pocket, and John started hammering the lids back on. They strong-armed the boxes back into their hiding place, and looked around them to be sure nothing was out of order. John boosted himself out of the lazerette and gave Brie a hand up. They replaced the hatch, and John took the camera back down to the saloon. Brie climbed down to the skiff. John pulled the ladder up after she had descended, and put it back where he had found it. Then he went over the starboard gunwale the same way he had gotten aboard, using muscle only.

As they rowed for shore, Brie was silent, wondering how their discovery, other than confirming what she had come to believe, actually furthered her investigation. An angry gust of wind rocked the skiff. Brie looked at John, glad he couldn't read her thoughts—know what she knew. What she knew was that a person who had killed twice would have few qualms about killing again.

Chapter 23

B rie and John tied Blake's skiff off to the dock and made their way back to the truck.

"Want me to drive?" John asked.

"Sure," Brie said. She fished the keys out of her jeans and tossed them to him. "We need to stop by Harriet's place. She will have heard about Amanda."

"That's fine," John said.

They headed back down Blake's driveway and turned left onto East Island Road. Brie pulled her lucky rope from her jacket pocket and worked the line into a Carrick Bend. Her eyes drifted to the bouquet of flowers on the floor. She hadn't even considered Doug McLeod as a suspect. *Why not?* she asked herself. *Was it because of his overtures toward her?* No, that was ridiculous. She could never be blinded by something so transparent. She knew the reason. He was Wendy's brother, and in her mind, he could never have killed the woman Wendy had made into a mother figure. But Brie could conceive of a very reasonable motive. Maybe Doug needed the money from the smuggling operation to raise Wendy—send her to college. Maybe Harold's snooping had jeopardized that. *But killing Amanda. Why? Wouldn't he be shooting himself in the foot?* It just didn't make sense. But Brie reminded herself that murder often didn't.

Just before they got to Puffin Point, John turned right and headed across the island. "You're awfully quiet over there," he said.

"There's something I'm missing," Brie said. She stuffed her rope back into her pocket. "I need to go back to Harold's journals. I fell asleep last night before I could finish the last one. Then, after all the excitement with the fire, I never gave them another thought." She was thinking about them now, though. She could picture them sitting on her berth back at the ship.

"Do you think there might be something there? Something important?"

"Probably not. But it's a stone I haven't turned."

"Well, it'll be time to head back to the *Maine Wind* after we stop at Harriet's. The rest of the guys were going back to the ship when I started for the village. George is planning some kind of a dinner extravaganza. I think he said something about Italian."

Brie's stomach started to rumble at the mention of George's cooking. The small sandwich she'd eaten with John on the bluff in front of the keeper's house was long gone.

"I was thinking about Doug McLeod and whether I've considered him carefully enough."

"You mean for the murders?"

"No, for a future liaison—of course for the murders."

"Lover boy falls from grace," John muttered to himself.

"What was that?" Brie asked.

"Nothing. Just wondering why you're raising the alert level on him."

Brie shared her thoughts briefly on why Doug might be a suspect. But they had arrived at Harriet's driveway, and she decided not to pursue the topic right then. John pulled up beside the wood pile. Fudge's battered red jeep was parked ahead of them.

"Frannie must be here with Harriet," Brie said. "I'm so glad she's not alone."

They walked around to the front door and knocked. Within a few seconds Frannie opened the door and spoke in a hushed voice. "I came over to Harriet's right after you left the Scuttle-butt. I knew how terrible this would be for her," she said.

"Is she okay?" Brie asked.

"I think so. After we talked for awhile, she seemed to be doing better. She just went to take a nap about twenty minutes ago. Poor thing. She's a strong lady. But how much can one bear? Especially at her age."

"We don't want to disturb her," Brie said. "We just wanted to be sure she wasn't alone with the news about Amanda."

"That's very kind of you, Brie," Frannie said in her affection-ate way. "I'll be sure to tell her you came by when she wakes up."

"Thanks, Frannie. We'll be going then." She and John re-traced their steps to the truck. There was nothing else to be done, so they headed back toward the lighthouse.

As they drove free of the forest and approached the house, they saw Doug McLeod leaning against a pickup truck.

"Well, speak of the devil," John said.

"I wonder what he wants," Brie mused.

"I'll refrain from any snide comments even though several spring to mind."

They parked the truck behind the house and got out. John headed inside.

"What's up, Doug?" Brie asked as she walked toward him.

Doug was holding a thick leather-bound book that meas-ured approximately ten inches by seven inches. When he spoke, the confidence he normally exuded had evaporated, and he ac-tually appeared much younger to Brie than he had in previous encounters. "Have you ever gotten involved in something— maybe out of ignorance or even greed—and later wished you hadn't?" he asked. "But by then it's too late—too late to extricate yourself."

"I can't say I have," Brie admitted truthfully.

"I should have given this to you as soon as Amanda disap-peared, but I kept thinking everything was all right. That she'd turn up and no more questions would be asked. But now her boat's been found, and she's missing, presumed dead, although I haven't said that to Wendy. And to top it off, I find out you're a police detective." Doug paused and looked at her as if he hoped she'd pick up the ball, but Brie just continued regarding him from a place of neutrality.

After a few seconds he continued. "I stopped by Adam Blake's this afternoon to talk to him, see if he was as worried about the situation as I am. He was gone, but your truck was there, and when I walked down to the shore, I saw the skiff had been taken. I knew you'd gone aboard *Deep Blue*. I don't know what you know, but I need to tell you what's going on here. I don't know what difference it can make at this point, but I'm tired of all the subterfuge. I wanted out of the operation a while ago, for Wendy's sake."

"What operation?" Brie asked, even though she already knew.

"We've been salvaging treasure from a sunken ship—the *SS Ulysses*. The ship sank just after the Civil War in a bad hurricane that carried it north and into these waters. Amanda's mother had done all the preliminary research on it years ago. When she died, Amanda inherited all that research. She put together a team of eight people on the island to continue the search. We ultimately found the ship in the exact area her mother had predicted it should be. But that's when the bad decisions began." He paused and looked sheepishly at Brie.

"Go on," she said. She wanted him to tell the whole story voluntarily. It would play out better for him, and ultimately for Wendy, if he did.

"Well, there are certain channels you need to go through in these situations. Amanda knew what they were, but convinced *the group* that we could salvage the treasure and no one would be the wiser, and all of us would be a lot richer."

"What should have been done?" Brie asked.

"Well, first of all, there are certain circumstances in which a state can lay claim to a shipwreck. Amanda told us what those were: if the wreck lies within the state's territorial waters—three miles from any coastline—or if the sunken vessel is embedded in the ocean floor. If the wreck doesn't fall into either of those categories, then those doing the salvaging have to bring the case to court. That gives owners of the property or insurance companies the opportunity to come forward and lay claim to the salvaged goods. The court determines a reward amount that the salvagers are entitled to." Doug stopped and looked at Brie to see if she was following all of this.

"Go on," she said.

"The problem is, the process can take years to be resolved, and in the meantime the salvagers are left to cover the costs of the operation. It's a complicated system, and well, Amanda convinced us to skip the whole process. I was the youngest one in the group, so I had the least to say."

"You could have bowed out," Brie said. "For Wendy's sake."

"She was the main reason I went along with it. With our folks gone, I was worried I couldn't provide everything she needed. And I've made sure she doesn't know anything about our operation."

"You may believe that, Doug, but my guess is she knows a lot more than you think."

Doug lowered his head and scuffed the ground with his work boot.

"So, what do you have there?" Brie asked, gesturing toward the book he held.

"This is the ledger Amanda kept of everything we found, as well as what we collected for the sale of the treasure through her contacts in France. It also records how much money went to each member of the group. A couple weeks ago Amanda gave it to me for safekeeping. I wonder now if she didn't have a feeling something bad was in the wind. Anyway, she said she knew she could trust me and that, should anything happen to her, she wouldn't want it to fall into the wrong hands."

"Sounds like she knew she was in danger."

"She didn't say anything like that, but now I have to wonder."

"Did anyone but Amanda ever see this ledger?"

"Not to my knowledge. Amanda played things close to her vest. It was *her* contacts that made the operation possible. She distributed the money she received from the sale of the gold coins, but none of us ever received a detailed accounting. I guess it was the honor system."

Ha, Brie thought, *honor among thieves.*

Doug continued talking. "Anyway, we were all making plenty off the operation. So much so that Amanda encouraged us to put the money in the bank—not do anything too flashy with it, so we wouldn't call attention to ourselves."

Brie couldn't help thinking about Charlie Cappy's rather extravagant lobsterboat, the extensive improvements to the town library, and Adam Blake's schooner. But she shifted gears. "There's evidence that Harold McCann, the former lighthouse owner, knew something about your operation, and that his death was not an accident."

The color drained from Doug's face when she said this, and he took a step back. "I had nothing to do with that," he said defensively.

"I didn't say you did," Brie responded, watching him with interest.

"I should get back now. Wendy is home alone. What will happen with all this?" He gestured toward the ledger, now in Brie's hands.

"I honestly don't know," Brie said, "but you've done the right thing by coming forward."

Doug just nodded at that. "What happened here?" he asked, pointing toward the house.

"We had a fire," was all Brie said, watching him carefully.

"Is everyone all right?"

Brie noted the look of genuine concern and was glad to see it. "Thankfully, yes," she said.

Doug just nodded again. "Well, thanks," he said, although he looked like he wasn't exactly sure what he was thanking her for.

"Tell Wendy I'll come by to see her tomorrow."

"I will," he said over his shoulder as he climbed into his truck.

Brie watched as he backed up and headed the truck for East Island Road. Then she went in the house to find John.

Chapter 24

It was almost five o'clock when Brie and John left the lighthouse and started toward the trail that led down to the *Maine
Wind*. A mean northeast wind charged across the headland
and tore at them as they made their way along the top of the
bluff. Brie had given Amanda's ledger no more than a cursory
glance before they had left the house. Even so, it was clear to her
that *the group* had reaped a bountiful reward for its salvaging
efforts. She planned to look more carefully at the book when
they got back to the ship.

Right now, she was mentally sifting through everything
she had learned from Harriet and Frannie and focusing on her
gut feelings about Adam Blake, the schooner captain, and Bob
Weatherby, the owner of the bait shop. They both had sufficient
motives—one of them being her lover and the other her es-
tranged son—and Brie had been searching her mind for some
fragment of evidence, some nuance of behavior that would tip
the scale in one direction or the other. All things considered, she
felt the scale was listing a bit in Bob Weatherby's direction. Still,
she needed something to clinch the deal. In her business it was
called hard evidence. And that nagging feeling that she was
overlooking something was still with her.

John caught up with her and took her hand in his. That
small gesture gave her comfort out of all proportion to its size.
She didn't feel like talking, and John seemed to understand, so
they carried on in silence. As they reached the western boun-

dary of the island, the trail turned back to the north and started to descend toward the rocky beach they had been landing on with the dory. The *Maine Wind* still lay outside the cove where they had anchored her the night before. Sheltered in the lee of the island, off its western shore, the ship was protected from the increasing force of the northeast wind.

When they got down to the shore, they found the dory pulled up on the beach. The guys had obviously run a relay back and forth using the yawl boat, so they could leave the dory on the beach for them. They carried the dory down to the water, climbed in, and rowed toward the ship under a heavy, gray sky. The air here seemed unnaturally still, considering the gale force winds building in the northeast and already savaging the opposite side of the island. The stillness seemed oddly juxtaposed with the unsettled feeling steadily growing inside of Brie. She knew this feeling—it was the feeling of things coming to a head.

As they drew closer to the ship, she could smell the wood smoke from the stove in the galley. Since she'd been part of the crew of the *Maine Wind*, she had come to identify that smell with coming home. Oddly, it was the first time since she had left her parents' home, many years ago, that she'd had this sensation. Her apartment in Minneapolis had never offered that kind of comfort. She thought about the tiny berth that was her only space aboard ship when passengers were present, and realized that home is more a feeling than a place, and even the lowliest quarters can sometimes purvey a profound sense of comfort.

They came up to the starboard side of the ship, tied off the dory, and climbed the boarding ladder. Brie told John she was going below and headed for the aft companionway, where she descended the ladder to her cabin. The slight mustiness of the ship below decks provided another welcoming note. She stepped into her cabin on the portside of the ship, just beyond John's, and closed the door behind her. Harold's journals were there on her berth, and she laid Amanda's ledger on top of them.

She took off her jacket and hung it on one of the hooks next to the door. She stretched her arms overhead, hands clasped, and leaned to the left, then to the right, and then slowly bent over, keeping her legs straight, and placed her hands on the cabin floor. She stayed there a few moments, breathing in and out, and then rolled back up to a standing position. As she placed her hands against the edge of the berth and began stretching her legs, she could feel the tensions of the afternoon, and of her encounters with Summer Sanders, Adam Blake, Bob Weatherby, and Doug McLeod slowly dissolving.

After a few more minutes of stretching and breathing, Brie felt calmer. She pulled the band from her long ponytail and brushed her hair five or ten times before returning it to the ponytail. Then she tapped off a basin of water from the wooden cask that sat up on a shelf in the corner of the cabin. She splashed the cool water on her face four or five times, grabbed the soft towel from the bar next to the washstand, and patted her face. Feeling fresh and a bit restored, she left her cabin, climbed up on deck, and headed forward to see if she could help George in the galley.

When Brie came down the ladder into the galley, George was stirring a pot of tomato sauce and singing a verse from the "Octopus' Garden." She joined in, and the words made her think about being tucked away safe and warm beneath the sea in the galley of the *Maine Wind*. Before long, from his berth behind the galley, they heard Scott pick up the melody on his guitar and join them, so they finished the chorus as a rousing trio.

Clapping came from the companionway. Ben stuck his head down. "So, when's dinner, George?"

"Hey, Ben. Hope we didn't wake you with our rowdiness," Scott said.

"You know what, Scott? There's nothing I like better than the sound of young people enjoying themselves."

"We should be eating in about twenty minutes," George told Ben.

"So, what are we having?" Brie asked.

"It's spaghetti and meatballs tonight. Not egg noodles, but close enough, I thought."

"George, whatever you cook is bound to put a smile on my face. What can I do to help?"

"Why don't you assemble the antipasto salad. I've got all the ingredients out on the table. I'm just about to put the pasta in the pot and the bread in the oven."

Brie let all her thoughts about the case slip away as she focused on assembling the antipasto salad. In the large flat bowl George had provided, she built a base of lettuce and topped it with calamata olives, artichoke hearts, banana peppers, cubes of mozzarella cheese, and of course, small slices of pepperoni, the spiciness of which she could vouch for, having helped herself to a representative sampling.

Scott had come out to the galley when the singing started, and he helped Brie get the table set. John was nowhere to be seen. Brie guessed he was in his cabin taking a nap—something he was in the habit of doing during cruises after they anchored each evening.

When things were about set, Brie went aft to rouse him. She descended the ladder and knocked lightly on his cabin door. "Dinner's ready, John."

She heard an incoherent response mumbled from behind the door. When John opened his cabin door, he looked half asleep—tee-shirt and hair both thoroughly rumpled. Brie laughed. "Hey, sleepyhead," she said. "Dinner's on."

"How can you be so perky after we both slept on that cement floor in the lighthouse last night?"

"I've been cooking with George."

"Ah, that explains it," John said. "Tell the guys I'll be right there. Just want to splash some water on my face."

Brie headed back to the galley just in time to see George pulling a split loaf of cheesy garlic bread from the wood stove. The smell of it made her muscles feel like they were doing an imitation of the melting cheese. "George, I think I love you."

"Best not let the captain hear that, or I'll be losing my job," George quipped.

"Too late." The words preceded John down the companionway. "Careful, you two, or I'll have to make a law about crew members fraternizing."

"Wouldn't that be like cutting off your nose to spite your face?" Brie asked.

That got a smile from John.

"Okay, everyone sit," George ordered. He had set five places at the long v-shaped table. Outside, the sky was becoming increasingly menacing, so George had set a lit candle in the middle of the table, and it cast a homey glow on the golden wood of the table and interior of the galley. Ben slid onto the bench behind the table, followed by John and Brie. George and Scott each pulled up a stool on the other side. They passed around a big bowl of spaghetti topped with savory red sauce and large, tempting meatballs. Next came the wooden board bearing the garlic bread, and finally the antipasto salad that Brie had assembled.

Then silence, punctuated only by grunts and groans of satisfaction, fell as it always did at the beginning of one of George's meals. The meatballs had simmered long in the sauce, so they melted like butter in the mouth. The garlic cheese bread could only be described as heaven with a crust, and the antipasto played a nice counterpoint to the rich carbohydrates. Within twenty minutes they were all sitting silently with the dazed looks of pleasure George's meals were known to elicit.

"We're not quite done," George said, rising from the table and heading up the ladder.

The other four peered up the ladder with masochistic anticipation. They heard the chest cooler up on deck open and close, and then George came down the ladder carrying a delicate layered confection that Brie immediately recognized as tiramisu —a cake-like Italian dessert, in which coffee-soaked ladyfingers are layered with a rich custard concoction.

"George, you scoundrel," John said. "You're going to turn me into a fat, jolly captain, and I'm powerless to stop it. So, where are the plates?"

Brie laughed out loud. She liked this *defenses are down* side of John. It was quite charming. The whole dinner scene had lifted her spirits and removed her for a time from the specter of murder and misdoings ashore. She rose to get the forks.

George served up his delicious confection with cups of strong black coffee, and by the time they were done, Brie was leaning back against the bulkhead in what could only be described as a sated stupor. Then the yawning began, and it was so bad she thought her jaw might just lock in the wide open position. The day and the night before had finally caught up with her. She looked at her watch and was surprised to see that it was only seven o'clock. Another series of yawns began, but John interrupted them.

"Brie, for heaven's sake, you're exhausted. Go lie down. Scott and I will help George clean up."

"Well, okay, if no one minds," Brie said weakly.

"Go!" a three-way male chorus ordered her.

"All right then, you don't have to shout," she said good-naturedly. She slid out from behind the table and headed up the ladder without a look back. She was dying to crawl into her berth and sleep. She descended to her cabin, and once inside, peeled off her jeans and climbed into her sleeping bag. She lay there a few minutes staring up at the ceiling that was actually the deck overhead, feeling the gentle rocking of the ship.

The journals and Amanda's ledger were lying at the foot of her berth, and Brie knew she should finish reading them. Before long, the detective in her won the battle. She sighed, sat up, and reached down to retrieve the books. She propped an extra pillow behind her head and pushed herself up far enough that her head was erect and she could read easily. She clicked on the reading light above her pillows and opened Amanda's ledger.

This was truly Accounting 101, and it didn't take her long to realize there was some monkey-business going on. No wonder Amanda had been so guarded about the ledger. The distribution of the payoffs showed regular and rather sizeable extra amounts being funneled to Bob Weatherby. Was Amanda just trying to make up for the childhood she had never shared with him, or was something darker going on here? Was he extorting money from her?

The discrepancies in the ledger pointed to another motive Bob may have had to do away with Amanda. Maybe she'd had enough. Maybe she had threatened to tell *the group* what was going on. Then she remembered what Spencer Holloman had said at the meeting about Amanda wanting to meet with him the day she disappeared—something about a member of the group, he had said. This could be what she needed—hard evidence of a motive for Amanda's murder. She set the ledger aside and sat there for a few minutes, mulling over her line of thinking.

She realized there was only one stone left unturned. She hadn't quite finished Harold's second journal. She reached down to the foot of the berth and grabbed it. She had marked her place with a scrap of paper, so it was easy for her to find the page she had been on, dated September 7. It was hard to believe that she had just been reading the journal the night before. With all that had since transpired, it felt more like a week ago, or maybe two.

She nestled down in her berth with the journal and read again those mysterious words. *Thoughts of Grace consume me. I must let them go.* Last night, before she fell asleep, she had skimmed over the following pages, looking for another reference to the mysterious Grace. But she had been exhausted, and even though she felt little better now, she studied each page carefully, skimming Harold's entries for some other mention of the mystery woman.

288

She was nearing the end of the journal, and her hopes of finding out more about Grace were diminishing. Then in the middle of the penultimate page, embedded in a passage about *Deep Blue*, Harold suddenly diverged and wrote: *I'm so worried about Grace. I told her to destroy the letters, but she refuses.* That was all. The entry was as brief and mysterious as the first one had been, and yet, somehow, a faint echo reverberated in Brie's mind. She read the last page of the journal, dated November 8. There was nothing else of import. She knew Harold had died in April of the previous year, but his journal entries stopped on November 8. She could only guess at what had transpired in the months between those final entries and his death.

She set the book aside and lay there thinking about Harold's cryptic notation. Something troubled her—a little itch at the back of her mind she couldn't seem to scratch. But the warmth of her berth and the gentle rocking of the ship were working against her, clouding her brain like a thick fog bank rolling in. Finally, she let go of all thought, slid deeper into her bag, and drifted off to sleep.

Chapter 25

*L*ightning torches the night sky, casting shattered light on an angry sea. Thunder rolls over the roar of the waves. The wind, a lunatic banshee, howls in one low dissonant note. Brie perches atop a huge breaking wave in a tiny, oarless dory. She grips the gunwales on either side to steady the treacherous craft. Through a curtain of driving rain, she watches a terrifying drama unfold below her. Amanda Whitcombe floats on her back in the middle of a boiling sea. Not far from her, a flock of white envelopes slides down the back of a black wave, like oil on top of water. In yet another direction, so a nearly perfect triangle is formed, Harold McCann frantically rows his sinking craft, the top of which is shaped like a roll-top desk. He grapples with the oars, moving first toward Amanda, then changing course and struggling toward the letters, as if he can't decide where his first responsibility lies.

A loud thump on the deck overhead woke Brie. For a few minutes she lay in that nether world between waking and sleeping, the strange dream still vivid. As she pulled herself up to a sitting position, a thought slid into her mind as smoothly and cleanly as a round slides into the barrel of a revolver. It was the piece of the puzzle she had been looking for. Suddenly the picture was complete. She knew where to look for the letters, if in fact they still existed, and she knew who *Grace* was. She knew who had killed Harold and Amanda, and she knew why.

Brie kicked her way out of her sleeping bag, hopped off her berth, and grabbed her jeans off the floor. As she shinnied into them, she glanced out the small window that gave onto the deck. There wasn't much daylight left, but if she hurried it would be enough. She zipped her jeans stuffed her feet into her deck shoes, and checked her watch—a quarter of eight. At most she had an hour and a half before darkness fell. At this time of year, especially near the water, the last vestiges of light often hung in the sky till nearly ten o'clock, but tonight, with a nor'easter brewing, darkness would come earlier.

Brie grabbed her jacket off the hook, but thought better of that. She tossed the jacket onto her berth, grabbed her rain slicker, and went topside to find John. As she headed forward, she saw him emerging from the galley companionway. She was glad he was alone. She expected some resistance to her plan to go ashore and didn't want to deal with it in front of the others.

"John," she called. She waited for him amidships, not wanting the others to hear their discussion. She needed to do this alone. Potential danger always existed in these situations, and she refused to subject John or the others to that danger. "I need to go ashore," she said as he came up next to her.

"Why?" he asked.

"I just do. I've figured something out."

"There's a bad storm setting in. Can't it wait till morning, Brie?"

"It can never wait, John. When that break comes, you have to jump on it."

"It'll be dark in a little over an hour."

"That means I have to leave now."

"I suppose you'll refuse to let me come with you."

"It's best I go alone, and I have to leave now."

He was silent for a moment, staring down at the water. She knew he was waging an internal battle about whether or not to stand his ground. "I'll row you ashore," he finally said, "and I'll be back on the beach at nine, waiting for you."

"It may take longer than that."

"Nine-fifteen, Brie. Not a minute later. I'll bring the dory around to the starboard side." He walked aft.

Brie headed for the galley. George was at the sink when she came down the ladder.

"George, do you have something small I could use as a gift for Fudge and Frannie at the Scuttlebutt Café?" She needed a reason to stop by the café to make sure the poker game was going forward.

George dried his hands and turned to face her. "I have some homemade preserves. Would that work?"

"That's perfect. Could you get them for me?"

George went to a cabinet and took out two jars of preserves —one raspberry and one blueberry. He rolled each jar tightly in a paper bag for padding and slipped them into a plastic bag for carrying.

"Thanks, George." Brie took the bag from him and headed up the ladder. John had brought the dory around, and she climbed down the boarding ladder and stepped aboard.

They rowed silently toward shore. Brie could see John wasn't happy with the plan, but he kept his thoughts to himself. When they landed on the beach, he handed her his large flashlight. She knew it had a bright LED beam, and she was glad to have it with her. She hopped out of the dory and kissed him lightly on the cheek.

"Nine-fifteen, Brie. Not a minute later."

"Agreed," she said, and started up the path at a trot.

She could smell the storm coming—smell the rain that was imminent. The lightning that had been but a distant show when they had headed to the ship at five o'clock had advanced on the island, and now sent forth ominous rumbles that shook the air around her, making her feel strangely vulnerable. She had come to the top of the trail, where it bent east along the high bluff, and even though the forest sheltered her to the north, the wind from the east felt like a strong arm pressing against her chest. She hurried her pace, knowing that soon the storm would loose its wrath, and the heavy cumulus bladders overhead would release their dark torrent on the island.

She had reached the headland where the lighthouse stood. The forest fell away, and now the wind hit her full force. She leaned directly into it and headed for the keeper's house to get the keys to the truck. The front door was unlocked and she rushed inside, closing it behind her. She took a breath, happy for the momentary respite from the wind, and then headed over to the desk to snag the keys. She darted into the living room, grabbed the library book off the coffee table in front of the windows, and headed back out the front door.

As she came around the east side of the house, the wind tore at her, and she ran for the truck. She jumped inside and put the book and the bag with George's preserves next to her on the seat. Doug's bouquet still lay on the floor, now as wilted as her plans for a nice peaceful four-day break with John here on the island. She turned over the ignition, dropped the truck into drive, and stomped the accelerator. The truck jolted along the uneven ground, sending her dangerously close to the roof at times, but she didn't care. The clock was ticking; she needed to get to the other end of the island.

She rocketed down East Island Road past the turn for Puffin Point. Before long she sailed past the Sanders' place, then Adam Blake's driveway, and finally the signpost for the McLeods'. She hadn't encountered a soul on the road. She slowed the truck as the road swung west and dropped into the edge of the village. There was no one in sight; Barnacle Bay was battened down for a blow.

She pulled up in front of the library, grabbed the book off the seat, and climbed out of the truck. There was a light on in the building, so she headed up the stairs and pushed through the heavy door. There was no sign of Birdie. Brie called her name but got no response. *Must be downstairs*, she thought. She didn't want to linger, so she set the book on the counter. There was a pad of sticky notes on Birdie's desk, and Brie scrawled a brief note and stuck it on top of the book. She was out the door and back in the truck in less than a minute.

She turned out of the driveway and rolled down the road to the Scuttlebutt Café, a stone's throw from the library. There were several trucks in the small parking lot. With the impending storm, the poker players had obviously decided to drive. With George's preserves in hand, she climbed the steps. The red and green lanterns on either side of the door were turned on. *Port in a storm*, Brie thought as she pushed open the door.

The café was dimly lit, and she let her eyes adjust. The poker players were at the far end of the café, already so engrossed in their game that they didn't seem to notice her. Ranged around the table were all the men from *the group*— Spencer, Doug, Wade, Charlie, and Adam Blake. As she observed them, she saw Bob's truck coming down the road. He turned into the parking lot. Just then Fudge and Frannie came out of the kitchen carrying two trays with food and drink. Frannie saw her and bobbed her head in acknowledgement. At the approach of the food, Doug turned and caught a glimpse of Brie in his peripheral vision. He waved, causing the others at the table to take note of her, but none of them gave her a roaring welcome. *To be expected*, she thought.

After emptying their trays, Fudge and Frannie walked over to where she stood. She gave Frannie her small gift and thanked them both for their kindness, telling them she would be leaving the island the following day. They clucked over her a little, and then she was out the door. She had seen what she needed to see. The poker game was in progress and all *the players* were there. But there was another game afoot—one they knew nothing of— and in this game, she held all the cards.

She climbed back in her truck and followed the road out of town. She was unaware that the black pickup, ablaze with red flames, still sat running in the Scuttlebutt parking lot. As she rounded the bend at the far end of the village, it pulled out and followed stealthily in her wake.

Chapter 26

The wind had reached gale force, and it hurled all manner of small twigs and branches at the truck as Brie made her way out of town. Chances were good that anything not nailed down would be leaving the island that night via the nor'easter express. With the threatening sky, the forest was already on the shadowy side of darkness. Brie pressed down on the accelerator, knowing she was in a race against time.

She parked the truck down the road a ways from the driveway. She didn't want to pull up the drive and risk being caught there or boxed in. She checked her watch—8:15. She hoped she had time to find what she was looking for. She leaned across, pushed the door lock down on the passenger side, grabbed John's flashlight, and climbed out of the truck. She decided she'd travel faster without the rain slicker. She peeled out of it, threw it onto the seat, and locked the door.

Thoughts crowded Brie's mind as she walked south on the road. Thoughts of Amanda Whitcombe's cottage and a crime scene so subtle a less trained eye would have missed it; and of the beautiful castings the artist had created—the joyous lovers, the haunting mother and child, and the ship's prow, cast from aluminum sleek as a dolphin's back, sinking beneath the waves with its figurehead of the mermaid, kept too long from her watery realm. She thought of Amanda somewhere beneath the storm-tossed seas, and the strange dream of the letters cast adrift that had led her to the truth. Harold's touching statement from his journal played through her mind as well: *Thoughts of Grace consume me. I must let them go.* And Birdie's remark made just that morning—a remark that had helped her solve the mystery. *They'll never know the pleasure of letters from a loved one, long gone.*

Brie also thought about something Harriet had said. *There's a tendency when one returns to a place after many years to try and pick up where one left off*—words Brie had assumed referred to Amanda. But now she saw that those words could just as easily have applied to Harold, and she wondered whether Harriet had had her suspicions about Harold's death all along.

Brie had come to the driveway and started down it. She stayed off to the edge as she approached the house, even though she knew no one was home. She paused at the woodpile near which she had parked that morning. She flipped back the tattered black tarp and felt the wood. It was wet, as she knew it would be. The tarp had been removed Saturday night, the night it had poured rain. It had been removed to serve as a body bag for Amanda. The killer had used the tarp to drag Amanda's body down to the shore. She was sure the black fragments left on the path outside Amanda's cottage could be matched to this tarp.

She guessed the killer had towed a boat with an outboard motor behind Amanda's lobsterboat that night—a boat he had used to get back to the island after he'd dumped her body overboard and set *her* boat adrift. Brie shuddered at the coldness of it all, and at the pointlessness of rivalries taken too far. A compelling but sad picture was taking shape in her mind. A picture of jealousy, even hatred; a picture of one man determined to destroy another. She thought back on what Harriet had said about a pair of island boys, from two different worlds, growing up as friends. And the final piece—the haunting realization of who *Grace* was—to whom the letters had belonged.

This was a story of a man who had grown up poor, and his unrelenting drive, down through the years, to have another man's birthright—not just his paternal home, but also the woman he had loved from the time she was a girl. Brie remembered what Ben had told them the day they arrived, about how Harold had left the island as a young man, after having a falling out with some fellow over a girl. It must have infuriated Spencer that Harold's family still owned the lighthouse, and that Harold had come back to the island after so many years. Then Harold had formed a friendship with Amanda, and with Harriet and Bob Weatherby. He was reestablishing himself on the island. Brie guessed that was partly why Spencer had tried to burn down the keeper's house. She had thought his motivation had been to scare her off, but there may have been a deeper symbolism at work—an attempt to erase all vestiges of Harold from the island.

As for Amanda's murder—she had been collateral damage. She had unwisely engaged in a game of blackmail with a killer, thinking she was indispensable to *the group* and therefore safe. It was unclear what she had wanted from Spencer—possibly his position as town manager. Whatever she wanted, she must have threatened him—told him she'd seen him arguing with Harold at the top of the lighthouse the night Harold died. Maybe she planned to reveal what she knew to the others, or maybe to the police. Of Amanda's many errors in judgment, this had been the worst. This error had been fatal.

Brie made her way to the house and stepped up to the back door. She was counting on the fact that the islanders were in the habit of leaving their doors unlocked. She tried the door, and sure enough, it opened. She stepped into the Hollomans' kitchen and closed the door. There was still enough light coming through the windows to see her way around without the flashlight. She walked through the kitchen and into the dining room, wondering where to start. She went into the living room and searched Birdie's desk, even though she knew the letters would be hidden. She headed up the stairway that descended between the living and dining rooms. There was a large master bedroom above the living room. Brie glanced in and then checked the other doors. There were three other large bedrooms accessed from the central hallway. She saw no stairway to an attic.

One bedroom appeared to be a guest room. The twin beds were made; the room was meticulously clean and in order, and the closet was empty, except for some extra blankets stored on the shelf above the hanging rod. The next bedroom was set up as a workspace. There was a sewing machine, an ironing board, and a long table with gift wrapping supplies next to it.

The third bedroom was set up as an office. An imposing roll-top desk dominated the space, and a deck of cards was fanned in a sweeping arc on top of it. The lack of feminine touches told Brie this was Spencer's space. She was pretty sure the letters wouldn't be in here, but, remembering the dream, she noted the presence of the roll-top desk and took it as a sign. The closet door was slightly ajar, and following her gut, she walked over, opened the door, and stepped into a small walk-in space which measured about six by six feet. She reached up and pulled a hanging string that turned on a dim light bulb in the center of the ceiling. The closet contained several file cabinets, some stacks of boxes, and an assortment of outdoor coats, jackets, and hunting gear hanging on a rod, beneath which lay a jumble of shoes and boots that looked large enough to fit Bigfoot. She remembered Spencer and Birdie walking into the Scuttlebutt Café the day before, and how one of the first things she had noticed about him were the giant athletic shoes he'd been wearing, and how his every aspect had dwarfed the diminutive Birdie.

Brie opened one of the file cabinets and leafed through. It contained files pertaining to household bills and affairs. The next file cabinet contained information on island affairs, and a large amount of material on the upkeep of the town library, as well as information pertaining to the building of the new addition.

Brie moved to the boxes next. Kneeling down on the floor, she removed one lid at a time and searched the contents. The boxes contained household bills bundled by months and years, bank statements, and tax return information. One box contained photographs. Brie looked through a number of envelopes of photos from different time periods reaching back several decades. None of them contained any pictures of children, and Brie · realized that Birdie and Spencer had no offspring.

She closed the box, clicked on her flashlight, and scanned the shelf over the coats and then the floor beneath them. A glint of color caught her eye—something shiny or reflective. She knelt down with the flashlight and ran it over the area, and there it was again. She picked a black athletic shoe off the floor where it lay higgledy-piggledy in the corner with a pile of others. She shone the light on the bottom of the shoe, and when she realized what she was looking at, she drew in a sharp breath. Wedged in one of the rubber crevices on the sole of the shoe was a contact lens, blue as the sky on a trouble-free day. Amanda's missing contact lens—ironclad evidence placing Spencer at the crime scene.

A sound from outside the house drew Brie's attention from her discovery. She tucked the shoe back in the corner, clicked off the light, and went to the window. This room was on the back of the house that faced the driveway, and when she looked down, she saw Spencer Holloman getting out of his truck. She darted across the room, closed the closet door, and left the room, pulling the door shut behind her. She had seen a window with no screen in the front corner room—the one with the sewing machine. As she scurried across the hall, she heard the kitchen door open and close. She ducked into Birdie's work room and closed the door silently behind her. She prayed the window would open easily. She knew she had but a few seconds before Spencer started checking around the house. He would have seen her truck down the road and put two and two together.

She raced over to the screenless window and pulled up on the sash. It resisted at first, but on the second try, slid stiffly up. Brie opened it just far enough to get through. She leaned out and dropped her flashlight. It hit the ground and rolled into the undergrowth. Then she climbed out the window. Bracing her feet against the side of the house, she lowered herself till she hung at arm's length below the window, and then dropped. Her right foot hit a protruding rock as she landed, and she let out an involuntary cry as she rolled to break the fall.

She got to her feet and looked around for the flashlight. It was nowhere to be seen, and she didn't have time to look for it. Hoping Spencer hadn't heard her, she limped around the house, and staying to the edge of the driveway, headed for the road. When she heard a door slam and the engine start on Spencer's truck, she knew he had seen her. She tried to hurry her pace toward the main road, but sharp spikes of pain shot up her right leg. She gritted her teeth and pressed on.

She had reached the road and could hear the truck approaching. She knew she had parked her truck too far down the road—she'd never reach it. She limped across the road and dove into the forest undergrowth, wriggling forward on her belly to gain some cover. The truck came around the last bend, and Spencer paused a moment, looking down the road toward where she had parked her truck. "Please turn," Brie prayed. And then he did, obviously assuming she was headed for her truck.

Brie scrambled to her feet. She had to move—she knew he'd be back when he didn't find her at the truck. She hoped she had enough time to work her way deeper into the forest and hide. There was a long, dead branch on the ground next to her. She picked it up and snapped it in half across her knee. It would offer some support for her throbbing ankle. With the makeshift crutch at her right side, she started deeper into the spruce forest. She regretted not letting John come with her. She knew that in those moments she was governed by her cop's instinct to not put civilians in harm's way. Now she realized she had been foolish, but she had been following a hunch and hadn't imagined it would turn out like this.

The forest floor was blanketed with pine needles that muffled her footfalls. The wind had climbed to a strong gale, and Brie could hear the reports of trees snapping off, like tall, brittle bones. Darkness was descending, but not fast enough. Spencer would still be able to find her. She longed for the full cover of darkness—a darkness so complete he'd never locate her. The blackness of a dense forest on a moonless night is so profound as to offer nearly impenetrable cover to anyone hiding there. She thought again about that frightening night by Lake Superior and prayed for the darkness to shelter her one more time.

She hobbled forward on what she estimated to be a north-east heading that would take her to the other side of the island, where the Sanders and the McLeods lived. If she could evade Spencer, maybe she could make it to one of their houses and get help. But those thoughts were dashed as she heard a snap behind her in the forest. She knew it might be an animal, but she couldn't take that chance. She hurried her pace as much as her ankle could bear, trying to keep her footsteps silent.

She was hearing another sound now, and she focused on it. It was the sound of water exploding against rock, which didn't make sense. She knew she wasn't close enough to the other side of the island to be hearing that. As she was wondering about this, she saw what looked like an opening ahead. She limped toward it for about fifteen yards and stepped out onto the road. Her heart sank. She knew where she was now, and she knew what the sound was she had been hearing. It was the ocean rushing up the split. She'd forgotten about the gorge that ran inland from the shore for maybe a quarter of a mile, splitting the island into two rocky shoulders, and separating Amanda's property from the cottages to the north.

She knew she was trapped. If she tried to backtrack to the west and get around the ravine, Spencer would catch her. Any chance of getting to a house for help had just evaporated. She was completely isolated. All that lay between her and the end of the island was Amanda's abandoned cottage. And there was no help at the lighthouse—everyone was on the *Maine Wind*. Anyway, she doubted she'd make it to the lighthouse before he caught up with her.

She heard a muffled snap somewhere behind her. He was getting closer. She hobbled to the other side of the road and back into the darkness of the forest. And then the rain started down —a cold, drenching downpour that muffled all sound behind her. She knew she had to find a place to hide. Soon she wouldn't be able to see anything in the blackness. She turned north and headed toward the gorge. If she could find a spot, maybe a ledge down along the wall of the ravine, Spencer might pass on by, thinking she was heading for Amanda's cottage.

Lightning split the sky, casting a ghostly light through the forest. Brie glimpsed the edge of the gorge—she was close. She prayed the lightning would hold off, knowing that with each flash her chances of being seen increased. She hoped John would somehow sense she was in danger—that he would come looking for her. With her ankle injured, her chances of prevailing in hand to hand combat with Spencer were greatly diminished. Anyway, she was sure he had a gun; she had seen a gun case in their house.

There were thorny raspberries underfoot now—raspberries that needed sunlight to grow. They tore at her bare ankles and hands, but told her she was close to the split. She squinted through the rain and saw the lip of the gorge a few yards ahead. She hoped she still had enough light to find a hiding spot down along the rocky wall, because there was no time to patrol the edge. She was in the open now and vulnerable. She went to her stomach a couple of yards from the edge, crawled forward, and peered over. It was steep, but there were protruding rocks and roots that would serve as hand and foot holds.

She reached over and got hold of a sturdy root and eased her good leg over the edge, feeling for terra firma. As she slithered over the edge, lightning strobed again. In the brief flash she saw a slightly indented space to her left. Keeping a firm grip on the roots above her, she groped her way toward it. She prayed that the lightning hadn't revealed her location to Spencer. If he had seen her climb into the ravine, she was a goner.

She clung to the slippery wall and waited. Her clothes were soaked, and the northeast wind howled up the gorge with a vengeance. The tide was high, and waves exploded into the narrow rocky throat beneath her. If she lost her balance, she'd be crushed on the rocks below or swept out by the tide. She pressed herself to the wall, trying to escape the cold wind that clawed at her, prying at her tenuous hold.

She was unsure how long she had clung to the slippery wall, her hands slowly going numb. The bolt of lighting and explosion of thunder came simultaneously. Brie looked up and nearly plummeted off the cliff. Spencer stood directly above her, staring down like death incarnate. She saw the rifle at his side.

He laughed a slow, evil laugh. "You couldn't have picked a better spot for a tragic accident." His voice was bigger than normal—full of his imagined triumph, but colder than the north wind that tore at her.

"The only reason I'd be in these woods is if someone was chasing me."

"Who's going to believe that?"

"The Maine State Police, for starters." *Keep him talking,* she thought. *Assess your options.*

"Riiiight," he sneered dismissively.

"A detective was here this afternoon and visited Amanda's cottage with me. You won't get away with this."

"You already know what happens to people who threaten me. Harold's presence threatened me, and he's gone. Amanda threatened me—thought she could use what she knew against me. That was it for her. Your being on the island started as an annoyance, but now it's a threat. So this is the end of it."

The lightning flashed again, and in a surprisingly fast move, he gripped the rifle barrel and swung the stock at her head. Brie ducked, but the rifle butt caught the back of her head, carrying with it a bolt of pain that momentarily blinded her. As she clung to the tree roots, trying to regain her vision, she heard the unmistakable sound of a rifle round being chambered.

"Stop!"

That single word held her salvation. She shook her head and blinked hard, trying to clear her vision, trying to home in on the voice.

"Drop the gun. Now! Or I'll blow your head off."

Brie recognized the voice. It belonged to Bob Weatherby. In the next flash of lightning she saw the rifle stock still poised above her head.

"Okay, have it your way. You killed my mother. You killed my friend. You *should* die."

"Bob, don't," Brie shouted. The next few seconds morphed into slow motion. As the lightning flashed again, she saw the gun butt swing up. Bob fired. Blood exploded from Spencer's left shoulder. He went to his knees, but as he did, he raised the rifle to plunge it down on her head. Gripping the root with her left hand, Brie sprung off her good foot, grabbed the rifle stock and yanked with every ounce of strength she had left. Spencer, taken by surprise, didn't release the gun in time and plummeted over the edge of the cliff. Brie ducked into the wall and hung on, praying he wouldn't take her with him as he careened past. Still gripping the rifle, he fell to the rocks below. She heard a muffled thud, and knew it was over.

She clung to the tree roots, her eyes closed, grateful for the arm strength she had gained raising sail on the *Maine Wind*. That strength had just saved her life. Then Bob was there, leaning over the edge, an arm extended to help her up. She grabbed on, and her foot found a root that gave her a toehold on the slippery embankment. He pulled her over the edge and onto her stomach, and she moved her legs infantry style to scuttle away from the edge. She had just pushed herself up to a sitting position and leaned back against a lone spruce tree when she and Bob heard shouts in the direction of the road.

"Over here," Bob yelled. "Head toward the ravine."

They could see flashlight beams, and in a minute or two, John and Scott plunged out of the forest and spotted them. They ran toward the gorge.

"Brie! My God, are you all right?" John went to his knees in front of her and put his hand around the back of her head. He drew his hand away. "You're bleeding!"

"It's okay, John. Just a whack to the back of the head. Thanks to Bob here, I'm alive."

John turned to Bob. "Thank you. Thank you so much."

Bob said it was nothing, but of course, the evidence lying at the bottom of the ravine told a different tale.

"Why did you follow me?" Brie asked him.

"Just a feeling I couldn't shake after you left the bait shop. A feeling that you were in danger. I was just arriving at the Scuttlebutt when you drove away, so I followed you. I passed your truck where you had parked it, and then saw you headed up the Hollomans' driveway. I parked my truck around a bend farther down the road and walked back and hid nearby in the woods. When I saw you come down the driveway followed by Spencer, I knew you needed help. I raced back to my truck, grabbed my rifle, and tracked him into the forest. I just wish I'd had that same sense of danger when my mother needed me."

"Amanda would be proud of what you did tonight," Brie said.

John had stripped off his rain slicker and helped Brie into it, and now he and Scott got her to her feet. With one of them on either side of her, they helped her back toward the road. Bob went ahead and brought his truck around to meet them. John and Scott got Brie up into the front seat, and they climbed into the back of the cab.

"We need to go find Birdie and tell her," Brie said.

"Of course." It was said almost in a whisper, which told Brie that John understood how difficult the encounter would be.

"After that, I need to go back to the Scuttlebutt and call the Maine State Police."

"Can't that wait till morning, Brie?" John asked.

"It can't," was all she said.

Bob drove them back into the village. The lights were still on in the library, and Bob pulled up in front. John helped Brie up the steps and in the door. They broke the terrible news to Birdie. Afterward, they helped her close up the library and brought her with them to the Scuttlebutt Café. The poker game had broken up early, and Fudge and Frannie were getting ready to close up. Brie and John brought Birdie inside, and Brie took Fudge and Frannie aside and filled them in on the situation. She then placed the call to the Maine State police, telling them what had happened. She requested that Detective Dent Fenton be sent to the island the next day, and that he bring a search warrant for the Holloman property.

Seeing that Brie was soaking wet, Frannie brought her a bowl of chicken soup and made her sit and eat it. Brie willingly agreed. As she had hung on the side of the cliff, the cold wind and rain had chilled her through. Fudge went upstairs and came back down with a blanket, which he placed around her shoulders, and a walking cane that she could use to help support her bad ankle. Then he and Frannie went back to the kitchen to bring soup for the others. Frannie told Birdie Holloman that she would go home and stay with her that night, and Birdie, through her sobs, could only nod.

Bob drove John, Scott, and Brie back to Ben's truck, where the three of them climbed in and headed for the lighthouse. They helped Brie into the house, and John went upstairs and found a first aid kit in the bathroom. They cleaned and checked the wound on Brie's head, and decided it didn't need stitches. Scott went to the refrigerator and brought back a bag of frozen peas to use as an ice pack on Brie's ankle and gave her a couple of aspirin for the pain. There was no way to get her back to the ship with the bad ankle, so John sent Scott to let the others know what had happened, and to tell them that he and Brie would be staying at the house overnight.

After Scott left, John put a fire in the woodstove in the living room and went upstairs to Ben's room to find some dry clothes for Brie. He brought down a pair of flannel pajamas and some wool socks. He helped Brie into them and bedded her down on the sofa under several blankets. Then he hung her wet clothes near the woodstove to dry and pulled Ben's big armchair and ottoman over next to her. He added wood to the stove until the room became toasty warm. As soon as she was under the warm blankets, Brie started to feel better. As she drifted off to sleep, she was aware that John had settled into the chair next to her and covered up with a blanket.

Chapter 27

B rie woke to the sound of voices. Sunlight filtered through a broken cloud deck and dappled the floor of Ben's living room. The gale had blown itself out. Scott and George came into the living room and crouched down next to her like concerned big brothers.

"Hey guys," she said.

"How you feeling this morning?" Scott asked.

"Better than last night," Brie said.

"You have to stop scaring us like this," George scolded, but then added gently, "I brought breakfast."

"You did?" Brie pushed herself up to a sitting position, realizing she was actually quite hungry. "What are we having?"

"You'll just have to wait and see." George gave her a wink.

Brie sat up, put her feet on the floor, and tested her ankle. The ice pack last night had helped the swelling, but it was sore. Scott had brought an Ace bandage from the first aid supplies on the *Maine Wind,* and he wrapped the ankle for her and gave her a couple more aspirin for the inflammation. She stood up and found she could walk all right with the help of Fudge's cane. Scott admonished her that she needed to keep icing the ankle and rest it. She knew there were lots of loose ends to tie up today, but she promised him she would try to follow orders.

She shooed the men out of the room so she could get dressed. Scott, having seen her mud-covered clothes the night before, had brought her a clean pair of jeans, tee shirt and lightweight sweater, clean socks and underwear, and he'd thrown her hairbrush into the pack as well. She would have loved a hot shower, but the clean clothes would have to do till they got back to the ship later. She dressed and brushed her hair up into a ponytail.

She was picking up a wonderful smell from the dining room. She grabbed the cane and headed in there. George had baked a cinnamon crumb cake, which he had wrapped and carried up in his backpack, along with two thermoses of strong black coffee, and a tin foil packet filled with a pile of grilled ham. She could have kissed him. The cake was still wonderfully warm. They all fell to eating, and when they were done, not a crumb of the crumb cake remained. George beamed with satisfaction at their empty plates. "Good, nothing to carry back," he said.

They headed back into the living room to talk about what had to happen that day before they could weigh anchor and sail for home. Scott got the bag of peas back out of the freezer and made Brie put it on her ankle while they talked. John encouraged Ben to come back to the mainland with them, but he refused. "This is my home now, and I have to believe the problems are in the past. I'm going to hire Hooky Wilson to do the work. Remember, I mentioned him the night you arrived. He's the guy who struck a deal with me on the truck so he could propose to his girl at the top of the lighthouse."

"That's right, I remember," John said.

"Well, he's our island carpenter. He'll be the perfect guy to help me with the rebuilding."

"We don't know when Dent Fenton will show up to collect the evidence, but once that happens, the rest of what we have to do shouldn't take too long," Brie said. "I have to return Amanda's ledgers to Doug and say good-bye to Wendy."

John looked at her questioningly, and she knew what he was thinking. He was wondering why she wouldn't turn that information over to Dent Fenton. She chose not to comment on it, though. The fact that the murders had nothing to do with *the groups'* activities cast a different light on the situation. She had decided to talk to Doug and see if he had any plans to rectify the situation with the treasure salvaging. Wendy had lost enough, and Brie didn't want to think about her brother being in jeopardy as well. She was hoping they could find a different solution without calling in the dogs. She remembered that Amanda's ledger and Harold's journals were still on the ship, and asked Scott if he'd head down there and get them for her after they'd finished their discussion.

"We should call on Harriet and tell her what's happened," John said.

"Of course. That's very important," said Brie.

John and Ben had just started to compile a list of items they needed from the hardware store in the village when they heard a knock on the front door. Ben went to answer it and came back into the room with Dent Fenton. He was wearing the same blue jacket he'd had on the day before, but today he had a camera slung across his body, and an official Maine State Police cap on his head.

"So, I hear there was some excitement out here last night," he said. His eyes settled on Brie and traveled briefly to the injured ankle.

"Come sit down. I'll fill you in," she said.

Ben told Dent that he and John were going into the village, and Scott and George got up and said they needed to head back to the ship to get things ready for their departure later that day. Scott told Brie he'd stop back up with the ledger and journals within the next hour.

"That's fine," Brie said. "I have to accompany Dent over to the Hollomans' house and also to the gorge where Spencer fell."

They were discussing how to accomplish all this with only one truck when they saw Bob Weatherby cross in front of the picture window. John went to the door and ushered him in. Brie introduced him to Dent Fenton and told Dent that he had saved her life last night. Bob seemed uncomfortable with the praise—a reluctant hero.

"You should be proud of what you did," Dent told him. "Few people ever get to save a life. I *will* need to interview you to get all the facts straight, and I'll need your rifle."

"No problem. I'm at your disposal," Bob said. "I just stopped to see if there was any way I could help this morning."

"John and I could use a lift into the village," Ben said. "We need to get to the hardware store, and Brie and Dent need to use my truck. Maybe you could give us a lift?"

"Sure. No problem," Bob said.

"Could we all stop by the gorge first?" Brie asked. "Since it's a bit of a walk through the forest, and I'm lamed up, Bob could take Dent to the spot where Spencer went off the cliff. My guess is the body has washed out. There was nothing we could do last night in the middle of the storm."

"Of course not," Dent said. "We'll have a look, and I'll call the Coast Guard to search for the body if necessary."

With plans in order, they left the house. Brie was walking a little better but was glad she had Fudge's cane to take some of the pressure off her bad ankle. Bob took Dent and Ben in his truck and John drove Brie. They headed down East Island Road to where the road swung west around the gorge. At a point Bob pulled to the side of the road. John parked behind him, and all the men got out. Brie watched as they disappeared into the forest with Bob in the lead. The sunlight slanted through the trees and shone in the truck's side window onto Brie's face. The warmth of it comforted her, and she propped her head against the window and dozed off. She woke to the sound of voices outside the truck and was unsure how long she had been catnapping.

John opened the driver's door. "Hey, Snoozy," he said. "Sleeping again?"

"Somehow this *vacation* hasn't been very conducive to rest," Brie said.

"No kidding. I'm going to change places with Dent," John said, "and carry on into town with Ben and Bob."

"See you back at the ranch," Brie said.

"Okay, pardner." John stepped aside, and Dent climbed in behind the wheel. She had to wonder if the "pardner" business was for his benefit.

Bob walked over to Dent's window. "I'll bring my rifle when we come back from the village," he said.

"That's great. We'll talk then," Dent said.

Brie told Dent to turn the truck around so they could catch the junction road back near Puffin Point.

"Any sign of Spencer's body?" she asked once they were under way.

"Not a trace," Dent said. "When I get back down to my boat, I'll radio the Coast Guard to send a search boat. Chances are we won't find the body, though."

Within a few minutes they pulled into the Hollomans' driveway. Dent had obtained a search warrant for the property, and they approached the back door with it in hand. Frannie answered the door almost immediately and showed them into the kitchen. Birdie was seated at the big table in the kitchen with her hands wrapped around a cup of tea. She was emitting so little vital energy, Brie worried she might not make it through all this.

Dent offered his condolences on the tragedy and presented the search warrant as gently as possible.

"Oh, my, you didn't need that," Birdie said. "You can do whatever you have to. Take whatever you have to."

Brie told her they would need to take the tarp that covered the woodpile, but said that John and Ben were coming by later with a replacement. Then she accompanied Dent through the house and upstairs to Spencer's office, where she showed him the shoe with the contact lens embedded in the bottom. He snapped a few pictures of it and then placed it in a large plastic zipper bag he had extracted from his jacket pocket. Brie had no doubt the lens would match the one that had gone missing from Amanda's contact case when she was attacked.

Dent went out to collect the tarp from the woodpile, but Brie stayed behind to talk to Birdie. Frannie took a mug of coffee and sat out on the front porch so they'd have some privacy. Brie told Birdie she knew about the letters from Harold and asked her if Spencer had ever found out about them.

Birdie's eyes welled with tears, and she admitted that Spencer had found the letters when he had decided to rebuild some of the storage areas in their closet. "He had started emptying the closet one weekend while I was at the library. When I came home that night he was furious—irrational. It was raining hard that evening. A bad storm was moving in. Spencer said there was something he had to do." Birdie paused and looked at Brie with haunted eyes. "I begged him not to go out in that weather, but it was no use. It was the next morning that Amanda found Harold at the bottom of the lighthouse stairs. Spencer would never admit that he had anything to do with it, but everything changed between us after that." She stared into her tea cup. "He could never believe that I loved him; that I chose *him*."

Brie reached over and touched her hand. "I understand, Birdie." And she did understand. Even though Spencer had achieved everything he had aimed for in life, he could never escape the fact that he had grown up poor—could never escape the insecurities that that had created in him.

"Why did you save the letters, Birdie?"

"Oh, I don't know. If only I hadn't," Birdie said miserably. "I guess they were part of my past, my girlhood. Harold was my first love." Birdie's gaze came unfocused, and Brie could see she was remembering those early days. "Harold and Spencer were friends as boys, growing up together on the island. It turned into a friendly rivalry when they were teens. You know how boys are, always competing with one another. How could I know that Spencer would come to hate Harold so?"

Brie pulled out a chair and sat down and let Birdie talk.

"Harold and I went steady in high school. I always just assumed we'd get married. But then we had a fight the summer after senior year. We didn't talk for a month. That's when Spencer started coming around, bringing me little gifts, taking me to the beach for picnics. I guess Harold thought he and I were really finished, even though that's never what I intended. Later that summer he joined the Navy. I couldn't believe it—it broke my heart." Birdie's voice caught on the words. "I wrote to Harold when he left and he wrote back, and continued to write to me for a few years, but he never returned to the island. Maybe when he moved back here a couple years ago, Spencer felt threatened. And then when he found the letters, maybe he thought I still loved Harold. I don't know." Birdie looked down at her hands helplessly.

"You may never know," Brie said. "What makes people do the things they do is often hard to understand, and even harder to reconcile with what we thought we knew." She started to stand up, but remembered she hadn't asked her about the name in the journal. "Birdie, in his journals, Harold referred to you as 'Grace.' Why was that?"

"Oh, my," she sighed. "That goes back so far. Well, around the time Harold and I were entering high school, Grace Kelly married the Prince of Monaco. You'd be way too young to know about it."

"I *do* know about it, though," Brie said. "I've seen pictures of the two of them when they were young, and I've seen movies Grace Kelly made before they were married."

"She was so beautiful, so glamorous. Harold never thought the name Birdie was right for me. He used to tell me I was *his* 'Princess Grace.' " Birdie's voice broke when she said it.

Brie lowered her head. She knew nothing she could say would make a difference. Time alone would tamp down the pain. She was very glad Birdie had her library to keep her busy. Brie reached over and patted her hand. "I need to be on my way," she said gently. "I'll go get Frannie." She went out to the

315

front porch to tell Frannie she was leaving, and then headed around the house to find Dent Fenton.

As Dent steered the truck back toward the road, Brie told him about Harold's letters to Birdie, and the history of the rivalry between Spencer and Harold. She also told him what she'd learned from Adam Blake, about Amanda being willing to use blackmail to get what she wanted. "When he tried to kill me last night, he admitted that Harold, Amanda, and I had all threatened him and so, had to be dealt with."

"Holloman was obviously into power and control. Look what he did with Amanda's body—stuffing it into her casting of the ship. Says something about him, don't you think?"

"Sure does. It always amazes me, even after all my years in homicide, the lengths people will go to."

"I think all we can do is close the book on this one," Dent said. "We know Holloman killed Amanda. We have hard evidence. Since he and Amanda are both dead now, little can be gained from reopening Harold McCann's case. We can assume Holloman killed him, but we have no witnesses and no evidence to that effect."

Brie nodded her agreement. She had noted Dent's calm, methodical approach to the case, as well as the gentleness he had shown Birdie. Once again, she was struck by the feeling that this was a man she could work with—a cop who thought like her.

From Birdie's house they headed across the island to Amanda's cottage, where Dent took some pictures to add to the case file. Then they drove back to the keeper's house. Dent asked Brie to write up a report on all her findings in the case and mail it to him when she was done, and he encouraged her to contact him any time if she wanted information on the Maine State Police. Then Ben walked down to the cove with Dent to see him off.

There were just two more loose ends to tie up before they could leave the island. Brie needed to stop by the McLeods' and also pay a final visit to Harriet. She was about to head into the house when John came out the door with Amanda's ledger in hand.

"Scott brought this up from the ship along with Harold's journals. So, you want me to drive you to the McLeods'?"

"If you wouldn't mind," she said, tapping her bad foot lightly with the cane. "I'm eager to be done here and get back to the ship."

"Me, too," John said. They smiled at each other, and Brie realized how central the *Maine Wind* was to them. It lay at the heart of what bound them together, and she wondered if, without the ship, everything might not be different. Before they climbed in the truck she gave that last thought the old *heave ho*. If there was one thing she had learned in the last year and a half, it was to stop second guessing herself—to take what came and be grateful for it.

John drove her to the McLeods' and told her he'd wait for her in the truck. Brie got out with the ledger, and as she headed toward the house, Doug came down off the front porch. They walked up the steps together.

"Are you all right?" he asked, seeing the cane. "I think everyone on the island has heard about Spencer. It's hard to believe."

Brie didn't comment but handed him the ledger. "What do you plan to do about *this*?" she asked.

"I've scheduled a meeting with *the group* for tomorrow. I'm going to tell them that we need to report our find of the treasure. The matter will have to go before the courts. We knew it should have been done that way from the beginning, but as I told you, Amanda convinced us not to go that route. We'll be totally honest in our reporting; we have all the records. We'll take whatever reward is offered as our part of the salvage efforts, even if it means none of us will receive another dime. At least the operation will be on the up and up."

"I'm glad that's your plan," Brie said.

Just then Wendy came out the front door. She rushed over and gave Brie a hug. "Are you okay?" she asked looking at the cane.

"I'm fine," Brie said, "just a little twisted ankle. Are you okay, Wendy? I'm so sorry about Amanda"

"I know," Wendy said. "Me too."

Brie saw her swallow the lump in her throat. She put an arm around Wendy's shoulder to comfort her. She noticed Wendy's hair was wet. "Just get out of the shower?" she asked.

"Yup," Wendy said.

"How about that French braid?"

"Really?" asked Wendy.

"I'm game if you are," Brie said. So she sat down in one of the comfortable chairs on the porch. Wendy sat cross-legged at her feet, and Brie proceeded to work all that long brown hair into a perfect braid. Wendy asked if she'd visit the island if the *Maine Wind* came out their way, and Brie said she would try. Then she took her leave, and she and John headed over to the other side of the island to say good-bye to Harriet.

Like everyone else on the island, Harriet was already up to speed on the occurrences of the night before. Apparently, Charlie Cappy had elected to visit her and fill her in on what had happened. Brie wondered what kind of gaps that story might contain, considering the apparent gaps in Charlie's consciousness, but she let it go. She and John stayed and talked with Harriet for a few minutes, and then John went to replenish her wood supply.

While he was outside, Brie asked Harriet if she might find a way to tell Wade Sanders about his connection to Bob Weatherby. Harriet looked hesitant at first, but after thinking about it, her expression changed. "I believe you're right," she said. "I think it would be good for both of them." After John brought in the last armful of wood, Harriet shooed him out of the room and leaned over to Brie. "Don't be afraid to take that next step," she said, nodding toward the captain and giving her a wink. Brie smiled and gave Harriet a little kiss on the cheek.

"What was all that about?" John asked quizzically as they made their way back to the truck.

"Oh, nothing," Brie said. "Harriet's quite the gal, though, isn't she?"

"I'll say," John said.

They drove back to the lighthouse and were inside saying their good-byes when they heard a ruckus behind the house. The three of them headed out the door. A whole caravan of pick-up trucks was pulling up behind the house, each one loaded with people and supplies. Hooky was there with a load of lumber, his wife, and the McLeods. Wade Sanders and Bob Weatherby pulled in with loads of sheetrock, followed by Adam Blake and his wife, who carried tables and sawhorses in the back of their truck. Charlie Cappy was there, looking eager but mildly confused. Fudge and Frannie were last to arrive, and out of their jeep came baskets of food and containers of beverages.

"I don't think you'll be feeling like a stranger here anymore," John said, putting an arm around Ben's shoulder.

Brie noticed Ben wipe away a tear, so overwhelmed was he by this gesture of kindness from his fellow islanders. Best of all, it gave John and Brie a guilt-free exit, which they wasted no time in taking. Brie gave Ben a hug good-bye, and then she and John went to say good-bye to Fudge and Frannie. Brie tried to return the cane to Fudge, but he wouldn't hear of it.

"You just keep that cane, lassie, and when you don't need it anymore, you stow it. But think of old Fudge when you look at it."

"I will," Brie said. She gave them both a hug and thanked Frannie for all the help she had given her in the investigation. Then she and John headed around the house, and as they crossed the granite headland, she stole a last look up at the lighthouse. In the sunlight of that cloudless Maine day, the giant crystal eye winked and sparkled down at her. She and John picked up the trail and headed down to the cove.

Chapter 28

B ack on the *Maine Wind*, Brie wasted no time getting a shower, and afterwards, a nice long nap. Never had her cozy berth felt more inviting or more like home. She woke to the smell of hot coffee and lay there a few minutes enjoying the feel of the ship and the privacy of her cabin, knowing that next week it would be back to her crew berth. She caught herself on the verge of dozing off again and crawled out of her sleeping bag. With her bum ankle, she figured she wouldn't be a full participant in weighing anchor and raising sail, but even so, she put on a pair of lightweight cargo khakis that gave her lots of room for bending and stretching. She pulled on a clean, white tee-shirt and a navy blue v-necked sweater. She slipped her bare feet into her deck shoes, and taking fudge's cane for support, made her way up the companionway ladder to the deck.

John brought her a hot cup of coffee, and together they studied the chart spread out on the cabin top as he plotted a course for home. They planned to up anchor at dusk and do a night sail back to the mainland. The Coast Guard weather report was for moderate southwest winds—eleven to sixteen knots—and seas running two to three feet. Near perfect conditions. They decided they'd tow the yawl boat behind the ship rather than hauling it up onto the davits. With Brie out of commission, it was easier, and anyway, they'd need it in the water to maneuver the ship into port.

The sun was casting long shadows across the deck when George called them down to the galley for dinner. He was just pulling a loaf of rustic wholegrain bread from the wood stove and had put together a fresh green salad and a big casserole of his homemade macaroni and cheese. It was one of Brie's favorites—creamy and delicious with a crispy breadcrumb top, which George, in his best French accent, referred to as "gratin."

The sea air always gave Brie a roaring appetite. "George, it's a good thing there's plenty of work on this ship or I'd have to buy bigger clothes."

"Is that a left-handed compliment?"

Brie smiled and sat down on the bench next to John. His closeness filled her with a longing to recapture the time they had lost on the island. He reached for her hand under the table. She turned her head ever so briefly to look into his eyes, and there read a reciprocal longing.

The four of them lingered awhile in the galley after dinner, talking about the last few days on the island. There were lots of questions, and Brie filled the guys in on the fine points of the case. Then it was time to get underway. Brie stayed down in the galley and helped George clean up the dinner things, and Scott and John went on deck to get ready to raise sail. The *Maine Wind* still lay at anchor outside the cove, which made getting underway considerably easier.

George and Brie came on deck, and George helped John crank up the anchor and secure it to the starboard rail. Brie laid out the halyards for raising sail, while Scott went down the ladder to the yawl boat and fired it up. He butted the yawl up to the stern of the *Maine Wind* and began pushing the ship on a southwest heading away from the island. When they were clear of the island, he secured the yawl boat to the stern of the ship and climbed back aboard. The western sky was a wash of golden light as John and Scott began raising the foresail.

When it was time to raise the mainsail, Brie insisted on helping. She knew they needed a minimum of two crew members on either side of the deck to get the big sail up, and anyway, raising sail was all about upper body strength and getting in a hand-over-hand rhythm with your partner, who was sharing the halyard. As long as she had two good arms and one good leg, all would be well.

With the mainsail up, John took the wheel, and the other three sheeted in the sails and made them off. As John steered the ship onto a westerly heading, Brie heard the familiar groan of . timber as the sails filled and the *Maine Wind* heeled to starboard. The old ship came to life and began to make its music. They were underway.

As they sailed west toward the mainland, the sky repainted its canvas several times, looking for the perfect hue. George brought apple pie and coffee on deck, and they basked in the last vestiges of the July sunset. The moon climbed out from behind Sentinel Island, which was fast disappearing astern, and bathed the deck of the *Maine Wind* in light as soft as the southwesterly breeze into which they sailed. John assigned George to bow watch and gave Brie the night off, telling her she needed to rest her ankle.

At 10:30 p.m. he called Scott to take over the helm and said he was going below. Brie was sitting on the cabin top in the moonlight, and John paused long enough to look at her before descending the ladder. It was a look she knew she would never forget—one that held all things at once, both endings and beginnings—a look of pure possibility. Brie stayed topside for another twenty minutes, thinking about things, feeling the wind soft on her face, coming to know what she had known all along. Finally, she climbed off the cabin top, said goodnight to Scott at the helm, and descended the ladder.

John's cabin door was open. He was sitting at his desk reading. He didn't look up at first as Brie leaned against the door frame, but after a moment, he closed the book silently and placed it back on its shelf. Not a word was spoken as he rose and came toward her. The ship sang its song around them as he took her hand and drew her into his cabin. This time she did not resist.

Glossary of Sailing Terms

Aft—Toward the back of the boat.

Abeam—At right angles to the boat.

A-lee—Helm's a-lee or hard a-lee is the command for tacking or coming about.

Amidships—In the middle of the boat.

Bald-head rigging—A gaff-rigged sailing vessel that carries no topsails.

Beam reach—Also "reach." To sail across the wind, or with the wind abeam.

Bearing—The angle from the boat to an object.

Beating—Sailing close-hauled, or as close to the wind as is efficient.

Boom—The spar that extends and supports the foot of the sail.

Bow—The most forward part of the boat.

Bowsprit—Permanent spar attached to the bow, to which jib-stays and forestays are fastened.

Come about—Also "tack." To bring the boat across the wind to a new heading.

Cut—The shape or design of a sail.

Danger Sector—The fixed red part of a lighthouse's light shining over shoals.

Davits—Outboard rigging for raising and lowering the ship's yawl boat or dory.

Downwind—Away from the direction from which the wind blows.

Fore—Prefix indicating location near the bow.

Foremast—On a schooner, the mast closer to the bow.

Foresail—The sail that is rigged on the foremast.

Gaff—The spar that supports the top edge of a four-sided sail.

Gaff-rigged—A boat with four-sided sails rigged to gaffs.

Galley—A boat's kitchen

Grabrail—A handrail running along the edge of the deckhouse or cabin top.

Gunwale—(pronounced "gun'l") A boat's rail at the edge of the deck.

Hatch—An opening in a deck, covered by a hatch cover.

Halyard—A line that hoists a sail and keeps it up.

Head—A boat's bathroom.

Heading—The course, or direction the boat is pointing.

Heel—The tilt or laying over of a boat caused by wind.

Helm—The tiller or steering wheel.

Jib—A sail carried on the headstay or forestay.

Knot—1 nautical mile per hour.

Lace-lines—Also reefing lines. Used to secure a sail to the bowsprit or boom.

Lazarette—A small hold, usually in the stern, for stores and gear.

Lee of the island—The side of the island sheltered from the wind.

Leeward—Away from the direction of the wind. Pronounced "lu-ard."

Make off or Make fast—To secure a line to a belaying pin or cleat.

Mainmast—Mast farthest aft on a schooner. Carries the mainsail.

Mainsail—The sail attached to the largest mast on the boat.

Painter—The bow line on a dinghy.

Peak halyard—Raises the end of the gaff farthest from the mast.

PFDs—Personal flotation devices.

Port—The left side of the ship when facing forward.

Port tack—Sailing to windward with the wind coming over the port side of the boat.

Pulpit—A railed structure at the bow or on the bowsprit. Only seen on historic schooners that were fishing vessels and used harpoons for catching big fish such as swordfish.

Quarter—The side of the boat near the stern.

Ratlines—System of tarred rungs used to climb to the top of the mast.

Running—Sailing with the wind astern.

Saloon—The main cabin on a ship.

Scandalize the forepeak—On a gaff-rigged vessel, lowering the peak of the sail to slow the vessel.

Schooner—A boat with two or more masts: the foremast or forewardmost mast is shorter that the mainmast.

Scuppers—Holes in the rail or gunwale that allow water drainage.

Sole—A cabin or cockpit floor.

Starboard—The right side of the ship when facing forward.

Starboard tack—Sailing to windward with the wind coming over the starboard side of the boat.

Staysail—A small headsail set between the jib and the foremast.

Stem—The forward edge of the bow.

Stern—The aftmost part of the hull.

Throat halyard—On a gaff-rigged boat, the halyard that raises the luff or forward edge of sail along the mast.

Thwarts—The seats in a dory or dinghy.

Upwind—Toward the wind.

Windward—Upwind

Yawl boat—A small, powerful motorized boat used to push a motorless vessel.

Author's Note

Visit the author's website at:
www.windjammermysteries.com

Invitation to reading groups and book clubs: I will be happy to visit your book club, either in person or by phone, and join in your discussion of my work. To contact me, go to my website listed above and click on the author link, or e-mail me at:
info@windjammermysteries.com